Collections

Collections

MAGGIE SKYE

POCKET BOOKS

New York   London   Toronto   Sydney   Tokyo   Singapore

This book is a work of fiction. Names, characters, places and incidents are either the product of the authors' imaginations or are used fictitiously. Any resemblance to actual events or locales or persons, living or dead, is entirely coincidental.

An *Original* Publication of POCKET BOOKS

POCKET BOOKS, a division of Simon & Schuster
1230 Avenue of the Americas, New York, NY 10020

Printed in the U.S.A.

Quality Printing and Binding by:
Berryville Graphics
P.O. Box 272
Berryville, VA 22611 U.S.A.

To Gil and Harry
for a lifetime of love

Special thanks to: Cynthia Cowen and Rosemarie and Rafael Crisafio for their help and support; Jean-Pierre Radley of Pauline Trigere for his patience and humor under questioning; Ruth Finley of the Fashion Calendar for answering queries with wonderful directness; Mildred Marmur for being the perfect agent; and Isabelle Leeds, who opened a few doors and let us peek in.

CHAPTER 1

He sits in a wonderful old wing chair that is gloriously snug, feeling as he imagines the chair must: static and disinclined to move.

Then a slight change of mood as a flame in the fireplace catches a log with a joyous leap that broadcasts incandescence and deep shadow to the book-lined room. No warmth, however. Not needed in early September, in a New York town house, warmth, just *feeling*, character, the romantic flicker in a moodily lit, enclosed and private space. Egon Delville almost smiles, shifts a bit, crosses and uncrosses, then recrosses his legs on the ottoman. There's a slight numbness, nothing new, just sluggish blood making its leisurely journey around his interior passages.

The leather-bound journal almost slips from his lap. He rights it, reaches for his *digestif*, which—with its foul taste—he's begun to think of as medicine. He puts the glass down, picks up his pen, and begins to write. And having begun, like his conversation, the words run freely, a trill of words, a *scherzo* of words, clever and irascible.

September 8, Midnight: Oh, what a day, what a day, what a day. Decided intimations of fall when I'm not ready for it. And the dinner? Boring, utterly, thoroughly, incredibly boring, Kate excepted, of course. What's wrong with these people? What's wrong with them? This evening at Marguerite's was the after-dinner coffee you've always adored suddenly tasting like used rubber. Who are they, I asked myself mid-meal, glancing around at the dozen guests seated at table. Is this all it's come to, my wasted life? Stuck in a claustrophobic, candlelit room with a dozen power brokers, Annalise to my right and all I could hear was her chanting sagely about everyone from the English monarchy to the secretary of state. Success as a fashion designer has certainly made an expert on politics out of Annalise. And everyone within earshot nodding eagerly. Annalise Michelis, the Argentinian whore, puta (those heavy-lidded eyes, that salacious curve of mouth should tell all, but apparently don't), expounding to an ex-secretary of the United States treasury about how to handle the trade deficit. Her husband, of course, having decided to run for the Senate, was to be found at the other end of the table where state and city power was heavily concentrated. Can you imagine? The man could single-handedly balance the national budget, and yet there he was, servile and cringing for a nod from a couple of political hacks.

As for the secretary of the treasury, seated at Annalise's right, he listened, my he listened, his dazed eyes behind his rimless spectacles glued to her décolletage.

Well, how far she's come, our Annalise, how risen from the barrio in Buenos Aires, through the hellfires of German aristocracy and the French haute couture to meet yours truly, and all I could do, I did for her in New York society. I should have known, though, exactly how she'd turn on me. I still have her perfume in my nostrils. Not from Delville Perfumes, although, hoping to out-brazen me—good luck if she thinks age has dimmed my sense of smell—she insisted it was, when I accused her of treachery. Some special concoction, a little heavy on the frankincense and myrrh. She's planning to bring out her own scent—full-bodied and pure attack, no doubt—let her. What she sported was a sample of no value. They can take on Delville Perfumes all they want. It'll get them nowhere.

As for Marguerite, for once I was irritated with her because I know she can scarcely afford her haut style of living. I know for a fact she owes two months' rent on her offices, but in her own queenly way she refuses to acknowledge the trouble she's in.

Still, she plays the grande dame when she has guests for dinner, and while she uses Lalique crystal and antique plates, the dinner, for all its artful simplicity, set her back the usual pretty penny.

But it was Kate I'd come to see and whom I watched with veiled indifference all evening. Kate in warm plum-colored silk jersey without a bow or ruffle or pouf to disturb the line. Pure Vionnet, all bias cut and magic. Charming Kate with her jet black hair and Gypsy eyes, but, ah, the aching sweetness in her smile, as though life hasn't yet taught her its gloomier lessons.

At dinner our good hostess, with her usual intuition, sat Kate next to Frank More-Money-Than-God Lambert, the most insufferable old bore in the Western Hemisphere. Eastern, too, for all I know. Kate immediately fastened her grave, interested gaze upon him as though rubies dripped from his tongue, as though what he had to say mattered more than life itself. I've never seen him so animated.

It's a gift, that riveting attention, that slight bend of the head, that cutting out of the rest of the world. The operative word is charm. Kate does listen, she is fascinated, she comes away with an air of having *gained immensely from the encounter. It must be in the genes, although certainly not on her mother's side—the most egotistical woman alive.*

Egon pauses, tapping the pen against his upper lip. Kate should have it, he decides, everything, *tutti,* the whole Delville works. Clear up the debt and let her loose of that scum. Ira Gregory, with his thousand-dollar suits, ice blue predator's eyes, and courtly manners that didn't fool Egon for a minute. But wasn't that what he was doing anyway, spinning Ira Gregory off toward a black hole in the center of a galaxy at the far end of the universe?

The Delville Museum would have to go, of course, but now that he thought about it in the clear light of post-party reason, Egon Delville had the best immortality of all, a real flesh-and-blood piece of the future. Fancy that. And speaking of letting loose, getting rid of that blot hanging around upstairs. One might have to speak to the police commissioner if worse came to worst. No sooner said than done. But Winthrop Smith Six can have his week if that's what it takes to see the last of the treacherous little bastard. No one can say Egon Delville isn't charity itself, considering the circumstances. Imagine Winthrop taking Cliff Beal to bed and insisting, in his panic, that it was vice versa. I'll accept the vice, but that's all. Poor Ralley, thinking Cliff was straight all that time.

Life and its permutations never failed to amaze Egon. Amaze, amuse, and ultimately annoy. Then, as though the idea is not only brand new, but that he's the first person of money to think of it, Egon smiles with fresh inspiration. Of course, he must use his fortune in a more equable, a more loving way. Egon Delville, the ultimate ladies' man of no avowed sexuality. What a bloody, wasted life. Sixty-nine years old and it suddenly didn't look good. Well, there was time. He'd straighten everything out, for Kate, for Ralley, for Jaybee, decidedly for Marguerite, poor pet, carrying such a load upon her sagging shoulders. He'd see her first thing in the morning and offer—no, insist—she accept a check and his business advice. Hell, there was even something he could do for Annalise—offer assurance that she could let her guard down, that no one would ever know. And he would rewrite his will.

What was he going on about? His life wasn't about to end.

Egon smiles and closes his eyes. Call the attorney tomorrow, he tells himself, settle it once and for all. Call Kate, too, for lunch, call them all, let them know what to expect.

The leather-bound notebook slips from his grasp; the pen falls to the floor. The fire crackles, consumes itself greedily, and at last goes out. Egon's eyes are lifeless now, or those shapes that were his eyes. There is no grief upon his face, only a look of peace and of having at last settled everything to his immense satisfaction.

*   *   *

Shortly before midnight Win heard the old eunuch come in, the sounds of the elevator echoing up to the fifth-floor servants' quarters where he had his room. Not a servant, of course, Winthrop Smith VI. Just the genteel, impoverished guest of Egon Delville, the trouble being Win was supposed to feel grateful, and on good days maybe he had, but those days were now gone. Egon had said to get out of his house, his life, and particularly his checkbook. He wasn't about to back Smarts Gallery, not a day more.

Truth was, Egon Delville had been pretty generous. He never asked a sou of Win, or anything else for that matter, and had been liberal into the bargain. Win couldn't fault the old guy, couldn't even consider him a candidate for blackmail.

He collected pretty things, Egon. Men, women, whatever easy attraction he could lay those manicured hands upon, but not in a sexual way. Either Delville was a eunuch or sex scared the hell out of him. No matter. You can't tell the press that the ex-ladies' hat designer, the purveyor of Delville Perfumes, wasn't able to get it up with man or woman. Too bloody late, anyway. Egon was sixty-eight or -nine if he was a day. Who'd care? Not the women he surrounded himself with. Not the press. Anyway, why in hell was Win courting the idea of blackmail? The sixth-generation scion of the Cleveland Smiths might be down, but he wasn't a blackmailer, no way.

Yeah, blackmail was out; appealing to Egon's sensibilities was in. He'd see him, talk to him, be quiet, logical, apologetic, the whole enchilada, tell him it was all a stupid mistake. Grovel.

Win didn't move, however. He lay on his back, hands behind his neck, on the old-fashioned four-poster bed painted teal, in a room with yellow walls trimmed in teal as well. Swiss-inspired, he thought; if he looked out the window he'd find snow and the goddam Alps. Cabinets of oak, some black silhouettes in dainty frames on the walls, and an elaborate bouquet of silk flowers, teal outstanding, on the dresser. The room always smelled of starch and bleach, of wax, and of dust disturbed, then resettled. The maid made her way up once a week, sent by Egon to report, no doubt, that Win hadn't spilled coffee on the furniture or burned cigarette holes in the sheets. Not likely in a place Win couldn't call home, not a hot plate or a cookie tin allowed.

Yeah, it was a hotel bedroom, and in taste that was pointedly perfect. The trouble was Win liked it, felt comfortable there, rolled in tired late at night and slept like a top there. Where did Egon expect him to go now in a city of apartments only the big, bad, or beautiful could afford? Queens? The Bronx? Win wasn't even certain where Staten Island was.

He'd get down on his hands and knees and beg, apologize, ask Egon for immediate forgiveness, promise never to do it again, what in hell did the old fruit want? Did he think Win had no feelings, no passion, nothing?

Egon's attachment to Ralley Littlehurst was the catalyst that had brought things to a crashing end. Ralley shared her SoHo studio with Cliff Beal. For a moment Win's heart ached in a way that was new to him. They were still together, the artist and the tall, skinny fashion director. No breasts on Ralley to speak of, of course. Cliff laughed about it but in a bizarre, proud way. A very sexy lady with broad shoulders, slim hips, great legs, and no breasts, he said. Fashion stuff, he said. Looks great in clothes. Vice president of a big catalog house called Steyman's. Important to people who cared about those things.

Win turned on his side as if to ease the ache over Cliff, but it didn't help much.

This was nothing more than a cliffhanger, he thought to distract himself, no pun intended. Egon didn't care about Cliff, about Cliff's talent, about Smarts. He cared about Ralley and was furious over Win's taking on Cliff. But it was Cliff who made the first move—not that Win hadn't considered it, Cliff coming on like a battleship in the Mediterranean. Hell, Ralley would be the first one to admit her boyfriend was irresistible.

"She's out of town," Cliff said in that persuasive way of his, as if Win and everybody else in the world had lost their collective ability to reason. "That's the kind of job she has—Japan, Paris, San Francisco, you name it. When Ralley leaves town, man, she's *far, far* away."

Far away turned out to be Manhattan, the SoHo district, Ralley's big white loft, sparsely furnished, but a little crazy because of the giant riot of Cliff's wax and acrylic encrusted canvases. And Ralley walked in on him and Cliff, right in the middle of *everything*, her eyes popping, and man, mad as hell.

Cliff had to know, had to want Ralley to walk in on them like that, had to want Ralley to recognize his other tastes. Win, embarrassed and too stupid at the moment to think Ralley might call Egon to complain, had trouble climbing out of the queen-size bed, trouble finding his clothes, trouble getting into them. Ralley was as white as the walls. She'd just stood there and watched him, and Cliff hadn't been any help. He'd *laughed* and covered his face with the bedclothes.

Cliff would somehow manage to walk away from it all and never look back. Win loosed a funny little sigh that took him by surprise. It wouldn't even strike Cliff that he'd left a wasteland in his tracks. Big, good-looking painters with some talent had the world by the tail.

Right. The world by the tail. Yeah, the break would come soon, for Cliff and for Smarts. Win had to hold on, with or without Egon Delville. That was the scene in New York. You took what you could; it was the way things were done. Nobody expected anything different.

Win eased off the bed, went over to the mirror, and examined his face earnestly and with dispassion. Except there was nothing new to behold. He was thirty-seven years old and afraid of fading fast. Down on his knees to Egon, beg forgiveness, promise it was all over between him and Cliff—except that there hadn't been anything to begin with, just a lot of stupidity, and where in hell would he get eight thousand dollars for next month's rent if Egon didn't help him? It was Cliff who made the first move, surprising the hell out of a grateful Win, but what can you expect of an artist? They talk of the future and live for the moment.

Win went over to the door, opened it and paused, a handsome, slight, courteous man who looked ten years younger than his age.

Yes, no, what the hell. He stepped into the hall and made for the stairs. The Delville town house was a narrow five-story red-brick building on New York's Upper East Side. The kitchen and what Egon euphemistically called the servants' hall were a few steps below street level. The library, where he was certain Egon had gone, was on the third floor, as was Egon's bedroom, a small monk's cell draped in brown velvet.

In his way, Egon was a creature of habit. Every night at twelve, at least when Win was home, the elevator groaned its way up three stories. Every night the antique elevator gate was pulled open and then slammed shut. Egon went into the library for an hour or so. Then the well-oiled double doors were pushed back. Egon walked down the hall to his monk's room and bed. What in hell did the old man do in the library for an hour?

There was no sound of Win's tread upon the carpeted stairs. Past walls papered in yellow moiré above mahogany paneling and an expensively framed collection of fashion drawings. Down into the silence of the lower floors, with their scent of furniture polish and the perfumed candles Egon burned at his frequent parties.

On the third floor, Win walked carefully. No carpets, just a polished wooden floor with not a scuff mark on it. He found the double doors to the library open a slit. Win checked the stairwell and the door to Egon's bedroom off to the right. Absolute quiet. He peered through the narrow opening into the library.

Win had been there only once, and Egon had made it clear that the library —in fact, the entire town house—was off limits, with the exception of Win's bedroom and bath. If they met at all, it was in Egon's study, a small red room on the ground floor, filled with paintings and all manner of bibelots, with nothing more than a square foot of empty space for writing on a Spanish table that did for a desk. It was there Egon took an occasional accounting of the affairs of Smarts; it was there, in fact, that Egon, just the day before, had summarily dismissed Win from his life.

"Well, I won't turn you out into a driving storm," Egon said in his familiar overbearing manner, as though Win were an idiot, and hard of hearing at that, "carrying your infant child in your arms, but as far as I'm concerned, you've ceased to exist. Especially as you don't have an infant child. I'll give you a week to get your ass out of here. Don't even try to hit on any of my friends for money."

Egon paused, his face granite, the jaw, which was always a little soft-appearing, suddenly striking Win as stubborn and unbreakable.

"I don't know any of your friends, that's the trouble," Win complained.

"Thank the Lord for good favors."

"What in hell did I do, actually?" Win went on. He truly couldn't understand the fuss. After all, he and Cliff were adults, in charge of their own lives. "You're making a mountain out of a molehill," he said, keeping his voice reasonable, although he avoided Egon's eyes. "I got a month's rent coming due on the gallery, Eggie, you have to help me." Win remembered too late that Egon hated the nickname.

"Eggie. Eggie. Where in hell do you get the nerve? Order it wholesale from Sears? Case closed." Egon got to his feet, pushing his fingers through his thick white hair and glaring in a disconcerting way at Win out of bulging, darting eyes. "Eggie, *Eggie,* so help me, you've a penchant—no, a *genius,* a certifiable A-number-one genius—for saying the wrong thing, Winthrop. You're a fool and I'm a bigger one for pretending you weren't. May the good Jehovah forgive me my sins." He went to the study door and pulled it open. "One week. And incidentally, hand in the keys right now."

"Hey, come on, Egon, have a heart."

"A heart. I have a heart and I'd like it to keep ticking a while longer. Don't shorten my life, Smith the Sixth. I took you in—worse, you took *me* in—but it's over and when it's over it's over, Delville style. Keep the keys for one week. I'll remember to have the locks changed."

One week. One lousy week. Winthrop, who had no possessions to speak of, except his wardrobe consisting of expensive denims and even more expensive leathers, felt that the move, out of a lifetime of sudden necessary moves, was the hardest one he'd ever have to make. His family, a dozen years earlier, had told him to leave Cleveland and its precincts and never to come back, but they had at least given him a stake.

The slit between the doors gave Win a view of the book-lined library and the fireplace directly ahead. To the right, turned toward the fireplace, was a leather wing chair. Egon was asleep in it, slumped down, his head lolling against one of the wings. A pen lay on the floor along with an open notebook.

Win raised his hand to knock. From somewhere below he heard a sudden, muffled laugh—the valet and housekeeper in the servants' hall, no doubt. Egon didn't stir.

What the hell, just gently tap the old fellow awake. Win carefully slid the doors apart, stepped into the room, and just as carefully closed them. The fire had gone out, and when Win came up to Egon he was surprised to find the man's eyes open.

"Listen," Win began in a faintly apologetic tone, then stopped. Egon's mouth was open, a trickle of blood oozing out. Quite a smell from the old man, too; definitely not Delville Perfumes. The reality of the scene at last sank in.

"Hey, man, don't do this to me." Win didn't even know he spoke the words. His heart seemed to shake loose of its moorings, and he turned away in terror. What the hell was going on? Blasted luck, why did this always happen to him? Just his bloody luck he'd be caught and they'd blame the whole thing on him, that's the way it always happened.

He couldn't afford a run-in with the police, either. That one-way ticket out of Cleveland didn't necessarily mean the books were closed on him. He glanced around the room. Eight thousand dollars due on the gallery rent, and all this gone to waste now. He ought to take a little souvenir with him. He *deserved* it.

A smell of urine was getting to him. His eye lighted on the fallen notebook, which he picked up when he guessed Egon had been writing in it. Like the reader of mysteries who must peek at the ending, Win turned to the last page. Annalise, Marguerite, Kate, Ralley, Jaybee—the names jumped out at him. "Argentinian whore, *puta.*"

What the hell was he doing, reading Egon's journal while he lay dead a foot away? Win was about to put the book back when a fresh thought occurred to him. Egon spent every evening near midnight closeted in his library—and Win held in his hands the reason why.

He closed the notebook carefully and tucked it under his arm. Why he was so inspired Win couldn't have said. He wasn't a creative man, merely an opportunist. He picked up the pen, too, in a second wave of inspiration. On his way out of the library, Win caught a glimpse of half a dozen similar notebooks sitting on a lower shelf, half hidden by a row of signed photographs in elaborate frames. He recalled the only other time he had been in the library, when Egon had given him a tour of the town house, filling the air with carefree nonstop patter. At the time Win had been nervous but enchanted.

"Of course, I collect everything willy-nilly," Egon had said. "I'm one of those people. Let me think something is rare, show me two of them, and I won't stop until I've cornered the market." Egon paused and stared hard at Win, but not in any personal way. "Name it and I'll tell you I collect it. Go ahead, name it, anything." His voice was deep and very pleasant.

Win tried to think.

A finger was poked at him, and Win stepped back out of the way, as if Egon's next move would be to cut him through to the sternum. "Go on, you haven't been struck deaf and dumb, have you?"

Win shrugged and because Egon was glaring at him, stammered out the first thing he could think of. "Indian headdresses."

Egon rolled his eyes to the ceiling, shook his head, giving up. "Indian headdresses. For God's sake, if I wanted Indian headdresses there's a mess of smelly, moth-eaten ones at the Indian museum. If I were interested, all I'd have to do is get in the car and sail uptown. Small, *small*, this isn't the Louvre, Winthrop, not the Louvre. A man lives here, a collector extraordinaire, but we're fresh out of space for dinosaurs and the *Spirit of St. Louis*. Snuff boxes, Winthrop, and daguerreotypes, fashion drawings and old perfume bottles, Winthrop, and pre-Columbian statues—Mayan, to narrow it down, although no more since they discovered that fabulous what's-his-name in Mexico whose forgeries are in half the museums in America. All right," he added as if Win had forced him into a confession, "there are those items in Queens, but that's another matter."

Winthrop nodded, lost, trying to look interested, feeling as if he had been attacked by a horde of red ants.

"And I collect souls, Winthrop," Egon said suddenly. "My true hobby. All this is ephemera, if you understand what I mean."

"Souls?"

"You're a dolt, Winthrop. Good-looking, but a dolt—nearly my favorite kind of person. College-educated, right? Some smart smallish college your family forced on you, right? You got a degree in art history and you glide through life saying 'Gimme, gimme, gimme,' without the slightest idea of what it's all about. They have a word for people like you—'solipsistic'—but you should have grown out of that by now. How old are you? Twenty-eight? Thirty? Souls, Winthrop." He took Win by the arm and swept him out of the library, pausing only once to show him the row of leather-bound books. "That's where I keep my souls. You don't know what I'm talking about, do you?"

Win shook his head eagerly. One thing was certain, Egon didn't want him to understand. "I'm sorry, sir."

The answer seemed to satisfy Egon greatly. "Now, where the hell was I?"

Dead. Sitting in a chair dead, Winthrop reflected as he examined the spines of the journals. *Souls*—Egon collected them like everything else. Give him two and he cornered the market. Win was college-educated, all right. He wasn't a dolt. Maybe in the past things had a way of not working out, but Smarts could change all that. No, not a dolt, Egon. He removed the leather-bound volumes from the shelf and put them aside. A deft rearrangement of books and photographs, and the unwary would never know anything had been taken from the room. Not the valet, not the housekeeper, not the maid with her shattered nerves and long-handled dustmop. Would dust dare settle for long in the Delville town house?

Clutching the journals, Win made his stealthy way back to his room. He undressed and climbed into bed, taking the journals with him. He'd be out of there tomorrow, pronto, early, before anyone noticed. He'd sleep in the rear of Smarts while he worked out a way to procure the rent. Meanwhile he waited for the creak of elevator coming up from the servants' hall. The valet would be the one to discover Egon. Win was out of it. He opened the journal he'd found at Egon's feet to its last page and took in the spidery, elegant, determined handwriting.

> *But it was Kate I'd come to see and whom I watched with veiled indifference all evening. Kate in warm plum-colored silk jersey. . . . Charming Kate with her jet black hair and Gypsy eyes.*

Win settled back against his pillow. He wasn't at all sleepy, and his reading matter wasn't soporific in the least.

CHAPTER 2

Kate knew he was there the moment she opened the apartment door. She felt a rush of excitement because she'd been afraid he wouldn't come, and then was angry because he had.

The air was heavy, closed in, weighted with his scent—the fifty-dollar-a-bottle cologne, the monogrammed cigarettes hand-rolled to his specification —which announced Ira Gregory as sharply as a police siren.

She went inside, closed the door, and waited for a moment in the entry hall, keyed up as well because of the dinner party she had just left. They were always stimulating, those gatherings in Marguerite Varick's small—she called it *bijou*—apartment on Park Avenue. Her invitations were sought after; who was there and tidbits of conversation often showed up in Suzy's gossip column in the *Post* or William Norwich's in the *Daily News*.

The food Marguerite served at nine-thirty had been simply prepared in the best French manner, proffered hot and enticing on exquisite antique plates. The party had gone on longer than usual. Maybe it was the way the night air turned sweet and anticipatory, a night in which affection and good company made everyone reluctant to leave. Even Marguerite, who always expected her guests to be gone by eleven, allowed them to linger past midnight. Except for Egon, of course, who fussily left at his usual time and seemed annoyed that Kate stayed behind.

Now Kate listened to the familiar sounds around her: the faint honk and drum of traffic drifting up from Madison Avenue, a clock ticking, the hum of something doing what it should in the kitchen. Beyond, in the pale, comfortable living room with its big old sofa and roomy club chairs, she saw the gauzy white curtains shift under a slow breeze. The recessed ceiling lights, dimmed by the housekeeper before she went to bed, lent a staged, spectral mood to the night.

There were no sounds from her son's room or from the housekeeper's. She should check on Matt, make certain he was all right. Then a tiny, sleepy noise traveled down the hall, and she tilted her head to listen. A slight childish cry and she went quickly to his room. The door was ajar and in another moment Kate satisfied herself that he was asleep.

Outside her son's room, her hand still on his door, Kate remained very quiet. Where would Ira be? In her studio? In her bedroom?

This was her apartment, her territory, and he had taken it over with the same deft touch as everything else in her life. She had allowed him to weave a cocoon about her, the silken threads spun from his smiling mouth and Kate Hayden had twisted and turned, becoming more and more deeply entangled. She had foolishly given him the key to her apartment, had let the house-keeper know he would come and go as he pleased. But he was elusive; she never knew when he might be there or arrive when she was already asleep, to slip silently into bed beside her and kiss her awake. Kate had already learned nothing was steady about Ira Gregory; she might grab him and he'd be gone.

She had barely breathed from the moment she turned the key in the lock. She could sense the energy, the vibrations of the man. She wanted to cry out and knew she wouldn't. She turned and went quietly down the darkened hall to the rear of the apartment. Her bedroom door was open a fraction. He was there and waiting. She took in a deep, quiet breath, her eyes fixed on the doorway. One minute, two, an eternity. She heard a muffled noise and the door was swiftly opened. He stood there, a shadowy figure framed by a halo of light, sleek, ready to spring at the first sign of peril. It was that coiled energy she had noted first about him, and which now, as always, sent a sexual charge bolting right through her.

"You're late." His voice was deep and riding its sensuality and anger like a surfer's wave.

Kate experienced an unexpected flash of triumph. He wasn't quite in con-trol. "Is that all you have to say to me, that I'm late? I'd no idea you were waiting for me." Her tone was soft, careless. They were on even ground now, if only for a short time before everything shifted around her again.

He laughed deep within his body. She could see him clearly now, and she relaxed. Sometimes, when they were apart, she imagined him with a satyr's face, imagined that his hostility had become visible.

He was tall, intense, with sandy hair and blue eyes bordering on turquoise. His nose was strong and slightly hooked, his chin assertive. The suits he favored were expensively understated, and he was never seen at the office with a tie loosened or a pocket handkerchief out of alignment. Everything about him was studied and false; Kate knew that. She also knew he could do things to her no man had ever done. They were locked together; he owned her, he owned Kate Hayden, the company name as well as Kate, and for the moment she felt helpless and obsessed with him.

She moved past him into the room, aware of a welling up of desire that was crazy, beyond reason. The man was a liar; he had lied to her, and she was beginning to believe he was dangerous. She turned and faced him.

He regarded her with a slight smile. "Come here, Kate."

It was no use. A war went on constantly within her and kept her in a state of watchful anxiety. There were no winners, only losers burning with a craving that was never satisfied.

She kept her gaze bolted to his as she kicked off her shoes and ran to his outstretched arms, her lips connecting with his in a heated, deepening kiss. Smooth fingers drifted across the back of her silk dress and slowly worked the zipper down. Deep satisfaction pulsed through her as she felt his body tense against hers. And then it took no time at all. In lightning movements, he had her dress off and thrown to the floor, everything else peeled away until Kate stood naked in the circle of his arms. He held her tight, pinned to him. He owned her, and his kiss, bruising and insistent, left no doubt that he took what was his.

"Ira." She whispered his name and he lifted his head. He didn't loosen his grip, but his smile held brittle amusement. "I hate being naked when you're dressed." She glanced across the room and gestured to their image in a long oval mirror, her pale flesh pressed against his suit.

"Looks good to me," he said, "but you're right. It's a little like taking a bath with your shoes on." He laughed and his smile softened. In one quick action, he lifted her and kicked the door closed. He fell with her onto the bed and joined his mouth to hers, running his hand down the long curve of her body.

Kate felt the tension build. His touch always did that to her. She had never known anything like it, and even now wasn't certain it could exist outside her room. She crushed him close, not caring that he still lay over her fully clothed. She would take him any way she could, on his terms, anything.

He lifted himself and with his eyes still holding hers stripped off his clothes and tossed them to the floor. Kate gave a throaty laugh. "I can understand your throwing my clothes to the floor," she said, "but that suit? I'm flattered."

In another moment he descended on her and she lifted herself to him. She had been ready for hours but knew he was too experienced a lover to hurry. His hands moved over her flesh with a light, deft touch, as though outlining some exotic design meant to tease her, to increase her anticipation and desire. She reached down and let her fingers lightly encircle him—hard, warm, and pulsing.

She wanted nothing to interfere with the moment. She wanted no thoughts, just sensations. There were no abstracts like right or wrong, good or bad, love or hate. There was only the solid reality of his body and hers and the desperate need that fired from every nerve ending. And yet just when she knew she should be flying free, Kate caught sight of his dark face poised over hers and realized with a shock that his eyes had gone cold and hard and that his mouth had tightened into a grim line. She felt a string of fear and willed it gone.

Ira felt no need to confide in her, to explain their relationship. He could come and go in her life as he wished, totally in control. But she knew he needed her, too, and was angry about the other life she had without him.

He took her an instant before she expected it, and she couldn't restrain a sharp gasp. He was striking away at her and she gave in to it, as she knew she would. Time disappeared to some strange other place as Kate shut her eyes tight and let the fire consume her. Little licks of flame began somewhere deep, fanned by his relentless hammering. Just the right angle, just the right amount of pressure or pain, or whatever. She clutched at him, willing the heat, wanting it, not knowing how to make the sensation last forever. And then there it was, washing over her and leaving her breathless.

There were no words in the feverish darkness, but between them a recognition. Ira rolled away, pulling her with him. She knew his pattern. He'd wait until he thought she was asleep, then dress and leave.

His car was parked a discreet two blocks away, possibly with one or more of those men he called his associates waiting; there would be no questions asked, no excuses given.

She lay still, breathing evenly, feigning sleep.

"Kate, you're still awake."

"Oh, no." She mumbled the words. "I was just about asleep."

"Tomorrow, Kate. There's still time. I want that line opened up a bit. The operative word is 'bridge.' The career women we're trying to reach don't have the money for Kate Hayden, not as the line stands now."

"Too late." She reached out, gathered him close, and moved under him. "And it's in my contract. I'm creative director and you're to keep your nose out of my studio." She had rehearsed the words more than once, ever since he had broken the news to her about concentrating on the bridge—the area between designer clothes and clothes sold at middle-range prices.

"Fuck your fancy title, Kate. I've a couple of partners breathing down my neck." He caressed her for a moment, trying to soothe her.

"I thought you said they wouldn't interfere."

"Bottom line. That's not interfering; that's keeping the business afloat." He disengaged himself from her arms. "Gotta go. Don't even bother telling me you're going to think about it. It's sink or swim time."

She watched him dress, felt the bed move when he sat down on the edge. He was very careful about how he looked when he left her—shirt collar closed, tie knotted, hair combed. She closed her eyes as he came toward her, fully clothed now, the picture of married respectability.

"Kate, you have no choice in the matter."

"Haven't I?"

"No, baby, you haven't." He bent down and kissed her, then turned and left. At the sound of the door closing softly behind him, she flung herself across the bed and let the tears form in her eyes.

How in hell had she let it all get away from her? An affair with a married man who had no intention of leaving his wife. A liar who had told her he was in the midst of a divorce when he first took her to bed. A man she couldn't admire in any way but one. Her crazy, awful sexual obsession with him that had deepened rather than faded with time. Surely she had other choices, but knew it was too late. Unless Ira wanted her gone, she'd never be able to extricate herself. He did not give up his possessions easily and only when he was ready. And now this insistence on changing the line, with the spring showing two months away.

She was fully awake, although her limbs felt heavy. She dragged herself from the bed, went into the shower, turned on the spray, and spent a long time soaping and soaking herself, letting the tears wash away and water ease the ache. With her face uplifted, the shower pelting hard and sharp, she tried to tell herself she believed in free will. The choices had all been hers, beginning with the moment she had left her mother's house in Greenwich at the age of seventeen to begin her freshman year at the Fashion Institute of Technology.

"Private schools, Kate, with your fancy classical education, how could you?" Her mother, ChiChi, was appalled. She had been a fashion model when she was Kate's age and professed to an intimate knowledge of the way the industry worked. "Fashion, darling, it's the dregs of the universe. The absolute pit end dregs. It's all show up front and you sell your soul to the devil—the *devil*, the *mob*, you sell your soul to the mob just to get a leg up. And how in hell do you know you have a modicum of talent? I don't see it, Kate, and I'm in a position to know."

ChiChi had other plans for Kate. School in Switzerland, for one, where she'd learn to be a proper young woman with the proper social connections. ChiChi's spoken dream was Kate's marrying into a title and fortune, details unspecified, as in the most rewarding dreams.

"The Fashion Institute, New York, the streets, drugs. Graffiti. Drunks, Kate, *drunks*. Good Lord, that's depressing. Darling, you don't know what's out there. You have to be born with street smarts."

"ChiChi, I'm not a baby, I can take care of myself."

ChiChi tossed her long, thick golden mane. She was nearsighted but never wore glasses. "Look at you—tall, gawky, all neck and eyes, and God knows that hair will never be tamed, and you don't look a bit like me."

"No, I guess I don't," Kate said in a faint, apologetic voice as though she were personally responsible for not looking like her mother. It was the reason why she wanted to escape to New York. She didn't look like ChiChi, she wasn't formed like ChiChi, and she certainly didn't think like ChiChi.

Leaving had been easier than she expected, however. Her mother's third husband, it turned out, didn't want the teenager around. ChiChi cried, fussed, and bought her daughter a wardrobe that was, as usual, entirely too expensive and, as usual, too mature and not at all Kate's taste, that Kate discarded almost at once, presenting it to her willowy blond college roommate. "You should really be my mother's daughter," she said, and knew that ChiChi's disapproval would always haunt her.

But from that time on Kate wore only clothes of her own design, even when she worked for Domingo, who decreed that all of his employees were to dress in the current line. Domingo forgave her, though, and said her maverick talent reminded him of his early days in fashion.

"Darling," ChiChi would say in the rare times she saw her daughter, "I detest those unstructured styles you wear." Or "Darling, do something about your hair. Good *Lord.*"

Later, after Domingo died and Kate left the company to strike out on her own, ChiChi was on the telephone. "Darling, are you mad? Go into business for yourself? Who in the world would back you? You haven't the experience. But don't do a thing until you talk to Egon, promise me."

"Who's Egon?"

"Egon *Delville,* you little idiot. That does it: I'm sending him around to talk to you."

Kate thought of how ChiChi always talked about the owner of Delville Perfumes as though he were a great buddy, but she had never produced him. "You're *sending* Egon Delville, director of a grillion dollar corporation, to see *me,* not the other way around."

"Oh, darling, I've told you a thousand times, Egon and I are old pals. He'd do anything for me. And, darling, don't forget, fix your hair. You're not still wearing it blown out ten feet on either side, are you?"

"Mo-om." The drawn-out word expressed the old frustration over ChiChi's belief that her daughter had never grown up.

Almost immediately Egon called and invited her to lunch at Le Cirque. "I'll wear a white carnation in my lapel," he told her, "so you'll know me."

"And I'll wear one behind my ear, so you'll know me."

He laughed. His voice was warm and his laugh equally so.

"Anyway," she added, "I'll know you from your photograph in *W.*"

Egon then confessed to following the fashion scene closely and said he had seen her photograph in the same publication. "And in *VFF*," he added. "Marguerite Varick seems to think a lot of you."

And so Egon appeared in her life, telling her to turn a deaf ear to her mother and offering to finance Kate Hayden.

"Small scale to begin with, pet. That's how to do it. Afterward a frolic in the promotional fields. Leave everything to me. We'll want to talk perfume when the time comes."

She turned him down and refused calls from ChiChi for a month. She suspected Egon would interfere and take her autonomy away. He was clever and persuasive. Kate worried about her freedom. She had to hold on to the name Kate Hayden. Egon was obviously just a substitute for ChiChi.

Ira Gregory surfaced when an article appeared in *VFF, Varick's Fashion Forecast,* about her leaving Domingo to strike out on her own. She believed him when he said he could raise the necessary capital to underwrite Kate Hayden along with a budget to promote the line.

Egon had been furious when he learned about Ira Gregory. "Never heard of him. Where in hell did you dredge him up?" Egon fixed Kate with his bulging and unforgiving gaze. "I've been in the fashion business since Hector was a pup, a gleam in his mother's rheumy eye, and I've never heard of Ira Gregory."

"He's a businessman, Egon. Mostly offshore interests. He's from the Midwest, been in Switzerland with a company called DAS, which will finance me, and he's home now for good." Kate was aware of the tightness in her voice. Ira had been vague about details, merely smiling and saying things like "bottom line" and "the importance of sales promotion." She had been quite dazzled.

All she really heard were the magic words: he wouldn't interfere with the creative end, there would be money to set up business on Seventh Avenue, and she was to concentrate on her designer line. His partners would be silent, he assured her. And so they had been until recently. They were still invisible behind their initials and their foreign corporation, but now they had spoken, insisting upon a bridge line. Maybe Egon had been right all along.

"You what?" Egon screamed the words when she admitted she had given DAS the rights to her name. "My Gawd, your mother has a fool for a daughter after all."

"There's no *problem*," she explained, not hurt by Egon's tantrum, marking it down to not having things his way. Her contract with DAS gave her complete autonomy over design.

"Kate," he said, throwing up his hands, "I never thought you had your mother's talent for ignoring life's little realities, but I'm beginning to wonder."

"I have my father's sense of adventure," she said, furious over his reference to her mother, yet knowing it was true, and therefore making up qualities about a father who had left when she was five and whom she scarcely remembered.

"I think what you're doing is called suicide, Kate, wait and see," Egon said, "but not to worry. I'll be around to pick up the pieces."

Kate had the impression Egon would quietly investigate Ira and after a while, when he ceased alluding to him, she was relieved Ira could be trusted.

But the questions she wanted answered had never been. Had Ira set her up? And if so, for what purpose? She had caught him in his first lie when she discovered he was still married with no intention of divorcing his wife. Then he lied about giving her freedom to do an upscale line, going back on his word when Kate Hayden didn't burst upon the scene with a hundred doors nationwide.

When Kate stepped out of the shower, she was still too restless to sleep. She slipped into a soft flannel robe that made her look even younger than her twenty-nine years. She went barefoot into the hall and down to her son's room, which was small and crowded with toys. She switched on the lamp. Matt's bedcovers were on the floor and he was curled up at the foot of the bed, his pajama bottoms damp. He didn't waken when she gathered him in her arms and hugged him tight. Matthew Timothy Rearden, four and a half years old, still anxious over her divorce, with a wet bottom and a single mother and a father with visiting rights every other weekend. A father waiting to pounce if Kate made a wrong move.

She'd married Tim because it was what one did when one lived with someone for two years and became pregnant. Tim wanted the baby and convinced Kate that she owed it to him to see her pregnancy to term. Now, of course, Matt meant everything to her. And holding his chubby body in her arms, she wondered if she would be the perfect mother, be everything ChiChi hadn't been, neglectful ChiChi with too many husbands and a daughter who didn't resemble her in the least.

The loneliness she felt as a child still left a bitter taste in her mouth. Her mother was often away; she'd had a succession of husbands, two more since Kate left home, who told Kate to call them Dad, or Daddy, or Pop, or just plain Joe.

"Call me Joe, kid. You'd like that, wouldn't you? It makes more sense, right?"

"Right, Joe."

Her real father, ChiChi's first husband, had early drifted away, moving to France where he remarried and forgot to call or write or send birthday cards. Kate learned of his death two months after the event.

ChiChi, of course, was a wonderful, glamorous Hollywood kind of starring special event in the life of a little wide-eyed, straight-haired lonely kid. Kate remembered gazing one day past the library window of the ostentatious turreted pile of stone that ChiChi called home but was usually absent from. At Kate's side was a box of paper dolls with a hundred little paper outfits, some of which she had designed herself and colored in with marking pencils. Kate was waiting for her mother to return from her latest trip abroad.

The car came down the driveway and stopped. Her mother stepped out and as Kate jumped up to join her, the box went flying, scattering dolls and paper clothes all over the floor. She ran to her mother and was soon enveloped in her perfume, her furs, the tickle of her hair, the touch of moist red lipstick.

"Well, here I am. My, my, my, my, you're a good inch taller, little precious," ChiChi had cried. "Now, don't rush growing up, you hear? I don't want people to think I'm a hundred years old. And no more of that silly running around of mine." A touch of a finger to Kate's nose. "I'm going to just sit around and watch you grow. What I really need is time with my wonderful daughter. I love you, silly face, you know that." Another perfumed kiss, a blot of red on her cheek, which Kate wouldn't wash off.

There were always presents—this time a Madame Alexandre doll from Paris with a tiny Vuitton-style steamer trunk holding a dozen tiny couture dresses. Kate was thunderstruck. The paper dolls were swept up by a servant and thrown away. A long time passed before Kate remembered them.

Each reappearance of her mother was a child's dream of toys, of clothes, of books, and of promises to stay. Kate learned to be cautious after a while. So cautious in fact, that she developed the same self-centered drive as ChiChi. Kate's compulsion turned on her designing career and kept her mind in overdrive. And like ChiChi she'd never had a relationship with a man that was deeply satisfying.

Her son's head was tucked under her chin. She hugged him, promising herself that he wasn't going to pay the price for her mistakes as she did, *was*, for ChiChi's.

"That's not going to happen to you, kiddo," she told him. "You have my absolute, solemn, honest-to-God word that you'll always come first even if I have to breathe fire on the dragons." She took his small thumb from his mouth, smiling at the plopping sound.

Kate had taken a page right out of ChiChi's book by allowing Ira Gregory to come into her life and by giving him the key to her apartment. Matt had to be protected for more reasons than one. His father had never been satisfied with the custody arrangements and he'd made it clear he would jump at any chance to take the boy away.

"It won't happen," she crooned softly. "I'll change my life, grow up, accept responsibility for my actions, I promise."

"Everything all right?" Her housekeeper, in a flannel nightgown, came to the doorway, concern on her sleepy, companionable, middle-aged, middle-American face. Kate flushed. She *had* to ask Ira to return her key.

"Everything's fine, Jeannette. Matt's damp. I ought to change his pajamas."

"Here, let me." Jeannette took Matt out of her arms. The child moved but stayed asleep.

"Thank you," Kate said. She surrendered her son reluctantly, but the light in Jeannette's eyes had long before convinced Kate of the woman's genuine affection for the child. Still, Kate waited until Matt was back in bed, smelling of baby powder, his face ruddy with sleep.

She wandered into the kitchen and found it was nearly two in the morning. She was wide awake. Something about her mood had begun long before, over dinner, with Frank Lambert spinning some tale or other and Egon watching her covertly from across the table. He seemed dead serious as though he wanted to talk to her but couldn't work up the energy.

She returned to her bedroom carrying a cup of hot milk and settled in bed. She sipped the drink slowly, then turned the light out and slipped under the covers. She caught Ira's scent, but it wasn't his face she envisioned, only random patterns in a handsome piece of silk crepe she'd worked with that afternoon. She had ordered ten yards with the idea of using it in billowing evening pants. Before her eyes closed in sleep, Kate remembered the pattern was also available in a smaller design on wool challis. She fiddled with the idea of using the fabric for a spare little jacket to top the pants. There was a stripe in the pattern and she'd have to be careful about matching the stripes, which would mean using extra yardage. Ira occasionally complained of her profligate use of expensive fabric.

A bridge line didn't call for profligate yards of fabric, especially with the escalating price of silk. One took rayon mixed with a dollop of silk and used the bias very discreetly. How Egon hated synthetic fabrics, no matter how like the original they were. Too bad, Egon, she thought. You'll hate it if I have to do a bridge line. She inhaled a little breath not unlike a sob and fell asleep on the belief that the best laid plans of mice and fashion designers could sometimes go awry.

CHAPTER 3

The station sent a limousine for Annalise Michelis at six in the morning, although the television interview wasn't scheduled until ten minutes past eight. Annalise, dressed in a lightweight houndstooth suit of her own design and encased in a delicate, refreshing Delville scent as though it were a bullet-proof bubble, exited the apartment building on Park Avenue at a fast clip, her usual pace. She was perfectly groomed, blond hair parted in the middle and worn absolutely straight, like expensive silk curtains framing an impor-tant view. The view, in Annalise's case, was of wide black eyes in a face at once exquisite and thoroughly self-possessed. Her lips, which were very full, had been smudged, blotted, powdered, then smudged and blotted once more with lipstick selected to set off a soft, burnished complexion that was the most Latin thing about her.

The doorman saluted. "Morning, Mrs. Younger, fine day."

"Beautiful." She took in a sniff of air. A morning scent of wet green earth drifted over from the center divider, past the automobile fumes. A wonderful day, in fact. Perhaps she and Zack could get away to the country for the weekend. She suddenly ached for a chance to clip rosebushes or push a few spring bulbs into the fragrant soil. What was the color of the soil in Argen-tina? Gray? Black? Red? She no longer had any idea. Black, probably.

The doorman accompanied her to the curb and touched his hat once again. Annalise ducked into the limousine, remembering that Zack's calendar certainly wouldn't permit them to get away, nor would hers. She made a mental note to mention her husband's name on the television program. Viewers would be curious about Zack's seeking the Senate nomination.

"Everything here?" She asked the question of the head of her publicity department, who was waiting in the limo along with Annalise's assistant promotion director.

"Ready, willing, and waiting." Behind them was a panel truck carrying dresses, shoes, evening bags, tiny veiled hats, gloves, pins, scissors, tape, a sewing kit, an iron, and even a small ironing board. The truck also held a couple of assistants and a guard from Harry Winston with a small bag of precious jewels.

"Idiotic time of day to show a line of evening dresses," Annalise said, settling at the window and immediately opening her copy of the *New York Times*.

"Lots of yuppies watch," her press agent said in a carefully optimistic tone.

"At eight in the morning yuppies are on their way to work, just as they should be." Annalise, with an emphatic crackle of newspaper, turned to the business section. Locking her companions out, she was perfectly able, despite her usual four hours of sleep, to concentrate on stock market quotations.

Once she arrived at the TV studio, Annalise allowed herself to be taken in hand by a couple of wide-eyed production assistants who dripped interest and plied her with black coffee and understood it wasn't her first appearance before television cameras, that she was, in fact, a smooth old pro.

They powdered, combed, redid her lipstick, and ended up with a slightly exaggerated version of the Annalise Michelis Younger who had hurried out of her apartment building not a half-hour earlier. The camera was a great equalizer, and Annalise knew she would come across a little pale, tremendously swank and yet very human. As should, of course, the fashion designer wife of Zack Younger.

Zack's entrance into politics would change her life considerably. The idea of being a senator's wife appealed to Annalise. She had visions of evenings at the White House, of rushing to Washington on weekends and back to New York for five frantic days of work, of leaving no blank spaces whatsoever in her mind or on her calendar.

Sometimes, when maggots of doubt moved across the vision, she quickly told herself that the past was buried along with her grandmother, her mother, everyone from those days who knew and cared, or who knew and didn't care. The Annalise Michelis Younger now on center stage bore not even a passing resemblance to the thin, dark-haired creature with the wide, serious eyes who had once inhabited her skin.

At seven-thirty in the green room her favorite models were as restless as a remuda of horses spooked by coyotes. With deep red lips, clown-colored cheeks, and a heavy encrustation of color on sleepy eyelids, they sipped carefully at mugs of coffee and picked around the edges of Danish pastries, women on perpetual diets talking among themselves about inconsequential things, weekends away, and who met whom doing what where.

The clothes were luxurious silks in various luminous guises coating their slender bodies like mercury. Annalise had learned early on to inhibit a natural inclination to make simple dresses that would merely flatter by the clever manipulation of fabric. Her clientele wanted great gobs of heavy, jewel-toned silks gathered at the arms and shoulders, sparkles added, the sheer mass of shimmer meant to disguise poor coloring or an impossible figure or the incipient reappearance of wrinkles in spite of plastic surgery. In a way she envied Kate Hayden who had come blasting out of the starting gate a year before with an expensive but relaxed line that said, "Come and get me, I'm not giving an inch."

Viewers at that hour of the morning would be women whose idea of evening attire was cotton flannel pajamas beneath a well-worn chenille robe. Never mind, in less than a year, Annalise perfume, in its small round bottle with an orchid-shaped stopper, would be at every important perfume counter in the country. Even hausfraus had discretionary funds when it came to buying perfume. During the interview, she'd plug the fragrance more heavily than her evening gowns. *And* Zack, of course, *Senator* Zack Younger whose Latin wife Annalise designed those spectacular gowns for America's wealthiest women.

Annalise fussed over a creased velvet ribbon hiding a flat derriere. She insisted on steaming it herself right then and there on the model's figure, amid shrieks that the iron was too hot. Then she removed a diamond necklace borrowed from Harry Winston and replaced it with her own pearls, only to switch back impatiently, moments later.

She pushed up a pair of long white gloves, to scrunch them down again with a sigh. "Annalise, come on already," the model begged.

"You just sit there and look beautiful, that's all you have to do, Caroline." Annalise, who maintained friendly relations with her models, was both decisive and uncertain, an expert who knew there was more than one solution to any artistic problem.

Annalise silently rehearsed a few carefully chosen descriptive phrases while the production assistants continued to dance around her. She wanted the interview over, wanted to be at her desk with its spread of mail, fabrics, notions, drawings, with phones ringing, staff assistants badgering her with questions, lunch penciled in at Le Cirque, seconds, microseconds accounted for while she remained faintly removed, at the ready, in charge, missing nothing, and manipulating everything from her pinnacle.

"Ms. Michelis, will you come with us?"

She glanced in the mirror once before leaving the green room for the interview. With a characteristic gesture, using her index fingers, she parted the curtains of blond hair, peered at herself, and was satisfied. The curtains dropped back so that the edges of bright black eyes were hidden—Annalise Michelis keeping that necessary distance between herself and the rest of the world.

"Commercial break," the assistant whispered to her, leading her past a curtain to a small stage. There was no audience, just a platform to step up to and cameras with shadowy figures behind them. The set was simple, done in flattering beiges. A false window formed a backdrop with a serene sunset view of downtown New York photographed from Rockefeller Center.

Annalise cursed the sudden stiffness she felt, the fluttering in her stomach. She worried about her accent reappearing and whether she would stumble over English. Foolish thought, of course, and one born of stomach flutterings. She knew her English was precise and clear, her accent gentle and attractive. She thought of all those ladies in their curlers and chenille robes gripping cups of coffee, and how her sequins would brighten their morning. She told herself she had nothing to fear.

Tina Fletcher, the hostess of the program, was a young redhead with green eyes and a warm, friendly manner. They had met before and her greeting was relaxed and affectionate.

During the commercial break she beckoned Annalise to the upholstered chair on her right. "I'm thrilled you could come, especially at this perfectly ungodly hour. What do you think about Egon Delville?"

Annalise drew her brows together at the odd question, but at that moment Tina shook her head and pointed to the control room.

"Welcome back to *A.M. Today*," her hostess said in a natural manner to her invisible audience. "And now I *know* you're going to be as thrilled by our next guest as I am. If this is the year of the Spanish designer, then surely the interest in things Latin can be attributed directly to one of the most beautiful and talented women in the fashion industry, our guest—Annalise Michelis." She smiled at Annalise. "Welcome to *A.M. Today*, Annalise." Her tone was sweet and a little breathless.

Annalise smiled in turn. "Tina, I'm especially thrilled to be here."

Tina referred to some notes on a clipboard in her lap and then addressed the camera again. "Annalise was born in Buenos Aires. She lived in Paris and worked in several couture houses there, then came to the States where she set up her own business, Annalise, Inc. She's married to Zack Younger, and— correct me if I'm wrong, Annalise—there are rumors he'd like to run for the Senate on the Republican ticket."

Annalise was given no chance to confirm or deny. Tina went on. "And I understand you're coming out with a perfume called, appropriately, Annalise. When can we expect to see it? Or rather," she remarked with a laugh, "smell it?" Then, before Annalise could answer, Tina threw in, "How do you decide what kind of fragrance should represent your personal point of view?"

"To begin with, I don't think we'll see the perfume in the stores for another year," Annalise said. She wondered suddenly with a slight intake of breath, whether Egon was watching. "There are so many kinds of scents— floral, heady, light, sexy. You think of what your women want, what your

American competition is doing, what the French are doing, and ultimately what pleases you."

"What scent are you wearing now?" Tina Fletcher asked the question with a playful smile.

Annalise smiled as well. "A morning fragrance by Delville. My scent, Annalise, will be for late afternoon or evening—heady and very sensual." She could afford to be generous, especially since Egon had caught her the night before wearing a test fragrance that was similar to one of his own.

"Delville, of course. I should have recognized it," Tina said. She narrowed her eyes, seemed about to say something, then addressed the camera with fresh enthusiasm. "Annalise Michelis designs are worn by the most glamorous women in the world, a world of which she herself is very much a part. Annalise, as you must know, lives a life much like that of the women she dresses." She paused and smiled expectantly at Annalise. "And the best treat of all this morning," she added, "will be a showing of some of her gorgeous, *gorgeous*, absolutely *entrancing* evening clothes." Tina Fletcher paused, as though beyond the arc of cameras and personnel there was a large, applauding audience. The camera, like a slow, attentive animal, turned to focus on Annalise.

"Are our models ready?" Tina glanced at her producer and was rewarded with a nod. "Would you like to offer a commentary, Annalise?"

"Of course, Tina. I'd be delighted." How polite they were, how full of themselves, Annalise thought, herself not least of all. She was aware of the foolishness, the dishonesty. Eight in the morning evening gowns for tired hausfraus. And the knockoff artists, of course, would be ready with their sketching materials to copy her ideas. She remembered Marguerite's dinner the night before and the presence of Benjamin Keerman of Benkeer Fashions, who dispatched his sketcher to Saks with great regularity to touch, feel, and ultimately copy the details of Annalise gowns. Keerman had spent the evening smiling politely at her, flattering her at every turn. She had been equally charming but would cheerfully have plunged a dinner knife between his shoulderblades.

She was ready now. Annalise—concentrated, poised, and always serious— smiled once again, although any viewer wide enough awake at that hour, would catch the care with which the smile was given, and the wariness in eyes partially hidden by the protective device of that straight, center-parted drape of blond hair.

Caroline, in a slender waterfall of pale blue sequins, came out from behind the curtains.

Tina took in a breath. "Beautiful."

"Caroline is wearing a sequined gown of Tahiti blue," Annalise began.

In exactly seven minutes it was all over. Afterward, her staff saw to the packing of garments and accessories and the dispatching of the jewels back to Winston while Annalise hurried to the elevator. It had been a typical, effusive, vapid interview, but she was pleased with the plug for Zack and for her perfume. She was riding high, at the peak of her power, of her success.

Still, she would have to talk with her public relations staff. "Elegance" should be the key word. Serious fashion treated seriously. Barbara Walters, *60 Minutes*, public television—only important interviews from now on.

Her own chauffeured limousine was waiting at the curb when she came out of the building and she hurried toward it, aware of the curiosity of passersby. That was part of it, wasn't it, the curiosity of strangers? Being the mysterious beauty who hurried out of a building into a waiting limousine? The end of a long dream that had become reality.

Annalise, surprised to find her nineteen-year-old daughter Elizabeth tucked into the corner as though she were trying to hide, was struck anew by the thought that Elizabeth was the only person she had failed completely.

"No class today?" Annalise asked the question more briskly than she intended. She took her seat in the caramel-colored interior of the limo and offered her cheek to be kissed. Elizabeth's lips were thin unyielding edges, little razor blades designed for cutting.

"I have class," Elizabeth said. "I figured Robert would drop me off."

"Since when can't you get to school under your own steam?"

"I can, I just figured . . . oh, what's the difference?"

Annalise's briefcase, crammed with papers, lay on the seat between them. She imagined Elizabeth had gone through them in a desultory, uninterested way.

"What's that awful little outfit you're wearing?" she asked her daughter in an irritated tone. Elizabeth was dressed in a cotton beige layering of safari clothes, skirt, blouse, overblouse, and wide man's vest over that. Her brown hair, arguably her best feature—a long, thick mass of uncombed, or over-combed, curls—was partially hidden under a narrow-brimmed black bowler.

"This is neat," Elizabeth said, scowling anew. "It's what *we* wear. *We* don't wear couture clothes to school. We don't wear couture clothes out of school, either."

"Elizabeth, I don't expect anything from you except that you graduate and get on with your life."

"I need fifty thousand dollars if we expect to finish that film."

We, that imperious *we*, a ragtag group of kids with angry faces and funny haircuts. Annalise cast a glance at the chauffeur, knowing he couldn't hear them; still her eye caught his through the rearview mirror and she had a momentary shock at the intimacy of that shared glance. He was merely the chauffeur, a man nearing retirement who was married to her housekeeper, that was all, but it took her back to that other life, a thousand light-years distant when a glance out of hooded eyes had struck her with terror.

"Don't get hysterical," Elizabeth was saying. "We'll pay back every cent. I have complete faith in the project. Mom, it's important." Her implacable manner told Annalise that the film would change the world forever.

Annalise leaned back and took up the leather briefcase, tossing open its creamy flap. "*Breathing*'s important," she remarked. She remembered the film project now, something about the early fight to unionize the garment industry. Clever of Elizabeth to ask her mother for money to fund such an enterprise. "Fifty thousand dollars, is that all?"

"To launch that perfume is going to cost you twenty million dollars."

"It's a lot more complicated than that, Liza. The perfume is licensed. We're dealing with other people's money."

Elizabeth's sigh was audible. "Right. Other people's money. Leveraged buyouts, I know all about it. You're not interested in anything I do. I figured as much." She leaned forward, tapped the glass separating them from the driver, and spoke into the intercom. "Robert, I'm getting out at the next corner."

"What does your father say?" Annalise asked. She had no desire to detain her daughter.

"He's not my father, and I'm not about to ask him."

"Funny, he'd be more likely to hand you the money if you could show him why you need it and how you intend to use it."

Elizabeth stepped from the limousine. "It's all right," she said. "I haven't promised anyone you'd come through. I didn't think you would. After all, the ladies must be dressed in their stupid sequins, they must wear that—that perfume you're developing. God forbid you'd see your way to funding something really important. Your pal Egon said he'd help, but now he's dead and I'm stuck coming to you, but forget it." She slammed the door.

"What did you say?" Annalise put her hand to her forehead, unable to take in the meaning of her daughter's remark. "*What do you think about Egon?*" That was Tina Fletcher, wasn't it, back at the studio? And now Liza, telling her Egon was dead.

Annalise called out after her daughter, but Elizabeth kept walking.

"Shall I get her for you, madam?" Robert, who had come around to the passenger side, regarded her through the window.

"No, thank you, it's all right, Robert." She gazed after her daughter, the little baroness, a small, plump, truculent figure with her German father's puckish face and indignant manner and none of Annalise's polish.

Egon? What in the world was happening?

"Robert," she said as the chauffeur settled back into the driver's seat, "better keep going to Eighth and then back east to Seventh on Thirty-eighth. Otherwise we'll never get there. I've got a meeting. . . ."

"What do you think about Egon? But now he's dead." It couldn't be true. *But now he's dead, but now he's dead. Too bad about Egon.*

From the first, Egon understood her need to control everything around her. Hubris of that sort was harmful, he told her; if she was afraid of advice, of disagreement, she wouldn't learn, wouldn't grow.

"Annalise, don't hide behind pride; use it to your advantage. You have beauty, brains, and talent, and guess what?" he'd said in a tone that expected no answer. "You don't need a farthing because you have Egon Delville."

One never *had* Egon Delville, not totally. One had Egon's flitting, careless attention, and occasionally some good would come of it. He had introduced her to New York society, and to Zack, beaming like a proud father when she landed the wealthiest, most eligible bachelor in town.

"This is merely the beginning," he said, and yet the night before at Marguerite's shot daggers at her because she planned to come out with a rival perfume. How proud he was of his *nose* and how much she wanted his opinion of the scent she wore. Instead, at the last minute, she insisted she was wearing Delville, daring him to call her on it. He hadn't disagreed, merely disapproved.

She gazed out the window, unable to repress an unexpected smile. He was just being bitchy, but then, so was she.

The sidewalk was crowded with the clothing trolleys that daily made passage impossible in the garment district, yet no one had found a better way of moving clothing from factory to showroom than out in the open, on the street.

As the limousine edged its way crosstown, Annalise plucked a computer printout from her briefcase and was deep into sales figures when the limousine drew up at the big granite building on Seventh that held the offices and showrooms of Annalise, Inc. She slipped the printout back into her briefcase. She hadn't been concentrating; she had been thinking about Egon Delville.

CHAPTER 4

The kitchen was old-fashioned and sunny, with high white wooden cabinets and white tile behind the sink and stove. Like the rest of the prewar apartment, its windows were filled with plants, in this case herbs that kept the kitchen fragrant with the scent of basil, oregano, and rosemary, which now mingled with the aroma of coffee and toast.

At eight o'clock Kate, dressed and ready for work, sat in the kitchen with Matt, supervising his breakfast. "Nothing wrong with your appetite, is there, my man?"

"I'm not a man, I'm a little boy."

"Well, so you are, a big little boy, though."

Matt looked at her seriously. "You can't be a big little boy." He pushed his spoon through a bowl of cereal, managing in spite of the mess to down half of it. He was a stolid child with pale strawberry blond hair like his father's, golden skin, gray eyes, and a serene expression that matched his temperament. In spite of the divorce, in spite of his mother's absence through most of the day, he was playful, bright, and self-confident. Leaving him, however, was so wrenching that Kate once considered turning a back room at work into a nursery where other employees might also bring their children. But Ira had given the idea an unconditional no because of the cost of insurance and qualified personnel.

She leaned over and kissed her son's cheek, taking away the taste of cereal on her lips. "What are you going to do at nursery school today?"

"I don't know." He bunched his shoulders together.

"I Don't Know. Hey, that's my favorite game—I Don't Know. Let's see, as I recall I Don't Know is played with a rubber ball and a stick and there are three men on first base."

Matt giggled. "That's no game." He began to push the spoon around his cereal bowl again. "Don't go to work," he announced with an unexpected frown, not looking at her.

Kate was taken aback. Her son usually ran happily ahead of her when she dropped him off at nursery school. "Darling, I'm afraid I have to. I thought you liked nursery school. After all, Teddy's there. He's your best friend, isn't he? Don't you want to see Teddy?"

"Can I go to work with you?"

At that moment the housekeeper appeared. She took the spoon out of his hand and removed the cereal bowl. She contended that Kate fed him entirely too much. "Time to go," she announced. "They're having a clay-mushing contest today, remember?"

Matt nodded enthusiastically and climbed off the chair. "Yay, clay-mushing."

"What kind of contest is that?" Kate asked Jeannette on the way back to her room.

"Mushing clay, I suppose."

"Well, thank heaven for whatever it is, anyway. He was making noises about my staying home."

"He'd make noises no matter what you did."

The intercom connecting her apartment to the lobby buzzed twice signaling the arrival of her cab.

The intercom buzzed again, then rapidly a couple of times more. When Kate came out of her room she found Jeannette replacing the intercom receiver. "What was that all about?"

"Mrs. Varick is on her way up."

"Marguerite Varick?"

"Sounds like it."

Matt came into the room carrying his security blanket, a pale blue tatter of wool. "Darling, leave the blanket at home."

"No."

"You might lose it."

"No, I won't."

"Somebody else might want that blanket just as much as you do. Then what would happen?"

"No, they won't."

"Jeannette." Kate turned an imploring eye on her housekeeper whose glance told her not to worry; she'd handle the boy. The doorbell rang. "I'll get it," Kate said, wondering what Marguerite wanted at such an early hour. After all, they'd been together the night before.

"Is everything all right?" she asked, frowning when she saw Marguerite looking paler than usual.

"You haven't heard, then." Marguerite moved past her into the apartment, a tall, erect woman in her sixties with a mop of short curly hair dyed to resemble a cloud of red-gold—she referred to it as her signature color. She was smooth-skinned, a dramatic woman for whom cosmetic surgery worked.

She dressed in black and wore masses of bracelets, chunks of real gold that clanked with each movement like Indian chimes played by the wind.

"Heard what?" Kate followed her friend into the living room.

Marguerite turned peridot green eyes on her. She regarded Kate with an odd expression on her face, as though she had second thoughts about the visit.

The intercom buzzed twice. "That's my cab," Kate said. "Let me drop you off. We can talk on the way. I've got to get going."

"The cab will have to wait." Marguerite spoke imperiously in a thick French accent leavened with British pronunciation. After thirty years in America her speech was the same as when she had first arrived: the French *r*'s and the ends of sentences inflected as though she were asking a question in a girlish voice, with an added "eh" for emphasis. If angry or frustrated or emotional, as now appeared the case, her accent became more exaggerated.

Matt, still holding his blanket, came into the room and bumped up against his mother. "Matt darling, say hello to Tante Marguerite."

He went over to Marguerite and politely put his hand out. Marguerite spontaneously bent down to kiss him. "How are you, *mon petit chouchou?*" Matt stared at her.

"Matt, put your blanket in your room. We're going to leave in a minute. Jeannette," Kate added, shrugging helplessly. The housekeeper took the boy by his hand and with a soothing word led him back to his room.

Kate felt palpable tension in the air. She thought of Ira, of a fashion award she stood a good chance of winning; she thought of the end of the world and realized her hands were shaking.

Marguerite went over to the living room window. She turned to Kate and regarded her silently. "You don't know."

A chill came over Kate. "What don't I know?"

"Egon is dead."

Kate stared at her friend, bewildered. "What?" The word came out fainter and at a higher pitch than usual.

"Last night."

Kate picked up the telephone, punched in Egon's number, and after two rings, slammed the receiver down. She went over to Marguerite and put her arms around her. "I'm totally blank. I can't seem to take in what—what you just told me." After a moment's silence, during which they stood holding on to each other, Kate murmured, "It's not possible. It can't be. He was— We saw him— He was with us last night. I mean he looked *fine*. I mean a little off his feed, but—"

"He died at home, sitting in his favorite chair. About midnight."

"You know all that?"

"His valet called me. Woke me up at two this morning. He thought I should know. Kate, I've been up all night."

"Was it his heart?"

"So the doctor believes. He was an old woman," Marguerite added impatiently, as though anxious to impart blame to Egon for dying without warning her. "And secretive."

"Secretive! Marguerite, he lived in the public eye, reveled in it."

"You learned only what he wanted you to learn. He held things back."

Kate frowned. Marguerite was apparently taking Egon's death as a personal affront. He had managed to die without Marguerite's permission, all alone in his library at some unwholesome hour.

"And he took things from you—your life, your secrets, so that you had to depend upon him," Marguerite went on, her voice rising. "He was the repository of your soul."

"You're not making sense, Marguerite."

The woman gazed at her with surprise. "Think about it, my dear."

"He was a mentor to me," Kate said slowly. "My backbone in a way." But so was Marguerite, two mentors moving her career along. And neither cared a dime for Ira. "Damn, what will I do now? I never felt the collection was ready without his approval. Oh, Lord, I can hear his voice. 'All right, kid, you're good, but what are you doing for an encore?' That was Egon being Humphrey Bogart. I think an out-and-out compliment, given right up front, would have killed him. Killed him. Dear Egon." Her voice fell away. She felt she should cry, but her eyes held no tears.

"With Egon gone, nothing will ever be quite the same," Marguerite said. "We need a court jester. The life we lead needs a court jester, someone who can tell us how empty all this is and what tremendous fun."

"We used him, he used us. Oh, hell, what are we talking about? I hate consigning him to the past. There's so much I meant to talk to him about."

Egon had often pressed Kate about putting her name on a perfume. "Don't wait. It's the single most important thing you can do. Get you out of the clutches of the Ira Gregorys of this world. I'll help you. I'll lend you my nose."

"Keep your nose, old dear." She always laughed and refused to take him up on it. Licensing would come later, when her name was firmly established. She needed to win a few more prestigious awards, make the cover of *Vogue*, have a boutique on the fourth floor of Bloomingdale's. Egon was supposed to live forever.

"Mommy." Matt stood at the door without his blanket.

She glanced at her watch. "Marguerite, I have to take Matt to nursery school."

"Yes, of course." Marguerite enveloped Kate in her arms for a moment, then with a quick kiss on her cheek released her.

Kate took her son's hand and headed for the front door. "Marguerite, I was going to call you. I need your advice about a whole bunch of things." She needed to talk to her about designing a bridge line and whether it was an appropriate move.

"And if Egon were alive?" Marguerite asked. "Would you have gone to him first?"

Kate was astonished at the question. "Egon? About this? No, never, absolutely never."

At nine Ira Gregory opened the door to Kate Hayden's busy workroom and peered in. "Got a minute?" She had a mouthful of pins and it took her a few seconds to stick them into the wrist pincushion she wore but invariably forgot to use.

Kate always draped on a live model, Vivian, her favorite, who was bony, leggy, lazy, and able to stand, trancelike, through long fitting sessions. "Come in," she told Ira, still eyeing the soft, bias-cut drape of lightweight emerald silk that would evolve into a figure-flattering dress.

"In here," he said, coming quickly through the busy atelier and opening the door to her office. There was no particular firmness in his tone and no familiarity, either.

Kate adjusted the drape at the shoulder and then excused herself. "Back in a minute." Her staff barely glanced up from their work.

The studio was a busy, disordered place filled with sample clothes and bolts of fabric, mannequins on which half-finished dresses had been pinned, and sewing machines that produced a faint, pleasant hum.

"Oh," Kate said to her model, "Vivian, could I ask you a gigantic favor?"

"Anything, Kate."

"Don't move."

"Don't move!" Vivian gazed around the room as if entreating the others to help her, and said in her warm, languid voice, "Ka-ate, how can I move? These dumb pins. I'll bleed like a pig if I move."

"Be right back." Kate walked into her office, closing the door behind her. Her office was orderly and modern. A couch upholstered in white linen stood against the wall, flanked by a couple of sleek white chairs. Her desk was a slab of Lucite on a steel pedestal. When she sat behind it, one could see her shapely legs and her feet shod in expensive pumps with very high heels.

"You've heard about Egon," she said. Ira stood behind her desk, reading her mail.

"Hey." She went up to him, giving him what she knew was a false smile. "You don't know the meaning of privacy, do you?"

"Privacy?" He came around the desk and took her in his arms. "After what went on between us last night? Privacy the lady wants. There isn't anything about you I don't know a hundred different ways." His mouth was on hers. She heard a sudden inconsequential laugh on the other side of the door leading to the showroom. Kate was acutely aware of the view outside her window and the building across Seventh Avenue where someone might be watching them. She was aware of both unlocked doors to her office, of the possibility of someone popping in unannounced.

She pulled away. "It doesn't mean anything to you that one of my closest friends has died."

"At the risk of having you offer me your charming frown, I'd say it didn't happen a minute too soon."

"I could slap your face for that remark."

"You'll do better without him. I never liked him, and I never liked his interfering in our business."

"He never interfered, and I valued what advice he did give me. And I'll miss him, dammit, and I don't want to hear one more word from you about Egon Delville."

Ira merely laughed and reached for her. He had her in a vise, she thought, in more ways than one, as his hands closed tightly around her arms. "I hope he left you a bundle in his will."

"Why in hell would he do that?"

"He was in love with you."

"You bastard." She had promised herself to end it with Ira and to demand her apartment key back. She was about to say something when his lips descended on hers. Kate felt her muscles and her will give way. She was certain the whole world knew and was talking about her foolhardy affair with Ira Gregory. She moved against him and cursed her craziness as his tongue searched hers out, his body hard and ready. She allowed him to draw her over to the couch, to press her with his body into the down-filled linen.

The moment of urgency threatened to come with expected swiftness, that moment when all sense would disappear and she'd have him quickly, with her staff laughing on the other side of the door, Vivian waiting to be unpinned, voyeurs watching from across the way, and the possibility of someone coming through the unlocked door. And the damnedest part was suddenly not caring in the least. She would have him as desperately as she had the night before, without thinking of the consequences.

Ira's moan was low in his throat. He fumbled for her blouse, the madness ready to repeat itself with everyone outside listening for the moaning, the struggling.

And Egon was dead. Egon who for reasons never explained had despised Ira. She pushed hard against Ira, dragging her lips away. "Is this what's so urgent I had to drop everything?"

"It always is." But her remark spoiled the moment. He rolled off her, laughed, and got to his feet.

Kate stood up, straightened her skirt and blouse, and went over to the mirror to correct her makeup and comb her hair. She was still wearing the pincushion on her wrist, like a thick, exotic bracelet. She wanted him, she didn't want him. She loved him, she didn't love him.

Ira came up behind her and placed his hands on her breasts. He watched her in the mirror. "He's gone, Kate. He was destructive. Your talent is supposed to flow free, not depend upon the idiosyncrasies of one crazy old man."

She whipped around to face him. "He wasn't old and he wasn't crazy."

"But he is dead."

"Yes, he's dead and I'll get on without him, but his was the approval I sought, Ira, not yours." Time to ask him for the key, to be brave about fresh beginnings. Egon was dead. She had to rid herself of Ira. "And I agree my work is supposed to flow free, Ira. I don't like having limits put on me."

"I'm only asking for a line apart from Kate Hayden that will start money flowing in."

"It's too late in the season. I've got ninety garments to produce between now and November. I want to be able to cull from a lot more than that. I don't have time for bridge lines or any other damn thing."

His look hardened. "Too late isn't in my lexicon. I want you to sketch the collection and have your staff work up the models. And I need models to send to Hong Kong for pricing out, Kate. You're too goddam slow in the best of times."

"I know what I'm doing. I think you forget that I managed my life pretty well before you stepped into it. I'll have everything ready on time, if you'll just get off my case."

He studied her for a moment, then said in an unexpectedly casual tone, "Incidentally, the IRS is coming to look at the books next Monday."

"The IRS?" An alarm ticked off. She glanced at his eyes, but all he gave her was an untroubled smile. "What's the problem?"

"There isn't any."

She felt the familiar twinge that reminded her she had signed away too much of her power too quickly. She had walked away from Domingo because she wanted autonomy, and now the only autonomy she had was whether to drape to the right side or the left side. "So the IRS wants to look at our books."

"I welcome the opportunity," he told her. "But I don't want you around for the week or two they're here. It's the perfect time for you to fly to Hong Kong with the models. I want you to see our factory, talk to the manager, learn the operation firsthand. You're too distanced from what's going on there."

"That's on the heels of trying to force a bridge line on me. You're something, Ira, you really are. You tell me there isn't any problem with the IRS, but I'm not supposed to be around when they show up to examine our books. Mind explaining yourself?"

"You wouldn't know a spreadsheet from a racing form. Your absolute ignorance in money matters is appalling, Kate. I don't want them interviewing you and having you say something stupid."

"Stupid!" She felt a surge of pure anger. "I don't know what the hell's going on because you keep telling me, 'Create, baby. Don't worry about the finances.' " Not worrying, she realized, because all she wanted at the moment was to see the collection a raving success, her name on a label, Kate Hayden *everywhere*. Pick up a dress, check the label, and there it would be, Kate Hayden, Kate Hayden, Kate Hayden.

"What's wrong with wanting you to keep your mind off the finances, to create, nothing else, no worries, nothing? We've been operating on that principle for the better part of a year, Kate. I haven't heard you complain before."

"I'm complaining now. I want to see the books before the IRS does."

"You're going to Hong Kong. You won't have time."

"You really believe I'm capable of saying something stupid to these—whoever they are."

"You know what I mean."

"No, I don't. Anyway, why would they interview me if all they want is a look at our records?"

"I'm booking you into a suite at the Majestic in Hong Kong for a week, Kate."

"I'm not going to Hong Kong," she said. "Not now. You go to Hong Kong just as you've always done. And I'm not leaving my child here while I pop off to the other end of the world and have my ex jump a lawsuit on me claiming neglect."

"Neglect? Leaving your child for a week so you can earn enough money to keep him in luxury, something that lout you married can't do? Just give me a week by staying out of the way. It won't be the first time you've been away from your son."

"It's not overnight to Podunk."

She noted, returning to her desk, that a couple of incoming calls were being deflected by her secretary, as she had requested. "I've got to get back to work." All this anxiety so she could amuse herself draping lengths of fabric that had absolutely nothing to do with the way the world turned. "Which set of books are you going to show them?" She made the remark as a joke, not daring to note his reaction. She picked up the telephone and punched in her secretary's extension number. "Any messages?"

"The phone's been ringing off the wall all morning, Kate."

"Let me see what you have."

Ira cocked a finger at Kate. "Lunch," he said with an expression on his face that told her she had no choice in the matter of Hong Kong, the bridge line, or anything else. Exiting the office, Ira winked at her secretary, who was on her way in.

"No, I . . ." Kate began and then finished lamely, "have an appointment," but he didn't hear her.

Ira was beginning to be a problem, and she no longer had Egon to verbally kick Ira around. She'd been angry and amused over the license Egon took, but with him gone she had no one besides Marguerite who'd give a damn. It was about time she began to show a little muscle. She wasn't going to Hong Kong, she would say no to the bridge line, and the next time she saw Ira she'd demand her key back. That was a start, wasn't it?

CHAPTER 5

You heard," Dell Stanche said as soon as Annalise stepped out of the elevator into the busy reception room.

"About Egon? Yes." Annalise handed over her briefcase and went rapidly through without looking right or left.

The showroom, with its gray Ultrasuede walls and thick gray carpeting, was an open ell visible from the reception area. Deserted at the moment, a buyer from a Scottsdale, Arizona, boutique was expected in at ten that morning.

"I haven't quite taken it in yet," Annalise said, going quickly down the corridor.

"The clothes looked gorgeous on TV," Dell said. "We watched in my office. Your voice comes across really creamy. Your accent is so beautiful."

"Everyone talks about my accent, and I keep thinking I've lost it."

Dell waited a beat as though to catch her breath. "Anyway, I called the *Times* to check about Egon. They said it was a heart attack."

"We were together at Marguerite Varick's last night," Annalise said.

"Was he all right then?"

On either side of the gray-carpeted corridor were offices. At the far end were the workrooms from which issued a pleasant muffled sound of sewing machines and voices, and a scent of air-conditioning, coffee and perfumes, all of which Annalise took in unconsciously. Heads whipped up when she passed, smiles were given, heads ducked down. Someone came running toward her from the sample room carrying a sheet of vellum with a watercolor on it, the new young assistant she had hired away from Oscar de la Renta. "Could I speak with you for a few seconds, Mrs. Younger?"

Annalise shook her head, glancing at the watercolor upside down. "It'll have to be sometime late this morning. How are you working out?"

"Fine, it's just—"

"About eleven." Annalise gave a smile she knew was patronizing. "Dell," she said to her assistant, walking quickly on, knowing the young designer stood there looking worriedly after her, "what about lunch for our friends from Scottsdale? Have you penciled it in?"

Dell pushed open the door to Annalise's private suite of offices. "They said their schedule's too tight this trip around and thank you kindly."

"We're laying on coffee and pastry, though."

"Kitchen's handling it."

Her secretary jumped up and rushed to unlock the door to her office. "I'm sorry about Egon Delville. I still have that message on my pad to put a call through to him today."

"I guess you can scrub it," Annalise said, a little too sharply, realizing she didn't want to discuss Egon, not quite yet, not until she could digest the news properly.

"Can you imagine? He was a bachelor, wasn't he?" Dell paused, then added, "Wonder who inherits?"

Annalise sailed into her office, but not before casting a look of annoyance at her assistant. Who indeed? Egon had probably thought he'd beat the devil by ignoring him.

Morning sun obliquely lit the neutral taupes and grays of her office, and the faint disarray she encouraged: sueded walls backed by cork upon which had been tacked Annalise's witty sketches of the resort line, a long narrow ribbon of antique silver sequins thrown carelessly over the back of a couch, piles of silken fabric on a chair in the corner.

She remembered Egon rushing in earlier that year after his return from the Milan collections. "Houndstooth and plaids, Prince of Wales *principally*, Annalise, everything terribly British country." She'd had no doubt he was right, and he was. Damn him for dying.

Standing at her desk, she checked through her messages while Dell and her secretary breathlessly recited phone calls. The press had been calling all morning, *W*, the *New York Times*, *New York Newsday*.

She found a message from Marguerite Varick who'd undoubtedly be planning a commemorative issue around Egon for *Varick's Fashion Forecast*. Ralley Littlehurst had called. She'd want to meet Annalise for a strong drink raised to Egon's memory. Since there was no family to call or console, his friends would have to meet merely to talk about him, to wonder about his meaning in their lives.

She supposed she'd hear next from Kate Hayden. And Jaybee Olsen. Their phone calls formed a kind of round robin. Damn Egon, she'd miss him, the silly, lovable, overbearing fool. Had he been the one who held them all together? Was he the glue of their tenuous friendships?

"Get me Ralley Littlehurst," she said to her secretary, flipping through her calendar. "Then Marguerite Varick, then Kate Hayden." She'd hold off on Jaybee, whose truculence could be unbearable sometimes and who would have a lot to say about Egon, scarcely any of it good.

They'd all been at Marguerite's party the evening before, but hadn't said much to one another. Marguerite's dinners were carefully choreographed; she frowned upon women chatting up other women for any length of time.

"Miss Littlehurst must be at work now," her secretary remarked. Ralley was fashion director of Steyman's, a large retailer with a successful high-priced mail-order operation. "Oh, and don't forget your appointment at ten. Lowry's, Scottsdale."

"Just find Ralley, please, and get her on the phone." Annalise reached for the folder that held her morning mail. She turned to her assistant who had disappeared for a moment to return with a pack of photographs. "Check to make sure everything's ready for Lowry's. Models, too. Are they here?"

Her secretary nodded. "No sweat. Your husband said to call him at his office first thing."

"Ralley, then my husband."

"I'm sick over Egon," Ralley said at once, without waiting for preliminaries. "He didn't tell you anything was wrong, did he?"

"Egon equated being sick with old age, and he never figured on growing old," Annalise said. "Let's not talk now. Meet me for lunch. Raven's, noon."

Her husband, reached at his office, asked at once, "How'd it go?" His voice was deep and assured. He had been taking speech lessons from the top image maker in the country and only faint traces of his New York accent remained.

"You didn't catch it, then." She tried to contain the exasperation in her voice. All through the interview she believed he'd been watching.

"Sorry, love, I couldn't catch it, but I set the VCR. We can admire it this evening. Incidentally, I heard about Egon. A pity, I liked him, in spite of everything."

"In spite of everything, oh Zack, how could you?" She took in a short breath. Dell, along with her promotion director, newly hired chief executive officer, and premiere were standing at the corner window with its view down the avenue of the Twin Towers in the distance. They were examining transparencies held up to the light and whispering among themselves.

"We'll find you someone equally charming," Zack said. "Elizabeth called and mumbled something about fifty thousand dollars, then said I should forget it and hung up. Know what that's all about?"

"She called, did she? Well, will wonders never cease? No need to worry. Our daughter's an entrepreneur. We'll talk about it later."

"*Our* daughter, is it?" His voice was both wary and pleased. "Look, Annie, how about lunch? This thing with Egon, maybe you could use a good shoulder to cry on. No, dammit," he said a second later. "Lunch at Gracie Mansion. Somehow I don't think—"

She could see her secretary being detained at the half-closed door by the director of marketing. She hit the button on her telephone. "Is it true?" she asked Marguerite at once.

"Merde," Marguerite said. "You'd think he'd tell us what his plans were. So unlike Egon." She began to sob quietly and then, after a moment, said, "You were sitting next to him last evening. Did he say anything—complain, eh?—about not feeling well?" In speech, her syntax was often deliberately clumsy, although she wrote grammatically perfect English.

"No. He wasn't much fun, but I figured his nose was out of joint for one reason or another. You know Egon, you either run the whole works or sit back and sulk."

"I've got to get the *Forecast* out, no matter how sick I feel. I'll need a quote from you, Annalise. Egon was one of your earliest friends when you came to the States. Just a few words, a little *quelque chose,* how his famous exquisite taste affected your work, et cetera."

Annalise thought for a moment, but suddenly didn't want Marguerite to know how much she had depended upon the man's approval. "Darling, make something up for me. You're so good at that." Marguerite would rewrite whatever she said, anyway.

"Yes, of course, my dear, if that's what you want. I'm feeling pretty low. When can we have lunch?"

Annalise didn't want lunch that day with anyone but Ralley, who would mask her sorrow with crisp humor. "Later this week?"

Marguerite seemed satisfied. "I'll call you."

After she hung up, Annalise sat quietly for a moment, removed from the activity in her office, from the people waiting politely for her word, good or bad. She knew that Marguerite didn't hold her designs to be of much worth and thought Annalise used Paris as too close a reference point. Annalise disagreed. Her ladies wanted Paris fashions with an American hand, and that was just what she was giving them in this, the year of the Spanish designer, according to Tina Fletcher.

The light blinked on her telephone again. Her secretary, instead of reaching her through the intercom, opened the door and smiled in at her. "Mr. Younger on six."

Annalise frowned and reached for the receiver, wondering what her husband wanted. He had said something about lunch with the mayor at Gracie Mansion. The door to her office was still open, and she could see her secretary once more detained by the director of marketing. She hit the button on the phone, not realizing it was the wrong one.

The man's voice at the other end was quiet and light, altogether polite and appropriate, which threw her off guard. "Ms. Michelis? I didn't think I'd get

She interrupted him. "Zack, I'll see you at dinner. Incidentally, I managed a plug for your Senate race this morning."

"In between the sequins. Of course, I knew you'd come through."

She laughed. "Of course. Oh, and remember tonight's concert. Well, maybe not, because of Egon." Her hand was on the disconnect button before he could say another word.

Her staff, at the window, turned and looked at her expectantly. "How are they?" she asked, referring to the transparencies.

"Sensational."

"Fantastic, Annalise, fantastic."

"We're going to crop Stargaze for the *W* ad, put the emphasis on the three-quarter view. Want a look?"

"Just a minute."

Her premiere, Nance Ulanov, came toward her entreatingly, holding a large cutting of a silken-look jersey. Dressed all in black, she was a sober, intense woman whose blunt-fingered hands produced the models for the evening collection.

"This jersey," she said of the swatch she proceeded to squash in her hands, "I don't care if it's made of silk or spiderwebs, it wrinkles unmercifully." Her manner with Annalise was easy and familiar. "The pattern's flattering and so's the way the fabric takes color, but you get this bunching under the arm." She shook the material out, but the wrinkles remained. "It's a bitch, Annalise. You'll have your ladies cursing you senseless."

"They'll wear it once, give it away and it's the ladies at the resale shop who'll curse me senseless. What is it? Silk and what else?"

"The ticket says silk, sheer wool, rayon."

"Get me Isabel," Annalise said, referring to her fabric stylist. She took the swatch and rubbed its silkiness. "Too bad. It has a wonderfully light hand and takes that beige beautifully. How'd she let it slip by?"

"Didn't wear it under her arms. And believe it or not, the damn thing has a sheen. You have to treat the fabric like velvet. We won't get good cutting."

"I want something like it, though."

Her premiere nodded. "If possible. You know, that's a corollary to Murphy's Law. If it's good, they'll build a flaw in it."

"All right, we'll see what Isabel has to say." Her secretary opened the door, and a maid wearing a dainty starched uniform came in with coffee and a few dry biscuits for Annalise.

"Marguerite Varick on six," her secretary said.

Annalise glanced over at the window where her employees still waited. The maid placed the cup in front of her and poured coffee from a delicate china pot. "Anyone else?" Annalise asked, reaching for the telephone.

through so fast. I figured I'd have to pass a battery of lieutenants or the palace guard at least."

"Who is this?" The voice wasn't familiar, but Annalise was instinctively on her guard and couldn't have said why.

"I just wondered," her caller said after a slight hesitation, "if you could tell me what the word *puta* means."

CHAPTER 6

The freight elevator clanked slowly up, stopping on the second floor to let out the driver from United Parcel wheeling a handcart loaded with packages. The elevator stopped again on three. A woman entered clutching a sheaf of papers. She cast a worried glance at Pete Frank as if being alone with him were a date with murder, then pushed five, stood close to the door, and hurried out without a backward glance when she reached her floor.

Pete was pleased. He obviously looked the part. Studded denim jacket, tight jeans, luxuriant tough-guy mustache, hair a little long—your basic trucker on his way to give a payoff, or accept one. A thrill raced through him of heightened sensibilities, of adrenaline pumping as smartly as Mobil at the local gas station, the excitement of the risk-taker doing what reason and his boss had told him not to do.

"I don't want to hear about anything illegal, Pete," Tess Cristaforo had said. The United States Attorney for the Southern District of New York knew he was a maverick when he transferred to New York, but she apparently hoped he'd operate within the law. "I've got a hundred thirty attorneys to worry about, and how come they can all toe the mark but you?"

"Maybe they lie about their toe-marking. This is the way I do business."

"I said I don't want to hear about it. And as in the best spy fiction, if you're caught, I'll disown you."

"Tess, we're dealing with creeps—mob creeps. You don't handle them the way you do normal criminals."

"I'm not listening to you, Pete."

Pete believed in hands-on experience, even if little came of it. This one could mean nothing or an invitation to a drowning in the East River. Just before he stepped out of the freight elevator on the eighth floor, Pete Frank slipped his hand into his leather jacket pocket and flipped on the tape recorder. Then he waited a moment while the huge doors clanged shut and the elevator moved slowly upward. A pile of neatly stacked dress boxes lay on a handcart to his right. A couple of clothes trolleys to his left held an array of garments under plastic covers. Dead ahead—in front of a blank wall broken only by a well marked-up girlie calendar, a cluttered bulletin board, and a double set of doors—was a small metal desk covered with shipping papers. Behind the metal desk sat an overweight fellow with a shiny pate that echoed his belly in shape and size. He was blind in one eye, which gave him a malevolent look, turned now upon Pete Frank advancing to the reception desk.

"Yah?"

"Name's Don Assorio," Pete said.

"Congratulations."

Pete gave him a broad grin to let him know he appreciated New York humor. He felt the false mustache move on his upper lip and gave it a light press as though he had just finished a beer with a thick head on it. "Right. Of Assorio Trucking." Then he fished in his jacket pocket for a card, which he presented. "Based in Brooklyn, with two brand-new GMC trucks. You'll find our prices competitive. More than competitive. Who do I see around here?"

The man took the card, scarcely glanced at it, and handed it back. "You're in the wrong place," he said. "We're very satisfied with our truckers."

"To get a foot in we'd be willing to talk price," Pete persisted. "How about letting me see your boss?"

"Forget it."

"Come on," Pete said, leaning on the desk in a friendly way. "You've only been in business for what—one year? You don't even know if you're happy or not."

"You from the South? I mean, you new in town? That southern accent? Straight off the farm, is that it, don't know your way around and you figure you'll get a little action in the garment district, right, am I right, of course I'm right. Jeez, they don't teach you to take no for an answer down there, do they?"

"Hey," Pete said, "those are a lot of questions. I'm just after a piece of the pie; there should be plenty around for everybody."

"What's that pie they eat down there, pecan? Yeah, I remember that from the army." He turned his one good eye on Pete's face. "Now, get lost, Mr. Assorio, and if you want my advice, you'll stick to Brooklyn or Queens with your brand-new GMC trucks. Traffic's lousy in the city, no way a man can make a decent buck." He stopped and looked back as the double doors were pushed open and a man came out in a rush, carrying some papers. He was dressed in an expensive gray suit with shot white cuffs and a deep red tie of lustrous silk. "Listen, Hal," he began, then stopped when he saw Pete.

"He was just leaving, Mr. Gregory."

Ira Gregory, the man himself, Pete realized, straightening and digging into his pocket for another card. "Just tryin' to sell my truckin' service," he said, exaggerating his North Carolina accent so that he sounded as if he'd come straight out of the marshes of Louisiana.

Gregory, whose eyes were a striking blue, studied the card for a moment, then handed it to Hal. His words were polite but with a firm edge. "We're happy with our current truckers," he told Pete. "Appreciate your stopping by."

"We do long-distance hauling. We're competitive with Federal Express, UPS. Try us, you'll like us," Pete added.

Hal pushed his chair back and with surprising speed stepped out from behind the desk. "What say you take your ass out of here right now, Mr. Assorio?"

"No sweat," Pete said. He turned and went back to the freight elevator. Ira Gregory had disappeared behind the double doors. As Pete waited for the elevator to lumber back to the eighth floor, he was aware of Hal standing behind him unmoving.

Well, Hal was in possession of his business card and maybe he'd make a phone call and maybe he wouldn't. Perhaps next time Pete would enter Kate Hayden through the reception room. Wear a thousand dollar suit and blow-dry his hair. Pretend to be a buyer from Beverly Hills with cash to spread around.

Tess would split a gut.

The reporter from *Mirror* magazine was thin, serious and clearly a bright young man. David Orenstein also slouched in his chair and complained about having a bad back. He sipped black coffee from a Styrofoam container that left a fresh circle on Pete Frank's desk each time he picked it up. The steno pad in his lap was opened to a blank page.

Pete's fault, of course, the blank page. He scratched his ear and kept his expression deadpan. The article Orenstein was researching on the way the mob ruled New York's fashion industry and how it was getting away with murder, could land him in a lot of trouble with the wrong people. Whether the reporter didn't care or was suicidal, Peter Frank couldn't tell, but he wasn't about to help Orenstein on his way.

Orenstein shifted awkwardly in his chair, as if wondering whether Pete Frank's silence was arrogance or worse. "I need help," he said at last.

Pete thought about telling him to lay off, that racketeering and corruption in the fashion industry was one area from which even the Manhattan district attorney's office stayed a respectful distance. Pete wasn't with the local D.A.'s office, however. He was an attorney with the U.S. Justice Department and had been recently assigned to the Southern District of New York. His opinion didn't quite mesh with the city's of the way the fashion industry was conducted. The city considered itself lucky enough to keep alive the remnants of its fashion manufacturing business without muckrakers like Orenstein embarrassing anyone into a full-scale investigation.

The President was committed to cleansing municipalities of corruption. In his inaugural speech he stated that racketeering wouldn't be tolerated, which was why Pete was in Manhattan with a commission to rake over the garment industry under RICO, the 1970 Racketeer Influenced and Corrupt Organizations act. RICO was originally enacted to root out criminal interests that had taken over legitimate businesses. An anonymous source, three months previously, had contacted the government about Ira Gregory. The source, a well-placed businessman with no ties to Ira Gregory, refused to name *his* sources. The attorney general's office had been impressed enough to go ahead. The Internal Revenue Service, following leads of its own, suspected that DAS Limited, Zurich, the parent company of Kate Hayden, was part of a money-laundering operation.

Kate Hayden was as good a place as any to start an investigation into money being cleansed in and around the Seventh Avenue rag business. And why, to keep the mission quiet, Peter Frank on a warm fall day had to lie through his teeth to one David Orenstein, journalist.

"I don't understand it," Orenstein was saying with a look behind thick eyeglasses of genuine confusion. "You guys know what the hell's going on. Why can't you pick these people up, put them through the wringer? I mean they're scum, a blot on the city's landscape."

"You can't prosecute if no one complains."

"Get a couple of men in there."

"Where?"

Orenstein stared at Pete as though at a bona fide idiot. "Inside, in the shipping room. Have them observe payoffs. TV, tape recorders, the whole works. Take one company at a time. They'll all fall over like dominoes once you make your move. Christ, it looks easy, which is why nobody bothers. Back street sweatshops," Orenstein went on, "the works. The mob's tentacles spread out. Take a look at the way clothes come in from abroad dismantled and are stitched together here to avoid customs duties. Man, there's a book in it, a Pulitzer Prize. I can take you to Chinatown," he added with increasing enthusiasm, putting the Styrofoam cup on the desk to create yet another ring. "You'll see sweatshops—one, a dozen, you name it. Out in Queens, for instance, there's an ex-movie house hiding behind a supermarket, cleaning store, and greengrocer. Gnomes working long hours for a pittance—no benefits, nothing. Sweatshops wherever the hell you look. Why don't you get your people out there?"

"See the Queens district attorney. I've heard he's a gung-ho type."

"I came here for a story, Pete. Why isn't the IRS involved?"

"Ask the IRS. Have what you came for?"

"Sure, one blank page. Quote: Peter Frank of the Justice Department refused to cooperate. End quote."

Pete laughed.

The journalist angrily snapped his notebook shut and got to his feet slowly, like an old man, one hand pressed against his lower back. "The Manhattan D.A.'s office refuses to cooperate with my investigation. Ditto the Justice Department. Doesn't matter. I have my story; I just could've used a little help, a little input, a little feeling that there's going to be a follow-up. I've focused in on one independent trucker and the way he lived—wife, couple of kids in a Maspeth two-family, and how when he asked for a little piece of the trucking business on Seventh Avenue and was told to get lost, he threatened to go public, and how he got blown away for his trouble."

"If you have any particular details, I suggest you see the Manhattan D.A."

Orenstein shook his head. "What you have in the trucking business is a case of graft being unionized. You don't go into business for yourself—not in New York City. And if you go into business, you definitely don't go after the garment industry. Sure, I've got the probable names of who did what and where they are and why they haven't been caught. Just wanted the district attorney's opinion on it."

"I'm with the federal government," Pete reminded him.

"Yeah, right, and I wanted your opinion, too." Orenstein went over to the door. "You think you're operating sub rosa," he added, turning around and fixing a cold, level gaze on Pete. "You're not. What justice is doing this time around is already on the grapevine."

Pete went to the door, opened it, and accompanied the reporter down the hall to the elevator. "Wish I could help." He obligingly pushed the Down button.

"I still don't get it," Orenstein said. "You're fighting mob corruption in everything from the drug business to porno, but when it comes to Seventh Avenue, it's hey, we don't know nothin'."

The elevator door opened. Orenstein stuck out a hand. "Look, if um—"

"Right," said Pete, shaking his hand. "You can count on me." He waited until the door closed and then went, fists dug into his pockets, around the corner to the office of his boss, Tess Cristaforo. Sure, he'd like to talk, grab headlines, grandstand, but the fish he and Tess were baiting would make headlines later if not sooner.

Tess was on the phone, but when she saw Pete at her door, she beckoned him in. "What's up?" she asked, obviously still listening to the voice at the other end of the line. She was a small light-skinned black married to an

Italian-American lawyer. Her voice was deceptively soft, so that her toughness always came as a surprise.

"Reporter named Orenstein was in my office," Pete began as soon as she hung up. "He's researching an article for *Mirror* magazine on the way the mob controls the trucking business in the garment industry. Incidentally, his story will focus on a trucker who was killed in the line of not doing his duty— that is, in all innocence he went to some firm and asked for a piece of the trucking action. Refused, he said he'd go to the police, the papers, whatever. Result, he was wasted. How in hell, Orenstein asks, does the fashion industry manage to exist on a bed of corruption and racketeering without the D.A. cracking down?"

Tess looked shrewdly at him. "And what did you say—I don't know nothin'?"

"Precisely. I also reminded him that I'm with the Justice Department, not state and not city."

Tess was immediately distracted by another phone call and Pete walked out, telling her he'd see her later.

Back in his small office Pete spread the files concerning Kate Hayden on his desk. He was contemplating them as though they were a splendidly painted landscape of Seventh Avenue when Tess came in and sat down. "Okay, what have you got? Can we roll with it?"

Without further preliminaries, he opened a folder and began to read. "Kate Hayden was twenty-eight years old and head fashion designer for Domingo until she quit suddenly a year ago. Salary at that time was a paltry sixty thousand a year, which she spent on your basic messy divorce. Prior to going into her own business, she bought a co-op apartment on upper Madison Avenue, which is expensive as hell to maintain, so we have to ask ourselves where she got the down payment and the monthly upkeep. Of course, her mother has money and may have given it to her. Then there's her son, his nursery school, and a housekeeper as part of basic expenses."

He and Tess regarded each other for a time. Then Tess said, "Doesn't exactly add up, does it?"

"Well, it leads to why she quit Domingo. She wants the kind of life only an entrepreneur can afford."

"Always thought his clothes had a certain relaxed flair," Tess said of Domingo, who had died of AIDS almost two years before. "Too bad about him; he was pretty talented."

"So is Kate Hayden, according to the scuttlebutt, but what the hell do I know about fashion?"

"Kept the image alive, I'll say that much for her," Tess grudgingly admitted. "Jeez, that stuff's expensive."

"In the restructuring of Domingo about a year after he died, Hayden asked for the title of head designer, a share of profits, and publicity in her own right. She was refused, and instead of engaging in a little haggling, she quit outright. Apparently a mistake on the part of Domingo's executors, as she had a lot of good press."

"Dummies," Tess threw in. "Greedy dummies, but we're not concerned with Domingo, are we?"

"The company's being run by Domingo's lover, it's in disarray, and after floundering about for a couple of months, they set out feelers for Hayden to return. By that time she'd come up with Ira Gregory and DAS," he went on. "DAS on the surface looks good. They have an operation in the Philippines making children's clothes, low end, in full production, chief markets the United States and Europe. They also have a factory in Hong Kong that handles the Kate Hayden line, as well as contracting with Japanese and Swiss apparel manufacturers. Gregory is out of Chicago and is president of Kate Hayden. We know Gregory traveled for DAS, we know he operated for a while out of their Zurich office, but outside of his birthplace, Chicago, U.S. of A., he's an unwelcome blank."

"Kate Hayden's a class act from everything I've heard," Tess said. "Nice stuff, nice. I mean, she's designing for yuppie women; price no object. Wonderful draping, wonderful fabrics. You could have a figure like Quasimodo, you step into a Kate Hayden original, you're Christie Brinkley. There's always money for a class act with a successful background in this industry and why she dredged up Ira Gregory beats the hell out of me."

"He found her, I suppose. It wasn't a secret that she had quit Domingo and needed start-up money and plenty of it," Pete said. "Incidentally, besides talent, she has something else going for her."

Tess said nothing, merely watched him curiously.

"She's quite a beautiful woman."

"You've met her."

"I've got a picture of her."

"Show it to me."

Pete hesitated. Then he rustled through the file folder and came up with a rather formal black-and-white of Kate Hayden, clipped from a fashion magazine. He'd known precisely where it was the whole time. He slid the picture across his desk.

"One of those long necks," Tess said with noticeable envy. "Must be hell swallowing. You take a bite of steak, three years later it meets up with your stomach juices."

Pete laughed, the tension of his own making quickly subsiding.

"Those looks and talent . . ." Tess left the sentence unfinished.

Pete reached for the photograph and studied it as he had a dozen times before. Dark, luminous eyes and a wide, generous mouth revealing something a little shy and vulnerable.

Tess broke the silence. "When is the IRS moving in?"

"They already have. They asked to see the books. Gregory requested a postponement, and the IRS gave him an additional week."

She pursed her lips, stared down at the display of folders on his desk, and got to her feet. "He needs time to cook the books."

"He's cooked them already."

"Good luck. I think Ira Gregory is going to be a clever, tough adversary."

"The kind I like best."

"Oh, incidentally, Egon Delville died this morning."

Pete looked at her blankly, and Tess gave a weary shake of her head. "You macho types, what did you give your wife for Christmas when she asked for perfume?"

Pete shrugged, a little disconcerted by the question. He never talked about his ex-wife, but Tess seemed to take a perverse pleasure in bringing her up. "My ex never asked; she told. And she came supplied with her own perfume."

"Ah, sexy, sexy, sexy." Tess studied him with interest. He was just under six feet, of athletic build; his eyes were dark and thoughtful and women referred to his mouth as sexy.

"Her old man ran a drugstore," Pete added. "You'd be surprised what you can pick up in a drugstore. Who the hell is Egon Delville?"

"Owns—*owned*—Delville Perfumes. *Delville*—you know the name."

"Ah, okay, okay, I've got it now."

"Well, twenty-five, thirty years ago or so he was a hat designer with what perfumers call a nose. Created a couple of great scents, one of which he named after his own good self—Delville. Expensive but great. You can put it on your Christmas shopping list for me. My father decidedly doesn't own a drugstore. Anyway, Delville Perfumes made him a fortune. But I only mention the man because his funeral should bring out just about everybody who's anybody on Seventh Avenue."

"And?"

"It would be interesting to see the players."

Kate Hayden. The thought came unbidden.

"I'll need a guide," Pete told her.

"I've no doubt you'll find one."

"*If* there's a funeral."

Tess shot a finger at him. "Right."

Before she was out the door, Pete was checking his watch. Eleven o'clock and he had an appointment in a half-hour with someone in the mayor's office, J. B. Olsen, who was a liaison between city government and the garment industry.

J. B. Olsen turned out to be an attractive brunette in a tailored suit padded heavily at the shoulders. She had a dimple in her right cheek, her voice was warm, and cultured. Pete sensed a kind of unyielding air about her that was puzzling and decided she'd be a difficult woman to know.

"Have a seat, Mr. Frank."

"Pete."

The mahogany-paneled office occupied a corner on the seventh floor with a view of City Hall across the square. Sparsely furnished, in good taste, it held a large, well-waxed mahogany desk, Queen Anne chairs upholstered in sage green, a Persian carpet, and in one corner the flags of the United States, New York City, and the state.

"What can I do for you?" Jaybee asked, once she was seated behind her desk. Her manner was faintly adversarial, which made Pete lean back and relax. She was defending her territory, he decided, that was all.

"I was wondering what I could do for *you.*"

She frowned. "What in hell's that supposed to mean?" Then she let out a laugh. "Oh, I get it. You guys are about to come onto the garment industry like a swarm of locusts and you want a little direction from me."

Pete gave her a smile that was encouraging and full of admiration. "A reporter came to see me from one of the local magazines. He's doing a story on corruption in the trucking industry in New York and its ties with Seventh Avenue. He seems to think we know all about it and that, like the Manhattan D.A.'s office, we're being paid off to stay back."

"David Orenstein," she said with an air of disapproval.

"He saw you, too."

"Oh, he'll leave no stone unturned. Coffee?"

He shook his head, then consulted his watch. "I'd like to buy you lunch, however, Ms. Olsen."

"Jaybee. Everybody calls me Jaybee." She leaned over and checked a desk calendar full of scribblings that Pete noted upside down had something marked in at noon. "Sure, a sandwich downstairs, maybe."

She wrote a few words on a slip of paper which she handed to her secretary on the way out. "Move this date up for me, okay? Check my calendar so we don't conflict."

In the elevator she turned to Pete and said in a crisp manner, "I told Dave Orenstein and I'm going to have to tell you. My job in the mayor's office concerning the garment industry is strictly one of liaison. We see no evil, hear no evil, tell no evil, and insist no evil exists."

"Exactly what does 'liaison' mean, Jaybee?"

"Have lunch with guys like you and tell them that the fashion industry in New York is alive and well and up and taking nourishment. There's a deli on the corner that serves a whopping pastrami on rye," she added when they reached the lobby. "How about it?"

"Sounds great. When in New York," he said, touching the small of her back and noting a slight stiffening in her body as they went along, "do as the natives do."

"Where are you from, Pete?"

"South of the Mason-Dixon line."

"Figured as much. Where, exactly?"

"Charlotte, North Carolina."

"Nice accent."

Once they were in the crowded deli, tucked into a booth on hard fake-leather seats, with a large bowl of pickles between them, Jaybee said, "Orenstein insists the Justice Department has been told to clean the garbage out of Seventh Avenue. What are you having? I'm ordering grilled cheese on rye, and coffee."

Pete checked the menu over and settled for chopped liver on rye.

"Onions," Jaybee warned him. "Filled with onions."

"I'm going straight home after work."

She glanced at his third finger left hand.

He offered her an apologetic grin he didn't feel and had the impression she wouldn't care one way or the other. "Nobody's there but a philodendron that came with the sublet. I try not to talk to it."

She smiled, relaxing visibly, but waited until their order arrived before getting down to business.

"What's left of the fashion business in New York, with all the rest in the Far East, has made it more or less mean and lean. It works, and if the governor or the President or the attorney general or whoever thinks his interference would be appreciated, forget it. The industry works fine just the way it is. The firms that are meant to prosper do so. The ones that couldn't cut the mustard are long gone. Right now it's a healthy, viable industry. Investors invest and get their money back. Designers design and are paid well for their talent. Cutters cut, pattern makers make patterns—"

"And women with no green cards from the Orient and Latin America work long hours in sweatshops for a pittance."

Her look was black and Pete stopped dead. He wasn't intimidated; he just knew he'd come up against a brick wall.

"The system *works*," she reiterated.

"Illegal immigrants don't pay taxes; they're an underclass being exploited."

"They put money into the economy. U.N. delegates don't pay taxes, either, but you don't see anybody telling them to get out of town. Hasn't it occurred to you guys to stop trying to beat the garment industry dead? Even if the top echelon isn't—*wasn't*," she corrected herself, "exactly one hundred percent clean, who's hurting?"

"Oh, you paint a rosy picture indeed. Obviously we have a stalemate here." Pete took the chopped liver sandwich in hand and realized how hungry he was. "Incidentally, I like the perfume you're wearing. Chanel?"

"Delville."

Pete faked a frown. "Didn't he just die, Delville somebody?"

Her eyes lit up. She seemed triumphant for some reason, as though she had either wished him dead or had won a bet with him about who'd go first. "Egon Delville. Yes, suddenly. Amazing nobody can believe it. He was only sixty-nine, but you'd think he'd been around forever."

"Are you going to his funeral?"

"Sure. Certainly. Egon Delville?" For a moment a veiled look came over her eyes, but she went on talking. "It's going to be some circus. He knew *everybody*, I'll say that much for Egon. He'd like to know he went out in style. You want to learn about the up side of the fashion business in New York?" she asked, then answered her question. "Come along, whenever it is. You'll see a lot of tears shed, crocodile and otherwise."

He waited a beat before replying, even anticipating the slight tightening at the corners of her lips. "It's a date, Jaybee."

CHAPTER 7

"Hats, get everything we've got on hats in the forties, fifties; that was his heyday. Too bad, with the latest fad he'd be on the cutting edge. He talked about coming out with a line."

"Cutting—funny."

Marguerite Varick looked up at her assistant, a rangy, attractive, independently wealthy blonde in her early twenties who accepted without complaint the pittance paid her to work on the publication. "Jackie, for once I wasn't trying to be funny."

"Oops, sorry about that. Forties and fifties, Egon Delville hats. I love his perfume, very sexy. Now, how do you suppose he knew so much about what turns a man on?" She regarded Marguerite and the quick frown that passed over her face. "I mean, you know what they say about him."

"For heaven's sake," Marguerite said in an exasperated manner. "A man does not marry—"

"Anyway, they say men who don't marry die younger. Nobody to take care of them properly. I mean, does a valet really care whether you take your heart medicine or not? *Oui, madame, je sais, je sais, tout de suite,*" Jackie said to the vexed look Marguerite gave her. "Get everything on hats, forties and fifties."

Once she was alone in her office, Marguerite stood at her desk and allowed a worried expression to cross her face. Her heart was sore. It pained her each time she lost a friend, but with Egon the pain was particularly great. He was forceful, clever, a witty companion, irascible, and full of surprises. No one would replace him. He was the only one who hadn't cared who she was or what she knew, and she had liked having someone around who reminded her of reality from time to time, even Egon's skewered view of reality.

Strewn over her desk—as always inches deep with press releases, fabric swatches, photographs, original fashion sketches, pieces of jewelry, rubber bands, clips, pens, Scotch tape, an old-fashioned telephone, and one satin shoe decorated with rhinestones—were photos of Egon, young, old, alone, and with others. She reached out and with the tip of a nail pushed some aside, pausing at a photograph here or there, bemused by some and nostalgic over others.

Here were some stills of the squat, arched bottle that held Delville Perfumes, a small flacon of crystal with a round stopper, a carefully tied silk ribbon at the neck, and two tiny pom-poms, assembled by delicate fingers at a factory in Grasse. Powders, soaps, and colognes were all available in the trademark shape, offering the subtle, slightly naughty scent meant to drive men wild.

Marguerite sifted through more photographs until she came across one of Egon at the Metropolitan Museum of Art with Kate Hayden on his arm. Kate photographed well. She had ChiChi's bone structure, which caught light and shadow in a flattering way, if not her vapid blond beauty. Kate was dressed in a long, pale silk crepe de chine gown with the classic bias cut that had been invented by Vionnet and which scarcely anyone understood how to use correctly. Kate had that instinct, of course. Marguerite was certain the talent was God-given and that with the freedom Ira Gregory was apparently giving her, Kate Hayden might just turn the fashion world on its head.

In the photograph, with his white hair, prominent eyes, and determined jaw, Egon managed to be both distinguished and theatrical. And how regal they looked together. Marguerite checked the caption on the back of the photo. Of course, the photo was taken when Kate won the Fashion Industry Award just after she left Domingo for the collection she had done the previous year. The ceremony was an annual event at the museum and a prestigious one.

"Egon." The name came out softly. "You lovable old fool, and what's going to happen to your Delville Museum?"

"Marguerite, I must have it. For my museum." Egon crowed with pleasure the day—had it only been a year ago?—Marguerite pulled an original Delville hat out of an original Delville hatbox. It was small and black and worn tilted on the head, with a great black feathery pouf over one ear.

"It's perfect, *perfect*," he cried. "I remember now." He grabbed the hat and checked its label, grinning with pride. "Brand new, not a hint of dandruff anywhere. This has to be twenty-five, thirty years old. I called it something like Pouf Perfect. Let's see, we sold it in black, red, navy of course, pale beige, and I think some outrageous deep turquoise. A bitch getting those feathers dyed to match, as I remember. And ChiChi, photographed on ChiChi in a three-quarter view with her retroussé nose. Hundreds of units— they *flew* out of the stores. Marguerite, you angel, I ought to kiss you to kingdom come. How in hell did this surface? You didn't get it from me. I'd have remembered."

"I bought this at Saks," Marguerite said, deftly removing the hat from his hands. "Paid for it with my own hard-earned cash, and never once had it on in all these years."

"Never wore a genuine Egon Delville you paid for with your own money?" He pretended to be crushed.

"Sorry, I have no idea why, as a matter of fact. I do remember it was about the time I went back to Paris to try to resurrect *Cachet* magazine. I was gone a year, and when I returned the world had gone hatless. But of course, Egon, I'd never have given away anything of yours. And just what do you mean, your museum?" she had asked him. "Did I hear right or am I going deaf?"

"A fashion museum. The Delville Fashion Museum, to be exact." He grinned and rolled his eyes.

"The city already has quite enough in the way of fashion museums," she commented dryly, "quite enough. New York isn't Paris, you know." Egon was always full of plans that fell through. Only Delville Perfumes had lasted.

"Charles James, Mainbocher, Claire McCardell." He rattled off half a dozen names of designers long gone. "We've had our share of great designers, Marguerite, and it's about time someone in this city took the matter in hand."

"The Metropolitan Museum does. The Fashion Institute does, or haven't you noticed?"

"Mine," he said starchily, "will be independent. It will contain a library as well as exhibition space. I've given this a lot of thought. For instance, *jeans.* The history of jeans. Good Lord, they should be enshrined in glass cases. Jeans have changed the way the world dresses. I can see the exhibit now—a cowboy sitting on a rail fence, wearing jeans. Longhorns in the distance. Little children will be brought in by their mommies to see the origin of jeans in situ. And Marguerite," he added with increasing enthusiasm, "my town house is going to be the home of the Delville Museum. What do you think of the idea?"

"I don't. Let it drown, Egon." She discouraged him out of hand and could not exactly say why. "I always said you had funny ideas about how to spend your millions."

"Listen," he had said, suddenly serious, "I'm not kidding. New York's the center of the fashion industry. What doesn't it have? A fashion museum."

"Exactly what do you call the Costume Institute at the Metropolitan?"

"It's an archive. What the latest fad was in Egypt at the time of Herod. It has nothing to do with Seventh Avenue."

"There are fashion archives and fashion exhibitions all over the city, including every department store window, Egon. Do you know how much it costs to run a museum?"

Egon, his eyes raised to the ceiling, waited until she simmered down.

"Marguerite, you believe so much in your own publicity, we'll have to have you stuffed and waxed soon and sent to Madame Tussaud's for display. Or if you wait long enough, we'll set you up in the library of the Delville Museum."

"Go ahead," she said, scarcely hiding her impatience. "I'm listening."

"I've been kicking this idea around for a long time. I've this warehouse in Queens—did you know that? Stuffed to its proverbial gills with antiques, books, clothes, shoes, hats, you name it, all to do with American fashion. Fabrics, *fabrics*, glorious lengths of silk from the twenties. A stole like cobwebs that predates the Civil War. We'll need a fabric conservator—the best. I'm not kidding, Marguerite."

"I believe you," she said, allowing the acid to bite into her tone. She knew all about Egon's neurotic compulsion to collect. "But a warehouse in Queens? You are a secretive little beast, aren't you? How come you never told me?"

"The past year I didn't want to tell you, I've been collecting on a serious level. Serious, Marguerite. Bidding against my competitors. There are people all over the place scouring for the best stuff, taking it off the market, pawing it in private. Fashion? That's the last domain of the world-weary who can't afford van Gogh sunflowers but who want to collect something, anything. My warehouse is chock full of vintage stuff," he went on. "You'd be surprised at what's waiting to be plucked."

"Really. Well, you are curious," she said coldly. She didn't like secrets and suddenly felt that Egon had cut her out of something important.

"You might as well know everything. I want an American museum strictly devoted to fashion on this side of the ocean. It's a big story. Try not to discourage me, Marguerite. You're a witch. You hate anything new you haven't thought of first." He took up the hat and balanced it on his index finger. "This hat is vintage Delville, and it's mine, you must let me have it. I'll pay you for it," he added with a triumphant smile.

"I have an uncommon affection for that hat."

"Marguerite, I want you as curator."

The words took her by surprise. She was flattered for a moment, but then shook her head. "All that for a hat?"

"Forget the hat. I'm serious."

"What are we talking about? I have work I really care about and that affords me a living."

"Really? A living? You're in debt up to your ears."

She flushed, yet knowing it was an open secret, her being in debt up to her ears. "I pay my bills," she said defensively. "Besides, what business is it of yours?"

"It isn't. If you need money, you can always come to me. I'm serious."

"Yes," she said, regarding him with respect. "I suppose you are." He was right. *VFF* barely paid its way and she spent sleepless nights worrying about it. Her subscriber list included people in the industry, the wealthy, and fashion educators. *VFF* was published bimonthly in color—twenty-four pages of forecasts and commentary on dresses, coats, shoes, hats, gloves, bags, belts, jewelry, maquillage, perfumes, and hairstyles, as determined by one woman— Marguerite Varick, arbiter elegantiae. To maintain its standards and credibility, *VFF* accepted no advertising. Its subscription price was high but worth it to the ten thousand readers who considered her taste impeccable, her sense of the fashion future infallible.

She was perpetually broke, perpetually chasing after cash, because the daily costs of producing the magazine depended upon its subscription price, upon the lecture fees that Marguerite commanded, upon the perennial sale of a landmark fashion book she had written in the seventies, and upon the cleverness of her accountant.

"Chief curator and director of my museum all rolled into one," Egon had whispered. "On a steady salary, a generous salary, and money enough to see the museum through from the beginning to the end. And, my dear, as an added fillip, I want you on the board of directors."

"And when will this extraordinary event take place?"

"Perhaps it'll see the light of day in another year or two. At any rate, it's in my will."

She had paused for a long moment, then said, "Are you planning on exiting soon?"

Egon shook his head. "Give me the hat, and I'll move the launch date up."

She still owned the hat. In the year intervening, the matter of the museum hadn't come up again, and although Marguerite often found herself wondering about Egon's plans, she thought it judicious not to bring the subject up.

She turned to her typewriter and began the story that would grace the front page of *Varick's Fashion Forecast:* "Egon Delville, a famous hat designer of the forties and fifties, whose line of perfumes is known worldwide, died suddenly in his New York City home today. He was sixty-nine years old."

She was interrupted by a light knock on her office door, signaling the arrival of her accountant and, she supposed, his weekly serving-up of the bad news.

"*Entrez.*"

The door opened and Sol Greenspan stood before her, grasping a worn leather briefcase, his arms thrown wide. He was dressed in a baggy suit, his horn-rimmed glasses pushed high into gray curly hair, a natural comedian with a rakish grin and a forthright manner. "Hiya, Marguerite sweetheart. It's your Bad News Bear." He closed the door behind him and came over to her desk, slapping his briefcase down and then leaning across so that his nose was inches from hers.

"Sweetheart, I'm telling you, you have two choices: sell the damn thing to Libby Publications, they'll keep you on as editor, after all, they're not buying twenty-four double pages; they're buying Marguerite Varick. Or take in advertising like the weekly wash, for chrissake. You won't be putting your soul on the line; you'll be *saving* it, you won't be losing your independence, just gaining cash flow. Think about it, Marguerite, it's time. Old Man Winter is breathing at the door, you're not, what shall we say, in the first blush of youth, and the truth of the matter is, you ain't got no choice. You listening to me, sweetheart? I hate it when you shake your head as if you agree with me when I know you'll go your merry way as soon as I'm out of here."

"I'm not deaf and I'm not senile yet, Sol, not by a long shot."

He threw his hands in the air and stepped back. "Hey, hey, did I—"

"I hate you forty-year-old punks acting as if you had the exclusive on youth and smarts. I'm sorry," she added contritely. "I'm a little upset today. Did you hear about Egon Delville?"

"Right. Tough. Met him but didn't know him personally. A little too fey for me. I mean, that smooth pink skin, that mop of white hair. Styled, I suppose. He always looked slightly boiled to me, like a young lobster."

"Sol, the man's dead."

"Right. I gather he never did anything halfway. Papers said he didn't have any direct heirs. You knew him pretty well, Marguerite. Call his lawyers to see if he cut you in for something."

"Sol, *tu eres imposs-ee-ble.*"

"No, I'm not, just realistic, Marguerite, love. You're gorgeous and the trouble is you're stubborn. It's grown on you like a tumor. Your bank account looks like the Gobi Desert, and your subscription list hasn't grown enough to make a dent."

"And what's the good news, Solly?"

"My firm just won the Annalise Michelis account, thanks to you."

Her face lit up. "Wonderful. I won't say she's the cleverest designer around, but I would say she's the richest. Well, it's her husband's money. I'd guess Annalise, Inc., pays its way barely. How many ten thousand dollar gowns can you sell to how many wealthy women?"

"We could pay you a commission."

"I had nothing to do with it," she said stiffly. "I don't take money for making phone calls."

"Kidding, kidding. My God, you're sensitive. I mean honesty and integrity have their limits, too."

"Am I supposed to look something over, Solly?"

He groaned and rubbed the back of his neck, a forty-year-old with too much weight on him and too much angst over his clients' problems. "Nothing, darling, unless you admire zeros. I'm going to call Libby, how about it?"

"No," she said sharply. "Not yet. Let me think." Egon's fashion museum, his will, wanting her to be curator—she had to think. How long would it be before the will was read and probated? What an awful bitch she was, Egon scarcely cold and not even in his grave. What about his funeral? How she dreaded that, how she dreaded all funerals—and there had been entirely too many lately.

"Marguerite?" Sol was watching her, concerned.

"No, don't call Libby."

He shook his head. "You're making a mistake. Look, I don't know from fashion, but I know *VFF* performs a function in our society. What the hell that is, don't bother telling me, but if it's important to you, then it's important to me. That's why I'm after you to take on a partner."

"Sol, let me think about it."

He went to the door. "Look where thinking got you, Marguerite. Nowhere."

She laughed softly. "Nowhere? That's news to me."

"See you, sweetheart."

CHAPTER 8

Annalise spotted Ralley at once at one of the window tables at Raven's; as usual, her heart leapt a little at the sight of her closest friend. She and Ralley took the greatest pleasure in each other's company and had done so from the very beginning, from their first polite handshake those many years ago in Paris.

As she made her way across the room, she took the time to note the way Ralley was dressed, in a black suit with a draped closing on the jacket. She recognized it as a Donna Karan. Ralley—with thick, curly dark hair cut short, a tiny nose, a wide mouth, and slanted, clever eyes—never quite understood how beautiful she was.

Annalise was also aware of the effect of her own entrance, not upon Ralley, who couldn't have cared less, but upon the other diners, who whispered in discomfort as she went by, stirring up the air with her narrow, shapely figure, her straight blond hair, her perfect posture, her impeccably tailored houndstooth suit, the judicious dab of Delville daytime perfume. That, she thought with satisfaction, was what fashion was all about—sheer show and mystery, panache and mirrors.

"Sorry, sorry, sorry," she said when Ralley raised her hand and mimed the time on her wristwatch. "Traffic."

"Forgiven," said Ralley, her eyes troubled in spite of her smile, "all is forgiven. I thought I was going to be late. Stasio's in town from Milan with a retinue of five *hundred*, and I'm not exaggerating one little bit. Publicists, models, his son, his son's mistress, who is his son's mother's age, and Stasio's current lover, in this case a certain movie actor who'll remain nameless. Stasio checked into the Carlyle with his lover and put the rest of his pals, including his son and said mistress, at the International Motor Inn on Tenth Avenue. And, he wanted me to come over pronto to talk about old times. Isn't that a bitch about Egon? He loved Stasio—I mean, not in *that* way."

Her voice was deep, warm, and rough-edged, the voice of a woman men fell easily in love with but scarcely dreamed of having. There was something faintly mysterious about her, as if her coolness, her insouciance, her ability to get along with people, masked a deep and delicate hurt. And no matter how sophisticated Ralley made herself, Annalise sensed that underneath was the scared little girl with the crazy mother.

"How'd you manage to put Stasio off?" she asked.

"I said that my dearest friend had passed away and that I'm much too upset at the moment. What I am is smashed"—Ralley reached for her martini glass—"and I've a meeting at three with the merchandise manager and our beloved elder Steyman. You know I never drink at lunch, but then, how often do we lose the likes of Egon Delville?"

A glass of white wine stood at Annalise's place. She raised it. "To Egon." The sudden catch in her throat surprised her and for a moment she couldn't speak. "Is he really gone, the old reprobate? I'll miss him, dammit. There wasn't anyone funnier, livelier, bitchier."

"To Egon," Ralley said, "in spite of the bone I had to pick with him. I mean, not Egon's fault about Cliff," Ralley added, "but it was that creep living upstairs in his attic."

"What the hell are you talking about?"

"That shit Egon put in business with Smarts. I never really understood Egon, did you? I mean, I don't think he liked little boys. You know, no sexual drive," she went on, putting the emphasis on "sexual" as if it were separate words.

"You didn't know him in his heyday," Annalise said.

Ralley raised an eyebrow. "And you did."

Annalise stiffened slightly, not at Ralley's offhand remark, but at the memory of what she was and where she was in Egon's heyday. And the telephone call that had her on edge all morning. *Puta.* She had slammed the receiver down but not before hearing her caller's laugh. He hadn't expected an answer, much less a definition.

Ralley reached out and touched Annalise's arm. "Hey, you should see the look on your face. I was kidding. You're upset, aren't you? I mean about Egon."

"Aren't you?"

"*Le maître,*" Ralley said. "I needed someone in my life with better fashion sense than I have." She screwed up her eyes and examined the glass she held. "I think that's what I mean."

"An anchor," Annalise remarked quietly. "Egon *was* pushing seventy," she said, staring severely into her wineglass. "Anyway, who's this 'shit' you're talking about? What do you mean Eggie put him in charge of Smarts?" Annalise knew about the gallery, knew that Egon was backing it, had even promised him she and Zack would appear at Cliff Beal's opening, but that was all she knew. It was possible Egon had said more, but Annalise was often uninterested in what other people, even Egon, had to say.

Ralley signaled for a fresh martini and ordered another glass of wine for Annalise. "This creep he felt sorry for, who convinced Egon to back him in Smarts."

"Who was he? Where'd Egon meet him? I hate half-finished stories, Ralley."

Lighting a cigarette, Ralley took a deep drag, knowing smoking was an unfashionable enterprise, very lower class, and therefore precisely what she *would* do. Annalise, with her characteristic gesture, used her index fingers to part the blond curtain of her hair.

"I'm beginning to think that Egon was a very large drum against which we slammed ourselves, and what echoed back was us, not Egon," Annalise said, "ever."

"For a lady whose native language isn't English, you express yourself remarkably well," Ralley said.

"What about Smarts?"

"Winthrop Smith," Ralley went on, "the Sixth, mind you. Can you imagine five others coming before him? I have no idea how Egon met him. Maybe Win just showed up on his doorstep one night. Egon knew everyone. I think Win wants, or wanted, to be an actor. I suppose he came packaged with a letter of recommendation, maybe from an actor, maybe from a director, I haven't a clue. Egon took him in, let him use that guest room on the top floor of the town house—you know, the one with the framed silhouettes? All I know is Cliff wandered into Smarts one day before the gallery opened. He had a portfolio with him and his slides. The carpenter had just quit, and Cliff rolled up his sleeves and went to work building racks. Win was impressed and after that Cliff was a shoo-in." She paused, laughed bitterly, then said, "In more ways than one." Her eyes were frank, a deep gray, the lids feathered with long black lashes. She turned her pained gaze directly on Annalise. "Look, I couldn't talk about it before, even to you. I came back to the studio last week and found them in bed together."

"Cliff and Egon or Cliff and the shit?"

"Winthrop Smith the Sixth and Cliff, the only one of his kind. I remarked, en passant, that I found them in bed together. Aren't you going to say anything?"

"I believe you. If it's any consolation, I'll add I never liked Cliff."

Ralley flushed and seemed about to admonish Annalise, but then sank back in her seat and reached for her glass. "You never met Win, and Egon your favorite pal? He's been living Chez Delville for half a year—more, maybe. Slim, good-looking, pale hair, mustache, a bit of a ditz. He'll tell you his whole bloody boring life history if you give him half a chance. Very friendly, takes you in, and it's a long time before you realize his ozone level's a little low. Cliff said his family threw him out because he hocked a portrait of Great-Great-Grandfather Smith for some coke. I'd be a little upset myself under the circumstances, given that the portrait was by Rembrandt Peale. I wonder who inherits the Delville fortune?"

Annalise frowned, shaking her head. Egon talked incessantly. He was witty, cruel, clever, took everything from you, and when you got down to it, gave nothing of himself back but his amusing company, his impeccable taste, and an occasional expensive gift. And all the while he had someone living on the top floor of the town house.

"You don't suppose he left it to this Smith character?"

"He never said anything to you, then."

Annalise shrugged again. "Neither about Smith nor his will. As far as I know, Egon had no family."

"Maybe he did. You have a habit of tuning out everything that doesn't interest you."

"What are you talkin' about?" Annalise looked bewildered.

Ralley patted her hand. "Come on, you know me. When I'm in my cups I'll say anything."

"As a matter of fact, Egon touted Smarts on a couple of occasions when he met me with Zack. He said we should quit collecting phony Renoirs and specious Rubenses and begin to collect the neo-expressionists, neo-*modernes*, neo-geos, whatever. Zack laughed. He always laughed in Eggie's company. But tell me about Cliff," she said when she realized Ralley was only half listening to her. "Is he still with you?"

A long pause while Ralley studied her martini. "No, I don't want to talk about him, and yes, he's still with me."

"Why don't you throw him out?"

"Followed by his seventy-foot canvases, just chucked down the stairs. I've dreamed of it. I've dreamed of slashing those—those—those *works*. They're ugly, and he's so smug and self-righteous about what he does. All that empty talk. 'I have to work out from within, ya know?' " she said, imitating him. " 'I mean, like, ya know, ya don't paint the reality around you, ya, you, ya paint the reality with*in*. Deep inside, man, the soul. I mean, ya know, ya know?' Translation: he can't draw worth a damn."

"Do you hate him?"

Ralley shrugged.

"Love him?"

"I've never been able to figure it out."

"Obsessed with him?"

"Afraid of AIDS, maybe."

Annalise stared at her, horrified. "Oh, Ralley," she began, but could think of nothing else to say.

"I can't worry about it," Ralley said. "I can't afford to. We had a big blowup. He swears he never— I believe him; I have to." She stopped, then said, "Let's not talk about it. You're not going to treat me like a pariah, are you?"

"Oh, for heaven's sake."

"If they ever found out at Steyman's—"

"Oh, for heaven's sake."

"Right. Forget it, Annalise, forget it. Say something amusing about Eggie. Oh, wait, about your husband's running for the Senate: Mr. Steyman doesn't like the idea one bit."

"I didn't know the elder Steyman was a political beast."

"He isn't," Ralley said. "He's worried about giving you the front cover of our spring catalog."

For a moment, Annalise's face lit up with the surprising news. "Front cover? Well, that's fantastic. . . . Okay," she added after a moment, "what's the catch?"

Ralley shook her head slowly, as if knowing Annalise's immediate reaction would be one of distrust. "I said I'd try and I did. Steyman agreed. You passed Donna Karan, Bill Blass, Oscar de la Renta, and jail on your way to winning the cover. However, you won't collect two hundred dollars; you'll probably have to part with a lot more. We'll want an exclusive gown, of course, and there'll be all sorts of caveats. Steyman's afraid Zack will win the Senate nomination and you'll decide to follow your husband to Washington and quit designing after we've made the commitment to Annalise."

Annalise stared at her in astonishment. "Follow Zack to Washington? Give up designing? Is the elder Steyman turning senile?"

"Yes, but I'll need your assurance that you'll meet your obligations, in writing, in triplicate."

"Zack is merely trying to secure the Republican nomination," Annalise reminded her. "The primaries won't be held until next year. And winning the Republican primary is no guarantee he'll win the race."

"I'm only reporting Mr. Steyman's worries. However, first things first. We meet with Papa Steyman, caress his ego, give him what he wants, and you'll have the cover of the spring catalog. *Voilà*. Listen, I'll want something in green, very Easter egg but definitely not bilious. A long gown, *très simple* but *très frou-frou* at the same time. Chiffon with a sensational skirt even Ginger Rogers would love to wear while dancing the night away with Fred. I'll get you a color sample. The green's a given, but if you want to add flowers or whatever, that's okay. The catalog, in case you ever consulted it, always has something romantic on its spring cover. Just keep to this year's signature color, like Marguerite's hair. Now that that's out of the way, let's talk about Eggie."

"Funny," Annalise said. "I've wanted the cover of Steyman's so much I could taste it, but do you know whom I was suddenly thinking about? Thierry Saul."

"Thierry," Ralley said with a wistful smile. "Hey," she added, "we've come a long way since Thierry. Did you ever imagine it?"

"Yes," Annalise said simply.

"Of course, I remember your ambition."

"I've always worn it on my arm like a vaccination mark."

"So you have, Annalise. I never did. I'm the result of hard work and sheer luck."

It was in Thierry Saul's Paris showroom that Annalise and Ralley had first met. Thierry's star was in the ascendancy and Annalise was his assistant. Ralley had come to Paris with Marguerite Varick, who had hired her as an associate editor on *Cachet*, although she'd had no fashion experience. She'd been hired merely because Marguerite thought long-legged, straight-nosed California women the most beautiful in the world. Ralley's face also bespoke intelligence and Marguerite quickly became her mentor.

"Thierry," Ralley said. "He wanted to set me up as his mistress."

"And I talked you out of it. I saw no future for you in being the mistress of a fashion designer who had no intention of divorcing his wife."

"I thought you were jealous."

"Because I'd been his lover first? But I understood all along that he never loved me, Ralley, and that he certainly loved you. I thought we were bosom buddies. How come you never told me you didn't trust my motives?"

"Because I think all of us have pockets in which we hide our real feelings. Nothing wrong with being jealous. I'm jealous of a silly little queer called Winthrop Smith."

"Are you?"

Ralley winced and ferociously stubbed out her cigarette. "I'm not quite used to my lover's bisexuality, that's all."

"Don't get used to it. Dump him."

"Easier said than done."

The waiter came by and Ralley had to poke Annalise to remind her he was there. Annalise opened the menu, selected a salad of fruit and cheese, and coffee. The waiter leaned forward to take the menu from her hand. He was young, slender, a toreador with a narrow bony face and black hair. He smelled faintly of musk. His eyes glistened when he found her gazing at him, and then slid away. Ralley was chatting on, something about Thierry, and for a moment Annalise seemed to hang suspended in a kind of terrifying, haunted space between reality and the past. Before lunch ended, she would do what reason told her not to: she'd reach into her bag and extract a small card with a telephone number on it. It would be handed surreptitiously to the young waiter along with a generous tip. She watched him as he made his way back to the kitchen. Broad shoulders, small rear end—the combination never failed to excite her.

"Whose funeral?"

"Egon Delville. You know, Delville Perfumes?"

"Egon Delville? I thought he was dead."

"He is dead, you jerk, that's why they're having a funeral for him."

"No, I mean like twenty years."

"Don't you read the papers? Listen, the guy was rich as Croesus. I mean, with all this homeless around, you'd think he'd show a little compassion. A museum of fashion! A museum of *fashion*. I mean, talk about not knowing what the hell's going on around him! Who'd he think he was? Louis the Fourteenth?"

"What in hell are you talking about?"

The two strangers moved away from the church out of earshot. Pete Frank stood off to the side, barely repressing a smile. Louis the Fourteenth had left Versailles behind, although given the choice there wasn't any doubt he'd have taken it with him. From the rumor in the *Times* that morning, Egon Delville had apparently left his fortune and his East Side town house for the establishment of a museum of fashion. Pete hoped the story was apochryphal. New York, which had more museums to the inch than any other city in the world, could have used a museum for the homeless in the form of housing.

The gray stretch limousines disgorged fashionable women and men who hurried up the steps of the church with grim expressions on their faces, chins tucked well in, as if trying to hide from the paparazzi taking pictures, and exposing the best possible view.

Chic funeral. The words kept going through Pete's mind as he waited for Jaybee Olsen. She arrived at last in a cab, which pulled to a stop halfway down the block, away from the crowd. She was dressed from head to foot in a sober burgundy dress that flattered her olive complexion and made her look feminine and pretty.

"Welcome to a high-fashion upscale New York funeral," she said cheerfully, "in which they come to praise Eggie, show off their costumes, and then rush away while the flashbulbs are still popping. Eggie would've loved it."

They climbed the steps to the red granite church and entered the sober High Episcopal precincts where emphasis was laid upon ceremony and not upon sermons. The building dated from the turn of the century, and the interior smelled of incense and old polished wood. Someone was playing Bach on the organ in a gentle, lugubrious manner.

A scattering of mourners sat in the front pews. Others were clumped about in groups, talking quietly. Jaybee led Pete to a pew on the side aisle, halfway down. "Can't find anyone around so far who's worth pointing out," she said. "That sour-faced individual off to the right is his valet, but he won't have any trouble getting another job. Who the others are, I can't say. Anyway, among his friends, I can assure you, nobody wants to be first, everyone wants to be last." She checked her watch. "Ten minutes more. Funeral's scheduled for eleven."

"If he left no relatives," Pete stated, "who's going to sit in the front row?"

"His lawyers, I suppose. And Delville's CEO and all the other highly placed executives and accountants who were his dear and personal friends. Marguerite Varick, I imagine, a close pal."

"I read about the museum of fashion he's giving to the city of New York."

Jaybee laughed. "Leave it to Eggie. He was a sly old fox."

"You mean you approve."

"Approve? Sure, I approve. It'll be good for the garment industry, that's all I care about."

There was a sudden shuffling at the back of the church, and Jaybee said, "Here they come all at once." As the ushers quickly tried to direct people down the center and side aisles, Jaybee began murmuring a litany of names: prominent dress designers, socialites, real estate tycoons, actors who were familiar to Pete and some who were not.

"Will the mayor be here?" Pete asked.

"Oh, he'll show, all right. He read the *Times* this morning."

Pete, however, hadn't come to view a political parade; he had come to see Ira Gregory and Kate Hayden in the flesh.

"Annalise Michelis Younger and her husband. He's running for the Senate," Jaybee pointed out. "She's a fashion designer. Good Lord, Annalise moves as if she's going to faint in another minute."

"Which one is she?" Pete asked.

"The blonde in the big black hat. Black suit, not a crease. That's Zack Younger with her. Also not a crease. He's strictly Savile Row. Annalise is rather fascinating. Very centered."

Pete looked them over. The woman was quite beautiful, he thought, then realized her eyes were hidden by the wide brim of her hat and that he actually had no idea what she looked like. Aura, he supposed that was what they called it. He'd never seen anyone quite like her before. As for Zack Younger, he was familiar from photographs. The would-be senator's expression was extremely serious; he kept his eyes down, as though afraid someone would ask him what he thought of the dead man and of funerals in particular.

"What do you mean by 'centered'?" he asked. "As in *self*-centered?"

"No, as in knowing just what she wants and how to go about getting it, and never straying a minute from her goals. It's about total concentration on the object at hand, namely Annalise, Inc. Okay, that's Marguerite Varick of *Varick's Fashion Forecast,*" Jaybee said of a tall red-haired woman wearing a black hat with a feathered pouf on one side. She came down the center aisle leaning on the arm of a slender, handsome youth. "She was one of Egon's closest friends, and she's what you'd call the ultimate fashion expert. Short skirts happen only if Marguerite puts her imprimatur on them. Skirts down to your ankles? Blame Marguerite. Up to your pupik? Blame Marguerite. Does she do it out of a sense of duty, out of a sense of fashion? Who the hell knows? I don't suppose even Marguerite does. Power, maybe that's what it's all about. She has no money to speak of but plenty of power, worth a hell of a lot more. Oh, and under that nifty little hat you'll note a head of red hair that glows in the dark. Her *signature* color is what they call it in the fashion industry. You'd know Marguerite anywhere. If her black dresses and red hair don't do it, then certainly the clang of her bracelets will. I wonder if she's wearing them today. Perhaps not. The noise would certainly interfere with the service, and she was devoted to Egon. Anyway, her taste is impeccable. Note how young she looks, my dear, what a nip and tuck won't do. Get that stunning figure, but she always dresses in black and always has some gorgeous little cretin at her side." Her companion guided Marguerite to a seat in the front row. He was dark-haired, with soft, even features and pale eyes beneath black brows.

"He's the latest in a long series. I mean," Jaybee added hurriedly, "I think she keeps them around as pets, you know, her private escort service. Teaches them the business, then unties their moorings after a while. Remarkable lady," she added. "French. Knows everything, knows everybody. Am I helping you?"

Pete turned to Jaybee. "Immensely."

"Going to do something with all this information?"

"Write a book."

"Funny." She pointed out other figures to him, but Pete was still waiting for Kate Hayden and Ira Gregory.

"Okay," Jaybee said at last. "Coming down the side aisle—just like her to try to avoid the limelight; I'll bet she walked here—that's Kate Hayden, very talented designer. The best, according to Marguerite, and Marguerite seldom goes all out for anyone."

Pete took a moment to find Kate, surprised at his reaction and the measurable quickening of his heartbeat. She hurried down the aisle to take a seat directly behind Marguerite Varick, whom she tapped gently on the shoulder. In the morning light sifting through the stained-glass windows, her hair took on a high sheen. She was dressed in a sober gray suit and wore no hat. Her skin was pale, of the shade referred to as alabaster. Her eyes were hidden behind dark aviator glasses. He caught her profile and realized he had memorized the full-face black-and-white photograph and now had to discover her all over again. Her nose was straight and small. He remembered Tess's comment about her long neck, which was arched and gave her a certain grace.

"You should have seen her way back when," Jaybee said. "She worked for Domingo, you know, he died of AIDS. She was quiet, without the least glamour, the little girl from Greenwich, Connecticut with golden fingers, always dressed in her own designs, not Domingo's, and he let her get away with it. Now she's well on her way to the top of the world, thanks to Ira Gregory. And that's the great man himself, coming down the aisle with his wife."

Pete drew his eyes reluctantly from Kate to Ira Gregory. He felt a slight tick of annoyance that had nothing to do with confronting the man he was after; it had to do with an unexpected image of Kate Hayden in the man's arms. He brushed the thought away and concentrated on the man he had met briefly on his foray into the shipping department of Kate Hayden. Impeccably groomed, Gregory wore a dark tie against a white shirt, his cuffs shot neatly out of a thousand dollar suit that announced its tailoring like a large neon sign. His thick hair was expensively cut by what Pete supposed they called a stylist.

"Wouldn't want to cross her," Jaybee whispered of the woman with Gregory. "That's his wife, ex-showgirl, dancer, Las Vegas, tough as nails. Supposedly doesn't know about her husband and Kate."

Pete was careful to contain the surprise and unexpected irritation he felt, although somehow it wasn't news. He regarded Ira Gregory through narrowed eyes, then slid his glance to Kate Hayden while the Gregorys took seats on the left aisle. Marguerite saw them and nodded to Kate, who turned. Her expression was immobile below the dark glasses. A slow flush of color suffused her face. She turned back quickly, bowing her head.

Pete knew at once that Kate Hayden had just been given her first sight of Mrs. Ira Gregory, who didn't know what her husband was doing behind her back.

"I'd call that drama of the first order," Jaybee said at his side. "Subtle, the stuff of Hollywood close-ups. Mistress glances at wife in the quiet of a church."

"Maybe you have it all wrong, Jaybee."

"The wife doesn't know, hasn't an inkling. Otherwise Kate Hayden would be dead."

"You're a regular font of information."

Jaybee colored slightly. "Everybody knows about everybody in this business. It's no secret. About Kate and Ira, I mean."

"His wife excepted."

"I'll hand you one other secret absolutely free. Egon was pissed at Ira Gregory just because he went into business with Kate."

The last of the mourners straggled in and took their seats quickly. "Staying for the service?" Jaybee asked. "If not, I suspect it's time to make a graceful exit."

Pete turned once more to Kate Hayden, but this time he was rewarded with nothing more than a glimpse of the back of her head. "Thanks for the tour. We'll have lunch," Pete said, flashing Jaybee a grateful smile.

She blinked once. "Right," she said. "Let's."

CHAPTER 9

"I was afraid you wouldn't remember me, Mr. Newcombe."

"Oddly enough," the lawyer said, looking across his desk at Winthrop Smith, "I had a call from Egon the day before he died. I was out of town and couldn't get back to him. Let's see." Newcombe had a computer and he busied himself pecking out information on his lap keyboard.

Win shifted in his chair, letting his eyes roam casually around the office, which was a paeon to conspicuous consumption in the realm of antique toys and old advertising signs.

"Ah," said Newcombe. He peered over his glasses at Win. "Just a memo saying he called about Winthrop Smith."

Win waited a moment and then, when Newcombe offered nothing further, said, "Right, well, that's what he told me. The rent's due on the gallery and he said something about setting up a fund so it would be paid automatically."

The lawyer raised his head a notch and waited.

"Smarts. That's the name of the gallery. Down in SoHo, on Broadway. The one he was backing." Win held his breath.

"Aha. Right. Seems there's a lease somewhere around." Newcombe, clearly proud of his talent with the computer, consulted it again, then picked up his telephone and politely asked the person at the other end to bring him the Smarts file. Win was impressed.

"It's a drag," Win ventured. "Every time you think you're ahead, the rent's due."

"Know what you mean." Newcombe waved his hand around his office to indicate he had the same worries. "How's the gallery business?"

"I mean so far, well . . . I mean Rome wasn't built in a day. It takes time," he added, stopping himself from going into further details.

Newcombe smiled for the first time. He was a pleasant-looking man with a pale face, horn-rimmed glasses, and something a little soft around his mouth, as though he cried easily. "If Rome cost eight thousand dollars a month, they'd have built it in a day."

Win caught the sarcasm and realized he was meant to. He smiled, too, glad of the opportunity. Evidently Newcombe knew everything about him, about Smarts, about Egon's signature on the lease. About the eight thousand dollars rent. But did he know that Egon had thrown him out?

"Egon figured as soon as we had the gallery moving and all the artists lined up," Win went on, "he'd give me a mailing list that would knock your socks off. We're open for business," Win added, "but business doesn't walk in off the street. I mean, it does to a certain extent. We have plenty of people coming in, looking around—you know, couples from the suburbs on Saturdays, Wall Street types during lunch hour. And tourists, plenty of tourists. But the big sales to collectors, you have to manage those, start out with the right mailing list, have big charity openings with the press attending. There are those out-of-town collectors, too, the serious ones. We have to reach them."

Newcombe nodded throughout Win's recitation, his hands glued to the computer keyboard. "You certainly seem to know the business, Mr. Smith."

"Right. Right." Win resisted the temptation to twist his fingers together, to wipe his wet palms along his trouser legs. He thought of mentioning his bachelor's degree in art history but decided against it. He supposed he'd have to mention a master's or a doctorate to impress Newcombe. "It's only a matter of time before it all pulls together," he mumbled instead.

Newcombe's secretary knocked briefly on the door before opening it. "The Smarts file," she said, coming rapidly across the room holding out a slender folder.

"We'll get this all on line yet," Newcombe remarked about the file, then removed the lease and spent a couple of minutes going through it. "Five more months to go. What kind of work do you show?"

"You know, eclectic. We're planning a big opening for Cliff Beal." Win said the name importantly, hoping the lawyer had heard of Cliff or thought he should have. "Large canvases and some drawings. Postmodern."

"Don't know the name. I'll have to ask my wife. Okay, Mr. Smith, get on with it. The estate will pick up the tab on the gallery because it was obviously Mr. Delville's wish, at least through the end of the lease. After that we'll have to see."

"About a salary . . ."

"Mr. Delville pay you a salary?"

"Well, yes—no," Win said lamely. He'd been living on unemployment insurance, which would run out in another month. Egon never asked where Win was getting money to live on, but between the room at the top of the town house and the gallery expenses assumed by Egon, Win never dared to broach the subject. Besides, he hadn't been above explaining to Egon the importance in Cleveland of six generations of Smiths named Winthrop. There was no way to admit his family had disowned him a long time before.

"What's your address? Still at the town house?" Newcombe drew his brows together. "No, of course not, except for the caretaker, the place is unoccupied. Better let me have your address."

"The gallery," Win said, feeling the heat rise to his face. "I've been bunking down there working forty-eight-hour days."

Newcombe stared at him. Win could imagine him calculating the cost of heat, electricity and hot water on tap twenty-four hours a day. He decided not to bring up the matter of insurance. A long chill slid down his back. The lawyer's soft crybaby mouth worked into a thoughtful pursing. "You have a bed in the back or what?"

"We always kept a cot there," Win improvised. "Sometimes an artist comes in from out of town broke, that sort of thing, we put him up."

"Well, can't help you with a salary, Mr. Smith. I have it in black and white that Mr. Delville picked up the rent and utilities, and here's an insurance policy that covers liability, fire, and theft, standard issue. Due . . . ah, in five months. I'm going to assume Mr. Delville wanted to continue the gallery until the end of the lease. At any rate, the lease is unassignable and it would cost us just as much to break it. Why in hell he signed such a document without consulting me . . . Oh, well, no one ever told Egon how to live. He had it all locked up. How to die, too, I suppose." He gave Win a companionable grin. "I have no reason to suppose he wanted to put you on salary. So." He put the lease back in the file. "Submit bills pertaining to the gallery—openings, mailings, heat, electricity, whatever—directly to me. Don't go overboard. I'm not Egon Delville, and I'm out to see that the estate isn't drained by anybody or anything."

Win got to his feet. Except you, he thought and wondered what he would discover about Reuben Newcombe in the leather-bound journals.

At the door Win turned back with a puckish smile, but Newcombe was already intent on tapping something into the computer.

Win let himself out of the office and didn't breathe deeply until he hit the street. Five months until the lease ran out. He had five months to get his act together, if not one way, then another. And he'd have to find some way to bring in a little extra cash.

"What do you drink?" Annalise wrapped her fingers around the ice cold crystal goblet and shook it gently. She kept her eyes on him, knowing once again she had made a mistake, knowing once again it couldn't be any other way. The pattern was too repetitious to be accidental, too self-destructive to be anything but a fun-house distortion, a crazy, rippled mirror of the past.

"What do I drink? What are you offering?"

He leaned back against the hand-carved eighteenth-century French headboard. Annalise had found the piece at Chordivan's on Second Avenue. Cherubs cavorted with pleased smiles over what had just taken place below their distended bellies. It was ugly but exactly right for those heads of thick hair that leaned against it.

Annalise examined him dispassionately. He was really quite good-looking. His eyes were a trifle vacant, but she liked it that way.

"A line, if you have one," he remarked, smiling. He clasped his hands behind his neck.

"Forget it," she said tersely.

"Just thought I'd ask."

"Don't ask again." She never left cocaine around the place and wasn't about to feed his ego. One snort and he'd think he owned her. Amazing how she always picked the same ones over and over again. Now, why would that surprise her? Men asked for the same woman time and time again. Send me a blonde, good tits, not over twenty-five. They could be eighty, requiring the blasting power of a nuclear missile to get them started, and still they knew exactly what they had a right to.

"Stoly on the rocks."

She went into the efficiency kitchen and busied herself with the drinks, watching him covertly through the door. He was trying not to seem impressed. He didn't want to appear too interested in the fact that the small apartment reeked of money. Somewhere along the way he'd drop a light question like a throwaway.

They never asked the right questions, either, and never knew when they were close to the truth. She didn't mind talking about herself afterward. Sometimes she even told them the truth, but it sounded like a lie, and they didn't know how much they could believe. They'd remain very still, preparing to earn every penny. A fuck wasn't enough. They had to seem *interested.* "So tell me about yourself." The postcoital inflection just so. She knew the act by heart. Waited for the raised eyebrow, the even white well-tended teeth. The wide smile giving off the message that sex had opened up new vistas; it had never been like this before; eyes focusing on the person who called the shots.

You relive your past, she thought with a sigh, unexpectedly reluctant to go back to him. You relive your past over and over again, always trying to get it right.

Years before, when Annalise was in their position, she had wanted to escape the dark meanness and uncertainty. She'd never had the nerve to ask questions. She'd been just as scared afterward as before. You never knew when they'd become vicious, never knew when they'd decide once wasn't enough and they needed it some other way.

The uniforms, the shiny boots, the limousines waiting with impassive chauffeurs, their eyes catching hers when she slipped into the quiet interior. No words exchanged, nothing expected, just the unsaid message hanging in the air that she was dirty, physically dirty, and they expected her to leak semen on the carefully brushed upholstery. She'd sit huddled in a corner waiting for the limousine to take her back to the white villa in Recoleta and then, more often than not, the driver didn't even get out to open the door for her.

"Hey, you growin' it or mixin' it?"

His question brought her back to the present. In spite of his slang, she recognized an actor's trained voice. Its resonance hit the walls and reverberated off the dozen layers of carefully applied shiny green paint. She came back into the room with the Stoly and a glass of scotch for herself.

"Ah," he said and lowered the sheet so that it barely covered him. He reached for the vodka.

Annalise raised her glass and looked at him through a prism of color. A painting now. Degas. No. She shifted the glass. Renoir, a male by Renoir. If she could keep him quiet long enough, let it happen again, but she knew what was going through his head. He had finally lucked into a real one, with money and a need for hard young flesh. If he played his cards right, he might . . . maybe . . . if only . . . He couldn't make a mistake. This one was real; she might never happen again. Time was fleeting. How long was he going to be twenty with a schlong that didn't care where it was half the time?

"Hey," he said, drawing his brows together in a parody of thoughtfulness, "haven't I seen you somewhere before? Wait, I'm not kidding. I thought that in the restaurant, you know? You're famous, right?"

Annalise stayed quiet, watching him, not allowing a muscle to move.

"You're somebody's wife."

She felt a jolt of real fear. It had to happen. Flashbulbs, television cameras, the wife of the candidate, the one with the curtain of blond hair that was a dead giveaway.

She forced a laugh. "And you're somebody's little boy. Here." She lowered her voice, giving him a come-on, playing the game exactly the way he expected her to play it. Turning the tables. She loved it. She wet her lips slowly, letting the tip of her tongue move easily along the edge of her mouth.

"What the hell, who cares who you are?" He took a drink, then put the glass on the night table. She let her dressing gown fall open. Her breasts were still young and firm. The gown opened fully as she came toward the bed. She watched his eyes widen, and nearly smiled at his inadvertent gulp. She placed her glass next to his and sat down beside him. She raised a finger and slid it inside the sheet, feeling the rigid muscles of his stomach contract.

"Lady, you sure—"

"Why don't you shut up?" She lowered her finger, keeping his gaze until she found the crisp hairs and the root of his penis. Perhaps twenty minutes had gone by, and he was as hard as a rock again. Annalise hadn't been with anyone so young and easily ready in a long time. She let her fingers glide with feather touches until she reached the tip, then ran them back and forth in a soft, expert way. He drew in a breath and pressed her hand down, telling her he wanted long, hard strokes. She fully encircled him, and he began to move his pelvis as he reached for her, but with a light, deft movement she pushed him back, then dropped her robe and leaned over him.

He rolled his head back, and she slipped the tip of one breast into his mouth. He sucked hungrily, pulling at the other. Then drawing both breasts together, he took the nipples into his mouth.

Annalise felt a sharp sexual charge, almost painful in its intensity. She heard her own lustful cry and pushed him down so that he lay flat on the bed, his rigid member stabbing the air.

"Come on, baby," he said, reaching for her. She opened the night table drawer to retrieve a condom. Before he could object, as he had earlier, she slipped it on. She bent to wet it with her tongue. They ought to do something about the taste, she thought as the familiar powdery, rubbery scent filled her throat. In another instant she was over him, reaching down and placing him at the mouth of her vagina. He used his fingers to open her. In one thrust he was in her, grunting, holding her hips in place and letting her ride him in a blindingly frantic way that almost blotted out memory.

It was good. For a moment she lay against him as though they could make a night of it. He put his arm around her, rubbed her close, but the movement disgusted her. She drew away, sat up, retrieved her robe, and slipped into it. He removed the condom and held it up. She reached for the wastebasket and he dropped it inside.

"I didn't finish my drink," he said. "Man, you work up a thirst." He made a grab for her.

"Forget it." Her voice was stony cold now. It was over and she wanted him gone. He frowned, clearly unable to figure out what had gone wrong. Nothing, that was the trouble. He had given her just what she wanted. Twice, in fact.

"Man, you're a bundle of contradictions." He swung his feet over the side of the bed and reached for his pants, which had been carelessly thrown on the floor the first time, when there'd been no preliminaries, just a handsome hulk coming into her apartment, his tight pants revealing what his part of the bargain would be.

With a frown, he slipped back into his pants. Annalise almost felt sorry for him. She knew the routine by heart, knew exactly what he'd say to her if she gave him the chance. She should want to see him again; he had even taken his time with the foreplay, waiting for her to say it was okay. He'd had women like her before; they came in a rush of screaming and pounding, and they couldn't get enough.

She could. She had. She did. She glanced at her watch. Zack would be expecting her, and she needed to shower again. The kid was stalling and if she didn't get rid of him soon, he might become a problem. She had run into that before, and it was never pretty. But worse than that, he thought he recognized her. Perhaps she had ridden the waves too long, kept her frail secrets until she no longer thought of them as dangerous.

"Just when you think you're safe, the devil takes his due." Her grandmother had issued the warning in her dark, superstitious way.

"You can't hide, *niña*, ever."

"I don't know what you're talking about."

"You don't know now, but you will soon enough."

Screwy old woman, she'd never been wrong about anything, sitting in that dank, dark hut with a black cat as old as she on her lap.

Annalise pulled a pair of hundred dollar bills from her wallet. He was buttoning his shirt, pretending not to notice her gesture. "You were really very good," she said softly, holding out the money.

The corner of his mouth turned up in a grin she might even have called endearing if she dared. "Listen," he said awkwardly, "you were pretty good, too."

Annalise trilled a laugh. "Oh, well, I was inspired. Here, this is for you."

He eyed the money, but didn't reach for it. "So, can I see you again?" A hopeful note crept into his voice. His eyes took in the room again and its expensive furniture and bibelots. He might not let go quite so fast as she hoped. And he knew the place, knew the address, could come back and wait for her one night. She vowed never to take such a chance again; there was too much at risk. But she knew it was a vow she'd break all too easily.

She shook her head. "No, let's just remember today as something special for us both."

"I've got a friend," he said in a more desperate manner, not moving, although Annalise had already walked to the door. "Together we can take you to the moon."

Annalise shook her head. "I've been there."

"Hey, you didn't even ask my name." He came over to her.

He seemed genuinely hurt, and she remembered how young he was. She reached up and drew her fingers through his hair. "What's your real name?" she asked. She pressed the money into his shirt pocket.

"I told you on the telephone. Avery Bennington."

"Okay, Avery, if that's how you want it."

"Oh, hell, that's my stage name."

"Believe me, I know your real name."

An incredulous expression crossed his boyish face. "So, look, who are you? I've seen you." He almost reached for her and then apparently thought better of it. "I mean, you come into the restaurant with your friend and you spend the entire lunch hour looking at me. A big tip with a card that has only your telephone number on it. Clever. An answering machine. 'I'm not in now,' " he said with a near perfect imitation of her accent, " 'but if you'll leave your telephone number I'll get back to you.' Beats the hell out of me. So you call, make a date, and we fit together pretty good, so what's the problem?"

"None, none at all." She tried to keep her tone light, but she recognized an edge of fear that created a fresh excitement. "I sleep with young men like you once in a while because I need to . . . I need to—well, I need to have it in a certain way."

His face turned ugly. "Shit, next time advertise for it."

"I paid you. What did you expect?" His gaze swept over her. She took in a breath, realizing that she was tingling, that it was part of the routine, the reliving part—pushing them, backing them into a corner until they lashed out. "I don't want you to call me or to try to find out who I am," she said in a low voice. "I know who you are and if you ever bother me or call me, I'll see you finished. Do you understand me?"

He watched her through half-open eyes, too dumbfounded to speak.

"As for a job, acting or waiting, your name will be mud in this city. Now turn around like a good little boy and get out of here."

"Hey, you're really some kind of bitch, aren't you?" His cheeks were red, and for a moment Annalise thought he was going to hit her. Her heart pounded. The tingling wouldn't go away, but he drew back and reached for his jacket. "Stupid cunt."

The words hung in the air as he went out the door, slamming it behind him. She heard his tread on the stair, heard the foyer door open and slam shut, then the street door. Stupid cunt. No, not stupid. She went over to the window and drew the curtain aside. Below, the tree-lined street was in shadow. She had forgotten the time and looked at her watch once again. Nearing six. She had to get home. The kid came out of the building, hands dug into his pockets. He stopped and checked one way, then the other. He turned right, toward Lexington Avenue. His step was jaunty, and Annalise knew he had come to terms with his little adventure and would never bother her again. He had made it twice in the space of an hour and had two hundred dollars to show for it. It beat waiting on tables any time. But there could be trouble: he'd know her the next time he saw her picture in the paper with Zack.

"Hey, that's . . . hey, man." She could hear him, the triumph and the uncertainty.

Annalise let the curtain drop back into place, went into the kitchen and poured herself another drink. She should be more frightened than she was, but in fact she felt remarkably good. The boy had been expert; he had stamina and a certain finesse. For a second she toyed with the idea of calling him again, but that would have been a most dangerous thing to do.

She put her glass down, knowing that as soon as the effects of the sex wore off she'd be depressed again. She was reluctant to remain in the apartment, however. It was on the second floor of an East Side brownstone, a floor-through with two large airy rooms plus a kitchenette and a tiny bathroom.

Expensively decorated, from the draperies that kept out the daylight and street noise to the oversize bed, there was no hiding its purpose. You stepped inside, you were confronted with a lair filled with rococo gilt and silk and satin and the scent of sex. There were no preliminaries here, no pretenses. Clothes were shucked off, the bed bounced; the heavy floors and thick walls muffled sounds or sent them back.

It was a pied-à-terre, her foot on a piece of earth, unlike the sky-high triplex she lived in with Zack and the baroness. Once in a while she came here alone, without dragging some kid by the horn. It reminded her of Paris, of Buenos Aires, of longing, and the belief that just beyond the curtained window lay something *fulfilling*.

She showered quickly, then dressed, gathered her bag and jacket, and left the apartment. The evening was incandescent and warm. All the same, she pulled her jacket collar up around her neck. She walked, as she always did, to the corner for a cab, her heels clicking on the pavement; the street, which was completely residential, seemed unusually closed in and empty. Lights cast through windows appeared to issue from something warm and uncomplicated inside, something she envied without questioning why. As she passed a tall modern apartment building that took up the northwest corner of the block, her eye caught a flash of movement through its front entrance. A tall, slender man, his hair graying at the temples, stepped through the glass doors onto the street. She had no idea who he was, a resident of one of those apartments she envied, no doubt. His eye caught Annalise's and he tilted his head, his gaze narrowing as he took her in. A smile traveled across his face, the smile of a man admiring an unknown, pretty woman, yet Annalise felt a shiver course through her. It was in her walk, her carriage. She was the secret whore whom men everywhere recognized.

She bowed her head and walked quickly on. She would hail a cab at the next corner.

CHAPTER 10

E gon Delville, late owner of the giant perfume corporation, Delville Perfumes, earmarked the bulk of his estate for the founding of a museum of American fashion. Site of the museum will be Delville's town house in the East Sixties."

Shit, thought Win, dropping the newspaper to the floor. He should have taken Egon's address book, not a bunch of fairy diaries about the most sodden bunch of human beings who ever lived. Except for Kate, whoever she was. Egon *loved* Kate. And Ralley, too, because for all her boniness, her lack of breasts, she was the all-American rose, complete with thorns.

Win lay on the cot in the back of Smarts, surrounded by the smell of paint, glue, the sweet pastiness of casein, and the pungency of varnish. The time was early evening. A naked hundred-watt light bulb overhead did little to dispel the gloom and, in fact, added to it. Stacks of artworks filled the newly built wooden bins, some large enough to hold Cliff's monolithic paintings, which Win had begun to call Neo-Ego.

On a hook behind the door to the gallery proper hung Win's clothes, fresh from the cleaners and covered with plastic. Win had a thing about personal cleanliness.

Moving into the back of Smarts hadn't been a good idea, merely the expedient one, given the state of his bank account. Behind a steel door painted white, a toilet and a worn porcelain sink were the only amenities.

Four and a half more months were left on the lease and Win's bête noir was an intractable lawyer who was not about to spend one cent more than he had to on Smarts. Meanwhile Win was living on the proceeds of a painting sold to a midwestern couple who had wandered in one Saturday afternoon. The money was enough to keep him in food and cleaning bills, but an apartment was out. And besides, he hadn't yet paid the artist, Maxi Franilero, who called him daily and had begun to make threatening noises. Win had run out of excuses, and because Reuben Newcombe refused to pay for printing, the four-color invitation on shiny stock ordered for Cliff's vernissage would take up the bulk of the cash left.

"The artist is responsible for his own mailing," Reuben said.

"No, not true, Mr. Newcombe. Good galleries take up all costs. Sales promotion, advertising, everything. I mean, we're running a class operation, Mr. Newcombe."

"Wish I could help you, Win, but no instructions to that effect from Mr. Delville. You get the artist to pay," Newcombe added with a cold smile that closed the matter.

Win needed a power mailing list; he should have scoured Eggie's library for his address book. Sat up and copied the addresses instead of walking out of the library, arms around a matched set of leather diaries. Copied the names and then placed the book on one of the hall tables on his way out.

"And remember, keep away from my friends," or words to that effect. Egon had warned him not to hit on any of his friends for Cliff's exhibitions. Well, Win could now, if only . . .

He sat up, swinging his feet over the side of the cot as though ready for action. But Win felt full of malaise. He'd been so close and so stupid. All that bloody money to a fashion museum. Cheap bastard, Egon could've supported Smarts until the twenty-first century. All Win had come away with were a bunch of journals about *putas*. He remembered Annalise Michelis's intake of breath when he'd whispered the word into the telephone. He'd felt a little thrill then but had quickly turned scared. After all, she was a pretty important lady; Zack Younger had even more money than Egon. Money meant power. Power could mean extermination, like swatting a fly, with Win the fly. He decided he was getting too old for games.

Though the night was warm, the wide, high-ceilinged back room of Smarts felt chilly. Depressing, too, full of canvases with dun-colored backs. No use contemplating the mistakes he'd made in his life. Win had to think about the inheritance he had at hand; think about half a dozen leather-bound journals and how he might turn them into immediate cash. Less than five months to make a go of Smarts was no time at all unless he had the addresses of all the right people and the wherewithal to make them show up at Cliff's opening three weeks away. And attending the opening needn't be enough. They had to be convinced to *buy*. Convinced. That was the key word.

"Everyone here? Settled nice and comfy, wing chair excepted?"
The voice on the tape was certainly Egon's, whose deep and theatrical tones filled with an eerie reality the crowded library of his town house. Kate, sitting in a corner chair, half expected him to explode into the room with his usual restless energy, eyes wide with amazement, his white hair crowning a sanguine complexion. She could all but see Egon in a dark pin-striped suit, perfect cravat, and a collar that would never dare to have a ring around it.

But Egon was dead and his voice issued from the tape recorder on his desk.

Kate shifted in her chair, caught Marguerite's eye, and at the same time noted the stiffening of Annalise's back. Ralley, on the other hand, affecting a weary, uncertain air, lit a cigarette and without apology expelled a stream of smoke.

Kate gazed around the warm, book-lined room with its *faux-marbre* fireplace and ornate Regency desk. Egon's leather chair was still in front of the fireplace. She thought, with a slight shiver, that gold braid with silken tassles should have been strung across the seat from arm to arm, as in museums. Egon Delville Died Here.

She remembered her first visit to the town house. Egon had recently given up smoking. Despite an affability that struck her as faintly forced, she had the feeling he'd been looking forward to the visit. She brought Matt along and he'd immediately climbed onto Egon's chair. Egon took a step forward, then stopped, smiling indulgently.

"That chair is usually reserved for me and the queen of England," he stated. "And since her royal highness shows every evidence of keeping her job . . . ." He gave an apologetic shrug.

"Matt, come down off the chair."

Egon scooped the child into his arms. Matt stared at him in alarm. At the time Egon had no experience of children and her son none of elderly white-haired gentlemen. The moment became awkward. She rescued her son by taking him into her lap.

Egon slipped into his chair and put his feet up. "Shall we talk mortgages?" he asked her.

She nodded, embarrassed over the reason for her visit. She had recently gone into business with Ira Gregory and was taking home a nominal salary. The mortgage payments on her apartment, purchased when she worked for Domingo, were becoming increasingly oppressive, particularly because maintenance costs had risen. Egon generously offered to lend her money to pay off the mortgage. Kate had repeatedly refused until Marguerite got wind of it.

"Don't be a fool, Kate. Egon can be as generous with his friends as he is niggardly with his enemies. He's taking the pressure off so you can get on with what's important in your life. You'll pay him back, he's not worried."

But Kate wondered now, sitting in his library, whether the bill wasn't about to come due. Egon had given her the money without interest and had put off asking her to sign a document making it a straight business deal.

Egon's voice broke the silence once again. "And so you've gathered together under one roof, the important players in my life, Kate Hayden, Annalise Michelis, Jaybee Olsen, Marguerite Varick, Ralley Littlehurst, Mortimer Quinlan, Locke Warren. Zack Younger probably isn't here, but I expect that.

Let's see, have I left anyone out?" A long pause ensued as though Egon were counting on his fingers.

"Egon from the grave." The speaker, Mortimer Quinlan, chief executive officer of Delville Perfumes, was a charming Irishman with a Cambridge accent and a head of beautifully coiffed steel gray hair. "He always liked a little joke."

"I could do without the whole business." Jaybee Olsen sat, like Marguerite, in a stiff-backed chair that faced Egon's desk. "I don't know what I'm doing here, anyway. Here's where they found him, isn't it?" She nodded toward the empty wing chair.

"Don't be morbid, darling," Marguerite said irritably. "Wnat does it matter where he died? *Le cher maître* is gone, and obviously he does not want us to forget it."

Once again Egon's voice, with its cosmopolitan accent and emphatic lilt, spoke to them. "Ah, of course, Reuben Newcombe. The one person I've always taken for granted."

Reuben, sitting at Egon's desk, scowled and ran a hand through his thinning hair.

"Let me add that I expect Reuben to outlive me. After all, he's in possession of a beautiful wife, and statistics on mortality aren't on the side of the elderly bachelor."

A pause followed, as though Egon didn't believe his own words. The tape ran on with a faint scratching sound. Reuben raised his hand to tell them to expect more.

Kate could trace Egon's growing interest in her to that first visit when she had come with Matt. It had struck her powerfully then just how lonely Egon was. How, in fact, he regretted his independence and the self-centered life he had led. It had made taking the money a little easier, but Kate never quite rid herself of a certain guilt, as though she owed him something more than money.

"Of course there's lots of yours truly to be left behind as well," Egon went on. "You, Mortimer, know that better than I. And Reuben, who'll make himself fat and comfortable administering the estate. Delville Perfumes and all its scents, all its packaging, its soaps and lipsticks, its powders and sprays, its *deodorants*— mustn't forget the underarms, so important in the afterlife."

A pause, then some faint Bach, a recognizable air from one of the Bradenburg Concerti. "Better," said Egon. "Fits in with the general mood. By the time you hear this tape, you'll know the terms of my will. Been shocked, annoyed, enervated or energized by it, each according to your expectations. Admit it, all of you. You've spent plenty of time speculating on the disposition of my estate. Well, now you know. You are sitting in the future site of the Delville Museum of American Fashion.

"And Reuben will have explained that all my employees—salesmen, promotion people, stylists, clerks, secretaries, bookkeepers, trainees, and executives—will share in my largess; I've left lump sums to them all. The remainder will be used for the establishment and support of the museum."

Kate heard an audible sigh from Marguerite, sitting next to her. She turned. Marguerite had her hand to her lips. Her face had gone completely white, except for two red spots of color on her cheeks that stood out like apples fallen on a blanket of fresh snow.

"Trinkets, bibelots," said Egon, "ornaments, frippery, foofaraw, gingerbread, you name it, Egon Delville collected it.

"Well, I'm gone now and only *le Bon Dieu* knows where. Do I sound morbid? Maybe it's the late hour. Of course one continues to hope what lies out there will reveal the grand hand of a master architect: Doric columns and beamed archways, with togas stitched up by Coco or Mainbocher.

"Ah, well, if Houdini didn't make it back with a report, neither shall I, I'm afraid, but perhaps one day we'll all meet at a celestial showing of shrouds."

Another pause. "Egon could really wax eloquent when he wanted," Ralley said.

"All that's left is the wax, I'm sure," Annalise said. "I wish he'd get to the point."

"Won't be long now," Reuben said cheerfully.

The tape resumed. "Well, enough of that. No one ever said I was boring. I'd hate like hell to bore you from the grave. What I want, my darlings, what I expect, is an active board of directors for the Delville Museum. You'll record the entire history of American fashion from the first settlers to—well, to Annalise's latest bit of puffery."

"Puffery!" The word spilled from Annalise's lips. She almost started from her chair, but Locke Warren, a thin, square-jawed member of the city's ruling class, and president of the School of Fashion Design, put a finger to his lips.

"Those impossible sleeves your ladies love," Egon continued with a laugh in his voice, as if he had heard Annalise's outburst. "Well, never mind, I've spelled out my wishes concerning the museum quite clearly. Truth is the name of the game. No revisionist history. We want to show what the middle class wore and the other classes, high and low. I've given you a start. We'll purchase, beg, borrow, or steal the rest. We." There was another pause as Egon apparently contemplated his use of the pronoun.

"We," Kate echoed and said it once again for good measure. "We. No doubt we'll never be able to make a move without some kind of reference to Egon, his approval or disapproval."

Egon's voice broke in. "The chief executive officer of Delville Perfumes will be chairman of the board; the lawyer who administers my estate will be executive secretary, and the president of the School of Fashion Design will be treasurer. One member of the board will come from the mayor's office, the person in charge of liaison between the city and the fashion industry. Additional directors will come from the fashion industry and at the moment I've designated these directors to be Kate Hayden, Marguerite Varick, Annalise Michelis, Ralley Littlehurst, and Zack Younger. Well, have fun, my darlings. I won't say good-bye, since I'm still in the here and now and maybe I'll outlive you all. Like Picasso, I somehow believe I can beat the system by living forever. However, unlike Picasso, I've no kith and kin to battle over the remains of Delville Perfumes, hence the care with which I want the estate to stay out of the hands of the court. No, I won't say good-bye. If I can somehow part the curtain, I'll peek through."

Reuben quickly put his hand on the stop button. "That's it," he said.

Kate glanced down at her hands, stretching her fingers out, noting her blunt-edged nails, kept short because of the delicate fabrics she handled. Talk erupted around her, but she paid no attention. Her relief was overwhelming. All Egon wanted was that she sit on the board of directors of his museum. The bill for her cooperative apartment hadn't come due, after all. But she swore to herself that she'd pay it back to the estate just as soon as her collection was off the ground.

Ralley, at Egon's desk, reached for a tall marble obelisk that stood among a collection in various materials. "Get this," she said, holding it up so that everyone could see. "What a lovely bunch of phallic symbols our Egon had." She glanced around the room and spotted others on the bookshelves. "Naughty, naughty Egon. My, my, my, I never realized the significance of these before. God knows I've seen them enough times. My, my, my, what will all those eager little students think of our Egon when they go trooping through the Delville Museum of American Fashion?"

"They are not significant, Ralley, not in that way," Marguerite said with an air of impatience, taking the obelisk out of her hand. "The man collected everything." She set the object down on the desk.

"Oh, and I just remembered the auction at Sotheby's," Ralley said with the brittle enthusiasm that was her trademark, "Tuesday, isn't it? The Havemeyer collection. Poor Eggie wanted to go. Jewels, my dears. He adored jewelry, especially Deco. Think of all that yummy stuff he must have sitting in his safe. Will we have access to it?" she asked Reuben Newcombe.

"Probate first. After that, the museum gets everything."

"We should go to Sotheby's en masse," Ralley went on, "in memory of

Egon. Call for a couple of minutes of silence. Can we bid on anything, Reuben? For the museum, I mean."

"I'm afraid you'll have to let the Havemeyer collection go under the gavel without the Delville Museum."

"I can't possibly sit on the board of any damned museum," Annalise said. "Egon never even consulted me or Zack. He only wants Zack's money, it's quite obvious."

"Wants?" Jaybee raised an eyebrow. "*Wanted* would be more appropriate, Annie."

"Just a minute." Marguerite's imperious voice broke through the chatter. "It is not necessary for you to get high-handed on us, Annalise. You'll sit on this board just as you sit on half a dozen other boards, some of which are far less consequential. Did he mention a director for the museum?" Marguerite directed her question to Reuben.

Kate noticed the rigid way the woman stood, hands clenched. So that was it. Marguerite had known about the museum all along, and Egon had promised her something. The directorship, possibly.

Reuben shook his head no. "Up to the board of directors. That sort of appointment would be."

"Odd for a man who was so careful about everything else."

"He never said anything to me," Reuben remarked. "The will is a couple of years old. Egon fumed and sputtered every now and then about changing this or that, but he never did. Hell, he called me the day he died and said he wanted to see me. Oh, right, that was about something else." He looked intently at Marguerite, then slid the tape recorder into his briefcase. "As I said, there's probate to get through. I doubt if there'll be any trouble, but then, you never know. One thing I can say about Egon—"

"Only one?" Annalise shot in.

"Organization," Reuben continued. "The man knew what he wanted. Everything is ready to go once the will is probated."

"Everything," Marguerite said, "except the choice of director and curators. Ralley is right, of course. We could be letting something go at Sotheby's that—"

"All in good time, Marguerite, all in good time." Reuben closed his briefcase with a flourish.

"Well," Mortimer Quinlan said to Locke Warren, sticking out his hand, "I think the idea will perpetuate the name of Delville and that's all we want."

"Frankly, the money could've been used for the design school building fund, to say nothing of scholarships." Warren spoke with a sour expression on his face.

"Egon never discussed his plans with me," Quinlan went on, "so I'm not certain what his agenda was, but as for the school, the company will always have scholarship money."

"Personally I'm thrilled and honored with Egon's plans and his including me among them," Ralley said. She draped an arm across Annalise's shoulder. "Think of all the fun we'll have looking through Egon's personal effects. I'm dying to find out what kind of undies he wore. Calvin Klein pink, I'd imagine. Come on, I'll buy you a drink. You guys want to join us? We can get drunk and try to figure out what the hell kind of monument Egon really wanted erected in his good name." She grinned at the collection of obelisks on his desk.

Kate followed Marguerite to the door. "I'm expected at home, Ralley. Matt's waiting to go to the park."

"How about coming over tonight? You know, we're having the usual suspects."

"My son's with me," Kate said, referring to the fact that Matt stayed with his father on alternate weekends. Of course, Jeannette, who had the afternoon off, would be back around nine that evening. Kate could use a little fun of the kind Ralley dispensed. A lot of good talk or no talk at all, just relaxing in the midst of the SoHo scene. She caught Annalise's eye and the faint shake of her head. Ralley's way of life was never for Annalise in spite of their friendship. Annalise traveled in a more rarefied atmosphere.

"I'll try," Kate said at last. She wondered what Ira was doing that evening. He had been vague when she asked him, mentioning family business as though it were a duty and not a pleasure. But then, family business was the umbrella excuse he had used from the start.

When Kate left the town house, Marguerite was at the curb looking vainly for a cab.

"We'll try Madison Avenue," Kate said, tucking her arm through Marguerite's. "Anyway, I want to bend your ear a bit. There's been so much going on in my life." They began to walk down the quiet tree-lined street passing handsome old row houses that were lovingly maintained.

"Girl talk," Marguerite murmured.

"No, not that. What's odd is that the whole structure I'd been building seemed to begin to collapse the moment Egon died."

"Nothing to do with your child, surely."

"No, Matt's fine. It's Ira, actually."

Marguerite turned sharply toward her, opened her mouth to speak, then seemed to think better of it.

"Ira's beginning to pressure me about things I don't want to be pressured about. We had a big thing about whether or not I'm going to Hong Kong. Oh, damn, I might as well tell you everything. The IRS wants to see our books. In fact, they're coming in on Monday. Ira's decided I should stay out of the way, all the way to Hong Kong, mind you."

"The IRS?" Marguerite shrugged. "They've looked me over any number of times. They cannot understand how I manage to operate at a loss or a near loss year in and year out. Is he worried?"

"Enough to insist I fly to Hong Kong for a week. What in hell he thinks I'd say to them—"

"Never mind. Tell him you cannot go. Remind him that market week is around the corner."

"I did. We had a battle royal yesterday. I dug in my heels and I won. He's fuming because he has to cancel arrangements for the trip. As if that wasn't enough, Ira now says the designer line won't make a profit for a couple of years. I don't know what he expected. Apparently, though, his money men are beginning to balk. He's talking about my doing a bridge line."

"Wait until your name is established, Kate. Don't spread it around like margarine."

"I know, that's what I keep telling him. Then, when he lost on Hong Kong, he began on a new tack: he wants me to go private label for Saks, Kate Hayden for Saks. Sounds great, but I don't want to, not yet. Let me have a boutique on Saks' designer floor and then I'll talk about private label."

"How far ahead are you on your spring line?"

Kate groaned. "I want ninety pieces, which means a minimum of a hundred, hundred ten to choose from. I've got sketches for seventy-five, but you know the way I work. Then there's the possibility of something startling from Paris or Vivienne Westwood in London that has to be taken into consideration. I like the way they're using brocade in Paris."

"Don't worry about what Paris is doing. Or Vivienne Westwood. You have your own flair. Dramatic, au courant, youthful. Worrying about the European collections isn't going to help."

"I don't want to have a line of wide-legged pants only to discover Karl Lagerfeld has gone all skinny-legged."

"He has and he will," Marguerite said dryly. "Don't worry about him. As for draping on the model, get yourself a good model-maker and you won't have any problems, Kate. Have your sample-maker work from your sketches, like everybody else. Don't be such a prima donna."

"I like draping on the human figure. Anyway, Ira's already making noises about that. He even talked about moving my sample room to Hong Kong where I could be close to the factory. But the pressure's beginning to build, Marguerite. Then this nonsense of Egon's—a museum. I don't know how Ira's going to take my sitting on the board."

"It's none of his business."

"He thinks everything I do is his business." The remark was the closest Kate had ever come to admitting how much control Ira had over her.

Marguerite let a few seconds of silence go by, then said without preliminaries, "Egon wanted me to be director of the museum."

Kate was surprised; Egon had never said a word to her about the museum. "You mean he told you about his plans?"

"Last year. And he made it quite clear he wanted me as director."

"Why didn't he say so? On the tape, I mean."

"Because he thought he was going to live forever and he had plenty of time. I wish he were around so I could kill him." Marguerite made the remark with a flourish of her delicate pink-tipped fingers.

"Why didn't you speak up back at the town house?"

"I have nothing in writing."

"Doesn't matter. Everyone knows how scrupulous you are."

"We were in my apartment when he told me. I fed the sly beggar enough times. It all happened over a hat, a Delville I've had for centuries. He insisted I give the hat to him for the museum. I didn't."

Kate looked curiously at her mentor. "Do you want the directorship? Wouldn't that mean giving up *VFF*?"

"Yes."

"But . . . *VFF* is your *life*."

"So it is. I may not actually want the directorship, but he offered it to me, and he should have put the fact in writing."

"When the board meets," Kate said patiently, not certain she understood the fine points of Marguerite's argument, "I'll bring up the subject."

Marguerite laid a hand on Kate's arm. "No, don't. My experience of in-fighting leads me to believe I'll have to handle the appointment differently."

Kate stood stock still. "I don't get it. You don't want the title but you want it."

"My accountant calls me daily to read me the mordant figures on how *VFF* is doing."

"All you have to do is open the pages to advertising."

"Or sell. I've had an offer, a good one. I no longer have the stomach to turn *VFF* around, to hire an advertising person, to argue with a staff of strangers, who suddenly appear one day and treat me like a relic."

"Marguerite, you're the doyenne."

"Spare me, Kate. I am the doyenne they will treat like a relic. No, I have lost my stomach for battle, I think. But Egon has disappointed me."

Marguerite treated her to a fond smile before peremptorily jumping into the street and hailing a cab. "Yes, I may have to sell *VFF*, and I may try to beat Egon at whatever game he's playing."

"Marguerite, Egon's dead."

As she pulled the cab door open, Marguerite turned to her with a smile. "Yes, of course. How amazing that I should forget for just that one little second."

CHAPTER 11

Central Park, with its soft green hillocks and thick-trunked, thick-limbed trees, seemed to sop up the Saturday afternoon crowds like blotting paper: elderly strollers, children and dogs, balloons, nannies, teenagers, lovers leaning against trees and kissing. Squirrels, too, fearless of people, dogs, and children, intent upon cadging food.

"Yay, squirlows." Matt tore after one, chasing it up a tree. The animal did an about-face halfway up and clung motionless to the trunk, staring down at Matt who watched raptly.

Kate waited on the path, knowing that if she didn't keep an attentive eye on her son he could disappear in an instant. After another moment she headed for a bench that held one other occupant, an elderly man reading a newspaper. The warm sun sent its rays through the leaves and left patches of light on the grass.

"Hey, Mommy, look." Matt called to her with awe in his voice. He pointed excitedly to a man crouching on a grassy knoll, feeding squirrels from a paper bag. Matt began to run toward him at a fast clip, shouting something she couldn't make out. Kate got quickly to her feet. Telling her son to stay away from strangers was an exercise in futility. Alert, friendly, and trusting, Matt spoke to everyone without fear. The problem lay in teaching him to be discreet without becoming paranoid. She hadn't quite figured out how to handle the problem. When she came close, Matt had already been offered a handful of peanuts and was happily tossing them afield.

"I'm sorry," Kate said apologetically to the stranger. "My son really is a little beggar." She stopped when he turned a friendly, interested gaze on her.

"Have some," he said, offering her the bag. "There's more than enough to go around." She detected a slight southern accent, which struck her as nonthreatening.

She dug her hand in and fished out a handful of peanuts, which she scattered around. "Squirlows—I mean, *squirrels*—are my son's passion. I really ought to bring peanuts when we come to the park. Perhaps I've been depriving him of some of the best moments in his life."

"Ah, but then I wouldn't have the pleasure of offering him my largess."

Kate gave an uncomfortable laugh and thought, glancing overtly at the stranger, that he was attractive, less perhaps because of his physical attributes —which were many, for he was tall, lean, and broad-shouldered—but because of his evident charm and easygoing nature, the intelligence in his clear, open gaze, and his mouth, which was decidedly sexy.

She was concluding recklessly that he was a man who could be trusted, when Matt came up for another handful of peanuts.

"They're taking them," he announced in an important tone as some squirrels ventured close.

The stranger hunched down and held out the package. "Here, give them the whole works."

With a look at his mother, who nodded, Matt took the bag and enthusiastically began scattering the nuts.

"How about saying thank you?" Kate called to her son.

Matt turned around and regarded the stranger for a moment. "Thank you," he said in somber voice, then with a sudden broad grin went back to his work.

"Cute little fellow you've got there. Your eyes."

"Thank you. I hope you didn't hand my son your lunch."

"Fed squirrels the same way when I was a kid. I'm afraid it's a habit I can't break. And I've already had lunch, thank you."

"I wonder what memories Matt will have," Kate mused. "He much prefers this to the zoo."

"Pretty logical when you think about it. Squirrels are small, manageable, uncaged, and they have a deceptive way of appearing friendly. That wide-eyed stare of course is all alertness and distrust."

"Perfect behavior for a denizen of Central Park."

"I suppose that's what you have to teach your son."

"Not quite yet. I'd hate to have him grow up with a fear of strangers. Right now he's always with me or his nanny or at nursery school." Or with his father, who might have his own priorities.

"Well, I'm glad you've delayed the lessons a bit," he said with a smile.

Matt had emptied the bag and shaken it upside down a couple of times. "In the litter basket," Kate told him. He trotted to the litter basket, stood on tiptoe, and dumped it in.

There was an awkward moment between them when Matt came back, fished his ball out of his pocket, and threw it into the air after casting a shy glance at them.

"I've been in New York a year," the stranger said. "The city takes a little getting used to."

"Most glamorous city in the world," Kate said with a certain amount of pride, suddenly aware that she was talking to a perfect stranger. In New York one didn't trust strangers past casual conversation, no matter how attractive they seemed and no matter what she had or hadn't taught her son.

"It's a city for being young or rich in. There's no middle ground left," he remarked. "If you're young, thick skin protects you. If you're rich, you see only what you have to. The rest doesn't exist."

"Maybe I ought to amend your remark," Kate said. "It's a city to be young or ambitious or rich in." She sensed they were engaging in the empty, polite talk of partners at a ball performing a stately dance.

Matt, with a giggle, tossed the ball to the stranger, who tossed it back. Kate stood to one side watching them, wondering who he was, where he came from, what he did. And why, in fact, he was playing ball with her son.

Her mind went quickly to Ira, to her husband, and back again to Ira. She stared at the stranger. He hadn't enticed Matt. He'd been merely tossing peanuts to squirrels. No, her curiosity was something more than that. She was *interested* in a total stranger her son had picked up in the park, and that would never do.

"Matt." She held out her hand. "Time to go."

Matt pouted and seemed ready to cry. The stranger handed the ball to Matt and, taking him by the hand, led him over to Kate. "I didn't realize the time," he told her. "I've got to get a move on." He reached out and tousled Matt's hair. "You play a mean game of catch."

Kate lifted Matt up. "Come on, killer, we have a busy day ahead of us. Thank Mr.—" She stopped. "I'm sorry, I don't know your name."

He gave her a slow grin. "Pete," he said just before he walked away. "Pete Frank."

"Katie, love, how are you, how's my darling Matt?"

"Mom! Wonderful, where are you?" The trouble was, Kate thought, her mother's voice over the telephone wasn't preceded by the bleep that usually accompanied overseas calls. That meant she could be around the corner or across the continent.

"Beverly Hills, just in from Acapulco. How's my darling grandson?"

"Handsome, all grown up. We just came in from the park where he was feeding the squirlows. You can talk to him for yourself."

"Katie, just a minute, before you put Matthew on, answer one question. I'm devastated about Egon, of course, but I just heard the most extraordinary thing. A museum of fashion, was he mad?"

"I think he knew precisely what he was doing."

"He left every blessed cent to the museum, is that it?"

"He was pretty generous to his employees, as a matter of fact."

"I see." Her mother was quiet for so long that Kate began to think they'd been disconnected. When she spoke at last, it was in a querulous tone. "You heard the will, I suppose."

"Only the part pertaining to the museum. It seems he appointed me to the board."

"What about your apartment?"

"He didn't call in the debt."

"Well, thank goodness for that. Now put my grandson on."

"Right," said Kate, calling out to her son. She didn't want to know when ChiChi would return to New York. While she loved her mother, she preferred her in minuscule doses.

CHAPTER 12

The vast, spare, white SoHo loft belonging to Ralley Littlehurst was jumping. Something rap, with a heavy, relentless beat and a voice spewing out anger, shook the walls and Cliff Beal's massive encrusted wax and acrylic paintings. Despite windows open to a warm, soft night, the scent of marijuana drifted heavily on the air. Ralley, ever mindful of the elder Steyman and with enough in her past to crucify her, allowed no other abusive substances. Cliff, in fact, had posted signs around the loft to that effect. He had also managed to cajole Ralley into letting him remain at her loft until after the exhibition at Smarts.

It was a typical Saturday night at Ralley's, where twenty or thirty people gathered to shout their opinions at one another over or under the music, to eat potato or taco chips, and to drink. Ralley never prepared food; the word "cooking" wasn't in her lexicon. In Ralley's crowd, hard liquor was mostly out, and so the scents of marijuana, beer, and wine. Except for Ralley, however, who mixed a particularly lethal Gibson for herself, but drank it out of a wineglass with the inconsequential onions nestled cozily at the bottom.

The crowd was a blend of lanky models, Ralley's friends from Steyman's, actors, a sculptor who taught at the New School, a writer or two, artists; this night Kate had come by late and alone. Jaybee was there, too, as well as the man who ran Smarts, Winthrop Smith.

"Why is he here?" Ralley asked Cliff in a reasonable tone when she discovered Win sitting in a corner with Jaybee.

"What?" The music was loud, but Ralley had asked the question at top decibel.

"You heard me, you son of a bitch." Cliff had sworn there was nothing between him and Win, had sworn he'd never bring him around again and yet there the worm was talking eagerly to Jaybee of all people, and there wasn't a thing Jaybee could, or would, do for him.

"C'mon, Ralley, Win's my *dealer*," Cliff said, "the only one I have."

"He's not going to do a damn thing for you. He's a loser."

"What?"

"I said you heard me, you bastard."

"C'mon, Ralley, part with a couple of names and addresses of your pals. You know everybody. Just get them to the opening."

"Openings mean *nada*, how many times do I have to tell you? Nobody *buys* at openings. Nobody *comes* to openings. Tell your friend to have a small, intimate vernissage for a select list of patrons, it's the only way."

"He'll do it, he'll do it," Cliff said enthusiastically. "Just give him some names."

"Over my dead body. I suppose you turned the place upside down looking for my address book."

He gave her a sheepish grin. He was a tall, beefy man in his mid-twenties with a perpetually tanned face and dark ringlets that gave him the look of a merchant prince as painted by Hans Holbein the Younger. Cliff's black-fringed eyes were of an unclouded brown that made him appear smarter than he was. His teeth were even and white, his smile eager and almost childish.

"Let him get his own list of names," Ralley said, turning away and melting into the crowd. She wanted Cliff's exhibition to be a failure, not because he was a bad artist, which he was, but because success would only make him more insolent.

She had long before given up any notion of attracting the right kind of man. The men she fell in love with were all losers, men who were uncertain of themselves, or too certain, who were weak or mercurial, or had only their sexuality to recommend them, men who used her up or whom she used up, who were half-crazed to begin with, and about whom the beginning and end of each relationship were well established before its inception.

Jaybee, a faintly sour expression on her face, sat on a large white ottoman with an eager and attentive Win crouched next to her. The trouble was Win had something engaging about him, although anyone meeting him a second time would realize how dusty and unvisited his attic was.

Jaybee didn't care for men, that was common knowledge, but she had come that evening with a tall, very attractive man she introduced as Pete Frank. Ralley had been trying for an hour to catch his eye; then Kate walked in and Pete disengaged himself from the group he was chatting with and made his way over to her.

Ralley, from across the room, had seen the surprised expression on Kate's face and the rise of color to her cheeks. She was wondering if Kate knew him when she felt a hand on her neck. A voice whispered in her ear, "Cliff's paintings stink, you know that, don't you? Man has no talent what-so-ev-er."

She turned to find leering at her the sculptor who taught at the New School. "You don't know what you're talking about," she said, suddenly defending Cliff and not quite certain why.

"Nobody's buying or even looking at monolithic garbage anymore. Nowadays it's neat, cute, adorable still lifes. Lit-tul real-as-anything paintings. Tell Cliff to quit while he's behind."

"If you know so much," Ralley said, trailing her fingers up his chest, along his neck, over his beard, along his clean-shaven upper lip and his bulbous nose, "why aren't you painting cute little still lifes and making a million dollars?"

He smiled. "Because I spend too much of my time womanizing with the gorgeous likes of you."

"Yeah," she said, moving off, "I've heard about you and your seventeen-year-old students."

It was all hype, painting or clothing. Maybe if she dispensed a few names to Winthrop Smith, Cliff would meet the right kind of people and either shape up or ship out. She wouldn't bet the rent money on which. At the moment, however, she hated Win and Cliff equally. Even so she couldn't quite part with Cliff, if no longer letting him make love to her, and insisting he bed down on the couch.

The music stopped, there was an instant of silence, and then something fresh began; Cliff had carefully spliced together a parade of rap music, and Ralley, standing alone at the edge of the crowd, eyed the stereo. She suddenly wanted to race across the room and rip the tape off. Instead, she took a sip of her Gibson, straightened her shoulders, and plunged back into the crowd, fishing up across the room to where Kate sat on the window ledge.

The loft was five stories above the street. The downtown section of the city closed up at nightfall, and for once there wasn't even the sound of a drunk being rolled. Kate had her fingers wrapped around the stem of a wineglass. She was regarding Pete Frank with an unusual light in her eyes. Jaybee had left Win and was standing with them. Ralley joined the little group, putting a hand on Jaybee's shoulder. She was, as usual after a couple of Gibsons, feeling faintly adversarial.

"Hey, if Annalise and Marguerite were here, we'd have a quorum," she said. "We could dissolve the Delville Museum and donate the money to charity, which is where it should have gone in the first place."

"What charity?" Kate asked, looking interested, as if it might be a possibility.

Pete Frank, holding a can of beer, gave Ralley a bemused smile. "How about a charity for the hearing impaired, namely the current generation?" He referred, of course, to the music. Ralley held his eye for a moment, sensed the appreciation directed to her, and at the same time knew his remark was meant for Kate, whether it had relevance or not.

"I'd lower the music," Ralley said, still holding his eye, "but I can't stand the sound of my guests thinking."

"They think, do they?"

"Jeez, Pete," Jaybee said, "you talk like a philosophy professor a hundred years old instead of a lawyer."

"A lawyer?" Kate studied him, pressing the wineglass against her cheek. Ralley, watching, thought she had never seen Kate looking so beautiful. She wore a long-sleeved black silk collarless blouse with military epaulets and a wide high-waisted black skirt. Her complexion glowed. She resembled the women she designed for—young, restless, successful, and self-possessed. But that she didn't know Pete Frank was evidenced by her question. Ralley was mystified.

"Pete's with the U.S. attorney's office, Southern District of New York. Better watch out, you two," Jaybee said imperturbably, taking Ralley and Kate in at a glance. "Rumor has it he's coming down hard on the garment industry. You know, mob money, stuff like that."

"I work for Steyman's," Ralley said, "a highly respectable mail-order house with absolutely no ties to the mob. We don't manufacture; we buy." It wasn't quite the truth, since Steyman's had its own private label line designed in house and manufactured in Hong Kong.

"We in the Southern District of New York," she added, "never take bribes from manufacturers and make barely enough to support us in our cold, shabby bohemian lofts."

"I haven't said a word," Pete remarked, "but I've apparently come on like gangbusters."

"Oh, knock it off, Ralley," Jaybee said. "You make more money than God and are extremely profligate with it. She's a vice president of Steyman's," she explained to Pete, but he was no longer listening.

His attention was centered on Kate, and even unmindful of both Ralley and Jaybee. Ralley drifted away. Men never wanted brittle women, and she was brittle all right. Alone in the middle of her own party, clever, brittle, not-so-bad-looking Ralley Littlehurst, who wandered through life dispensing brittle cheer because it was what she had taught herself to do best. She needed her drink replenished was what she needed.

Kate left the party soon after. Jaybee's offhand remark about Pete Frank had ruined a harmless flirtation and made her suspect that their meetings, both in the park and at the loft, were setups. She had nothing to base her fear upon except the fact that the IRS was scheduled to examine the company books on Monday, books she'd made no effort to understand, perhaps out of fear of what she'd find. Even though Ira had backed off about sending her to Hong Kong, as if the idea hadn't been a good one to begin with, the sense of unease was difficult to shake. Kate felt as though she were in the calm center of a storm that would carry her along and break soon enough.

She ran down from Ralley's fifth-floor loft rather than wait for the clanging freight elevator and its difficult-to-manage door. It was nearly eleven and there were no cabs cruising through. The dark, dreary street was silent and empty. She drew her jacket close and took a firm grip on her shoulder bag. A glance upward revealed the bright lights of Ralley's loft. She'd been a fool to rush away alone when she could have phoned for a cab. She contemplated going back, but didn't want to see Pete Frank again. He was the reason, after all, why she left. She resolutely began to walk toward the busier cross street. Sitting in a doorway was a drunk who called something out to her. She hurried by. Someone, a man in an old overcoat, began to weave toward her diagonally across the avenue.

"Ho, listen," he called in a cracked voice. She bent her head and quickened her pace.

"Hey." He stopped and began to shout obscenities at her. A moment later footsteps moved up behind her, quick steps that would overtake her in seconds. She reached the corner and ran out between two parked cars into the street, hoping to find a cab. The street was empty in both directions. She headed quickly for West Broadway staying in the center as an urban guerrilla was trained to do. Her heart seemed to pound in her ears and she almost missed hearing her name called.

"Kate." There were a million Kates in Manhattan.

"Kate, hold it." She recognized the voice and hesitated a moment, but then quickened her pace. She couldn't have said whether it was an unconscious running away or not, when what she wanted to do was turn around and say it was okay.

"You're giving me a run for my money."

She whipped around to face Pete Frank. "What the hell do you think you're doing?" She lashed the words out, thinking at the same time that perhaps she was glad to see him after all. "You scared me," she said lamely, a second later.

"Sorry. I was following you, along with a wino and a kid who looks as if he means business."

No, she thought, he'd been tracking her, which wasn't the same as following her. "I'll take my chances with them, thank you." She turned away and began heading for the brightly lit avenue, knowing he wouldn't let her go on alone.

He caught up with her. "Just let me see you safely into a cab."

"I don't want to have anything to do with you," she said. "You've made an absolute fool of me. Pretending to feed the squirrels, using my son to meet me, then showing up at Ralley's, and now this. What in hell do you want?"

"Hey, wait a minute, you're a little confused." He put his hands on her arms and wheeled her around to face him. For a long moment they stood regarding each other. She caught a look in his eyes, soon veiled, a flicker of interest that had nothing to do with mobs and the garment industry, and that every woman recognizes. She thought with surprise that if she played her cards right she could connect with him.

"I think," he began in a measured voice, "that I want to get to know you."

"Because I work on Seventh Avenue?"

He laughed. "That's as good a reason as any. I could use a contact."

"I'm a designer, and I don't work for the mob."

He brushed a stray bit of hair from her face. "Whom do you work for?"

"I work for myself."

"Nice. Something I always wanted to do."

She turned, and heading toward West Broadway, matched her pace to his. "The company's called Kate Hayden. That's what you want to know, isn't it?"

"Sure," he said in a tone meant to placate her and convince her she was all wrong, that they had met through one or two of life's little coincidences. They reached West Broadway, a wide avenue that was well-lit and busy. Kate went over to the curb to hail a cab.

"I'd like to buy you a cup of coffee," Pete said.

A cab drew up. Kate opened the door and stepped in. Just as she was about to slam the door shut, she cast a glance at Pete. His hands were jammed into his pockets, his shoulders hunched. He was waiting. The notion occurred to her that she had lost the ability to look at a man, receive his look of interest, and work with it. Perhaps it had something to do with a lousy marriage and a disgraceful love affair that tied her in knots so that she was unable to respond the way an available woman should.

"Okay," she said, moving over. He climbed in after her. "There's a bar on Third Avenue," she said. "Comes complete with a jazz pianist, suit you?"

"Suits me fine."

After giving instructions to the driver, Kate settled back in the seat, arms folded across her chest. So far he had given her no reason to trust him. She had to know what he was doing in her life and what he expected to find out. Ira would want to hear. The excuse for being with Pete Frank seemed reasonable. That she had a desire to connect with him in a totally different way was pushed to the back of her mind.

The bar was crowded. Kate ordered a wine cooler, Pete a Dos Equis. There were no seats available and they pushed their way over to the window.

"How'd you meet Jaybee?" Kate asked.

"I think you know how."

"If the Justice Department is going to investigate the garment industry, you begin by making friends with the mayor's office."

"You're a smart lady."

"You knew who I was in the park, didn't you?"

"Yes."

"You were following me."

"No."

"You just happened to be feeding the squirrels when Matt and I came by."

"It's a small world. I live on the West Side close to the park. Where do you live?"

"On the East Side close to the park."

"Case closed. How *do* you know me?"

"I read *VFF.*"

"I'll bet."

The jazz pianist floated up a few notes, then launched into an old Bessie Smith number, something bluesy about her man doing her some kind of wrong. "New York's a small town," Pete said.

"So small you show up at Ralley's, which is miles and a couple of a million people away in SoHo, and there I am."

"Lucky me, batting a hundred twice in one day. Fashion industry's small, too."

"And you're going to cleanse it of mob influence. *If* there is such a thing as mob influence."

"Tell you what, Kate, let's talk about jazz or Bessie Smith or what you design and why, but let's not talk about what I do for a living."

"Why not? It's why you picked me up, it's why you're following me, and it's why I agreed to have a drink with you."

"You're wrong on two counts."

"How do you go about discovering mob influence in the garment industry if you announce yourself with bullhorns?"

"That was Jaybee's bullhorn, not mine. I may just have to cream the lady or worse, put a muzzle on her."

"The cat's out of the bag. Isn't your whole operation tainted?"

He hesitated, as though she had said precisely what was on his mind. "We're up against people who weren't born yesterday. They take their meetings at midnight on downtown streets, not on the telephone. They cover themselves in ways we can't even imagine. They're worthy adversaries, Kate. Meeting you is pure coincidence. Our having a drink together is pure pleasure."

She waited a beat, then, moving an inch closer to him, said, "Work much with the IRS?"

She caught a slight shading in his eyes. He bent over and placed his lips lightly against hers in a momentary kiss, pointedly ignoring her question, which made her wonder whether she was right. "I've been wanting to do that all evening," he said. "No, scratch that. I've been wanting to do that ever since I offered you a bag of peanuts in the park."

A girlish warmth suffused her cheeks and she looked away. The kiss felt entirely too good. Ira's kisses were rough and self-serving, meant to bring her to heights that would satisfy him.

"How about another drink?" Pete asked, although her glass was still half full. She shook her head. There was a long, awkward silence between them he made no effort to break.

"Music's great," she said at last.

"I'm a big jazz fan. You?"

"I don't have time to be a big anything anything. My work and the life attached to that work pretty well take care of my time."

"Including Saturday evenings in SoHo?"

"That's networking, and besides, Ralley's my friend. It's necessary that I see what people on the street and at parties are wearing. One doesn't work in a vacuum. I'm designing wide-legged pants in my studio; they're wearing leggings in the real world."

"They tell you what they want to wear, in other words."

"They suggest they prefer tight pants."

"And you can't convince them otherwise."

"I'm not out to reinvent fashion, only interpret it. Why are you with the Justice Department and not a big Wall Street law firm?"

"That sort of thing impresses you, I gather."

No, she thought, studying him. Worrying about the IRS and the Justice Department looking into mob control of the garment industry impressed her. "I just wonder, given the choices . . ."

"You mean between big bucks and a five-figure salary?"

"Yes."

"I grew up in an atmosphere of community service. My father was a doctor during the civil rights demonstrations in Selma. I was with him when he volunteered his services in the ensuing riots. I was a kid but he figured I should learn something about how people act toward one another. We traveled around a lot. I learned."

"You're going to clean up the world," Kate said. "As fast as you clean it up, that's how fast it's going to become dirty again."

"You think I should quit the sanitation brigade and do a little littering myself. That's success in your book."

She reared up, supposing it was exactly what she meant. "I don't think I dump on anybody."

He repressed a smile.

"I don't," she continued. "I like ambitious men . . . *people*. Anyway, I don't know what we're talking about. I'm afraid I haven't given much thought to cleaning up the world, just dressing it."

"Kate, I'd hate to think you and I have such differing views of how to live the good life."

"I don't believe I hurt anyone with what I do," she said. "All I've ever asked was to be allowed to express myself as a fashion designer."

"And you don't give a damn about the route your clothing takes to arrive at the point of sale. It's none of your business." He said the words quietly and then, as if realizing they were on dangerous ground, backed away. "Forget it. I seem to remember wanting to keep our conversation superficial."

"Agreed. Are you married?" It was the one question she hadn't bothered asking Ira until too late. She cast a glance at Pete's ring finger. There was no ring, not even the outline of one.

"Divorced. You?"

"You know I'm divorced."

"Now I do."

"Anybody in your life?"

"Not until today."

"You might ask me the same question."

"I'm afraid to."

"Then you understand." She put her drink on the window ledge. "I have to go now."

"Kate, stay awhile."

She regarded him without a trace of a smile. She liked his mouth, the unwavering gaze in his eyes, and the look of interest he no longer made any attempt to hide. But all the revelation did was confuse her, tell her she had made two too many mistakes with men, that she had lost her talent for loving anyone or anything except her son and her work.

"It's late," she said. "I promised Matt an early start in the morning." She put her hand out and he grasped it warmly.

"You're very beautiful," he said.

She felt herself blush and was glad for the subdued lighting in the bar. She whispered a thank-you and turned away. He followed her out of the bar. "I live just a couple of blocks away," she told him. "I can manage."

"There are winos and hoods around here, too," he told her, drawing his hand through her arm.

When they neared her street, however, Kate had a sudden unreasonable fear that Ira or one of his men would be watching the front entrance. She stopped. "Thanks very much," she told Pete, pulling away from him and simultaneously offering her hand. "If you don't mind, I'd rather go on from here alone."

"Right." He pressed his lips together. "Right." He turned and walked abruptly away.

Kate gazed after him, wondering why he had given up so easily. Then she walked rapidly around the corner to her building. She did not look for Ira's car; it was Saturday and he spent weekends with his family. Besides, when he did show up, he'd find his key no longer fit the lock.

CHAPTER 13

"Forget it." Ira Gregory, seated behind his desk, used the tone of undisguised irritation with Kate that he had adopted increasingly of late. "Twenty-nine years old and you've been invited to sit on the board of a fag hat designer's museum. Gives you a sense of importance, does it?"

"Egon didn't know he was going to die. And what the hell does my age have to do with it?"

"On the one hand you're telling me you can't work on a bridge line, and on the other you're taking a seat on a museum board to satisfy the whim of a dead man. A fashion museum. Little kids dying of AIDS, the streets thick with the homeless and panhandlers, and your brilliant pal wanted a fashion museum so the world would remember him. Now I know I've heard everything. And sit down for chrissake. I hate you hovering over me like that."

Kate leaned across his desk, pressing her hands against its surface. "Kids with AIDS? The homeless? I had no idea you were such a charitable creature." The words popped out. Kate had no stomach for an argument. She merely wanted Ira to know about her appointment to the museum's board before he heard the story from someone else. However, she had chosen the wrong time, the wrong day, and the wrong subject. Promptly at eight-thirty that morning, a team from the IRS had moved into the accounting office.

A decided bustling about the offices of Kate Hayden ensued, albeit accompanied by a hushed and wary air.

Ira had swung through the offices wearing a smile as though it were a war decoration. The staff, always watchful of Ira's moods, scented the menace even when he was smiling, as he smiled at her now. It sent an abrupt chill along her spine that told her not to cross him.

"Look," she said, "what I do on the board after hours won't interfere with my work. Preparing a new bridge line without an augmented staff *will*, and you know it."

He brushed her remark away. "Spare me the details. Just get moving. They're squawking in Hong Kong for the models."

"I'm still waiting for fabric samples, Ira. Half a dozen cuts I ordered from Besson haven't arrived."

"Get Elfie on it," he told her, referring to her assistant who served as fabric stylist.

"Speak with the head office," she said. "Maybe they can light a fire under Besson."

"Get Elfie on it."

She closed her eyes for a second, unable to go on fighting him. He reminded her of Matt when her son was three, resisting authority, arguing over every issue, whether it involved putting his socks on or eating his dinner.

"Speak to publicity about the museum," Ira added unexpectedly but in a grudging tone. "Might as well make the most of it, but after the show, kid, I want that bridge line for summer. Kate Hayden New York, Kate Hayden Sport, Kate Hayden You Name It—I want you to start thinking about it now." They stared at each other for a long moment. Then his telephone rang. As he reached for it, Ira asked in a surprisingly conversational way, "Incidentally, how was your weekend?" Before she could answer, he told his secretary to hold the call.

"My weekend?" Had he been spying on her? The thought frightened her. "Much as always," she said, watching him closely. But it hadn't been as always. She'd met Pete Frank of the U.S. attorney's office, Southern District of New York, Pete Frank, Justice Department lawyer, who made no secret of the fact that he was investigating mob infiltration into the garment industry.

"Matt okay?"

"Fine. And your weekend?" She headed for the door, silently mouthing *family business.*

"Family business."

"Wedding? Funeral?"

"Kate, don't pry."

"You're right, it's in bad taste." She reached for the doorknob, then whipped around. It was now or never. "There've been a couple of burglaries in my building," she said, her heart pounding, "in spite of the doormen and elevator operators. I've had my lock changed." She tried to keep her voice matter-of-fact but felt its tremble.

"You'll have to give me a new key, then."

Kate fought back the desire to run away without having to finish what she had started. "Sorry, but that can't be."

"Is your ex making noises?"

He wouldn't face the truth and, in fact, preferred a lie. "Yes. Matt said something to him the last time he was there. And I think my housekeeper is a little upset, too. I can lose just about anything, but not my housekeeper."

He let out a bellow. "Your housekeeper? Who gives a shit about your housekeeper?"

"I do. She's responsible for my son's well-being, and he cares about her."

"You don't mean your housekeeper. I've charmed a lot less than she. It's your ex-husband. You're letting him pull your strings, Kate. If I didn't know what you were like in bed, I'd say you still want him around."

"Guess what, Ira, you haven't hit my Achilles' heel. And, to take a page out of your notebook, I don't want to discuss Tim with you."

"Touché. You're right. What we have between us exists in its own little bubble."

He wouldn't let go easily, either because he cared about her or because she was all the investment he had, Kate couldn't be certain which. The hint of a smile on his face showed no warmth or humor, only triumph of a sort she couldn't understand.

Before she could offer a suitable response, his intercom buzzed. He picked it up with an irritable motion and barked at his secretary for interrupting him again, then in another moment instructed her to send Vivian, Kate's model, to the showroom. When he replaced the receiver, he told Kate that Ralley Littlehurst was in the showroom with Richard Steyman. Relieved, she opened the door and slipped through. She had come to tell him about the museum and the key, but it was the Internal Revenue Service that sat most heavily on his mind.

Ralley was picking her way through the clothing rack when Kate came into the showroom. "You know Richard Steyman," she said without looking up, referring to a handsome, friendly man in his forties who was sipping coffee from a porcelain cup. The heir apparent had recently been made executive vice president of Steyman's in charge of merchandising. He and Ralley were on the prowl for their spring catalog.

"Yes, we've met," Kate said, extending a hand and offering him a smile. He wore aviator glasses and an expensive hairpiece, and seemed charmed to see her again.

"We're heavy into silk chiffon, charmeuse, linen-looks," Steyman said at once, as though it were an extension of a conversation they'd previously had. His speech was polished. He was well educated, and there was no doubt he'd inherit the business from his father, although he was the younger of two sons. "We're emphasizing colors on the pale side, exceptions: red on the order of russet, navy, and a green bordering on sunny."

"We thought about a blouse and pants," Ralley said, all business. "Figured we'd find it in your resort collection."

"Small but choice," Ira said, coming quickly into the showroom and giving them his disarming smile.

Kate saw Ralley brighten with his entrance and knew that the same fascination she had first felt with Ira intrigued Ralley, too. Sex appeal or ego or energy, or all of them put together; Ira made the room come alive and Ralley responded. She suddenly wished something would come of that electric moment and then was ashamed for wishing it.

Just then Vivian came into the showroom looking combed and beautiful.

"Try this," Ralley said, handing her a beige blouse and deeper beige pants. "How'd this sell?" she asked Ira.

He had to walk a fine line, telling her the style had sold well but wouldn't be seen everywhere. "I'll check. The whole resort collection did very well."

"We'd want it in an exclusive color-fabric combo. Some subtle changes, absolutely Steyman's."

"No sweat."

Vivian, holding the clothes, silently exited. Kate caught up with Vivian outside and asked her to look for a pair of beige high-heeled shoes. "Check the accessories closet for shimmery nude stockings. I think we have a couple of pairs, and the pants show just enough ankle to be interesting."

"I have a heavy gold chain for around my neck," Vivian suggested.

"No," Kate said. "I know Ralley. She's already figured something out."

"Kate could sketch something up for you," Ira was saying when she came back into the showroom. "We can fax the sketch to Hong Kong along with fabric information and they can come up with a price."

"Right," Steyman said, looking interested. "We'll see the day when we can fax the fabric and findings while we're at it."

"Reproduction's getting pretty good," Ira said. "You never know what they'll come up with next."

Ralley caught Kate's eye and shook her head slightly. Kate caught the message. Ralley would save her the trouble of designing something new by steering her boss onto a garment already in production. "I'm thinking of something more along this line," she said, diving into the rack again and coming up with a wide-legged jumpsuit and a blouse taken from a three-piece suit. "Use the blouse as a lightweight jacket, in a smoky gray see-through, maybe chiffon. Beautiful, Dick, n'est-ce pas?"

Steyman seemed impressed but added, "I'd like to see it in that russet red. What do you think?"

"Stunning," Ira said, casting a glance at Kate that told her to agree.

Kate had no objection at all and thought Ralley was clever; she might mock up something similar for the spring collection.

"Not red," Ralley said. "Kate?"

"I've been thinking of drop-dead colors in a softer range, frankly."

"Well, let's keep our options open." Ralley never kidded around when it

Steyman and Ira had repaired to the window and were conversing in low voices.

"That was some hunk Jaybee showed up with on Saturday," Ralley said. "Where in hell does she find them?"

"Definitely not crawling out of the woodwork."

"Did you get any more out of him?"

Kate frowned. "About what?"

Ralley cast a glance toward the window, clearly meant for Ira. "About investigating Seventh Avenue."

"Why would I even want to know?"

"You're kidding, Kate."

"We're owned by a Swiss corporation. They're a very uptight crew."

"That's there; here's here. What did you talk about? He followed you out, didn't he? Was that prearranged? Jaybee acted as if she couldn't care less, but then, she couldn't care less."

"We prearranged nothing. I'd just had a long day."

"But he caught up with you, don't deny it. Does he have your telephone number?"

"No." Kate realized she had used the word too sharply. "Why would he?"

"You didn't know him before Saturday night?"

"No." Kate pulled a navy jacket and skirt from the rack and held them up. "We met that afternoon in the park, that's what was so weird. I mean he was out there feeding squirrels and Matt picked him up."

Ralley examined the jacket. "Gorgeous drapery, you genius you, but it'll photograph like a nun's habit."

"We'll produce it in something pale and pretty, ninny."

"No, I mean it's sedate and we're up to the gills with sedate for the upwardly mobile. We'll find something, Katie Kat, and order up a nice number of 'em. What do you mean he was feeding squirrels and Matt picked him up?"

"I don't know what I mean, but that's what happened."

"He's in love with you."

"What?" Kate said the word so loud that Ira turned, frowning. Kate felt herself coloring. "Where in hell did you get that idea? You know you have a brilliant way of exaggerating people's behavior. In love! I've only met the man twice."

"He is or is about to be. You walked into the room, he pushed three people to the floor to get to you, stepping over their dead bodies on the way. When it comes to vibes between men and women, I'm the expert." Ralley put the jacket and skirt back. She found a sleeveless dress with a long pleated chiffon skirt. "This," she said, "as a jumpsuit. Change nothing but sew a seam up the center and turn it into pants. I see it in palest plum—pale, pale, pale, a sprinkling of dust over it to keep it clouded, with a velvet ribbon at the waist in a red bordering on fuchsia, perhaps nipped at the knot with the funkiest little bouquet of turquoise flowers. How's that?"

"You don't just sew a seam up the middle, Ralley. Look at all that pleating."

"You can do it, love."

Vivian came back into the room, modeling the jumpsuit and blouse.

"Stunning," Richard Steyman said, coming over to them. He looked hopefully at Ralley.

"I'm for this," she said, holding up the chiffon dress. "As an evening jumpsuit. In palest dusty plum with a bissel fuchsia at the waist and a bisseler touch of turquoise right there," she said, pointing to the satin belt that came with the dress.

"Kate?" Ira raised an eyebrow in a suggestion that she agree.

"It can be done. We have to send the fabric out for permanent pleating, Ralley. This doesn't come off the loom pleated."

Ralley laughed and tucked an arm briefly through Ira's. "Your head designer's a genius, Ira. You know that, don't you?"

"My life, which is on the line, says it."

Vivian continued to walk languidly up and down the length of the showroom. "Shall I try it on?" she asked Kate.

Kate looked at Ralley. "No," Ralley said. "Stitch it up and send it over with the other jumpsuit. We'll show them at our merchandise meeting end of the week. We'll have to work out color, fabric, and trim. Palest, palest, palest plum—I'm fixed on it."

"What do you project for the first order?" Ira asked Steyman.

"Go with the fabric you have for the time being. Let's have a ball park price based on a first order of . . ." Steyman paused and consulted his pocket calculator.

Ralley took the opportunity to draw Kate aside. "I still want to know about Pete Frank."

"Well, I'd like to, too," Kate said, "but I can't help you."

"And what Jaybee was doing with him."

"Call her."

"If I did and he was up for grabs . . . ?"

Kate gazed at Ralley. "Exactly what are you asking me, Ralley?"

At the question, Ralley abruptly deflated. "I don't know," she said on an expelled breath. "I just wish someone who looked like him would look at me the way he looked at you."

Kate gave Ralley a guarded smile. Suddenly, unexpectedly, she didn't want to talk about Pete Frank.

"Ralley?" Richard Steyman was checking his watch.

"Right," Ralley said. "I think that about wraps it up."

CHAPTER 14

E gon's journal:

January 14, 1984: Mortimer Q, my general factotum, told me I must rouse myself from the usual torpor and make that trip to Buenos Aires. He's run out of excuses, and they're planning a new Delville boutique in Alvear. Torpor! The man knows not of what he speaks. I reminded him that two intense hours daily at the office plus all those power lunches with the ladies and all those power dinners with the mighty demonstrate anything but torpor.

However, I can arrange the trip around Mardi Gras time, stop off in Rio, visit a few clients in Venezuela, as long as I'm roused from my torpor, and finish up at the Reynolds compound in Acapulco to rest the weary flesh.

Well, be that as it may, I had a sudden inspiration and acted on it. Told Mortimer to put Annalise on the payroll as a consultant and I'll take her with me to Buenos Aires and then on to Rio. It should be a gas.

January 15, 1984: Annalise arrived on these shores six months ago from Spain, divorced (again) and with that sniveling young baroness in tow. The girl must resemble her father since she has none of Annalise's beauty and not an atom of her grace. Annalise set up housekeeping at the Carlyle, although Marguerite, who knew her in Paris, told me she was flat broke, living on some change and a pocketful of chutzpah.

Her first marriage was to a dissolute German baron, the father of Elizabeth, the second to a Spanish playboy dazed on wine and drugs. Apparently he opened his eyes long enough to catch his wife in bed with a toreador, a bit of bull he didn't take to very kindly. The marriage ended quickly, leaving Annalise broke but for certain jewels she had squirreled away.

Being a sucker for women determined to make their way in this world by charm and guile, I pulled out all the stops to keep her on these shores.

The lady, after all, had worked as Thierry Saul's assistant and certainly knew her warp from her weft.

She refused all offers to play second fiddle in any of the couture houses to which I introduced her. Figured the lady had a lot more money than I was led to believe, but Marguerite insists not. She has something on her mind, Annalise, some master (or mistress) plan, but I'm not quite sure what it is.

She needs money to keep up the Carlyle life-style and the kid at Dalton.

"I'll put you on the payroll at Delville," I told her this morning. For a moment she brightened. I thought it was what she was waiting for. Hell, easier done than said. "I'm off to Buenos Aires," I went on, expecting her to burst with enthusiasm, "and you're coming with me. We'll have a high old time."

No one has ever accused Annalise of showing any emotion other than Latin charm. The lady paled. I believe she shrank two inches.

"No." Her answer was curt enough and sharper than the proverbial two-edged serpent's tooth.

Yours truly is seldom at a loss for words. My mouth opened, then closed without a sound expelled. Well, well, well, said I to myself. The woman doesn't want to go to Buenos Aires. Now, what do you suppose that means?

The batch of witty drawings of flat-chested, narrow-waisted women with stick legs and broad shoulders were tacked neatly to the wall above Annalise's drawing table. Her spring collection could be seen at a glance, revealing a range of color flowing from taupe to navy with her characteristic pulsating flowered limes and chrome yellows on some of the jackets and evening clothes. Attached to each drawing were fabric swatches, buttons, trim, tiny notes indicating the name of the garment, suggested accessories, and who was scheduled to model it. The sketches were Annalise's, rendered in her meticulous hand so that no one would doubt which gown was meant to bell, which skirt grazed the knee, or which dress was fluid or stiff. There were seventy-five in all, beginning with day dresses, working through suits, pants, and coats to evening clothes and ball gowns, her specialty.

Annalise, leaning back in her chair, surveyed the drawings in the company of her premiere, Nance Ulanov, and other members of her staff.

"That's it," she said of the collection. "Any comments?" There was a murmur of approval, which Annalise expected. The meeting was the first time her staff viewed the collection as a whole, although they had shared in the process of working it through.

"How's the production coming along?" her CEO asked.

Annalise glanced at her *premiere.*

"If this is it," Nance said, "we have a month. We'll manage handily, we always do." She referred to the clipboard in her hand. "The trapeze dresses are almost ready, but we're missing some of Abraham's brocades. Also, those mother-of-pearl buttons, forget it. Poor quality, but we talked about that."

"Any other anticipated problems?" Annalise asked.

"The anticipated problems are the easy ones."

"Don't keep anything from me," Annalise said. She turned to Dell Stanche. "Okay, croquis of *tutti* to everybody concerned and nobody who's not concerned."

"And we're presenting at the Plaza," her CEO said, "on November third, four P.M. We'll close market week with a triumph. The models we're booking in from the Paris showings will already be here and no headaches anticipated."

"When can they be here for fittings?"

"We're working on scheduling now," Dell put in. "Count Lela out, however," she said referring to a popular French model. "She met a movie producer, from what I hear, with a line that's as ancient as Methuselah."

"She's young and stupid," Annalise said in a quiet voice. "In a few months she'll be strung out on cocaine and finished as far as a career is concerned—modeling, acting or otherwise."

Dell looked curiously at her, but before Annalise could react, her intercom buzzed. Annalise jumped at the sound, wanting both a drink and an aspirin.

"I've got Maia Harris on two," her secretary said. "She said not to disturb you, but—"

"One minute." Annalise nodded to her staff. "Let's continue tomorrow morning at nine *al punto.* Go on," she said to her secretary.

"Okay. Mrs. Harris wants to borrow Dress Blue, the one with the military buttons, for a dinner at the White House. Want me to put her off?"

Annalise bit down on her lip: she hated being taken advantage of, especially by Maia Harris, who was infamous for borrowing dresses and returning them weeks later wrinkled and stained. The woman, however, was invited and photographed everywhere. An original Michelis worn to the White House generated the kind of publicity designers coveted.

"No, tell her she's welcome to the dress but add politely that we'll send someone over for it the following day, so as to save her the trouble of getting it back to us."

"Gotcha."

Annalise picked up a pen but couldn't remember what she was going to jot down.

Puta. Ever since that call right after Egon's death, she had reached for the telephone with trembling hands. She'd always been so careful. None of those boys she played with had had the sense to trace her. The voice was American, yet the word *puta* was straight out of her past. Someone knew all about her and Buenos Aires. She closed her eyes and struggled against remembering.

Annalise had escaped the dark, heavy-lidded look of her grandmother and reached back into the unknown ancestry of her Spanish forebears. The inhabitants of the port city of Buenos Aires were a mix of Italian and Spanish, English and German, Slav and Jew, and the *indigénas* with their burnished skin and implacable gaze.

She was christened Nina Santana and raised by her grandmother in one of the *villas miserias* on the outskirts of the central city. The barrio had been there forever, with its iron corrugated shacks and its poverty. Hunger and the notion that something tempting, something brighter, must exist beyond the meanness and unrest, had kept the blood dancing in her veins. For young girls there was always the model of Evita Perón.

Annalise never knew her father; he could have been any man within a two-mile radius of her grandmother's shack. Her mother disappeared when Annalise was three years old; the only memory left her was of thick, deep red hair, a smile, and soft white flesh.

She was a dreamy child, given to fantasy and hope, to believing that the world outside was full of glitter and happiness.

For Annalise Michelis, sitting in her showroom high above Seventh Avenue in the most exotic city in the world, the slums of that *villa miseria* were as real, as pungent, as close to her skin as the Delville perfume she wore.

When she was eleven years old her grandmother took her to a wealthy family named Rosario in the Barrio Norte, in Recoleta, which bordered the Río de la Plata. Their Parisian-influenced villa off Avenida Córdoba was to be her home now, and it was there that she was apprenticed as a servant. The heavy doors of the servants' entrance closed behind her and on her grandmother's encouraging smile.

When Annalise was thirteen her grandmother died and the Rosarios gave her money to pay for the funeral. By the time she arrived at her grandmother's house, every bit of furniture, every small possession, had disappeared and a new family already occupied the shack. After the funeral Annalise returned to the villa in Recoleta.

When Annalise was fourteen, Señora Rosario found her husband trying to seduce the unwilling girl and packed her away at once to the home of a friend, an officer in the army, Colonel Antonio Guzmán. He soon finished what Señor Rosario had begun. Later the colonel installed Annalise in a small apartment near Palermo Park, a pretty section of the city known for its artists and culture.

Guzmán, who visited Annalise almost every evening, would be heated and quick, and when he left, there was always money for clothes or treats.

When a year had passed, he brought an even younger girl to the apartment. Annalise heard them making love as she sat outside the bedroom door, wondering what he had in mind for her.

She learned, not long after, upon his returning one day with a kindly, effusive woman whom he introduced as an old friend, Señora Girard. She seemed enchanted with Annalise almost at once.

"Beautiful skin, beautiful hair," she said, reaching out and touching her as though she were an animal at auction. "And are you very clever, my dear?"

"My friends saw to her education," the colonel said, referring to the lessons Annalise had been given along with the Rosario children.

"I think she'll do very well. We'll see what we can teach her."

She was taken to a handsome white casa grande in Calle Alejandro, again in Recoleta. Her education as a whore had begun. Annalise no longer had any memory of how many men took her. She learned to be good at her trade, to laugh and flirt, to do what made them breathe harder and gaze at her with glazed, grateful eyes.

Annalise stirred herself from the memories of a past that never left her. And as daylight faded, even knowing how tight her schedule was for that Friday, she felt the need for something, some pick-me-up to brighten her mood and bring back her control. She was due at Marguerite's for dinner. Zack couldn't make it, and there would be time if she hurried. She reached into her desk drawer and pulled out a small blue book. She flipped through the pages and then picked up the phone. A young male voice answered on the second ring.

Marguerite's party that night had been spontaneously arranged for the French designer, Thierry Saul. Both Annalise and Ralley had come, along with several of his favorite American customers. Annalise, Ralley, and Thierry spent the greater part of the evening huddled together on the couch, often erupting in hilarious laughter, the causes of which they refused to divulge. Marguerite, who liked a flowing evening in which politics or the latest books were universally discussed, turned an impatient eye on them every now and then. Still, the evening was a success by her usual standards. She expected one of her guests to call Suzy the next morning with a report about the three tittering fashion experts.

Even so, at eleven, the party was over. Thierry and his entourage, including Ralley, were heading for a downtown nightclub. Kate was invited but begged off, and Annalise offered her a ride home.

Although Annalise lived on Park Avenue within a half-mile of Marguerite, she always arrived and left by limousine. Kate, on Madison Avenue, lived within the same radius and ordinarily would have walked home even at that time of the night, but she accepted the offer quickly.

"I suppose I could have gone with Ralley. I have the whole weekend to myself," she explained once she settled back into the limousine. "Matt's with his father, and my housekeeper is off visiting her sister. But I'm going to shut myself off from the world and try to concentrate on the spring line, see that it's all of a piece. Of course," she added, glancing at Annalise and finding a rather dreamy expression on her face, "in the old days Egon always had something doing, and if he had nobody else to haul along, he'd invite me. It's only now that I realize what a circumspect life I lead. I'm not famous enough to be invited everywhere, and I don't have what passes for a social life."

She found herself wanting to talk, to say things to Annalise she could never say to Marguerite, had never said to Egon. She didn't want to return to the empty apartment to work all night on the collection. She turned to Annalise and took her hands. "Damn, in some ways Ira frightens the hell out of me."

Annalise looked surprised. "Has he ever beaten you?" She asked the question in a matter-of-fact way that startled Kate. It was as if Annalise might expect beating to be part of a relationship—not acceptable, perhaps, but part of one. "Good Lord, no." She laughed at the idea. "No. Beat me? Hurt my designing arm? No, never."

"Then what are you afraid of?"

"I don't know. There are times when I wonder if he's *savory*."

To Annalise's frown, she added, "I keep my head in the sand. I don't want to know what's going on. That's dumb, but I'm so desperate to see the line succeed. I've nothing else on my mind." She released her hold on Annalise, leaned over, and gave her a light kiss on the cheek as the limousine pulled to a stop in front of her building. "Never mind. I'm really together. It's merely the pressure. Market week's only four weeks away and it's do or die as far as my line is concerned."

Their conversation had served no purpose but to tell Kate what she already knew: her affair with Ira wasn't the best-kept secret in the world. In spite of what she had just said to Annalise, as she hurried through the lobby, she had the odd feeling of expecting, of *wanting* Ira to be waiting for her. But of course she'd had the lock changed with the express purpose of breaking off with him and she was glad he had taken the news docilely. Perhaps he, too, was finding their affair burdensome.

Several feet from the door she stopped and dug into her bag for her key.

When she looked up, key in hand, she discovered that the door was slightly ajar. She frowned. Even if her housekeeper had returned unexpectedly, she wouldn't have left the door open. Reason told Kate to run away, to call the police. Yet she knew just what had happened. The building was a safe one; her remark to Ira about break-ins was pure expediency. After a moment's hesitation, she braced herself and stormed into her apartment.

"Ira! You son of a bitch, where are you?"

It took her a moment to realize he wasn't there, but his message was palpable. Nothing had been touched or stolen; she was totally alone. Ira had let her know that anytime he wanted her, he could get to her, and there was nothing she could do about it.

CHAPTER 15

Pete Frank leaned back in his chair, hands behind his head, feet on the office desk. He stared at the closed door opposite as though at an unfamiliar work of art. Kate Hayden was on his mind. No matter how he handled having exchanged some words with the designer, meeting her on Saturday wasn't an accident as the law and Tess might define accident. He'd been a damn fool and there was no reasonable way to explain his behavior either to himself or to Tess.

He could saunter into her office, slouch into a chair, talk of sealing wax and cabbages and kings and then throw in as an afterthought, "Incidentally, through no fault of my own, I met Kate Hayden. Reason to be worried?"

Then again, he might experiment with tossing off a casual remark as though it were a homily and escaping fast. "They state if you stand in Times Square for any length of time, you're bound to meet up with everyone you ever knew. Well, it wasn't Times Square and I can't say I know her, but guess whom I met today? Kate Hayden."

He could see the interested light in Tess's eyes. Framed in skepticism.

Stalking Kate in the park had been stupid, and he had gone right ahead and been stupid. The question was why. Learning Kate and her son went to Central Park on fine Saturdays when the child wasn't with his father was part of the general gathering in of information about Ira Gregory and the principals of Kate Hayden. What he engaged in was mere walking in the park on a sunny day. He hadn't enticed the son or his mother; he'd merely fed peanuts to squirrels. He was, in time-honored tradition, carefully and calculatedly in the right place at the right time.

Jaybee had invited him to a party at a SoHo loft and, once inside the door, let him know he was on his own. Although he knew Jaybee had more than a few friends in the fashion industry, Kate's arrival had stunned him. At that moment he should have waved good-bye to Jaybee and his hostess and retreated as far away as he could.

The question once again was why hadn't he retreated on both occasions? Perhaps it all came down to the expression in her eyes that revealed a certain amount of vulnerability. Pete was a sucker for vulnerability. She had run away when she learned who he was and what he did for a living. He had, stupidly, followed and caught up with her.

Kate was somebody's mother. Somebody's ex-wife. She was known to be the mistress of an insidious character, one Ira Gregory, who was married and had a couple of kids. Strike one for vulnerability; she obviously didn't mind having a married lover. But then he remembered Kate at Egon Delville's funeral, the bunching of her shoulders and the quick glance she gave Ira and his wife.

Pete at times felt he'd seen everything and been everywhere. There wasn't any congeries of events, evil or otherwise, that surprised him. He hadn't been surprised to learn of Kate's affair with Ira Gregory, either, until he met her and faced her wounded bird look, which made him suspect the lady had a tenuous hold on the way she was managing her life.

Pete pulled himself out of his chair and turned to the window. He pressed his hands against the sill and stared down at the traffic below. A taxi narrowly missed a woman wheeling a baby carriage. She scarcely noticed. Everyone was in a hurry to get somewhere—woman, taxi driver, maybe even the baby. All those clichés about the city rang true—big, crowded, anonymous, schizophrenic. Something was driving Kate, too. She was hurrying and perhaps once she arrived she'd find no one there. Which didn't settle the problem of telling Tess he'd met her on two occasions, neither of them in the line of duty.

He turned from his window, downed the last of his cold coffee, and was about to pay Tess a visit when his secretary buzzed him on the intercom. His contact at the Internal Revenue Service was on the line. The IRS had settled in at Kate Hayden three days before. Because the company had filed only one tax return, the auditors would not have to sift through mountains of paper. In fact, if Gregory was cooperative, and so far he had been extremely so, the investigation could be concluded in a week or two.

"Looks like we have something," were the first words Pete heard.

"Go on."

"That pattern you've been looking for that would make it easy for us to indict under RICO. Interesting gimmick. Infusions of cash from retailers out of the country—Brazil, Ecuador, Venezuela. According to the accounting department, retailers periodically show up on the doorstep of Kate Hayden with bags of cash. They order merchandise manufactured in Hong Kong, and the company is only too willing to oblige. Never any more than ten thousand dollars a pop."

"How do you know it isn't legitimate?" He was careful about getting excited. Ira Gregory wasn't a novice and he'd been decidedly too cooperative.

"We don't."

"I'll need a list of the foreign outlets."

"We'll fax them over this afternoon. We're only checking to make certain the company paid all its taxes on money taken in. My guess is Mr. Gregory is being very obliging because the company is an upright, tax-paying operation. The source of the money is another thing entirely."

"I take it you won't be able to get them on tax fraud."

"Profit in, tax dollars out—that's all the IRS wants. You can have the honor of taking him."

"Thanks, pal."

"Let you know when we're finished."

Pete put down the receiver and sat without moving for several minutes. A pattern of receiving cash could be enough to indict on RICO if it could be proved that the retailers in South America didn't exist or hadn't ordered the goods or couldn't explain why they paid cash. Provided the involved governments cooperated. The Justice Department was a long way from celebrating. Pete didn't bother calling Tess but took himself over to her office.

"Hey, don't look so gloomy," Tess said after hearing about the phone call. "We're aiming for patterns, we're getting patterns. We can take a comparable company and show it's not the way most dress houses do business. Pattern, that's all."

Pete pulled up a chair and sat down, his long legs stretched out, and wished for a cigarette for the first time in years. He told Tess about meeting Kate on Saturday, not once but twice. He didn't even try handling why he'd followed her out of Ralley's apartment.

"You, quote unquote, bumped into Kate Hayden twice on Saturday?" Tess regarded him out of narrowed eyes. "In a city of eight million people you bumped into Kate Hayden by accident twice in one day? Any more fairy tales you want to tell me?"

"In the park we discussed squirrels and her son and a bag of peanuts. At the party in SoHo we were surrounded by people and music loud enough to wake hibernating bears a thousand miles away."

"If you had asked me, I'd have told you to steer clear of Kate Hayden. A couple of wrong moves and we could jeopardize our whole case. Are you asking me to say it was okay for you to be seen talking to the woman?"

"I know what the law is and I understand the implications. Just hear me out, Tess."

"I'll hear you out, but first I'd like to remind you we're not some sub-rosa operation coming out of the White House basement. We have the President's mandate to run the mob to the ground but this ain't war and we ain't the army. Now, before you give me some cockamamie lawyer's argument about how important the meetings were to the case, let me fill in the blanks.

This Kate Hayden holds some kind of attraction for you, right? She look like your ex-wife?"

"My ex-wife is a small blonde with a pugnacious nose and a strong chin. Her eyes are blue, of the kind called icy once you slip out from under their first riveting effect."

"We can get Ira Gregory on RICO, and you're about to fuck up with Kate Hayden, if you'll pardon the expression. What party?"

"To begin with, Kate—"

"Oh, Kate, is it? Not Ms. Hayden."

He gritted his teeth and went on. "Kate Hayden knew I came with Jaybee Olsen."

"You're dating Jaybee Olsen? You get around. And to think I was worried about your being lonely."

"Only doing my job, boss. Jaybee told me the hostess was a fashion stylist named Ralley Littlehurst. Going to the party couldn't hurt, I told myself. It could only help. Kate Hayden arrived alone and left alone." He stopped, felt the faintest prick of conscience, and went on. "I expect you to make the problem disappear if there is one, which there isn't. End of conspiracy theory."

"Pete, we're close. We were praying for a pattern that Ira Gregory overlooked. Maybe we have it. And you'd better steel yourself, kid. We may also catch Kate Hayden in our net. The first question her lawyer is going to ask is, have you ever met Mr. Frank before? You fool, you damn fool."

"We're not picking her up, Tess."

"She signed her name, she gets the blame. What the hell is she, a newborn babe?"

"I don't want to mess up someone's life because she's stupid."

"Really? You're an odd sort of lawman. Good thing you won't be sitting on the bench when the case comes to trial, provided it comes to trial."

"I met her on Saturday afternoon at the park," he said with an exaggerated show of patience. "It was a nice day and I was taking a walk. All kinds of coincidences happen in New York on a nice fall day. I live on the West Side. She lives on the East Side. The park is in between. I walk there often. She takes her son there often." He stuffed his hands into his pockets. His fingers closed around his key ring and some change. "But since it did happen, what's the harm? We need a witness on our side. I haven't any doubt we'll manage Kate Hayden. She has a son and she's not about to leave him for a jail term. All I did was soften her up a bit. Part of the job."

"Soften her up? I thought it was peanuts and squirrels. You're some corker, you are. We haven't even indicted, but you're already hinting at immunity.

I've given you any amount of autonomy, fool that I am, knowing what you'd do with it, but I don't want to have to worry about your libido taking over."

"Don't worry," he said with a grin. He was off the hook, for now. "I won't do anything to embarrass you, even if I have to resort to self-abuse."

"Somehow I don't think that's a problem with you," she said, her smile showing she'd thought about it. "Every woman on staff has given you the eye, and the gossip at the water cooler has you playing no favorites and taking no prisoners around here. What I'd like to know, incidentally, is why."

Pete regarded her for a moment, then looked away. He hated like hell to think he'd been a subject of gossip around the water cooler or any other place. "I hate office politics and I've learned to be scared of office romances," he said.

"Pete, you're smart, you're quick, and you're good-looking, an irresistible combination for a jury. I just want you to take those blinders off. Every once in a while we meet someone we're not supposed to like and, whammo, the heart gives a little flutter." She smiled to take the sting out of her words. "Look at the lady but don't touch. Besides, she's in Gregory's bed. Do you want leftovers?"

A reaction like bile flooded his stomach. "I made a casual connection with one of the principals in a case we're working on," he managed. "I think the word for it is 'undercover.' "

"Undercover," Tess said. "Clever. Anything else you want to tell me?"

"Go to hell."

"You've got some kind of thing for the lady, and since this is my case—"

"Mine, too," he reminded her.

"—that makes it my business." She put her hand on his arm. She had spent her life in confrontational situations, a very smart, very powerful woman who clearly knew just what she had to do to intimidate. "I like you, Pete, and I don't want any trouble in my department. I call it as I see it."

"What in hell are we arguing about? This is a red-letter day, you said so yourself, red letters that spell RICO."

"Scarlet letters. And your friend Kate may be wearing them."

Pete held his tongue. Tess had a disconcerting habit of seeing right through to the truth. He went over to the door and opened it. "So long, teacher. I've got work to do."

He wasn't pleased to hear her last words. "I hope I won't have to put you back a grade or two."

His secretary stopped him on the way to his office. "That reporter, David Orenstein? He called twice. Want me to get him for you?"

"No. Next time he phones put the call through." Orenstein was becoming a problem. With a hundred other hot stories begging to be covered around town, Pete couldn't understand why Dave was bulldogging this one. He appreciated zeal but with Ira Gregory close to being pulled in, he'd have to put his thumb in the reporter's eye.

Pete closed his office door and sat down behind his desk. The talk with Tess hadn't accomplished anything in the way of making him feel better. The case could go down the tubes if there was any hint of collusion between Kate and him. Except there hadn't been any to begin with. He was trying to make sense of a beautiful woman with talent tying herself up with a mobster. In fact, he could make a better case if he faced her head on, told her what was coming down the pike for her if she didn't cooperate. Scare the hell out of her.

Kate's office number was scribbled on his calendar. Transferring it to his address book would be an admission of interest he wasn't about to make. He picked up his telephone and punched in the first three numbers. Then he let out a breath, tore the page from the calendar, balled it up, and threw it toward his wastebasket, which he missed.

CHAPTER *16*

Hot tongues of water cascaded over her body as Annalise, enclosed in a steaming circle of black mirrors, regarded her nude image multiplied a hundred times. Above the shower a domed skylight revealed the cool brilliance of a city night blinking to infinity.

Others might consider the triplex apartment the quintessential entitlement, with its art- and antique-filled rooms. Annalise knew better. It could all disappear in a crowded corridor suddenly filled with bad judgment.

When Annalise wanted to feel safe and secure from sensations that were as elusive and dreamlike as a sheltered childhood, she sought out the scorching heat of her shower stall. She wasn't quite certain why she felt safe there; perhaps it was reminiscent of the powerful, baking, sweat-filled memories of Argentina. All day she had felt the past moving toward her, engulfing her, then for a while subsiding. She wanted to wash remembrance away and yet embrace it, admit that it was the source of her ambition.

Somewhere in the apartment a door slammed. Zack, no doubt, turning restless. They were expected at a cocktail party at seven. At eight the assembled guests would troop over to Sotheby's for the charity auction of the late Mrs. Havemeyer's jewels. The guests at the cocktail party were what Zack called heavy hitters. They all wanted something one way or another, beginning with Zack. Nothing different there. Annalise had never met a man, penniless or wealthy, who didn't want more. "More" wasn't specific, either, a shapeless bit of canvas that hid the answer among its folds. Peek through and find the moral: Own enough and nothing can touch you.

Annalise understood something about herself, too. She needed the confetti of success and all its rewards: money, fame, awards. Her name—the one she had invented that fit her like a judgment but hadn't quite erased the past—was her "more."

She switched off the shower, continuing to study her reflection through the mist as if making a connection with someone she barely knew. She slid the glass shower door back and stepped onto a soft gray carpet, feeling the cool, shivery prickles as her body adjusted and awakened to the cooler air. She was adept at devising ways to feel. Back there, back in the whorehouse and not yet out of her teens, she had trained herself to numbness on command. Now it took patience and imagination to touch the nerve endings. She reached for a towel and patted her flesh dry, still watching the reflection of a body perfectly toned.

Her bedroom was large and high-ceilinged, with an elaborate sitting area at a bay window that looked out onto the penthouse terrace. At Annalise's insistence the room had been made to appear smaller through the use of warm, tropical colors. Walls were of melon silk, padded for a soft, fleshy texture. A green like the underside of new leaves had been used on flower-strewn curtains, bedspread, bed canopy, and even the French needlepoint carpet. Above the bed a Matisse odalisque peered languorously out of dark, bored eyes. There was a similar green in the painting, a green of the tropics, of the Riviera, of all the places that basked benignly under a swollen sun. Annalise came into the bedroom wrapped in a velour towel. She could see Zack at the door reflected in the Adams mirror on the window wall. He was wearing a silk bathrobe loosely tied.

Their eyes caught through the mirror. She paused and let the towel fall away as he came toward her. They were the same age, the same height, with equal ambition and similar appetites. Still, if she squinted slightly, as she did now, she could sometimes see her husband as through the small end of binoculars.

He was an attractive man with dark, heavy-fringed eyes and the shadow of a beard that required shaving twice daily. His hair had turned salt-and-pepper when he was still in his thirties and now was elegantly silvered. He had a good body, although he was fine-boned and gave the impression of being smaller than he actually was. His smile, which was deceptively boyish and disarming, took most people off guard. He knew how to be the person he was least expected to be, and yet power closed around him like an invisible toga. He was able, with a word, to emotionally destroy anyone who crossed him.

What Annalise admired most about him was his least likable trait: he possessed the reckless self-confidence of a gambler; he was certain he'd win and completely unafraid of failure. There was no way of coming out ahead with a man like Zack Younger. He knew the risks of losing and didn't give a damn. And now he expected Annalise to relieve his tensions.

Annalise had already decided to marry him before they met. Egon played the intermediary with high glee, arranging their introduction at a party in the Hamptons one hot summer day.

"You two really ought to get to know each other," Egon had said with a wink, as if the whole thing hadn't been worked out in advance. Egon loved to manipulate people, and with Zack Younger, the leverage buyout king, and

Annalise Michelis, the Latin designer with a somewhat mysterious past, he made what he called the high-powered introduction of the century.

"I've been wanting to meet you," Annalise said without preliminaries. She wore a sleeveless pink linen dress of her own design and looked fragile and cool on a very hot day.

Zack's dark, curious gaze took her in. Egon had warned her to go slow; he was no easy mark. His second marriage, to a woman almost half his age, had failed. It had cost him a fortune to bail out. Egon, however, sensed he was ready for a whole new life. It was an era of powerful men aligning themselves with dynamic women and Annalise knew what her competition was. She would bring no money to the marriage, but was certain she could offer him a brand-new kind of sex.

He expected everything from her and at once; his entitlement called for Annalise to show him what stuff she was made of, but she held off until the right moment, when he was most dazzled, most curious.

She had learned well in that whorehouse in Buenos Aires: most powerful men liked punishment—either to administer it or to receive it. And she had a whore's instinct for determining a man's unspoken desires. When she at last went to bed with Zack she knew precisely what he wanted.

Annalise understood how to smile at him, how to touch him, how to give him the message that only she could heat up the air for him. It was a package he bought quickly and, after four years of marriage, was buying still.

As he came toward her, he opened his bathrobe and dropped it to the floor. He was half erect. "I need this before we attack the Flaggs."

He sat down on the bed and she was before him, kneeling on the thick carpet. Even naked, he seemed powerful and in control. He parted his legs and she nestled between them. Slowly, as if each move were unrehearsed, her hands played along his thighs, her fingernails driving gently into his skin. She lowered her head and let her tongue, slippery and hotly wet, roll along his sensitive flesh.

His head rolled back, and she heard his breath pump heavily. She cupped her hand and held all of him encased as she ran her tongue softly along the side of his penis. He groaned and rolled back onto the bed, lifting her along with him. She lay for a moment on top of him, her eyes fixed on his.

She kissed his lips and drew herself to his side. The satin sheets felt like cool rolling waters. She bent over his chest to draw her teeth over his nipple. He lay still and her caresses became more fiery, as she lowered her head and covered every inch of his body with moist lips. She avoided his upthrust penis, allowing only her heated breath to touch it. Then with infinite care, she pressed her mouth to his groin as she gently probed his anus, coaxing a soft, almost exquisite cry of joy from him. He began to move his hips prodding her on, but she slowed. She had taught him to wait.

Had love ever been part of the bargain? They used the word with each other in a light way. "I'm waiting, love," he'd say. "Hurry." Or there was an occasional "We're good together, aren't we, love?" spoken after some successful dinner party. Statements of pride and ownership, which, with an occasional pat on the ass, were Zack's way of expressing affection. But real love, the kind that seared one's soul, no, Annalise knew enough not to expect it. Love would be an encumbrance in a marriage like theirs. Love meant taking someone else's feelings and desires into consideration. Neither she nor Zack would be good at that. Each operated in a high-power world with too much at stake and too much to prove.

Annalise raised her head and gazed at him. His breath was coming hard and fast. She reached for the silk cords that were tucked away in the bedside drawer. Straddling him, she tied his hands to the bedposts. He never spoke during those moments, although his eyes tracked her movements. Perhaps he was lost in a fantasy world she never tried to enter. The ropes were tight enough to cause pain. She saw him wince and suddenly wanted to call a halt to their absurd play. She had wondered often enough what their lives might have been like if she hadn't introduced Zack to her particular talents, if she had allowed herself to feel something for him in the region of her heart.

But he was as guarded as she; surviving in a hostile world had drained them of simple emotions.

What would loving him be like? She kissed his lips, but he merely regarded her out of glazed eyes. She bent back to her task, tying his feet to the bedposts so that he lay before her spread-eagled, a man high on a drug of his choosing, riding to the crest, to the far reaches of his soul. She studied him, unable to fathom his thoughts, incapable of reaching him. They never talked about the experience afterward; he had never told her what he expected or felt. His face was always a careful blank, and if on a rare occasion a spark escaped, she could feel its message as clearly and coldly as an ice shard: what happened was never to be discussed between them.

His penis was hard and he had trouble lying still. Annalise caressed him, murmuring in Spanish, which she knew he loved.

The cloying odor of warmed oils rose from the bedside table. Annalise raised herself and reached for a small emerald green bottle. Slowly, as Zack watched, she poured some of the oil and warmed it between her palms, then rubbed her hands over her breasts, pinching the nipples until they were taut. The oil ran smoothly down her fingers and onto her husband's body.

She took more oil and slowly spread it around his chest and down his stomach to his groin. He was moving slowly, his eyes closed. A small muscle twitched at the side of his face. He was holding back. She slid her hand down to his penis and held the tip tight between her fingers, a trick she had learned to delay the orgasm but not the sensation.

He moaned; his flesh was hot, pulsating in her hand. His breath produced the only sound in the room, yet she could shut it out as easily as blinking her eyes. She could touch another human being, sheath him with her body, and know that in her soul she was alone. There were nights when Zack came to her, usually after some particularly satisfactory business deal, and without talk, even without her cooperation, made violent love to her. It would happen quickly and passionately, the final consummation of the win. He was the victor in one hot burst of triumphant release. Annalise felt something for him on those occasions that almost erupted, but she didn't know what she might lose by uttering the words. Balance of power possibly. And then he seemed to need no commitment from her, just her body, a payback perhaps for all those other times.

She put her hand to his jaw and studied his face. He kept his eyes closed, perhaps sealing them against what he might see mirrored in hers.

She left him for an instant, reaching for a silver box lined in blue velvet and holding several gold needles whose heads were intricately detailed. She leaned over him, her breasts pendant above his mouth. He opened his eyes and met hers with a smile of intense and pleasurable gratitude. Yet Annalise saw something else, saw hidden in the black depths of his eyes the truth that if he could take the moment a step further, he might turn the tables and kill her.

While he continued to gaze at her, she touched the point of the golden needle to her clitoris, then to her tongue. Then with quick expertise she slipped the needle through his left nipple. There was no blood. She was an expert. Zack held back a cry and began writhing, his movement spasmodic. Annalise grabbed his penis and let him ride her hand. When he quieted, she took another needle and jabbed his penis with ever-increasing deliberation.

His moans turned to deep rumbles as he gasped for air. He gave one final cry, opening his eyes wide, begging for release. She knew precisely when to stop. She put her mouth to his penis and took him all in with a rhythm that sent her own body pulsating. He came in several hot spurts for a few seconds, then lay still, scarcely breathing. When he wanted to get up, he merely spoke her name. She slowly slipped the needle from his nipple, then bent and touched her lips to his chest. She untied him. He took her into his arms and kissed her deeply.

In another moment he eased himself off the bed upon which the carelessly thrown silken cords and gold needles still lay.

He picked up his bathrobe and went to the door that led to his room. "Half an hour," he said to her without turning back.

Annalise didn't move for several seconds after the door closed behind him. She lay looking at the ceiling, then lowered her hand. But it wouldn't be enough. The young, ready body she'd had earlier hadn't been enough, either.

For the moment she knew one thing only. She was in trouble, the kind she had never been able to avoid but would have to learn to control if she didn't want her world to fall apart.

Richard Oliver Flagg, a corpulent, homely man with an unpleasant mouth reported that he was delighted the Youngers had come. His unprepossessing bearing was more than made up for by his fourth wife, Luanne, who stood by his side in the large oval foyer of their Park Avenue triplex, loudly greeting their guests in her metallic southern accent.

Annalise should have despised Luanne but couldn't. That Richard Flagg had made an honest woman of Luanne must have been a surprise to her admirers in a certain seedy area of New Orleans. It was there she had begun and ended her career as a go-go dancer, famous for her naked backbends.

Unlike Annalise, however, who had gone to great pains to hide her past, Luanne flaunted hers, to the great amusement of her husband. Annalise couldn't help admiring her flamboyant charm, good humor, and penchant for high jinks. Luanne was the kind of woman who came into a room three feet ahead of her husband. She exuded an enormous confidence, built on nothing.

"Annalise, *ma chère petite* Annalise," Luanne shouted happily. She wore one of Annalise's late day dresses, a navy silk charmeuse cut off just above the knee to reveal long, well-shaped legs shod in custom-made shoes with heels high enough to make her a head taller than her husband. She was wide-mouthed, with brown eyes heavily made up. She wore her golden hair pulled back with a wide navy bow.

She dragged Annalise and Zack into the main salon where a dozen people stood chatting among gorgeous brocade curtains puddled on the gold-trimmed furniture, and expensively shabby antique carpets. The large Rubens on the far wall contained cupids, Ganymede, and several fair and epicene nudes in a country setting below billowing clouds.

Annalise found half a dozen power matrons among the guests, accompanied by their husbands or walkers, and heard a smattering of conversation like bits and pieces of a far-off explosion. No one seemed concerned about the price of beans, but then neither had she been for a long time.

In spite of the Luannes and Annalises who had made their way into New York society, the inner circle remained steadfastly incestuous. The same set met at all the right parties and openings, had been acquainted for years, and yet had never known each other well. This, in spite of the fact that they married and divorced within their small group, although occasionally a member who was big and powerful enough would bring in a woman from the outside world. If she was accepted, she'd become more like them than they were themselves.

They are the people, Annalise thought with amazement, who run the world, who determine whether you're going to live or die.

Annalise discovered the Noonans there, Ted's new wife wearing an Annalise, a pleated green chiffon cocktail dress with a sequined jacket. His first wife was present, too, wearing a deep red velvet shift, which she had put on backwards. Annalise, trying to conceal a smile, greeted her effusively and decided not to enlighten her.

The sight of these women wearing her clothes, backwards or not, to see their drape over living, breathing, moving beings, satisfied her deeply. No, she didn't have the creative talent of Kate Hayden, but she liked dressing dolls, always had.

Later, at Sotheby's, just prior to the jewelry auction, she wandered alone around the exhibition of Art Deco jewelry, her mind half on what she saw. What the other half was on, she couldn't have said.

"Russian Constructivist."

The words were spoken at her side in a soft, engaging voice. She turned, saw a slight fair-haired man gazing at a sliver of a bracelet with an alternating pattern of sapphires and diamonds. He wore a black turtleneck sweater and a dark suit in the current fashion of seeming several sizes too large at the shoulder and in pants length.

"The bracelet looks far too modern to be Russian," Annalise said.

"Russian Constructivist *influence*, I mean. Without the Constructivists where would anyone of us be?"

In spite of her best attempts, the courses in art and history, in philosophy and the social sciences, which she had crammed into her schedule, Annalise was aware of the gaps in her education. She remembered seeing a handsome collection of Constructivist paintings at the Wendels' and wished she had asked more questions about them. "Yes, of course," she murmured, "I see what you mean."

She was rescued by Zack who regarded the man curiously for a moment.

"I'm putting a bid in on the emerald necklace," he whispered in her ear, referring to a David Webb they had discussed earlier.

"Zack, it's not a good idea."

"Charity, love, it's all for charity." He brought her into the auction room. The crowd was there by invitation only, with a percentage of the proceeds to be donated to Amnesty International. Annalise had managed tickets for Ralley, who came in with Cliff Beal, and for Marguerite, who arrived with one of her young escorts.

Annalise and Zack sat in a reserved row with the Flaggs at their right and an editor of the *Times* and his wife at their left. Just before the bidding began, Annalise felt a tap on her shoulder. She turned to find the expert on Russian Constructivism behind her. "El Lissitzky," he said. "The power of clean lines, the simple statement, demolishing in a stroke the gilded imperial past."

She laughed, uncertain whether he was being funny or not. "Demolishing the past with diamonds and sapphires?"

"The auction will begin."

Annalise turned back, frowning. Zack was bent toward Luanne. Annalise could hear her generous laugh and knew by her husband's response that Luanne had said something off-color.

A quarter of the way through, the schedule called for bids on the emerald necklace. Annalise didn't want to appear greedy or interested. Perhaps it was the man sitting behind her talking about Constructivism and Russian imperialism. With a smile at Zack she got to her feet and left the auction room.

She went into the ladies' room and spent several minutes combing her hair and reapplying her lipstick, then returned to the anteroom and wandered without curiosity around a collection of Regency furniture scheduled for auction the next day. She felt aimless and a little light-headed.

"Of course it's all fallen apart, total chaos," the fair-haired man said, materializing at her side.

"We're not discussing Regency now, are we?" she asked, smiling at him in a conspiratorial way.

"I mean the contemporary art picture. I mean jewelry can't reflect in diamonds and sapphires what you see on gallery walls these days, can it?"

"Ah, I see what you mean. Postmodern kitsch. All those cracked plates and furry black lines."

"Of course I *could* be a little more discreet," he told her in a confidential tone. They had walked through an aisle of straight-backed chairs and reached the entrance to the auction room. "After all, I'm running an art gallery and where would we be without Neo-Ego art?"

"Neo-Ego?"

"Termed by yours truly. Well, of course who was a greater egomaniac than Gauguin when you come down to it? Willing his wife and all those kids to poverty just so he could paint."

"Perhaps," said Annalise, feeling quite wise and warming to the subject, "some sacrifices have to be made for the greater good."

CHAPTER 17

In the small, windowless private john attached to her office, Kate was on her knees heaving the remains of breakfast into the beige ceramic toilet. Her eyes teared; when at last there was nothing left inside her except a sour taste, she got slowly to her feet and flushed the sight away. She rinsed her mouth, washed her face, blankly reapplied her makeup, and went back into her office.

The article in *Mirror* magazine written by David Orenstein entitled "Mob, Money Laundering and Seventh Avenue" hadn't gone away. Her eye lighted on the paragraphs that had provoked such an abrupt, devastating reaction and left her shaking.

In 1988, a twenty-seven-year-old designer whom I shall call Holly Good quit her job as head designer for a major clothing manufacturer. Holly's greatest dream was to have her name on a designer label and Holly Good fashions hanging in every important store in the country. She had no doubt of her talent, having won the prestigious Fashion Council Award a year before, followed by the even more important Designer of the year plaque given by the Fashion Designers Association in 1988. Marguerite Varick of *VFF* had profiled Holly, calling her a major new talent.

In addition to her talent, Holly is young, beautiful and eager. Probably any major design house in the country would eagerly have signed her up, given her a line under her own name—Holly Good for ABC, or Holly Good for DEF—but she didn't have the name recognition of Donna Karan or Kate Hayden, which meant she wasn't a bankable star yet. The investment needed to launch a major line figures in the millions. Holly, however, believed in herself. She was prepared to wait it out, certain an offer would surface sooner or later.

Backing arrived in the name of an outfit that we will call PYN, a Swiss corporation with factories in the Far East. PYN gave Holly Good an offer she couldn't resist. All she had to do was sign on the dotted line, set up a workroom, and leave the rest to PYN. The Swiss company, you see, wasn't interested in fashion or names on labels so much

He nodded at the auction room. "You don't want to go back in there again, do you?"

He doesn't know who I am, she thought, feeling annoyed and yet faintly pleased, as though for a moment she could peel away the layers and be required neither to ask nor to give anything. "I'm sorry," she said, putting her hand out. "My husband's waiting for me. Good luck with your Neo-Ego."

"Perhaps you'll do me the honor of visiting my gallery," he said in a faintly self-mocking tone.

"I'm always interested in the work of new artists."

He broke into a grin and reached into his jacket pocket for a business card. "Smarts. It's in SoHo. You make your way down there on occasion, I hope."

"Smarts." She frowned and checked the card. His name was printed in the lower left-hand corner: Winthrop Smith—Cliff Beal's lover. Was it possible he'd come with Cliff and Ralley?

"Right. Owned by the estate of Egon Delville, Mrs. Younger."

Mrs. Younger. Somehow his knowing her name froze her. She handed the card back. "Thank you, Mr. Smith. I doubt I could manage it on my schedule."

"Buenos Aires, right? I was trying to figure out the accent."

"If you'll excuse me," she said, heading for the auction room, knowing she had to get away.

"Nina!"

She froze. There was a flurry from inside the auction room as though a valuable piece had just been sold.

Then the words came. *"Vos has hecho mucho con tu vida. Entendistes?"*

She felt her heart stop at the particularly Buenos Aires accent: "Nina, how far you've come." Then the macho, arrogant closing of the sentence. *Entendistes?* "Do you understand?" The meaning was perfectly clear: *You don't count.* The ultimate putdown, a word she knew well. She thought of the telephone call. She whipped around to gaze at Winthrop Smith and found herself staring into his friendly, almost blank gaze.

Her husband hurried out of the auction room, his eyes shining. "Ah, there you are."

"I suppose you won the bid," she said, shakily reaching out and pretending to straighten his tie.

"You wanted the necklace, Annalise, admit it."

She didn't answer but glanced back to where she was certain Winthrop Smith stood. He was gone.

as laundering. *Money*-laundering. And what better way to launder money than to pass it through a system already rife with mob activity, a system that New York's City Hall is apparently anxious to keep working?

Holly Good. Kate slammed the magazine shut and threw it into the wastebasket. When David Orenstein had requested an interview with her, he said he was doing a story on Seventh Avenue for *Mirror* magazine. He had never said he was a muckraker. She reached into the wastebasket, picked up the magazine, and opened it again to the offending page.

She wasn't even aware of Ira coming into her office until she glanced up and found him standing there.

"You're not taking any of that seriously, are you?" he asked, leveling a narrow-eyed look at her.

"You admit he's writing about DAS, then? That business about money-laundering?"

"He doesn't know what he's talking about. I've already had our lawyer on the phone. He said the writer covered himself with that reference to Kate Hayden. Very clever young man, Orenstein."

Kate checked the article again and picked out her name coupled with Donna Karan's. "Then I haven't anything to worry about." She collapsed into her chair.

Ira leaned across her desk, his hands splayed out on the magazine. "You never did. DAS is a respectable Swiss corporation trying to get a toehold in the lucrative American fashion market. You were their best hope. Still are."

"I gather the IRS agrees with you." Kate wasn't certain why she persisted. Perhaps it was the guarded expression in his eyes, in spite of his smile.

"Kate," he said, "design. Leave the rest to me." He rolled the magazine up and took it with him when he left.

Design. Leave the rest to him. She sat at her desk fingering a piece of Melton wool, reluctant to return to her workroom. It was the second week of October. Two weeks before, she had come back to her apartment and found the front door open. Ira had signaled his power over her; yet with consummate skill he had left her dangling, wondering what would happen next. Nothing had. They were at a standoff, a decided coolness for which she was grateful if vigilant.

Son of a bitch, he'd done it. Pete picked the magazine up and made his way to Tess's office. It was after hours and Tess was on the telephone. When she replaced the receiver Pete said without preliminary, "Who tipped the IRS to Ira Gregory in the first place?"

"Deep dark secret. I was told to get on to him by a Higher Authority, if you'll pardon the expression. Obviously someone with a score to settle."

"Whoever that is, he spilled to David Orenstein." Pete slid the magazine across the desk. "Dave covered himself pretty well by disguising the names, but he's talking about Kate Hayden and Ira Gregory and DAS. I don't believe in coincidence, but I do believe in settling scores."

Tess looked the article over. "The names have been changed to protect the guilty." She begun to read, " 'His body, when it was fished from the East River where it had lodged against a piling, showed no marks of violence. He did not wear cement shoes. He looked like a man who had crashed three days before off the pier on East Thirty-sixth Street in his 1989 Dodge truck—cost: thirty five thousand dollars, of which twenty-five was still owed. The medical examiner's office said he had probably been driving while intoxicated. Let's say his name was Buck Hanson.' " Tess regarded Pete. "Name changed to protect the dead."

" 'But Buck Hanson took on the mob in the wrong place—Seventh Avenue,' " she went on. " 'And what Buck ended up was dead, the perpetrators of the crime never found—it surely was crime—and with city government possibly in collusion with his killers. That's because Buck tried for a piece of the action in trucking in New York's garment industry. Apparently no one ever told him about a closed society condoned by the bureaucracy.' " Tess stopped. "Okay, the s.o.b. can write."

"That's all you can say. He's put the kiss of death on our operation."

Tess read on silently, Pete waiting at the window, staring down at the darkened street. When she finished, she closed the magazine carefully and slid it back across the desk. "Note the clever reference to Kate Hayden. Neat little ploy to protect himself against lawsuits."

"We're going to have to move fast," Pete said. "Ira Gregory can read, too."

Tess shrugged, then looked down at her desk and moved some papers around. "So move fast."

CHAPTER 18

The big question is who's Holly Good?"

Ralley glanced at her assistant, who had come into the roomy, sun-filled office bearing two porcelain cups filled with black coffee. "If you don't know, you're the only one in town who doesn't."

"Kate Hayden."

"Ira Gregory should be punching the writer's ticket"—Ralley stopped, picked up her small gold desk clock—"just about now."

Her assistant set the cups on the only clear spot on Ralley's disorderly desk, removed a pile of fabric samples from a chair, and sat down. Long-haired, pert-nosed, she was dressed in the Steyman statement: expensive, working woman, classical simplicity. The fact that she would inherit Ralley's job or earn one just like it was contained in a careless yet eager smile. "My boyfriend said there's nothing in the article you can't find in the record."

"Your boyfriend the lawyer."

Her assistant took a sip of coffee. "Uh-huh."

"There's one thing about finding the record, my love. Another thing to playing it in public. Ira's going to take out a contract on David Orenstein. Cross Ira and *brrr.*" The shiver she gave was exaggerated but real. Ralley remembered the glacial expression in his eyes when Richard Steyman had discussed their current preference for garments made in America. She found something more to his reaction than the mere mechanics of importing garments half assembled and now understood why. Money-laundering was a complicated business and it didn't involve turning cash over in the States so much as sending it abroad as soon and cleanly as possible.

"You know Kate Hayden," her assistant went on. "How's she taking it?"

"Pretending nothing has happened." Ralley's desk held a viewing glass against which she placed a sheet of transparencies. "Be that as it may, my dear, we've got work to do. I'm pissed as hell over Madeline Poe." She pointed to the model in the photographs. "She's positively anorexic. I don't care what she eats and doesn't eat, but what the hell happened between the time we booked her and she arrived for the shoot? Take a look."

Her assistant got quickly to her feet and came around the desk to examine the transparencies. "What's the matter?"

"You were at the shoot. You tell me."

"She looks fine."

"Anorexic. You couldn't tell?"

"We had to pin the clothes back," her assistant admitted.

"They don't drape right. Look at this bit."

The assistant squinted. The transparencies were tiny and it took an effort to read them. The model was a sophisticated blonde, her hair pulled back into a chignon. The navy and white Chanel jacket was too loose at the waist and the shoulders drooped.

"I wouldn't buy that suit if they marked it down to the price of a subway ride," Ralley said. She swept her hand across the transparencies. "There isn't one I can salvage."

"Are the rest of the models okay?"

"Could be. The beige Bill Blass jacket is tied wrong, incidentally. I'll get to that later. I'm not happy."

"You've always used Madeline," her assistant said in a defensive manner.

"I used the *live* Madeline Poe. This is the *dead* Madeline Poe. If I don't attend a shoot," Ralley added with an aggrieved air, "it's a guarantee something will go wrong."

Her assistant flushed and was about to mutter an apology when the intercom buzzed. Ralley shook her head and reached for the receiver. Whatever else was wrong with her life, she was on target with her job, a perfectionist with taste and an unerring eye. Her assistants never fulfilled her expectations, yet they would all go on to success, taking their ambition and lack of true commitment with them. "Yes?" Her answer was a little sharp, but her secretary was used to hearing an annoyed bark over the intercom.

"Mr. Krasmore called to remind you of this evening's appointment. Seven o'clock."

Ralley automatically reached for her appointment book. Drinks and dinner with Phil Krasmore, whose factory in Hong Kong produced Steyman's private label silk blouses and kimonos. Whenever he was in town Ralley went out with him for drinks and dinner, talked business, managed a few laughs, and wasted the evening pleasantly enough, considering he was a married man who didn't interest her in the least. "I have it. Thanks," she said.

Ralley replaced the receiver. "All right," she said to her assistant. "I'll go over the transparencies again, see if there's anything we can salvage, and rebook the rest. It's going to play hell with our budget." At issue was a small thirty-two-page catalog Steyman's sent out in January to preferred customers, and the production schedule was tight. "How's the copy coming along?"

"Due end of this week."

"I'll want to see it before Mr. Steyman does."

"Right."

Ralley picked up the telephone, dismissed her assistant with a half-smile, and dialed Marguerite's number.

"C'mon, Ralley, one more drink isn't going to hurt anybody." Phil Krasmore clapped a strong hand on Ralley's shoulder, trying to focus his watery, red-rimmed eyes on her. His sour breath was in a direct line with her nose. For the last half-hour, Phil had been acting as if he owned the bar of the Drake Hotel.

"You have enough gin in you to pickle a rhinoceros." Ralley crinkled her nose and fanned the air with her hand. "They're going to be closing the place soon."

"Who cares? I've got a room on the fifth floor. They can't throw me out, they can only throw me up." His words were slurred and he laughed uproariously at his joke. Ralley glanced over at the bartender, catching his sympathetic smile.

Because Ralley still hadn't straightened anything out with Cliff, she was determined to talk to him that evening. She was planning to leave Phil early, although she was admittedly having fun. Gazing at him through a haze caused by a bit too much gin, Ralley wondered why she hadn't noticed before that he had a very sexy jaw. According to Richard Steyman, who spent a good deal of his time in the Far East, Phil always expected the best of everything wherever he traveled. That meant the best restaurants, the best hotel suite, and usually the best hooker in town. When Ralley visited Hong Kong, however, she was rewarded with dinner at the Krasmore's five-thousand-dollar a month apartment, with his wife presiding.

"Hey, waiter," he called to a young man passing by. "Another round."

"That's a customer, Phil." Ralley reached for her bag. "I'm sorry. I have to be running along now. I have an appointment I can't miss."

"Hold on," Cliff had told her that morning. "I've got something sensational brewing. Everything's going to be all right, I'm telling you."

Sensational. If it had to do with Win Smith, it couldn't be all right. One minute she trusted Cliff, the next she didn't. Was it possible to have a single episode of ass-backward sex and that was all? It was nothing, Cliff told her. One of those unfortunate things that happen. Win was his lifeline to success. He wanted it, just a quick jab, that was *all*. "Only wait," Cliff said, "and you'll see what's about to come down the pike."

Hell, who was she to complain? There were episodes in her life she was glad she never had to explain.

The liquor was doing its work; she felt a light buzz that made her feel horny enough to want Cliff to scratch the itch.

Someone sat down at the piano and began a medley of show tunes meant to close out the evening. The lights dimmed. There were only four other customers and a couple of men at the bar who were laughing a bit too loud. They had come in separately, but she guessed they'd be leaving together.

Krasmore's groping hand found her knee. "Hey, got the blues, babe?" He leaned close, his eyelids blinking heavily like the slowly beating wings of an insect. "I've got the perfect remedy."

"Nothing I can't handle," she told him gamely and pushed his hand from her knee.

"Good, 'cause the night's just begun."

"No, really, I have to go. I work, remember? And I have an early shoot tomorrow."

"I'll give you a note. Even Steyman gives his employees a little head. Hey, that's a joke." He rolled with his own humor. Ralley reached for the glass the waiter put in front of her. She downed the drink faster than she should have.

"Listen, I've got some samples of a silk blend up in my room," Phil told her. "I meant to bring them along. Come up for a minute; I'll show them to you."

"You're coming in tomorrow, aren't you?"

"Can't, Ralley. Don't have the time. Tomorrow's booked solid."

"Look, don't start anything," she told him in an exasperated voice.

"You got a dirty mind." He turned away, insulted.

"All right, let's see the samples. I'm going to give you two and a half seconds."

"Make it three." He grinned, eased himself to his feet, and settled the bill. Five minutes later they were in his room and as soon as Phil shut the door behind them, Ralley knew she'd made a mistake. He pulled her roughly into his arms. "Gotcha, you gorgeous piece of silk goods." Her bag dropped to the floor.

"Phil, don't be difficult." She pushed at him, turning her head to one side so that his mouth landed on her hair.

"Come on, sweetie, you know you want it. I could feel the vibes all night." In a swift move he pinned her arms behind her back with one hand, the other hard on her breasts.

"No way," she managed just before his tongue pushed into her mouth. He squeezed and pinched her breasts. She twisted her head to get away from his stinking breath. "I said stop it or I'll scream."

He laughed. "Hey, go ahead, be my guest. I like a little fight in my women." Still pinning her arms, he reached down to unzip his pants and free his penis. Ralley managed to pull away, cracking him across the face with her open hand. He staggered back with a look of surprise as a trickle of blood oozed from his nose.

She felt the liquor well up in her mouth but still had to suppress a laugh. The expression on his face, coupled with his limp dick hanging from the open zipper, presented a pretty picture. Above and beyond the call of duty, she thought. This was the last of fraternizing with suppliers after hours, even if Krasmore produced the best-made garments in the Far East.

"Bitch." He glared at her, unaware of how foolish he looked.

She picked up her bag. "Don't bother seeing me out; I can find my way." Just before she closed the door, she added, "If you call me tomorrow with a sincere apology, I'll reconsider canceling that half million dollars worth of paper I was about to write."

She slammed the door hard behind her as something crashed to the floor. She hoped it was Phil Krasmore and that he had broken his cock off.

By the time she hailed a taxi and settled into the backseat, the tears came. Tears of relief, perhaps, of regret and self-pity saved up to be spilled onto the backseat of a smelly cab, the wet response to years of pentup disgust, disappointment, and dismay. The waste, she thought between sobs, the goddam waste. She cast a glance at the cabdriver but he was busy manipulating the Midtown nighttime traffic in a city that never stopped. She had spent half her life running away from everything that happened to her, all the while collecting fresh events from which to run.

California was ages ago and there was nothing in the air to bring the past back, but back it came, as clear as if she were standing on the beach at Malibu, waves washing over the skinny, isolated kid with the nutty mother who answered to voices only she heard.

Nicole Sanders was the mother no kid wants. Odd, wild-haired, and strangely dressed, her mother confusedly followed an arcane religion, her antics embarrassing Ralley in front of her friends. Yet she loved the loose-bolted woman with all the passion of a tender, strangled heart.

Ralley was christened Rachel Sanders, but chose the name Ralley early on because it sounded glamorous. A loner, she'd spent most of her time reading and inventing herself. She would become a very respectable person and she'd wear perfect clothes to prove she had quality and taste. In her dreams she had a perfect life, a father who loved her, and a mother she was proud of.

The cab reached Houston Street and stopped at a traffic light. Suddenly Ralley couldn't sit still any longer. "Driver, I'm getting out here. I think I want to walk." She took a bill out of her wallet. "Sorry."

"Lady, it's the middle of the night and this ain't a movie wonderland, you know."

"Thanks, but I'm only a few blocks from home." She handed him the money and got out. He shook his head and then moved on.

The neighborhood, which was well lit, wasn't entirely deserted. In the distance a siren sounded, then the rumble of a train, the screech of car wheels and beneath it all, a long, low buzzing persisted like a giant furnace fired in deep, subterranean passages. She liked that time of night best of all, still hours away from the raw, black loneliness before dawn when time stretched endlessly along shadowy paths of an all too remembered past. If only she could manage a bout of amnesia when it came to unpleasant memories.

"Taxi, lady?"

She turned. A cab kept pace with her as she hurried along the sidewalk. "No, thanks, I'm going in here." She gazed with relief at the bar on the corner, doors flung wide, the sound of a guitar drifting out. She could hear the soft peal of a woman's laugh and suddenly needed a drink and to be alone in the heart of a crowd. She wasn't ready to face Cliff and decision-making.

Inside, the bar was noisy and smelled of smoke and sawdust. A flattering pink light emanated from an arrangement of neon high on the wall. She took a seat at the back. When her drink came, she relaxed after the first sip and let the memories fill her veins and thicken her blood.

Her father. Even now Ralley couldn't bring herself to hate the man. It would mean hating the single bright moment of her childhood. She remembered being thrown high in the air and caught in strong arms. She remembered a deep, masculine laugh and a smile. That was all the memory she had of Major Severn Sanders who was gone by the time Ralley turned seven. He had left his wife and child without a word. Her mother never asked for support or even tried to discover where he was stationed. She prayed more fervently and held her head high in that fog of clouds that seemed to swirl invisibly around her, obscuring real life.

Ralley finished her drink, signaled the waiter to bring her another, and took a deep breath.

"We tried to stop her but she just seemed to want to go. We couldn't get to her in time."

"We tried to stop her she but just seemed to want to go." Ralley still remembered the warm sunshine of that California afternoon and the sweet-sour look of pity on the policeman's lined face. She remembered the air heavy around her and the way she gasped to fill her lungs, feeling the wings that beat in her chest, impeding each breath.

Her mother had walked into the Pacific Ocean and disappeared forever without a backward glance, without a word for her daughter.

The army informed her father in Germany of his wife's death and he reluctantly sent for Ralley. She was fifteen years old, tall, slender, and apparently beautiful enough to surprise him. "You'll be a bundle of trouble," he told her, "but not if I have anything to say about it. Just keep on my good side and you won't have a thing to worry about."

He was in charge of supplies for his command post. He had a mistress and was often away from home. He made no effort to get to know her, and once again Ralley was left to her own devices, the child of a disaffected parent, growing up awkwardly, surrounded by men who seemed to watch her and wait.

She wanted the memory to go away for good, to dissolve, to never have been, but Phil Krasmore's heavy touch had brought it all back, the time her father was away, the leer, the push, the power of stronger arms, the final terrifying moment when she knew her screams would not bring help.

"Miss."

Ralley gazed up into the eyes of a handsome, square-jawed young man who was smiling at her. "Sorry, we're closing." She was miles away and years beyond, carrying the scar tissue of pain, rejection, and questions that had no answers.

She knew Cliff was gone the moment she entered the loft. The lights were out but for one focused on his painting above the couch. The place had been straightened up—obviously his parting present to her. She found a note on the kitchen table, held down by a kitchen knife and scribbled in his familiar handwriting: "Ralley, I'm cutting out for a while. Things are just a bit too heavy between us. It's interfering with my art, and big things are coming down the pike. We'll talk soon and work things out. My love is still strong, so don't get any ideas. I'll come by for the paintings as soon as I can borrow a truck. Cliff."

Shit. She tore the note into little bits and let them flutter to the floor. She should have pitched him out long ago. She gazed at the painting above the couch. She hated his work, hated the swirling black impasto. The content was as vacant as he. The tears started again. Oh, Christ, why did things have to be this way?

She picked up the knife and advanced toward the painting.

CHAPTER 19

Win closed the gallery at eight o'clock that evening. Traffic along the avenue slowed down once darkness descended, but Win had waited hopefully for customers. The only people who walked in off the street, however, were some loud, high-on-grass skinheads Win was afraid had come to rip him off.

He'd mounted a group show of gallery artists, and the skinheads wandered around making comments that sent them into hysterical laughter. At the door on the way out one of them stopped and called over to Win, hovering anxiously nearby, "Nice, nice, I mean nice stuff, like." The critique caused further paroxysms of laughter. Win went outside, pulled the grating shut over the front windows, and bolted the door once he got back inside. He was beginning to believe the gallery scene wasn't quite what he expected. So far, glamour, prestige, money, and fame had failed to materialize. Boxed in, prey to the dangers of the downtown scene, he believed everyone was after something. A man couldn't be too careful. Win dimmed the gallery lights and retreated reluctantly to the back room, hating the place. *Plus* he was low on food, there was no booze at all, and his supply of snow was down to one snort.

And Reuben Newcombe had been on the phone earlier in the day. "Listen, Winthrop, I don't know what the hell's going on down there but who's this Maxi Frani-something?"

"Franilero. One of my artists."

"You owe him money?"

Win felt a bead of perspiration form on his forehead. "I don't *owe* him money. We sold one of his paintings. Plenty has to come off the top before he sees his money, that's the *arrangement,* and he knows it as well as I, Mr. Newcombe. I mean, face it, numero uno, the gallery gets half the sale price. Hell, plenty of galleries take that. Then there's the printing bill; he's in for the printing bill. I'm just waiting for the invoice. No use asking him to refund an overpayment later. Artists are like babies, and I can't operate on a deficit."

"We expect you to turn a profit, Win, but on the other hand I don't want whatever the hell his name is calling me at the office telling me Smarts owes him money or the estate of Egon Delville owes him money. Delville owes him bupkis. Pay the man, Win."

"Hey, right. He'll get what's coming to him." Maxi's paintings were careful renderings of satyrlike men standing in isolation in surrealist settings. Win figured on selling a few to the gay community and had been surprised when a hayseed couple from the Midwest walked in off the street and bought one on the spot, paying for the painting with American Express traveler's checks. The last thing Win wanted to do was turn off the Maxi spigot, but he had debts and they came first.

"I don't want any more phone calls from unhappy artists, Win. You're supposed to deal with them. How much time do you have on the lease?"

"Three months."

"How's business?"

"Great. Listen, I'll give you an accounting at the end of the month."

"Next week, Win. The estate expects an accounting, and if there's a profit, we expect to see that, too."

"Right, Mr. Newcombe, right. I'm telling you, Egon would be proud."

"No doubt," Newcombe said in a sour tone. "Just show up next week with plenty of black ink. Call my secretary on Monday for an appointment."

"Right, right, sure thing, definitely. No sweat, no problem."

Sure, no sweat, no problems, no business, and the whole enterprise sinking fast. And shit, why was Maxi so mad all the time? To Win, of course, he was a nonthreatening figure, small and almost as delicate as a woman, with high cheekbones and deep, lustrous eyes.

Things had started out pretty well between them. They had first met at a party downtown. At the time Win was trying to fill the gallery roster and to score while he was at it by playing the important art connoisseur.

The old gay bars near the waterfront had been closed down, and parties now were where you found them. This one was being held in the basement of an Off-Off Broadway playhouse that had been taken over by businessmen who knew how to make a buck. They had promised a show of the latest S&M paraphernalia.

Redone to resemble a Prohibition-era speakeasy, and with the smell of marijuana as thick as a Long Beach fog, the place was crowded with men in fringed and metal-encrusted leather and tight, ball-crushing pants. Mirrored ornaments twisted and blinked from the ceiling, reflecting the spotlights that circled the room, as voices screamed over the blare of canned music. Win's blood began heating up. Someone tapped his shoulder and asked him to dance. Win obliged, then danced with others who weren't his type at all. In fact, they scared him. One even looked as if he were still angry over missing all those good times during the Spanish Inquisition.

Then the spots flickered because the show was about to begin. "Exhibition" was more like it. Win wasn't much into the leather-sex scene, although once with Cliff he had really gotten off on being tied up and whipped. He didn't mind being a voyeur, though, what the hell.

The stage was dimly lit with a red glare slinking across the floor from overhead. Two bare-chested men came out, the taller in a leather face mask, evidently in control. Win sucked in a breath at the way leather pants stretched across muscular thighs and oiled glowing flesh contracted as their bodies moved.

The smaller one slid slowly to the floor on command and began licking his master's crotch. Both had strong erections. Win glanced around the crowd before lowering his hand to his own erection. Most of the onlookers were rapt. He noted a soft swaying as they took on the same pumping motion as the actors.

The air was heavy with heated expectancy as the man on the floor released the other's penis and took it in his mouth. It was then that Win first spotted Maxi, who was no doubt scouting the action. Win tilted his chin up in invitation, checking for the usual signs of preference, keys dangling from belts—on the left hip to signal the "master" role, on the right, the desire to be beaten. But Maxi carried none of the signs to show he was into anything that could smart. Win thought he'd lucked out when Maxi sauntered through the crowd, came over, and introduced himself.

"Maxi Franilero."

"Win Smith."

"Easy to remember."

Win laughed easily. "My parents thought of everything."

They forgot the show on stage even before it was over. The music began its erotic beat, some loud crazy group giving it their all.

"You dance?"

"Sure," Win said. He held out his arms. Maxi insisted upon leading, pushing him in one direction while moving his feet in another. Win felt as if he were holding on for dear life.

"Hey, ever use one of those cubicles?" Maxi was familiar with the place and nodded at tiny rooms that lined the far wall. "Used for privacy, man, if you want to, you know, talk without the usual racket around here. Man, you don't know how glad I am to find *you*."

"Let's *go*," Win said, heading for a cubicle that had just been abandoned.

As soon as he learned Maxi was an artist, he went into his routine about Smarts.

"Smarts? Hey, man, I know the place." Maxi was interested, said he'd seen the gallery sign go up and was planning on stopping by. He sold his paintings at an S&M shop, he explained, but he was a lot more ambitious than that.

It wasn't any time at all before they'd exchanged addresses. After a couple of minutes they headed for the sofa and had sex, using all the new rules. Win remembered thinking how the fun had really gone out of it all, though. Used to be you could range all over the place and not have to worry.

Still that was some evening with Maxi, Win remembered. He'd have to give him a full-scale show some time soon. He owed that much to Maxi.

He thought of his talk with Annalise Younger at the Sotheby auction. His carefully rehearsed Spanish in a carefully rehearsed Buenos Aires accent had scared her. Pity her husband had come along at the wrong time; all Win wanted was her mailing list and her appearance at Cliff's opening. He'd have to tighten the screws somehow.

The front door buzzer pulled him up short. Expecting Cliff, Win tucked his shirt into his pants and ran to the front. With a broad smile, he quickly unlocked the door. The smile died on his lips.

He gazed into a face that held a tight grin. Maxi Franilero stood there, wearing black leather pants and a black leather jacket.

"Hey, *amigo*," Win said. "How you doin'?"

Maxi stepped into the gallery and waved to a hulking shadow that suddenly appeared in the doorway. Win took a deep swallow. "Listen, Maxi, I swear I was going to send you the money tomorrow."

"Decided to save you a stamp." Maxi motioned the giant inside. "Now, Doherty," he said, slamming the door shut, "can you believe the coincidence? I call Win every day and all I get on the line is a machine. I drop by, the place is closed, I leave messages. I play by the rules and get nowhere. I show up with you and whaddaya know, the check is in the mail." He beamed at the giant who stood without moving, arms at his sides. "Oh, I don't think you two know each other." He gave an elaborate bow. "Chuck Doherty, this is Win. He owes me money and he's going to send it to me tomorrow."

Doherty drew out a laugh that rumbled from under a three-inch brass buckle holding up tight-fitting pants. His eyes were dim and yet held a gleam of anticipation.

"Yeah, Doherty, how ya doin'?" Win waited for an acknowledgment and, when it wasn't forthcoming, turned to Maxi. "Listen, why waste a stamp, you're right. I'll give you a check right now." He hoped he sounded convincing.

"Money, cash, moolah, the green stuff," Maxi said. "And eight percent interest compounded by the month. Round it out to, say, ten—no, twenty percent. I never liked that fifty percent arrangement, come to think of it. I do all the work and you sit back and rake it in."

"Listen, cash is impossible," Win began. "I mean you can see what it's like around here, nobody keeps cash around. I'd be ripped off in two seconds."

"Wish I could trust you," Maxi said, "but somehow I can't. You're an asshole." He spoke the last in a soft, firm voice as though he were passing out a compliment.

Win was about to turn away when Maxi reached out and gripped his chin between strong fingers. "You sold my painting and kept the money. I call that simple theft. Not smart but not complicated, cheating me. I'm a little guy, the kind you could push around, right?"

Win felt his eyes starting from their sockets. "Hey, take it easy. Look, man, we can talk. I put the check in the bank. It takes time to clear, man."

"Three weeks? You think I'm some kind of a cream puff." Maxi's voice rose. "You figure I don't know how to make a point. Get what's mine? Take him, Chuck."

"Hey, look," Win said, stepping back, "we're friends." The giant came closer. "Tell him, Maxi. We met at that party. We even had it on for a while."

"I meet a lot of people at parties. It doesn't mean we're friends and it doesn't mean you don't pay me the money you owe me."

Win kept nodding in agreement all the time Maxi was talking, but that didn't stop the giant.

"Hey, look, man, no oh, jeez." The first blow caught Win right under his heart. He felt a pain gallop through his body and take his breath away. The next blow smashed into his head. His eyes filled up with something that blinded him. Blood, he was dead, they were killing him. The blows came so quickly after that and with such intensity that he ceased to feel them. His body gave up and he slumped against the wall unable to move. Another blow slammed his head against a frame. He was traveling in and out of a black tunnel as the pounding crunched away at his brain.

"Now, listen, motherfucker, it's your last chance. If you make me come back again, your ass will never be good for anything smaller than a Mack truck. Get the picture?"

Just before Win blacked out he heard a distant voice say, "Hey, that's my painting. Grab it and let's get out of here. I think the check will certainly be in the mail first thing in the morning."

Then someone laughed and kicked Win in the ribs.

The phone was ringing. Something was ringing. Win tried to open his eyes, but a tight band kept them shut. Then at last a slit of light. He could barely move. First one leg and then the other. He was sitting in water. No, he had peed all over himself. He groaned as he shifted his weight and lifted his arms. By some miracle that ape hadn't broken any bones.

It took a full fifteen minutes to drag himself to the tiny john in the back room. The most excruciating pain he had ever felt gripped him as he spilled his guts into the toilet bowl. He got slowly to his feet and leaned over the sink. He splashed some cold water onto his face and with difficulty gazed at himself in the mirror. His eyes were nearly swollen shut. Blood that had oozed from his nose stained his upper lip.

"Shit."

He stumbled over to his cot and collapsed on it, tears stinging his aching eyes. He took shallow breaths and fell into unconsciousness.

When he awoke, it was daylight and Cliff was standing over him. "What the hell's the matter with you, leaving the door open like that? They could've come in and stolen my stuff right off the walls. Rise and shine, man, I've come for my paintings."

Win came to slowly, trying to make sense of Cliff's words. He swung his feet over the side of the cot. "Wait, gimme a second. Gotta get my act together."

"A sweet deal," Cliff was saying. "I've got a panel truck outside. She's got plenty of storage space, man, what a setup, what a setup. I mean, she knows *everybody*, all she has to do is snap her fingers, they come running. She takes maybe one or two new artists every couple of years. It's like a fucking miracle."

"What the hell are you talking about?" Win, through swollen eyes, couldn't quite make out what Cliff was doing, much less talking about. She? Ralley? Plenty of storage space?

"The May Collins Gallery over on Broome. She's taking me on, are you deef?" Cliff hauled a large oil through the back room into the gallery.

"She's what? Wait a minute." Win got shakily to his feet and went into the gallery. Cliff was already out the door, sliding the painting into a panel truck parked at the curb. When Cliff came back, he stopped dead at the sight of Win standing there.

"What the hell happened to you? Jeez, you look terrible. I mean, that must have been some party." He went past Win and came out a moment later carrying another painting.

"Hey, wait a minute," Win cried. "Are you telling me you're going with May Collins? I've got a show scheduled for you three weeks from now, you son of a bitch," Win said, trying to pull the painting away and knowing he was no match for the bigger, younger man. "I already ordered the invitations."

"Hey, come on," Cliff told him, wrenching the painting away and heading for the door with it. "You've got to be kidding, man. You don't think I'd give up a contract with May Collins for a couple of lousy weeks hanging in this

place, do you? You've got to have your head examined, Win. I mean those
S&M hangouts, they're doing things to your skull. Take a look at yourself."

"Go ahead, help yourself," Win said dully. "I'll get a court order."

"Don't even try, pal, don't even try. Now, if you'll excuse me, I've got to
get to Ralley's place for the rest of my stuff."

Win retreated to the back room and lay down on the cot. His head was
killing him; he had to think.

"Give it up, *chérie,* give it up. Or else *VFF* goes down the drain, taking
you with it, finished, *fertig,* ze end. Please, Marguerite."

"Sol, it's Sunday. *Je t'en prie.* Can't I sit with the paper and a cup of coffee
without having you phone me with bad news? Eh?"

Marguerite was at her kitchen table, telephone in hand and the *New York
Times* spread out before her. Freshly brewed coffee scented the air, taking
the chill out of Sol Greenspan's words.

"Sunday, schmunday, bubby, I said your life's at stake at this point in time.
You don't listen, darling. You get this faraway sound in your voice, tells me
you live by the sword, you're going to die by the sword. Get ready for the
sword and don't you dare hang up."

"What is it?" she asked after a moment.

"Money. Money, money, money. Three million big ones paid out over
time so you can't spend it all on one visit to the five-and-dime."

"By the time I pay my outstanding debts and taxes," she told him, "there
won't be three million dollars."

"Hold it, babe, don't jump to conclusions. You're a rare bird. Don't you
even want to know who's dispensing the largess?"

No, she thought, it hardly mattered. Someone who wanted *VFF* and was
willing to pay for it.

"Marty Farnstein of Libby Publications. You know, Canadian real estate,
married to the gorgeous Lelia, three feet taller than he?"

Marguerite managed a smile. Lelia, who wore Ungaro exclusively and who
showed more leg than the entire Radio City chorus line. "He wants it for
Lelia, I suppose."

"What do you care? He's willing to pay a price my conscience will agonize
over later. And that includes picking up all your debts, the name remains
Varick's Fashion Forecast and you stay on at a cool hundred thousand plus
expenses for a year, after which you'll negotiate."

Plus expenses. How remarkable. She thought of the upcoming Paris and
Milan shows she had to cover and the cost of looking as if she and one young
assistant could afford two weeks at the best hotels in both cities. "And they'll

botch it up," she said. "Take on advertising, go into collusion with designers over which clothes to promote—"

Sol's sigh was deliberately audible. "Marguerite, accept the offer. Farnstein is out shopping for a fashion publication and you're not the only one on the street."

"Only the most reliable."

"Right, Marguerite, the most reliable. Without you, would my wife know what length to wear her skirts? What in hell propels you, anyway? I mean who cares what length skirts are?"

"That's just the point. Nobody cares and everybody cares. Fashion's a business, *mon ami*, a fantasy, a dream, a crock of *merde*, it defines the way we live, it's a conspiracy, eh? A haven for homosexuals who want to—how shall we say?—express themselves on the backs of women. You understand?"

"Doesn't explain why *you* love it."

"Maybe because I love nothing else."

"Good answer, even if it doesn't make sense. And you think it's so important not to act in collusion with designers, you'd be willing to go down on a sinking ship, all the way down to the bottom where there ain't no advertising, no air, and no future."

"I made *VFF* in my own image, Sol. I can't just give it away; it's my life."

"It's your death, Marguerite. Sell to Libby. The real estate magnate is trying to put together a print empire. You don't want to make him unhappy, do you? And *VFF* isn't going anywhere without you at the helm."

"Perhaps I'll let *VFF* die a natural death," she told Sol, then added, "Did you know Egon wanted me as director of his museum?"

"Hey, wonderful. What does it pay?"

"As a member of the board of directors, I'll have to see it pays enough."

"Then you'll sell."

"I don't have the directorship yet."

"That should be easy," Sol said. "Who else would they want? Listen, sell *VFF* and back away from it if that's what you want, although Marty would still need your name on the masthead, director or whatever. Look, you're a class act. I bet if anyone knew you were ready for a fresh offer, you'd have them crawling in the window to get at you."

"I'm sixty-eight years old, Sol. There's no room at the top for what you say over-the-hill types, yes?"

"Listen," he said, "I'm on your side. Take the offer."

"Let me think about it."

"I'm giving you one day, Marguerite."

She laughed and hung up, then began to pace the length of her kitchen. She had invented *VFF*, never thinking of it as an investment, and now, unexpectedly, it would provide her with a comfortable cushion against whatever life still held for her.

During the lean years she had always managed to give the appearance of possessing wealth. It would be extremely pleasant, at last, to have more than enough. Until that moment, all she had of real value was the Park Avenue co-op, four large rooms purchased when she first came to New York with the money she had acquired from selling a consulting business in Paris.

She loved attending the collections and enjoyed the sight and touch of fashion; the directorship of the Delville Museum would allow the fantasy to continue. However, she would be dealing with the past more than the present. No more front seats at fashion shows. She would lose the deference paid her and the sense of power. If only she had accepted Egon's offer to back her. He would be gone, anyway, and *VFF* would still be hers.

What is there about fashion? Solly wanted to know. Ephemera, beauty, historical associations, a thing well done, perhaps the very reasons Egon established his museum. The director's title began to seem more and more attractive; she could actually determine the direction the museum would take. She had no doubt she'd find a quorum among the board to back up her policies. Now, knowing she could come away solvent from *VFF*, she felt a frisson of excitement. For the first time in almost half a century, she would be free, really free.

It took very little for Marguerite to step back into that distant time when the world exploded and the debris marched in with heavy leather boots and swastikas.

Artenay was fifty kilometers south of Paris. She was Marguerite DeLonge, born into an aristocratic family whose lineage could be traced back to the thirteenth century. Like the ancient family château situated upon a hill that overlooked the valley, the DeLonge line had survived wars, revolution, and the guillotine by shifting loyalties with the political wind. Her widowed father, Alexandre, was a tall, straight-backed man with white hair perfectly combed, a sharp, pointed nose inherited by Marguerite, and assessing gray eyes. His air of self-confidence masked the determination of a practiced liar, an aristocrat used to trading in other people's lives to survive. A successful businessman anxious to keep his plant running through the German occupation, Alexandre claimed his only desire was to protect his workers, to feed and house them during the long night.

But sensing trouble for his beautiful young daughter, he dispatched her to a convent seven kilometers away. Hidden in the convent were Jews and members of the Resistance; it was only a matter of time before the Germans came calling.

It happened without warning. When their voices were heard through the stone corridors, Marguerite ran in terror to a small broom closet beneath a stairwell. Crouched low, her fist in her mouth to stifle her sobs, she heard the bloody carnage that screamed through the ancient building.

Even now, in the deep black well of the night, Marguerite would awaken suddenly from the cries of terror in her dreams.

But this was Sunday morning, a clear fall day, and Solly had told her she could be free of financial worries forever. She pushed at the sleeves of her silk kimono and reached for the telephone. She had to talk; *had to have human contact.* She began to dial a number, then realized it was Egon's. She dropped the receiver and, after taking a couple of deep breaths, dialed Kate at home.

"How about dropping by?" she asked.

"Oh, you've seen Liz's column."

"No, I've been on the phone all morning with my accountant. He wants me to—"

"Better pick up the paper," Kate said quietly. "Mortimer Quinlan's newest pal is Tracy Lazer, she of the Westhampton Museum of Contemporary Art. Liz suspects Tracy is in line for the directorship of the Delville Museum."

Marguerite closed her eyes briefly. "Would you mind repeating that to me? No, it's all right, I'll check the paper. I'll call you back, Kate. *Je t'embrasse.*"

"Marguerite?" But Kate's voice came to her faintly, as if from a very great distance away.

"It isn't yours to give away, Mortimer."

Marguerite, although it was Sunday, had located the head of Delville Perfumes easily enough. She found Mortimer Quinlan where he always was: in his huge antique-filled office. He wore tennis clothes and greeted his visitor with a broad, charming smile. A mug of coffee sat untouched on his desk, along with a half-eaten sandwich. His youngest son, also in tennis whites, sat in a corner chair watching a soccer game on television.

"Good Lord, Marguerite, that was mere speculation on Liz's part. Sit down, for God's sake, and relax. Let's talk about this like two sensible people."

"I will not sit down and there is nothing to talk about. Liz cannot possibly speculate on something she knows nothing about."

"We're going to have to get busy with the museum, and hiring a director is our number one priority. Tracy could take a load off our hands. We've got a helluva lot ahead of us to make the ship run smoothly."

Marguerite collapsed into a chair. *"She'll* take a load off our hands?"

"All right," he said casting a glance toward his son, "I'll concede the point. The director, whoever that may be, will take a load off our hands."

Marguerite kept her voice steady, hoping he wouldn't notice her agitation. "Egon was very explicit on that one point. He wished me to head the museum."

She watched a slight flush of red rise along his neck and slowly begin to suffuse his face. Mortimer had been through an acrimonious divorce a year previous and had sworn never to marry again. He was probably ripe for someone to move in for the kill—someone like Tracy Lazer.

"Explicit? Ah, I see what you mean. You have something in writing. My dear Marguerite, why haven't you mentioned it before?"

"I have nothing in writing, merely his words to me. I didn't think it would be necessary to bring the matter up until the board met."

"Well, Egon was always a sly one," Quinlan said with an air of disbelief and real concern.

He wouldn't be an easy sell, Marguerite realized; this would be his first major decision without Egon. "Mortimer, you disappoint me. It's what Egon wanted, what he told me."

"And *VFF?*"

"Let's just discuss the matter at hand," she told him, recognizing the black look he gave her; he was settling in for a battle. "I think we will have to let the board decide whether I'm telling the truth or not." She stood up and went to the door. "Good-bye, young man," she called out to Quinlan's son, who turned to her and smiled. When she glanced back at Mortimer, she discovered him watching her, sober-faced, fingers tented at his lips. Life had taught her long before never to expect people to be anything but selfish. If Mortimer wasn't on her side, she knew five others on the board who would be.

CHAPTER 20

Egon's journal:

August 20, 1988. Dimples. I suppose I was always a sucker for them. Then the California tan and brown hair with touches of gold. And of course he exudes a certain innocent charm I don't trust one bit, but nevertheless can't resist. He's a wheedler, but then who isn't? Who doesn't look at Egon Delville and measure him for a touch of some kind? The idea is to be on my guard. I said he could use the guest room on the top floor for the time being. Laid down the law about the rest of the house: it's out of bounds. He looked properly contrite. He's a sneak, but his idea about opening a gallery in SoHo appeals to me and from the gallery personnel I've had the privilege to meet, he's no better and no worse. A little look into the Smiths of Cleveland; if he's a scion of that family, maybe he's not a liar and cheat after all.

Maxi was out there again with his pal, Chuck Doherty, rattling the wire grating, fiddling with the lock.

No one's here, Win wanted to scream. Can't you tell? We're locked up tight. I've gone to Timbuktu. There's no more Smarts, no more money, no more nothing. He sat shivering in the back room, in the dark save for the faint glow that was New York City.

Reuben Newcombe had come by that afternoon, stepping out of his chauffeured Mercedes to peer fastidiously through the window. The gates were up; there was a "Closed for Repairs" sign on the door, and Win sulked in the back room waiting for him to go away. The answering machine picked up threatening messages from Maxi and from Cliff every hour. It seemed Cliff was missing some drawings and was blaming Win, who knew nothing about them.

Win was hungry, cold, broke, and in pain. He lay cowering in the back of the gallery with nothing more than a few dog-eared magazines he'd fished out of a litter basket. Now, waiting for the roof to fall in, Win listlessly turned the pages of a fashion magazine. And hit pay dirt.

He had come across an article illustrated with full-color photographs of Egon's library and drawing room. He stared at the pictures as at some great work of art, feeling positively nostalgic for his old room with the silhouettes on the wall and the offbeat color scheme. He remembered the scent of the town house as if it were the Garden of Eden.

There was Egon's house standing unused, full of treasures, waiting to be turned into some kind of a ditzy museum, and here he was, in possession of the man's diaries when he should have helped himself to some of the valuable objects that covered every bit of surface in the place. Lost opportunities— Win could write the book on the subject. The trouble was he was too damn honest.

He backtracked along the article like a police dog sniffing out stash at the airport. He came across a paragraph devoted to Egon's idiosyncratic taste. Apparently a warehouse in Queens contained hundreds of dresses, shoes, and hats as well as countless antique buttons and trims. A curator had been hired to tally the collection, and was apparently ensconced in the warehouse. I could've done that, Win thought. Probably Newcombe had hired the curator, some upper-class brat with a useless masters in art history. The museum wouldn't be operational for a couple of years, he read. A board of trustees was already in place, and a director yet to be named. The writer speculated that Marguerite Varick would be chosen to head the museum. Maybe he should hit on her for a job, explain he knew the house better than anyone. He wondered if Newcombe would be a problem; if only he hadn't screwed up with the lawyer.

And to think he'd exited the town house with a useless collection of journals and nothing else. Egon's spidery handwriting was a chore to read; he'd begun a dozen times, only to throw down the journal in disgust. He'd been interested in Annalise because of the word *puta*. He now knew a helluva lot about her, but so far there hadn't been any payoff.

He had to think seriously about what the journals held for him and about the empty town house. Serious thinking wasn't possible in the back of Smarts with Maxi and Cliff calling for his blood. Once again he remembered the warm top-floor room and how happy he'd been there.

When the idea hit, Win didn't even try to examine it for flaws. He acted quickly, gathering his clothes, his shaving equipment, and Egon's journals. Mustn't forget the journals. After all, he had to put them back where he'd found them.

He slipped out the back entrance and closed the door behind him, locking it carefully. Hell, that was the least he could do. Which left him with a set of keys and two choices: he could toss them or mail them to Reuben Newcombe. He decided to deposit the keys in a litter basket on his way uptown.

He found a wire basket halfway down the block. In it he deposited all the keys on his chain but for three.

The magazine article had mentioned something about a caretaker living in the basement of Egon Delville's town house. If the caretaker caught him, Win would explain that he'd come in from the Ivory Coast, had just learned of Egon's death, and wanted to collect his things, thank you very much and good-bye.

The main entrance was up half a dozen steps and it was to this door that Win held his keys. He'd left his suitcase and the journals in a locker at Grand Central after panhandling the cost by explaining he was a traveler who'd just had his wallet stolen. Desperate times, desperate measures, Win decided; either the lock had been changed or it hadn't.

The door yielded to the two keys required to unlock it; with the third Win deftly turned off the burglar alarm. He was inside, the door closed behind him, the burglar alarm once again activated.

He stood for a moment in the entranceway, taking in the familiar scene. The air was dry, a little stuffy, and smelled as much of mothballs as of Delville Perfumes. There were no longer fresh flowers on the gilt hall table, of course, but the silver letter tray was still there, with, incongruously, an old *TV Guide* sitting in it. Win walked from room to room slowly, quietly, filled with nostalgia for what never was, admiring the small valuable *objets d'art* that covered every surface. He found no indication in the library that anything on the shelves had been touched except for dust. He cast a last respectful glance at the chair Egon had died in.

When he climbed to his own room, he found the bed made, the sheets clean, everything intact. The bathroom was shiny. A little drip in the shower faucet was still unrepaired and the mosaic shower floor was moist.

He might have to buy some towels, but he'd check the linen closet first. He would have to be very circumspect, but it could be done.

He moved in at ten that evening. Lighting was a minor problem: his bedroom window overlooked the courtyard and the curtains were opaque.

He was out early the next morning, calling Egon's old number from a corner telephone booth. The caretaker answered, a young, harried woman; he told her he was a reporter doing a history on Egon. When pressed, she agreed to show him around the town house if Reuben Newcombe permitted it. With further prodding, Win learned she went to school and was running late.

Saturdays and Sundays, he thought, since she could be home all weekend, might be a little sticky.

Win sold a small silver antelope in a downtown pawnshop that afternoon.

"A gift from my mother-in-law," he explained. "Can't stand her, can't stand that."

The hundred dollars would take the heat off, Win figured. Tomorrow he'd do some serious thinking about what to sell and how to sell it. He could live on three, four hundred a week. Life was expensive when you had to eat all your meals out. He'd need some clothes, too; he figured on getting a job in L.A. in a month or two.

Win was clean—no coke, no self-indulgences. He needed his wits about him at all times. He had a couple hundred dollars in his possession at the end of two weeks. Best of all, he had discovered a crawl space in the attic at the back of a small storage room that only someone looking for a hiding place would ever discover. It reminded him of the attic in the large house he had grown up in, with its gentle old-fashioned smell, as though surprises would be found in every corner, under old blankets and in leather trunks.

It was in this narrow space that he hid the leather-bound journals. He also repaired there when the unknown, unseen cleaning woman came twice weekly to make her way through each room singing and wielding a vacuum cleaner.

At the end of two weeks he heard new voices in the house. Voices sans radio and sans vacuum cleaner. Win repaired to his crawl space, leaving the storage room door slightly ajar.

He fell asleep in the nostalgic warmth. When the voices arrived on the top floor, he sprang awake, sliding to the deepest, darkest corner of the crawl space.

"Ralley, let me sit down awhile. I'm not as young as I used to be." The accent was French.

"I'm having a high old time, Marguerite. Now, what do you suppose he has in here? Ah, a storage room. Maybe this is where Egon kept the bodies."

Win held his breath. Damn, Ralley Littlehurst, his nemesis. What in hell was she doing there?

"Furniture," Ralley pronounced. "Come on in, Marguerite; you have your choice of chairs. Might as well poke in here, too. What the hell are you looking for, anyway?"

"I think I've had enough of Egon's artifacts," Marguerite said. "I'm sorry we came. I'm not certain what I expected to find, eh?"

"It's a job somebody has to do."

"It's a curator's job," Marguerite said dryly, "cataloging the collection."

"The curator is in Queens and can't be in two places at once. What worries me is all this stuff sitting around uncataloged."

"Not so, Ralley. You see why the museum needs a director. Egon has an insurance policy with a list of his possessions."

"You're so clever, Marguerite. Is it up to date?"

"Ah, no, I'm afraid not. Egon bought incessantly. He didn't expect to—" She left the sentence unfinished, then added, "I doubt his books are completely catalogued, but one doesn't know, of course."

"And I'll tell you something else, *ma chère amie*," Ralley said, "I believe a small marble and silver obelisk has disappeared, to put it mildly."

Win silently cursed and squeezed deeper into the recess.

"He had a dozen obelisks," Marguerite protested, "perhaps more."

"And I remember being especially taken with them when we all met with Reuben here. Egon and his phallic symbols, I remember quite clearly. Do you suppose the caretaker . . . ?"

"No, she's Reuben's niece, studying law at Columbia and hardly in need of money. As squeaky clean as they come."

"The cleaning lady."

"She'd be a fool to try."

"Let's get hold of the master list from the insurance company."

"I think we'll have to," Marguerite said. Then on a sigh clearly heard by Win, she added, "I wish things would move a little faster. Until some official word, I feel as if my hands are tied."

"You're in like Flynn, Marguerite. Even Mortimer Quinlan will support you when he thinks about it. Besides, you can count on the rest of us: Annalise and Zack, that inseparable Younger duo, so in love, don't you know; Kate Hayden, Egon's adored one; you, *moi*, and Jaybee-of-the-mayor's-office Olsen in the right-hand corner in the shiny red tights. Mortimer has no choice. Dig your heels in, Marguerite, that's all it takes. And while we're at it, we'll put in a recommendation that the director's salary should be set at something like a hundred thou. Come on, let's get a drink and plot strategy."

Their voices faded away. Win heard the familiar grind of the old elevator. A one hundred thousand dollar post as director of the Delville Museum? A hundred grand to do practically nothing? No one knew Egon's town house better than he. Wasn't he in possession of Egon's thoughts, preserved in the leather-bound journals? Who better than Win Smith to carry out the old man's wishes? He waited fifteen minutes more and then crept out. He wondered if he could retrieve the obelisk.

"Mr. Gregory?" Win's hand sweated a little on the telephone receiver that he held close to his ear.

"Yes, Mr. Smith, what can I do for you?"

"I wanted to read something to you."

"Just a minute, you did say you were from Dayton Hudson in Minneapolis."

"Well, yes, right, but how else was I going to get through?"

"Let me get this straight. You're not from Dayton Hudson."

"Actually, it'll cost you about ten thousand dollars to learn where I'm from, Mr. Gregory. But let me read you a little sample before you do, straight from the horse's mouth." Win realized his own mouth had gone dry and because he expected Gregory to hang up he began to read in a rush, not as he'd planned, straight from Egon's journal. " 'Giovanni Daguras, president of DAS Limited, Zurich, was never indicted in the Banco Ambrogliano scandal because he managed to make his way out of Italy before the news broke, taking his profits with him. Switzerland was only too happy to welcome him and his millions, but there are powerful men in Italy who feel Daguras took them—' "

Ira Gregory broke in. "I don't know who you are, and I don't know what you're talking about or what you're after, Mr. Smith, but if I ever hear your voice again, I'll track it right to its source and believe me, there'll be nothing left of you, not even a memory."

Win heard the click of the receiver and hung up quickly. He rushed across the avenue from the phone booth without looking back. He had never heard a voice so icy, nor anyone so sure of himself. Telling Ira Gregory he had the goods on him wasn't going to work. Hell, taking on the mob was pretty stupid. Egon had called Gregory scum and was out to get him because of Kate Hayden. Was the old man in love with Kate or something? Win decided to read the journals more carefully, take notes, map his next move. You had to hit somebody in the solar plexus if you wanted to make a living in the blackmail game. Besides, he had no idea what the Banco Ambrogliano scandal was about.

He thought of the bibelots in Egon's bedroom. And there was a tie he'd always liked.

"Nada, nada, rien, and *niente.* How do you say 'nothing' in Portuguese?"

"Beats the hell out of me," Tess Cristaforo said to Pete the day he showed up in her office with a list of South American boutiques claiming not to have written paper with Kate Hayden, as shown by Ira Gregory.

"I think we have everything ready for the federal grand jury," Pete said. "Can we count on them to come down with an indictment in a week or two? Anything more and I think he'll sniff us out and find he has to take a fast trip to the Continent."

Tess glanced over the list. "Okay, there's a distinct sign of furtherance of conspiracy, discrepancies between orders and billing, fabrics and nondelivery of fabrics for orders stores claim never to have made. I'm satisfied. Let Ira Gregory prove differently in a court of law."

"Incidentally," Pete said, "something else has surfaced, passed up from Rio. There's every doubt the boutiques in question would have left paper with a young, new company like Kate Hayden, since South America is a hotbed of knockoffs. If the stores want Hayden fashions, all they have to do is order a couple of pieces and copy them right down to the label."

"And no protection for the label, either."

"Hell, if anyone in Brazil thought there was a future in Kate Hayden, all he'd have to do would be to copyright the name and nothing could be done about it from here."

"Speaking of Kate Hayden—the person, not the label—is your friendship with her going to give us a tiny bit of trouble when Ira Gregory comes to trial?"

"Let the grand jury indict and we'll find out."

CHAPTER 21

A limousine from Neiman-Marcus was waiting for Kate at the airport when she arrived in Houston. Ira had made the date for her store appearance at an inconvenient time, however: only two weeks remained before market week. In those two crucial weeks she needed to cull ninety garments down to seventy-five, do model fittings and accessorize the complete line. *And* select her music. One day she'd have a staff to handle it all, if only she could hold on.

She was booked overnight into the Houston Sheraton, only a few steps from the exclusive department store. Scheduled for the designer dress department that afternoon, with Kate commentating, were fashion shows at one, three, and four-thirty. In between Kate had agreed to be available on the selling floor to talk informally with customers.

Ordinarily she would have been happy to make the trip even if it meant leaving Matt for a day or two. She wanted contact with her customers, wanted to see the way women dressed outside of New York, and wanted to talk seriously about her craft with people who were interested. There was another reason, however, why she had to be grateful for the booking.

Her relationship with Ira was coming apart at the seams; she was terrified to think their business partnership could collapse at the same time.

She promised herself that when she returned, she'd face the problem of Ira Gregory head on, find out what was bothering him, and tell him their affair was over.

She arrived at the store a little before noon. Just inside the main entrance she found an easel supporting a flattering poster announcing her appearance. The department store was modern, painted in soft hues, and pleasantly scented with a new fragrance being promoted that was light and dry, with a French floral undertone. Six mannequins in the center aisle were dressed in Kate Hayden evening gowns.

A vice president awaited her in the designer department, a tall, chic blonde in very high heels that brought her to well over six feet. She was dressed in a fitted Saint Laurent suit and, like Marguerite, heavy gold brace-lets clanged ceaselessly about her wrist. The department buyer, who was

younger and a great deal smaller, wore Kate Hayden, a bias-cut black silk
jersey with a skirt that flared below the knees into a tulip shape.

"My favorite," the buyer announced in a New York accent and with a
mischievous grin on a round, pugnosed face.

"I designed it with you in mind," Kate said, an untruth that nevertheless
went down well. They had met on a previous buying trip to New York and
had quickly established a friendly working relationship.

Before the show, Kate stopped in the buyer's office and checked her sales
figures. She found them typical; her day dresses and evening looks had better
sell-through than her sports clothes.

The show was to be held in a center aisle where a runway bordered by
several rows of gilt chairs had been set up. With only one customer in her
boutique, a faint panic began. Was this a ball to which no one would come?

In the dressing room they found the models in various stages of dress.

"Oops," Kate said of a skirt that looked too short, "I've a suspicion somebody's been hiking up the skirt."

The model, on her own, had turned the waistband up, hidden by the boxy
overblouse. "Ah," she said, disappointed, "I like them very short."

"Not with that top," Kate explained. "The look's out of whack."

She helped the fashion coordinator accessorize the fashions, agreeing to
most of what had already been done, but speaking her mind when she disagreed. At five to one she went back outside. Miraculously all the seats were
taken and there were standees at the back. She fished her notes out of her
bag and was suddenly very glad she had come.

Kate was back in her hotel room at ten o'clock, after having been feted by
the merchandise manager and vice president. She found two baskets of flowers in the room, one from Ira, the other from the department store. Seeing
Ira's name on the card only served to annoy her. Damn, she was thinking too
much without coming to a decision about just how to handle the man. She
kicked her shoes off and left a trail of garments into the bathroom. Thinking
too much without real action; that was it. When she returned to New York
she was going to take charge of her life. She showered, came back out, lay
down, and had to stop herself from placing her third call to her son. She'd see
him around noon, scarcely fourteen hours away.

The day, after all, had gone well. She was carving a niche for herself in a
crowded market. Women wanted well-made, easy-moving clothes that were
stylish and yet had a special slant, with unique but subtle colors and beautiful
fabrics. She'd been moved by the flattery and interest of her customers.

She lay back and switched on the television set, feeling somewhat ap-
peased. Flipping around the dial, Kate settled for a nature program on birds

and fell asleep almost at once. She awakened suddenly to the sound of people cheering. She discovered that an hour had passed. A news program was on, the cheering, local excitement over a college basketball game. With the commercial break, she began to drift off to sleep again.

"Now for national news." Kate stirred, opened her eyes and reached for the remote control. The announcer's voice was solemn with no hint of a Texas accent. "Federal marshals today moved swiftly into New York City's garment industry where they arrested Ira Gregory, chief executive officer of a fashion house called Kate Hayden. The government has been mounting an attack on mob infiltration into New York's fashion trade, and Gregory is the first to be indicted under the RICO law."

Kate felt a pain hit her stomach with such force she couldn't breathe. She sat up, her eyes glued to the screen as Ira and his attorney made their way out of the courthouse. He smiled with his usual assurance and headed for his Mercedes at the curb. She lost the announcer's last words; the picture flashed to a commercial. Pete Frank had moved into the garment industry to fight corruption and of all the fish he might have netted, the one he had apparently cast for was Ira Gregory.

"Sixty-third and Madison, please," Kate said, settling into the cab. The hustle of the airline terminal still jarred her nerves. She had taken the first flight out of Houston, numb with the fear of losing Matt and of having to deal with her ex-husband's inevitable threats to take her son away because of the notoriety. Nor had she any idea whether her business was intact or federal marshals moved in. She knew just enough about RICO to understand that a company's assets could be confiscated by the government under the law. And worse, Kate was furious at herself for ignoring the business end. Just like that, her life was in disarray.

The taxi maneuvered the circling roads out of La Guardia Airport, as a plane nosed up into the midnight sky, taillights blinking, the roar of its engines announcing dominance over the heavens. She watched the plane grow smaller, heading inland, to disappear somewhere beyond the Manhattan skyline.

She thought about how huge the world was and how many ways there were to make one's way in it. Seventh Avenue wasn't even a dot on the map. Damn Ira. Her greatest fear was that it would all be taken away.

Nor had she forgotten David Orenstein's article about mob control of the trucking industry and that she was Holly Good. Holly Dumb, perhaps, closing her eyes to everything but her feelgood exercises in creativity. She had a child to care for, and she was unforgivably careless with her life. She, who always judged ChiChi so harshly. More to the point, she wondered whether Ira had made her a scapegoat.

"Sign here. Sign there. Let's have your J. Hancock." Ira had shoved papers under her nose and she had signed without asking too many questions.

"You design, I run interference," he would say on the rare occasions when she questioned him.

He had dismissed Orenstein's article with a laugh. "He's a dummy, which is why he's making no money writing articles and you're going to own the world."

"You said Sixty-third and Madison," the driver called over his shoulder as they crossed the Fifty-ninth Street bridge into Manhattan.

"Right." She would go home, look in on her son, and then take a hot bath. She needed to hold Matt's sweet little body close and tell him that Mommy would take care of everything. He'd look at her uncomprehendingly. His head would fall to her shoulder. She felt moisture behind her eyes and knew in another moment the tears would come. She had come rushing back because staying another minute in Houston would have been torture, but now she was racing toward her son as if solace lay there.

Her ex would have heard the news report and she hadn't even worked out an adequate response to the call he'd certainly make. And she'd have to deal with her housekeeper's questions. The idea of arriving home when she wasn't expected, of having to face Jeannette before talking to Ira, was suddenly distasteful.

She thought of turning up at Marguerite's or Ralley's, but it was nearing three in the morning. The alternative was a hotel or the couch in her office. It was, she decided, no contest.

She tapped on the window, catching the cabbie's eye in the rearview mirror. "I've changed my mind," she said. "I'd like to go to Seventh Avenue and Fortieth Street."

She leaned back. There was no point in fooling herself. She had raced back to New York to see for herself whether Kate Hayden was still standing, whether the police had posted a notice on the front door or had the lock changed. If under RICO the government could confiscate the property of the person indicted, did she qualify as the *goods* of Ira Gregory?

The taxi turned onto the deserted block. "Which building?" the driver asked.

She pointed. "That one. It's all right, I've worked late before. It's open."

"I'll wait until you go inside." She paid the driver gratefully, adding a lavish tip, then grabbed her suitcase, and went to the front entrance. The taxi stayed at the curb. She had to ring the bell several times before rousing the night watchman.

"Harry, it's me," she said, peering through the glass.

"Oh, Miss Hayden, late for you, isn't it?" He unlocked the door. She heard the cab pull away from the curb.

"My show's in a week," she told him as he walked her to the freight elevator at the rear of the building. "I just came in from Houston and I'm wide awake. Thought I'd get a little work in."

He looked at her briefly and she wondered whether he had heard about Ira as well. "Want me to take you up? Charlie's off having his break," he said, referring to the regular night operator.

"No, everything's fine, Harry, thanks. I can handle it. I have often enough," she added, giving him a conspiratorial smile about Charlie's regular night breaks.

When the elevator came to a stop on her floor, Kate pried open the heavy gate. She stepped out into the shipping area, now empty of cartons and racks of clothes. She stood for a few seconds staring at the doors behind the reception desk. No tape, and no change of lock as far as she could tell. She carefully unlocked the doors, stepped into the shipping department and found it looking as it always did. Lights were always left on at night throughout the building, but the silence, the absence of familiar sounds, added an additional threat to her shredded nerves.

She went through shipping to the pattern room and then hesitantly crossed it, touching patterns and muslin, gazing at her sketches tacked to the wall. The sewing room hadn't been swept clean of bits and pieces of fabric and some machines still had fabric under the needle.

The accessory room just beyond was filled with shelves, each stacked with overflowing boxes of buttons, bows, belts, ribbons, anything that could possibly be attached to a garment. She discovered a shipment of shoes from Maud Frizon. She opened a box that held a fine pair of black suede pumps. Ira had recently been after Kate to design a line of shoes, but she had resisted for the time being. Now she supposed it was too late. Everything was too late, perfume, a bridge line, Kate Hayden for Saks. She covered the shoes with tissue paper and put the box down. She was touching things as if the life force flowing through her would somehow transfer to them, keeping them safe from harm.

Then, unexpectedly, a noise drifted back that set her heart pounding. She remained very still, trying to trace the source. Another sound, almost like a rumble of laughter, erupted from the direction of the company offices on the other side of the reception room. She crept quietly out of the accessory room into the corridor.

A laugh she identified as a woman's was joined by the deep sound of male chuckling. Certain it emanated from Ira's corner office, Kate wondered if he was there with his wife and friends. Possibly he was collecting some papers. She checked her watch. It was nearly 3:00 A.M. She hesitated, but another laugh, joined by more male laughter, breathless panting, and a woman's satisfied moan, stilled her heart. She headed almost unwittingly toward his office.

Somehow Kate knew what she would find but still she moved forward like a soldier in battle trained to advance no matter what the cost.

The door to Ira's office was slightly ajar, enough for her to see the sofa, its cushions thrown to the floor and three naked people thrashing around. She turned away, wanting to believe they were perfect strangers who thought the office empty and decided to spend the night. But even as the wish formed, she knew it for what it was, an invention designed to hide the truth. She recognized Ira's laugh, his sexual growl. She turned slowly to the scene again.

Ira's attorney, Len Burroughs, lay on his back, a girl, no more than a teenager, bending over him. He kneaded her breasts as she took his penis into her mouth and sucked vigorously. His head was thrown back and his mouth drawn tight in a rictus of passion even as his body bucked and he released himself into the girl's mouth.

Ira was in profile, behind the girl, entering her from the rear, slapping her buttocks and pummeling furiously. Then he reached under and grabbed her breasts. She lifted her face to the ceiling and gave a low, guttural cry as she twisted under the assault.

To Kate, watching mesmerized, they seemed to be engaged in a weird and terrible tribal rite. Wanting desperately to cut and run, the same powerful force that kept her rooted to the spot drove her to see it through, to recognize Ira for what he was. But what in hell had she expected?

Everything seemed to empty out of Kate, leaving a void that didn't even fill with anger. Ira laughed, a laugh she always thought of as dangerous. Now it had a mean, unholy ring. He withdrew from the girl, seized her and threw her on her back, straddling her, pressing down on her breasts. She laughed and arched back. Len slipped to the floor, watching them on his haunches.

Kate stopped breathing. The girl giggled and then began to tease Ira's penis with her mouth. He smiled at Burroughs, then spread her legs and plunged in deep.

"Atta girl," he said as he rode her.

Kate felt the bile rise in her mouth. She turned and gagged, swallowing the sour taste, pressing her fist against her mouth. She was drained of emotion, a wash of perspiration already cooling her. She had to get away. All she could think of was escaping quietly and unseen. She was in the reception room when she heard the lawyer's deep, self-congratulatory voice. "One thing about you, Ira, you really know how to pull off a celebration."

Only later, when Kate was inside her quiet apartment with her son in her arms, did she feel her blood warm up again. She kissed her son and put him back in bed. Jeannette came to her bedroom door, but Kate merely shook her head and went into her darkened studio.

Something had been released in her, something that had bound, stifled, and controlled her. She had been taken in and deceived. The trouble was she had aided and abetted the deception. None of it came as a surprise. Egon said more than once that she was selling her soul to the devil for a chance at the game. Egon was right. Egon was always right.

She thought back to the three naked bodies writhing on the couch. Remembering it, she smiled. Ira was more than a fool, he was a silly fool. She began to laugh, but the laughter stuck in her throat.

CHAPTER 22

You tickets, *madame*. We're on TWA to Milan tomorrow evening at seven. I've ordered the limo for five."

Marguerite took the tickets from her assistant. "Spare me the details, Jackie. Just make certain I'm out at the right time."

"Righto, will do."

Once the door closed behind her assistant, Marguerite picked up the telephone and dialed Reuben Newcombe's office. When she reached him, she came to the point immediately.

"Reuben, I suggest we establish a board of directors pro tem until probate is finished. You know the consensus is that I take on the title of museum director, which is what Egon desired. I also suggest we name a director pro tem, and I'm prepared to handle the job for the time being with or without salary, until the terms of the will can be met."

"That's a tall order. I'll have to think about it."

"Sol Greenspan has suggested I put *VFF* on the block, and he's come up with a buyer. I've decided to accept and I want you to represent my interests. I've agreed to stay on board for a year after *VFF* is sold. Indeed, the buyer will have it no other way. I am willing to donate my time as director pro tem until the year is up."

There was a long silence from the other end. "Selling *VFF*? Marguerite, I'm knocked for a loop. You've given it careful consideration."

"I can't afford not to sell. I've been operating at a heavy loss for far too long."

"Who's the buyer?"

"Libby Publications, Martin and Lelia Farnstein."

"Not bad. How much are they paying for the privilege?"

"Reuben, call Solly, have him go into the details with you. I'm leaving tomorrow for Milan and Paris to cover the collections. I'll be back in time for New York market week and when that's finished, I expect the papers to be drawn up and ready for my signature. After that, I'd like to think Egon's ideas aren't gathering dust. There's a great deal of long-range planning to do. Am I going too fast for you?"

"Not with my trusty old computer and tape recorder on hand. But this surprises the hell out of me."

"It shouldn't. You've taken care of my interests long enough."

As soon as she disconnected, her intercom went off. "Win Smith on three," her secretary said.

"I don't know any Win Smith."

"He says he's a friend of Egon's."

"Is?"

"Was?"

"Did he say what it was about? Never mind." Marguerite punched into the call, reflecting that Egon's was still a magic name.

"Mrs. Varick? Oh, hi, I'm Win Smith." His voice was light with a pleasant lilt. "Listen, I have a favor to ask of you but before I do, I want to read something to you."

"Read something? I don't understand." Instinct told her she must be annoyed, that she had a million and one more important things to do than be read to by a stranger, yet she unexpectedly lacked the will to hang up abruptly.

"Quote," the young man went on in his pleasant voice, " 'At times I'm sorry I have such a friendly, open face.' I mean," he interjected, "I'm reading this stuff, I mean about the friendly, open face. 'At times'—I'm still reading, quote, 'At times, I'm sorry to have been the confidant of the powerful and clever, but then, what life isn't full of angst and sorrow, my own included. Marguerite hiding it all this time under that aura of sophistication, of breeding, of sheer power and determination, the Creature Alone of Mysterious Origins.' That's caps, Mrs. Varick. 'Aren't we all?' That's part of the quote, aren't we all. 'Good Lord, it's all there, the stuff of which French movies are made—the beautiful young daughter of a collaborator manages to escape the wrath of her countrymen, becomes successful *après le déluge*, marries the wealthy Pierre Varick, late of Morocco. But suddenly her world threatens to fall apart and what does the woman do to keep it together? The unthinkable. The *unthinkable*. What it took her thirty years to confess. To me, I'm afraid, forcing me to share the burden.' Mrs. Varick, are you still listening?"

The receiver slipped in a hand that had lost all feeling. She heard the voice call to her again. She grasped the receiver in both hands and held it close to her ear. "Who are you?"

"Shall I go on reading?"

"What do you want?"

"Just to do what I'm best qualified at, and I need your assistance."

"How—how much assistance?"

"Hey, not money, what do you think I am? Just your vote of confidence, Mrs. Varick. All I want is a job. A job for which I'm well qualified."

"On my staff? I'm afraid I'm no longer—"

"The new Delville Museum," he said in a jaunty tone, the tone of a salesman who knew he had clinched the sale. "I've heard the directorship is up for grabs. I'd do anything to get that job, anything."

Stefan always let himself into the apartment, and Marguerite heard him at seven that evening bolting the door, a young stallion worth every penny of the one hundred fifty dollars an hour he charged. Self-absorbed and without scruples, he was—as Cissie Crayfield, who'd recommended him, had said— the man with magic fingers. One hour was all Marguerite usually needed under the gentle kneading that rejuvenated and calmed her.

She belted her robe loosely as she went to the bedroom door.

"Ah, Margi, *ma belle,*" Stefan said, greeting her with a kiss and a few more phrases in a bold and fractured French. Stefan Vyskocil was twenty-six years old, six feet tall, golden-haired, and fit. He had left Czechoslovakia three years before and learned English quickly, retaining a sexy accent and an occasional difficulty with diphthongs that added to his mystery.

Until meeting Cissie Crayfield, Stefan supported himself as a bartender, waiter, house-sitter, soft whoring, and assorted other ways of making money, legal and illegal. He had met Cissie while auditioning for a part in a Broadway play the wealthy, socially connected woman was backing. He didn't get the part, but Cissie introduced him to a whole new way of making money. There was no end to the number of women who were creaking under the weight of age, who needed tending much as would an abandoned house plant.

Stefan was made to order for the work: he loved older women because they were no trouble at all, never facing him with tears or accusations. They were uniformly appreciative, paid him when the hour was up, and asked no questions about his life when he was away from them. His magic fingers earned him money and the freedom to pursue his acting. He was a very happy man.

"You're looking gorgeous, as usual, Margi."

"Am I?" She asked the question while absentmindedly glancing at herself in the floor-to-ceiling mirror on the closet wall of her spare bedroom.

"You know you are. You know you're ze most gorgeous of my gorgeous clients." He reached into his duffel bag and pulled out the accoutrements required for his hour with her, a cache of emoluments in fancy jars, which he arranged with a certain amount of flourish on a high enamel-top table. He then removed a small, delicate pillow and a pristine sheet, which with carefully orchestrated movements he flapped as a toreador would bait a bull.

"So you're off tomorrow for Milan, Paris, London," he said, straightening the sheet on the massage table and adding the little pillow with a slight tap.

He began to remove his clothes, stripping to his blue and red striped Calvin shorts. He was slow, ritualistic, his manner that of one who expected her to watch hungrily, to focus on the firm bulge of penis beneath the tight-fitting briefs.

He was right, Marguerite thought, her eyes on his crotch; she could relax in his silly presence, forget phone calls, forget words that threatened to reorder her world. She opened her robe in the same ritualistic way and let it drop to the floor. She stood naked, hands at her sides, feeling no constraint as the robe lay at her feet. She knew very few women her age would have the nerve to act as she did. But Marguerite had lived the last thirty years of her life in a very careful way, attending to her diet and exercise so that her body was taut and smooth, the only concession to her age a slight droop of her breasts.

Stefan's leer was both wicked and amused as he helped her onto the table. "Margi, Margi, incredible, incredible." She lay on her stomach and closed her eyes. He draped a sheet over her lower body and began a slow, methodical rubbing of her shoulders.

He kept up a steady chatter, filling her in on gossip about his clients. For an especially interesting piece of news, Marguerite would add a generous tip. He was Lelia Farnstein's masseur, as well. She thought, drowsily, that she should really ask him a few questions about the woman but found it hard to concentrate on what he was saying.

He began to spread rose-scented oil across her back. "Roses for . . . for . . . what did Ophelia say?"

His fingers melded with her flesh, producing a soporific effect that further lulled her senses. She drifted in and out of a hazy zigzag of light and dark. Stefan's voice crooned above her as he kept her from wandering off into a past whose icy claim she desperately needed to avoid.

"In her apartment she's got two dogs that are built like Sumo wrestlers." His palms pressed into her waist. "And I don't think their only job is to guard the art, if you get my drift."

"Who?" Marguerite asked dreamily.

"You're not listening, Margi." He patted her behind. *"Ecoutes, écoutes, ma chère petite."*

"Yes, I'm listening, go on. I don't want to sleep. Who are we talking about?"

"Initials, R.M. After zat, my lips are sealed. All I can tell you is she's on more intimate terms with her pit bulls than with zat jackal she married. I hope she uses condoms or she's liable to spread disease among our canine friends."

"Stefan, you're incorrigible."

He laughed, "Careful, Margi, Margi."

She could still hear Win Smith's voice. How could he know? Who would have told him? She tried to remember the media interviews she had given over the years, fudging her history as best she could, yet everyone knew she was born in France and had lived there through the Second World War. But the word "collaborator" had never come into any of those interviews. How could it? She never talked about her father, only her work with the Resistance. As for her husband, no one could possibly know.

She shivered slightly under Stefan's touch.

"I've known worse than her," he said. "Did I ever tell you about the time I was hired for that last picture what's-his-name directed? The Roman epic they shot in Wales. I was the *present* for the star after a long day before the cameras. Some film debut. She relaxed by drinking a fifth of scotch, snorting an ounce of coke, taking on half the crew, male and female, and then getting a massage."

"Who?" Marguerite asked.

Stefan gave a deep sigh. "What are you thinking about, Margi? I believe you're the favorite of all my clients. You've got a lot of character. A woman alone making her way in the world and succeeding."

"A woman alone," she murmured. She had wandered crazily out of that monastery so long ago and had never returned to Artenay, had never seen her father again. It was only after the war that she learned he had been shot by the partisans. She had gone south to Biarritz, making her way down slowly, using her good looks to buy her food and lodging until she found La Girondelle, the house of a distant aunt outside the city.

"You're all tense, Margi." Stefan brought her back again, his fingers undoing the knots in her shoulders. "I think you need to unwind. Let Stefan handle everything." His tone softened. She felt his lips on her shoulder. "Come on, Margi, loosen up." He stood against the table, bumping suggestively as his fingers dug and pressed.

She willed her mind to go blank. If she didn't drag herself back from the past, there would be no going forward. Stefan's oil-slicked palms traveled along her back, but in a moment his touch changed to slow, rhythmic strokes that held for a moment at her waist, then went running around and under her. His fingers played lightly on her breasts. She couldn't remember the last time someone had made love to her—real love, not this patting, rubbing, stabbing, the equivalent of a whorehouse visit.

"Better," his young voice crooned. "I know when Margi is relaxing." His hands moved to her legs, coursing the flesh in and around her thighs and working up across her back. She felt herself beginning to relax under the light, persuasive touch of powerful hands. She eased herself into it and closed her eyes against the memories, knowing they would never go completely away. She was merely buying some time, some precious moments her body craved. She understood why she used Stefan. She was an ancient crone trying desperately to cling to life's bitter pulses. He was available and he served a well-paid purpose. The touch of another human being was sometimes more than necessary; it was essential to keep up the pretense that her blood could still heat.

His probing fingers circled slowly, targeting in. Marguerite groaned and arched her back. He wasn't in any hurry. His trademark method was slow and methodical, giving her an extra thrill by breathing heavily in her ear and pressing his body close to hers. She could feel his penis stiff against her side. He began moving his body with a cunning beat, and she heard a low hum as though he were accompanying himself with music drumming in his brain.

His hands were busy, one under her, gently probing, the other smoothly pressing slippery fingers into her moist flesh. Marguerite gripped the table and the echo of the oily telephone voice disappeared along with the murky shadows of yesterday as Stefan quickened his pace. He worked furiously, his breath on her neck, murmuring nonsense phrases in her ear. He called her *panenko*, telling her it was Czech for little doll, just when he brought a cry of release from her lips.

After a while she heard him pack his jars, the sheet, the small pillow, which had fallen to the floor. He would let himself out as usual and she would lay supine, prolonging the ecstasy, pretending her hour with a mere boy wasn't what it seemed.

A little later she rose and slipped into her robe. She had a way of putting time on hold, of stopping action while she figured a way to redirect fate. She would not let a disembodied voice block her moves.

And in another moment Marguerite understood where her caller had learned about her, why his words had rung so familiar. He possessed Egon's journals, the journals she had been looking for, Egon to whom she had once foolishly told everything.

CHAPTER 23

N inety," Kate said. "Now comes the hard part, knocking off fifteen models minimum. We don't have any choice, Elfie. The show can't be more than seventy-five garments at this point."

"It's not fair."

"What's fair? We're fighting for our lives. We'll be lucky if the show comes off."

"Kate, you're scaring me."

Kate, bending over her worktable, didn't even try to meet her assistant's challenge. For the past two days she'd been living on nerves, unable to eat, and walking around feeling slightly nauseous.

She still could see Ira being hustled out of the courthouse by his lawyer, the smile of triumph as he stepped into his Mercedes and then writhing nude on the couch in his office. And all she experienced from the memory was self-loathing. Once she had allowed him into her life knowing he was a liar and a schemer, nothing that followed should have come as a surprise.

The time wasn't right for falling apart. She couldn't afford the luxury of curling up in a corner crying her eyes out. Afterward, she promised herself, afterward she'd kick and scream and have a dilly of a nervous breakdown. Now she had to keep her mind clear and on the project at hand, the collection had to be ready for showing in two weeks' time.

She was, in fact, consumed by the desire to show the world that she was getting on with it and that she should be judged by the collection and nothing else.

Ira hadn't been in the office for the last two days, but he had let Kate know in one terse phone call—made from home and apparently in the presence of his wife—that the company was untouched by the government's allegations and that she was to plan the upcoming show as though nothing had happened.

"But can't they take everything under RICO?" she began.

" 'Innocent until proven guilty,' " he said. "They don't have a case," he said. "They're grandstanding, that's all. It's politics, as usual, and unfortunately I'm the fish that got caught in their net." He told her he'd be tied up with lawyers for the next couple of days but that if she had any questions he'd be available to answer them.

He cautioned Kate to act as if nothing had happened; nobody was going to put him out of business with a phony indictment; he was letting the world know Kate Hayden was intact and solvent.

He offered no explanations and no excuses. His arrogance was admirable, if nothing else about him was.

She felt exhausted and overburdened but knew she had to hold on, hope the newshounds would leave Ira alone, and pretend her staff wasn't whispering behind her back and wondering whether they would collect their salaries at the end of the week.

She had delivered a pep talk when she came in that morning, and her staff's assurance that they'd stay with her as long as she needed them was a measure of their warmth and trust.

Her calendar showed a date for lunch with Ralley Littlehurst and Dick Steyman. Ira hadn't cancelled the booking at Raven's. Kate was determined to keep the date and deliberately didn't call Ralley to confirm it.

The collection had been scheduled well on the Fashion Calendar, in the middle of the first week, early in the day when buyers would be fresh and wide-eyed.

The contingent she hoped to see included Marshall Field's, Joske's, Burdine's, Saks, Bloomingdale's, and a dozen other important names. The fashion publications had promised coverage, and Marguerite had suggested a couple of wealthy women for Kate to call and invite.

The showroom could hold a hundred twenty-five people at a sitting. Gilt chairs, giveaways, coffe, tea, pastries, music, jewels, scarves, hats, shoes, stockings—the work required to present the showing in a professional manner was overwhelming and Kate was understaffed. The models she booked were popular and expensive, and the schedules of two were tight. Prior to Kate's show, they were modeling a collection across town and a mile away at the Pierre. The logistics of moving them quickly had been solved after much consultation; she ordered a limousine and damned the cost.

Added to her worries was the fear the press might not attend, perhaps deciding that Kate Hayden wouldn't be in business long enough for stores to write paper on.

That morning, before she left for work, Kate was surprised to receive a call from Switzerland, from Giovanni Daguras, president of DAS, who assured her they were backing her one hundred percent.

"I hope you'll be here to see the presentation," she said.

"Yes, of course, all is possible."

All was possible. Tim had called her the evening before, asking for an explanation of what was going on.

She had felt her usual irritation with her former husband. His self-righteous tone dated from before their marriage, a certainty about the way he ran his life and the way he expected her life to go. Her ambition was only one of the reasons for their divorce. His stiff-necked personality was the other. "I'm afraid you know as much as I," she told him coldly, "if you've been watching the evening news. I'm sure you saw the interview with the Manhattan D.A. He said the Justice Department has no case."

"Somehow I don't buy that, Kate. I'm only interested in one thing and that's my son's mental health."

"Don't worry about your son's mental health. He's fine and he's happy. Don't look for trouble where there isn't any."

"I'm not looking for it, Kate, but perhaps you are."

She had hung up, knowing there was a grain of truth in what he said. She had sat staring at the phone, wondering whether to call Marguerite, her mother, or Egon. ChiChi was in Europe, Marguerite was out of town, and calling Egon required a spiritualist. She wondered how she could have an ounce of humor left in her.

Spread on the wall were Kate's lighthearted color sketches of the ninety garments in the collection, ranging from tailored dresses for business to evening clothes. Each sketch also held swatches of fabric and trim, as well as buttons, accessories, and the name of the model scheduled to wear the garment.

"Let's go, everybody." Kate turned to her secretary. "Take careful notes, because the way things are going, I'll forget what I said as soon as I've said it."

"Kate, do you think—" her secretary began.

"Everything's going to be all right. Let's just stick to the matter at hand." My life, she thought, that's all.

"Ten evening gowns," Elfie noted, coming in quickly, as though to defuse the moment. "We don't want to butt any of them out."

"Right. I wanted more, actually. But let's start with the suits. Let's see, I was never too nuts about number 5106, that's Desk Set. Neither here nor there." She referred to a tailored suit in a lightweight taupe linen and rayon suiting. She fingered the sample of fabric attached to it, then abruptly felt as though a light hand had touched her shoulder. She remembered discussing the fabric with Egon. He had disliked it intensely, picking up the small sample and wrinkling his nose in distate.

"The fifties were my time, Kate, and I can think of a lot of things I miss about it, but rayon . . . . ?"

"What's wrong with rayon? Mixed with the linen, it has a nice hand, takes color gorgeously, there's a lot less creasing and frankly you can't tell the difference except in the price."

He had stepped back, giving her his astonished look, forming a moue with his expressive mouth. "Nickle and diming your customers, Kate?"

"It's not the fifties, Egon. They're doing exciting things with rayon now. And there's a lot to be said for a linen suit that doesn't look as if it's been slept in five minutes after you put it on."

"The color looks washed out."

"It's supposed to look that way. Good Lord, you're a pain in the neck."

Out of pique she had ordered a sample cut because she wanted total control of her line. She made up the suit and now decided Egon was right, perhaps not about the rayon but about the way the suit had turned out. She'd been spooked from the start.

"This one goes," she said.

"Too fifties," her seamstress said. "Donna What's-her-name, the actress, wearing a wide-brimmed hat and carrying this huge bag under her arm—I can see it all now. Pocketbooks, they called them in those days, pocketbooks. Cute."

Kate groaned. Certainly spooked by Egon.

By eleven in the morning they had discarded nine pieces. Kate couldn't make up her mind about the rest. When a phone call came in she ordered a break and fresh coffee.

Ralley was at the other end. "Dick Steyman's a little prick, and that's for publication in case the operator's listening in."

"He wants to cancel lunch," Kate said. She'd been resigned to the call, knowing instinctively it was only a matter of time.

"Never mind. I told him he couldn't. Dick's too much of a gentleman to make a fuss. How are you holding up?"

"Fine. The Justice Department has made mistakes, you know." She thought of Pete Frank and knew he was a man who didn't make mistakes, not professionally, anyway.

"Don't worry about it. Dick's smitten with you even if he's a married man and doesn't know it, so smile at him in that way you have. Is there anything I can do?"

"Yes. Make sure we get the order."

"See you later, Katie Kat."

Raven's was crowded as usual, with a line of people at the door waiting to be seated. The noise level was in the high decibels, but the cheerfulness of the place was contagious. Crystal chandeliers glistened, walls were decorated with framed designer sketches, and there were vases of fresh flowers on each table. Kate smiled at the maître d' when he greeted her profusely. Like Kate, the customers were apt to be in the garment industry, and she nodded to a few acquaintances on the way to Ira's reserved table at a corner window. Smiles were a little rigid: they not only knew about Ira but worried they'd be next.

Ralley and Dick Steyman were already seated and deep in conversation. "Hi, you two." Kate stuck her hand out to Dick Steyman, who gave her an uncomfortable smile, his eyes darting with fury to Ralley for getting him into the situation. Kate leaned over and planted a kiss on Ralley's cheek.

"We started without you." Ralley pointed to her drink. "Where's the boss?"

"He'll be along. I like your suit, Ralley." Kate made the remark with a forced smile. The slim-line suit was from her fall collection, the jacket a collarless sliver of steel gray wool crepe with a side closing, and a narrow skirt.

"The designer has a lot of talent," Ralley said.

"Oh, she'll go far, no doubt about that." Kate noted the dark circles under Ralley's eyes and for a moment forgot that the world didn't revolve around her and her troubles. She'd have to call Ralley, have a long talk with her.

"What'll you drink?" Dick asked.

"White wine." He was too nervous. She felt the hatchet about to fall. "Sorry about Ira," she said, not even certain whether he would show up. "He's always very scrupulous about time."

"I have to tell you the truth," Dick said once her wine order was given. "You know how Steyman Senior feels about scandal."

"He runs a very uptight Republican catalog," Ralley threw in, dipping a celery stick into her Bloody Mary.

Dick shook his head lightly, catching Kate's eye as though she'd agree with him that Ralley was brilliant but crazy.

"Innocent until proven guilty," Ralley said. "The company will stay in business, and that's all Steyman Senior should care about."

Kate, glancing out the window, saw Ira's Mercedes pull over to the curb directly in front of the restaurant in a No Parking zone. She felt a thud in her heart and froze. She wasn't a good actress, and all she wanted to do was cut and run.

Ira stepped out of the car and had a word with his two associates in the front seat. It occurred to Kate that the action was characteristic and that she'd never paid attention to it before. As he headed toward the restaurant he gave a seemingly casual glance up and down the street. She even noted his easy saunter, his self-possession. He was totally unruffled, and she prayed that he would make things easy for all of them.

He greeted them with a smile for Kate and a kiss on the cheek for Ralley. Kate even had the impression that everything was settled and she had nothing to worry about.

"Sorry I'm late," he told them. He offered no excuses. She realized, not for the first time, that he possessed a kind of aura that riveted everyone in the room, and that even Dick Steyman relaxed a little. "Have you ordered?" Ira asked, nodding at the waiter who hurried over, his eyes glinting in an impassive face.

"We were waiting for you," Dick said.

Ira ordered a drink and another round for his guests. With the waiter's departure there was a moment of awkward silence. Then Ralley said, "Kate assures us it's business as usual."

"It always was."

"Steyman Senior sells the American Dream to millions of American women," Dick said. "You can't blame him for worrying about scandal."

"I don't blame him at all," Ira said. "Is there a scandal?"

Dick backed away immediately, reaching for his drink, clearly waiting for Ralley to lighten the mood.

Instead, Kate jumped in. "I had the oddest notion today that Egon was alive. I was culling the spring line with my staff and suddenly there he was, hand on my shoulder, reminding me of an argument we'd had over a piece of fabric."

"Who won?" Ralley asked.

"The argument? Egon, of course. I banished the design, after all."

"Marguerite said she almost dialed him on the phone last week," Ralley remarked.

"He's still pulling your strings," Ira said. "I never could see what the man meant to you, any of you."

"Fascinating character," Dick said. "Even Steyman Senior was impressed with him."

Ordinary conversation, Kate thought. Just four people on an ordinary day having an ordinary business lunch. She glanced out the restaurant window; even the weather was picking up. The Mercedes was still sitting in the No Parking zone. A policeman stopped and tapped the window. The window came down. He had a few words with the man on the passenger side and then moved on. The Mercedes stayed.

She watched idly as two well-dressed men came toward the restaurant. She studied their clothes—business suits that looked brand-new and were meant to impress with their cost. One wore a carnation in his lapel. As they passed the Mercedes, she saw one of them slide his eyes over to the passenger side. The man sitting there lifted a hand in greeting.

Then the Mercedes started up and eased away. Puzzled, she turned to Ira, but he was deep in conversation with Dick and Ralley.

The men came into the restaurant and nodded at the maître d', then headed swiftly toward Kate's table. There was a disconcerting feel to their fierce concentration on Ira, whose back was to them.

"Ira," she began, but before she could say another word, both men whipped guns from their jackets and fired at Ira.

A scream started in her throat. She gagged on it and pushed her hand into her mouth. Kate felt the warm splash of blood and gore strike her. Ira's head seemed to have exploded. He slumped to the floor. Around her the restaurant began to shift and move, although there was a sharp edge to the scene that made its way into her mind with mechanical precision. She heard screams and the sounds of people running.

Kate leapt to her feet, operating on sheer instinct. Dick Steyman, in horror, had pushed his chair back and was escaping to the far end of the room. Ralley was kneeling over Ira, the expression on her face as impassive and cold as a nurse in time of war.

Kate bent down in a trance. Ralley shook her head and opened her mouth. Kate supposed she said something but had no idea what. There was nothing left of the face she had kissed so many times. She reached out and touched Ira's shoulder and spoke his name again and again in a low chant.

He was dead. She wondered why all she felt was emptiness and a sense of not being surprised; of accepting the inevitable. The violence that had been a part of him had surfaced at last, although not in the way she'd expected. Her breath caught in her throat. She was in a nightmare that had turned real. Ira was gone and she was beyond feeling. That was when she heard the sharp, heartrending scream that tore from deep within her.

"Pete, come on in. Guess bad news travels fast."

From behind his cluttered desk at the Nineteenth Precinct, Captain Patrick Mallory motioned Pete to a chair. A twenty-year veteran of the New York City police force, Mallory was a big man with a broad, smooth face and an easy, familiar manner that Pete knew from previous experience could go hard in an instant.

"Here you Feds go and indict a guy," Mallory went on in his deep, nasa voice that told anyone familiar with New York just what part of Queens came from, "ten minutes later he gets it in broad daylight right in front half the city. Tut, tut, sloppy, sloppy. Kind of knocks your case right out the water doesn't it?"

"Not yet. There's a tie-in needs going into with the Swiss owner."

"The Manhattan D.A.'s sending someone over," Mallory said. "We can have a regular party. I hear you were at each other's throats over this one."

"Nah, don't believe everything you hear," Pete remarked. "We're working together to uphold law and order."

The captain gave a gruff laugh and rubbed his hand over his chin. "If I believe that, I believe in Santa Claus."

Pete knew they were questioning Kate somewhere close by. He was holding himself in, trying not to run to her rescue from a couple of cops who might think it cute to come down hard. Ira Gregory's murder was a prize that had fallen into their laps and if they could beat both the D.A. and Justice to a happy conclusion, it might mean promotions or at least the gratitude of the higher-ups. He took the stick of gum Mallory silently pushed across the desk, and gazed around the gloomy office.

The air in the station house was stiflingly heavy, saturated with the accumulated odors of ancient cigar smoke, the moldy rags of aggressive derelicts picked up for panhandling, and a thousand unsuccessful attempts at fumigation. Mallory's office wasn't much better despite an open window behind his desk.

Pete had been at the office when the report of Ira Gregory's murder came in. His first reaction was a sickening jolt in the pit of his stomach; if Gregory had been killed gangland style, then Pete bore some responsibility. His second reaction shocked him even more. Gregory was shot in a restaurant during a business lunch. He panicked, thinking that Kate might have been with him and might now be lying in a pool of blood. It took him five minutes to discover she hadn't been hit and precisely where she was. He raced out of the office before Tess had a chance to stop him.

"I understand the police were on the scene within minutes of the shooting," Pete said, already knowing the answer. "Get anything useful?"

Mallory shook his head. "Classic hit. Two fellows walk in, pull out Glock 17's and ruin all those expense account appetites. You should have seen the place. Some fag decorator's going to have to work overtime to get the establishment ready for tomorrow's lunch crowd."

Pete gave a low whistle over the use of the weapon that could fire seventeen rounds at a clip. "Glock 17's, state of the art. They could've blown away the entire restaurant if anyone made a wrong move. Get a make on them?"

Mallory shook his head. "You know the story. The restaurant was filled to capacity, yet most of the diners said they didn't see a thing, didn't notice a thing, were looking at their soup or the other way. The waiters gave us the usual schizo array of portraits." His broad laugh let Pete know they were on the same side. "Tall and short," Mallory went on, warming to the subject,

"fat and skinny, black and white, naked and dressed in tuxedos. Out of the lot we're hoping to find two that match and we can use."

"Let's see, you're questioning Gregory's business partner, Kate Hayden, right?"

Mallory nodded. "Right. She was with him and two buyers. A Miss Littlehurst and Mr. Steyman. He's the son of the owner of Steyman's—that's a big catalog house—and he let us know his father dines with the mayor, the governor, and the President of the United States, all at the same time. We managed to act impressed and questioned them both and let them go. Steyman was incoherent and told three different stories in succession. Littlehurst was facing away from the door and saw nothing until the shots were fired and even then caught only their backs."

"Have you been bombarded by the media yet?"

"You mean you didn't have to push your way through them to get here?"

"They thought I was the plumber."

"We questioned most of the witnesses in the restaurant, then let them go. We have a description from Gregory's partner, however. Kate Hayden saw everything. Saw the killers outside the restaurant, saw them come in, saw them head for the table, saw them blow Ira Gregory apart." To Pete's look of curiosity, Mallory added an explanation. "They were seated at a corner table. She had a view through the window and of the entrance."

"What about the diners at adjoining tables?"

"Everyone was into his wild rice and arugula salad and don't know nothing. Even the maître d' and headwaiter offered different descriptions." Once again Captain Mallory shook his head over the inability of the human mind to register facts precisely. "Would you believe a waiter standing near the door opened it for the killers so they could exit like real gentlemen?"

"I guess he figured they wouldn't be staying for lunch."

It took a moment for the joke to get through to Mallory. Then he grinned. "The way I read it," he said, warming up, clearly in his element and appreciating his audience, "the two torpedos were probably imported. The M.O. doesn't read like local talent. My guess is they caught the next flight out and are sipping martinis, even as we speak, poolside at the Mexico City Hilton. Whoever ordered the hit was broadcasting a message," he added. "I can think of half a dozen offhand, but you already know exactly what that message is, Pete. How about sharing it?"

Pete's gaze was level. He shook his head almost imperceptibly. "We indicted Ira Gregory under RICO; he was out of the federal courthouse in record time, and we were putting the case on the docket. That's all a matter of public record. Somebody figured he was a loose cannon and he'd be better dead and read about in the evening news."

"Think the order came from overseas?"

"Let's see who his godfather was first." Pete got slowly to his feet. "I'd like to talk to your witness now."

"Hayden?"

"She the only one you have?"

"The only one admitting to having seen the whole business from start to finish."

"I'd like to see her now."

"We've done your work for you," Mallory said, but got to his feet and opened his office door. "The lady's a bundle of nerves, but my guess is she examined the killers so closely that they're engraved on her memory. Which, incidentally, is food for thought." He led Pete down the corridor to the interrogation room.

"Paul, Mickey, this is Pete Frank. He's with the Justice Department," he said to the two men with Kate. "He'd like a word with Miss Hayden." Pete came briskly into the room, an airless cubicle, reeking of cigarette smoke. There were four straight-backed oak chairs around a table heavily scarred with initials, hearts and flowers, and some imaginative curses. The table also held several half-empty containers of cold coffee and an overflowing ashtray.

Kate sat at the far side of the table, her two interrogators opposite her, guns holstered and sleeves rolled up. Even in the yellow light bouncing eerily off stone-gray walls, Pete could see the bloodstains that were spattered on her pale wool suit. Her hands were in her lap, folded into tight fists. She held her head stiffly erect, as if one movement would shatter her control. She cast her eyes over Pete without the slightest hint of recognition. For a moment he thought she was in a catatonic state, then realized there was deep anger burning in her that had gone beyond pity or fear and that she was doing all she could to control it.

Jesus, they were pitiless, he thought of the two cops. She had, not an hour or two before, seen a man blown away, and they were expecting her to be calm, cool, and informative. But then, they couldn't know what he did, that she must be chewed up inside; to them Gregory was only her business partner.

The cops got to their feet reluctantly and just as reluctantly left the room with Mallory. The door closed behind them. Pete sat down at the table opposite Kate. She did not move. He was no longer certain what he wanted to say or know. He let the long silence lengthen between them.

"Am I being held for something?" she asked at last. "Material witness or something?"

"No." He got to his feet, scraping his chair back. "I wanted to hear the story from your own lips, but come on, I'll take you home."

Kate stood up obediently and drew her fingers through her hair. She reached for her bag and stalked over to the door, waiting silently while he opened it, then walking at his side down the corridor. He stopped at the captain's office, knocked briefly at the door before opening it. He found Mallory at his desk. "I'm taking Miss Hayden home now."

Once they were out of the station, however, Kate's demeanor changed abruptly.

"Mr. Peter Frank of the Justice Department. I think somehow I expected you to show up. You were behind Ira's arraignment, weren't you?"

Pete took her arm and tried to draw her down the street. "Come on, I'll take you home. You want answers; I'll give them to the best of my knowledge."

"First the IRS, then the indictment, and now this. And all the while you're hovering in the background like an avenging angel. I hope you don't have a decent night's sleep for the rest of your life." She turned and started to walk away from him, but he caught up to her, took her arm, and forced her to face him.

"Kate, cool it. They had you holed up in that place too long. You haven't had a chance to cry or rage. You want to pommel me to pieces or scream, go right ahead, I'm here for you."

She pulled out of his grasp. "I don't need you, dammit. I can take care of myself. I always have."

"Come on." He kept his voice calm and reasonable and suddenly all the fight went out of her. She allowed herself to be led around the corner where he'd parked the car grabbed out of the motor-pool. He opened the door and helped her in and closed the door softly. He saw her bend over, saw the tears begin to form, and turned his back while she cried helplessly behind the glass.

After five minutes, he went around to the driver's side and opened the door. He climbed in and put his key in the ignition. He heard her take in several gulps of air and, when he turned to her, found her gaze on him. Her eyes were red-rimmed, and her makeup had worn off. He felt like telling her she was beautiful, but some trace of sanity held him off.

"Tell me what you know now," she said.

He shook his head. "In time."

"I never saw so much blood in my life." She spoke so softly that Pete had to lean forward to hear her. "And it was all over so quickly. You'd think a human being would have a moment to contemplate what was happening, to know it was coming to an end, to say something, make things right."

"Make what things right, Kate?"

She didn't answer him for a long time, then said, "You know exactly why he died."

"I only know that he played with the wrong people in the wrong sand pile."

"He said the Justice Department didn't have a case against him."

"Kate, we indicted him under the RICO law. We have proof that he was involved in a scheme to launder money through—"

"Oh, my God," she said, burying her face in her hands. "Please, I believed him when he said it wasn't true, I believed him. How could it happen? We operate like any other dress house. Buyers come in from established stores. They place orders, we make up the clothes, deliver them. How can we launder money?"

"We have reasons to believe not every order was legitimate." Dammit, he thought, she'd better be innocent. He was climbing out on a limb with no place to go but down.

She stared at him, her mouth open, slightly moist. He wanted to reach over and push a wisp of hair away from her face. "I just never . . ." she began, then stopped, her shoulders drooping. "Does this mean the end of my company? I mean, should I call a lawyer? What kind of trouble am I in?"

"Kate, the government doesn't want to put anyone out of business except racketeers and criminals. The only thing we can be glad about is that you're safe." He turned away and switched the ignition on. "Come on, we can discuss this later."

"Why didn't they kill me?" she asked calmly.

"Because they're professionals and they don't get a kick out of killing. It's the kind of work they do and they don't pile up bodies for the thrill of it and they don't take prisoners. You obviously aren't a threat, despite what you witnessed. If you were, I'd be staring at you in the morgue right now."

"Ira left a wife and two kids. I suppose a couple of policemen just turned up at her door."

"It would be better than catching it on the six o'clock news." He eased the car into traffic. "Where's your son?"

"What day is it?" She shook her head groggily. "Oh, right, Wednesday. He's with my housekeeper. Wednesday she takes him to some kiddie movies at the museum. They should be back around dinnertime."

Pete headed across town; fortunately, the late afternoon rush hadn't begun. Fifteen minutes later he parked in a diplomat's space on East Sixty-third Street and helped Kate out.

She stood for a moment, her hand in his. "I'd like to see you safe inside your apartment," he told her. She said nothing, just extricated her hand and went into her building. He followed her through the lobby, into the elevator, and up to her apartment. When she opened the door she still said nothing. He came in and she pointed to the living room and left him.

In her big comfortable living room, he pushed aside a teddy bear and some picture books and took a seat on a chintz-covered sofa. The coffee table was covered with magazines and art books. A large abstract painting in soft water-colors hung above the sofa. White gauzy curtains at the window brought the late day sun into a homey room. Its slightly disarranged air was proof that the child was king and his comfort uppermost in Kate's mind; its unfinished look indicated that this was the living space of an artist who used her creative energies elsewhere.

While Kate disappeared into her bedroom, Pete thumbed through several issues of *Women's Wear Daily* and then some fashion magazines thick with Christmas advertising.

He'd been waiting for a quarter of an hour when the telephone next to him rang. After four rings, the answering machine clicked in with the audio on. He heard the caller, Annalise Michelis, ask Kate in a warm accented voice, to call her back. He remembered the name after a moment. Jaybee had pointed her out at the funeral, the blonde in a big hat whose face he never saw. After a few minutes the phone rang again and again the machine clicked in. In succession he listened to calls from Marguerite Varick, Jaybee Olsen, someone named Tim who sounded angry—her ex-husband, Pete thought—and members of Kate's office staff. He dug his hands into his pockets, went over to the window, and stared mindlessly down at the traffic for a long while.

When Kate came back out half an hour later, she wore a flowered kimono. Her dark hair was damp and hung limp on her shoulders. Her eyes hadn't recovered from the crying jag, unless, Pete decided, she'd had another in private.

The phone rang once again and Kate glanced at Pete before reaching for the receiver.

"Yes? Oh, hello Ralley." Her voice sounded dead. "I'm okay. Just got home. I'm okay, but I'm worried about you. You're sure you're all right." She cast another glance at Pete, who came back and sat down on the couch. He picked up a children's book and leafed through the pages. "Look, someone's with me at the moment. Let me call you back. . . . I don't know, in a half-hour or so. Are you at home?"

She replaced the receiver. "Can I get you some coffee, something?" she asked Pete.

He shook his head.

"They gave me coffee at the station house," she said.

"And a good grilling."

She managed a smile, then sat down in an upholstered armchair, tucking her legs under her. "I'm afraid so. They were very polite, though."

"The police in New York are much maligned."

"Am I still in business?" The question was posed in a direct way, her eyes on his. "I have to get in touch with my staff and it would help if I knew whether or not they have jobs."

"Keep operating," he said.

"Just like that."

"The RICO law is still too new to say things must be handled this way or that. My guess is the court will appoint a conservator until the details can be worked out. I've said it before and I'll say it again, the government doesn't want Kate Hayden to go out of business. It makes no sense to have forty people on the dole because the owner of the company was using it to transport tainted money. But while the case against your partner no longer exists, we have to find out whether there was collusion between the owners of the company, DAS, and Gregory." And you, he wanted to add, although the idea pained him.

"Can I pay my personnel?"

"Do you know anything about your company's finances?"

She pressed her lips together and looked away. "I can't tell you how much we have in accounts payable, although I suppose I can recite every account we have, how much in orders, how much about to be delivered, and how much in accounts receivable, paid and due." She turned back and gave him a sudden embarrassed smile. "I don't think you understand how tied up I am in what I do. But Ira handled—" She stopped, her eyes filling with tears.

"All right, we don't have to go on with this," he began.

"It would be no use explaining, anyway, how much I want the company to work."

"Try me."

She shook her head slowly. "I just saw my partner murdered. I can't get the sight out of my eyes."

"Kate, do you want me to call someone to stay with you?"

"No."

Studying her, watching the play of late afternoon light shadowing her face, Pete had no way of knowing whether those rumors about Kate Hayden and Ira Gregory were true. They were true, dammit. He'd be a fool to pretend otherwise. He found himself wondering what she was like in bed, knowing he was going to fall in love with her, that he was halfway there. The thought excited him. He had been down the road a few times, but now it had taken a different turn. His wife was one sort of woman, Kate another. There was no truth to the belief that one was attracted to the same sort of woman over and over. Pete had learned a lot in his years alone, ridding himself of a past that didn't work.

"I'm sorry," she said suddenly. "I was replaying the scene, trying to figure out why I didn't know what was about to happen." Her brow creased in a puzzled frown. "But you know, I did, I mean in a way. The killers knew Ira's men—incidentally, one wore a flower in his lapel, a carnation. I started to say something to Ira, but it was too late."

"Could be the carnation was the signal. Carnation to Mercedes, a hand signal to a shift of eyes, meaning Gregory was there, in Raven's."

She closed her eyes. He imagined her reliving the scene once again. "You have to go, you know," she said abruptly, without opening her eyes. "My son will be home soon and I still have the evening to get through, calls to make, things to do."

He got to his feet and pulled out his card case. "If you need me at any time, you can reach me at this number, or this one. . . ." He scribbled his home number and address down.

She took the card and touched the edge to her lips. "When am I to expect the conservator?"

"You'll get a call from the Justice Department tomorrow."

"A conservator means someone will be sitting on my shoulder all the time."

"Figuratively speaking."

"Damn." She gave a mirthless laugh. "That isn't what it sounds like. I've tried to keep myself free of artistic interference, but I don't seem to be destined that way at all."

"Did Gregory give you a hard time?"

"Are you always going to misinterpret what I say?"

"Not always."

She went past him into the hall, then turned uncertainly. "Look, thanks for picking me up at the precinct. I'm not certain I could have made it back here on my own."

"Kate, call me if you need me or if you think of something else."

She regarded him, her expression thoughtful. "Perhaps you'd like some coffee, after all." She reached out and touched his arm lightly. "No, no, forget I said that. Good-bye, Pete. Mr. Frank, I suppose we're on opposite sides of the fence now."

"We were never on opposite sides of the fence."

"It may have to happen," she said simply and stuck her hand out, yet when he grasped it warmly, she didn't return the pressure.

"Look," he began, "you're not alone. I'm here any time you want me. Weekends and evenings, too, just across Central Park."

"I can't trust you," she said quietly.

He dropped her hand and she went over to the door and drew it open.

"You can trust me, dammit," he said.

Her expression was totally without emotion although he saw her eyes begin to glisten with tears. He didn't want to leave her alone, but her telephone rang once again and he saw her take in a sigh of relief. Pete turned and left. As he pushed the elevator button he heard the door close softly. He drove all the way back to his office without even noticing it had begun to rain.

CHAPTER 24

When the phone rang Ralley had just stepped from the shower, her hair wrapped in a towel, the cold splash of cologne scenting her flesh. She grabbed a robe and ran through the huge spaces of the open loft, past walls now empty of Cliff's paintings, through seating arrangements of spare modern pieces, to settle on the sofa next to the phone. She had an odd notion Cliff was calling. He had been gone for a week and, she reasoned, should be hungry for pocket money. Cliff had never called about the damaged painting over the couch, which he boldly came back for when she wasn't around, and which he removed, along with every bit of money she had in the loft as well as some good jewelry and all her liquor.

Well, at least she needn't apologize for the slits she had carved into the canvas. Hell, they were an improvement. She answered the phone in a little girl's voice, hoping it was Cliff, knowing he was bad news.

"Hi, Ralley."

It wasn't Cliff but Win Smith, the termite Cliff had fucked right in her bed. No one could miss the puppyish, I'm-your-best-friend-you-do-love-me voice, whether on the phone or in the flesh. "I'm not talking to you, you little worm."

"Don't hang up. I've got information you might want."

He knew Cliff's whereabouts, then. She waited. Win was the kind of person it would be a pleasure to suck dry. "Make it quick, whatever it is."

"It has to be a sale, Ralley. I mean like barter. I have something you should know about; you have something I need."

"Don't give me a spiel, Win. I have a particular aversion to the sound of your voice."

"Hey, that hurts. Jeez, Ralley, let's let bygones be bygones."

"Win, I'm going to hang up and have my telephone number changed in three minutes, something I should have done weeks ago."

"Let me read something to you, Ralley. It's bloody interesting. I promise," he persisted.

She leaned back against the sofa, the receiver cradled against her ear. The pressed tin ceiling was painted white; she let her eye trace the diamond pattern. "I don't know what you're talking about, but it's your three minutes."

"Right. Jeez, Ralley, don't get sore. We're discussing business. Quote, now I'm quoting. Quote: 'Ralley's always been a bit too clever for her own good. With her looks and brains she should be running a Fortune Five Hundred company. The lady graduated summa cum laude from the school of hard knocks and acts as if she received an A-plus in every grade.' "

"Win," Ralley burst in, "get to the goddam point."

"Quote: 'Twenty years ago, a year out of college, with some newspaper experience under her belt, Ralley decided to do a story on the L.A. drug scene, hoping to turn it into a job on a national magazine. An inside story was the way she wanted to handle it, just like an undercover cop, even to the rock star she had to shack up with. There's a woman with balls.' "

Ralley's heart seemed to stop pumping for an instant. "I don't know what you're talking about," she managed.

"Hey, don't blame me, I didn't write this."

"Then who did, you nosy little bastard?"

"Just hear me out. I mean this is for *both* our sakes. Let's see now. Quote: 'And suddenly she was in the midst of a drug buy gone bad without knowing what was coming down.' "

Ralley held her breath, shutting her eyes tight. There were pinpricks of flashing lights behind her lids and a crushing pressure on her chest.

"Quote: 'She was there observing the life-style, objectively, the good reporter. The trouble, of course, was the law. Would the court buy the good reporter business? She was right on the premises when the police from the narcotics unit burst in. An exchange of gunfire ensued; one cop down. Everybody scattered, including Ralley's rock star lover, who was picked up ten minutes later and in a scuffle with the police died of a choke hold. Ralley made it out on her own and being brighter and ballsier than most, hopped the first plane out of Los Angeles before a warrant was issued on Rachel Sanders. She fished up in Paris six months later with a new name, the result of a fifteen-minute marriage in Manhattan that must have been performed at the airport chapel.' "

Ralley started to hang up but could still hear Win's voice and in an automatic gesture, brought the receiver back to her ear.

". . . no statute of limitations on murder," he was saying. "The case could be reopened anytime, anytime at all. Pity about Rachel Sanders, Ralley. I mean a whole career could go down the tubes with just a phone call to the LAPD."

"All right, Win, you've made your point. What's this barter business? If you want Cliff's phone number, you've come to the wrong place."

"Well, that's what I mean, Ralley. Cliff wasn't any good for either of us, right? I mean Smarts failed because of him. But I'm not mad any more. Smarts was a learning experience in more ways than one. Add the gallery experience to my B.F.A. and M.F.A., that job is right for me."

"M.F.A.? You?"

He was silent for a moment. "I'm not a liar."

"Win, I'm losing patience. Don't give me your résumé. I know all about you."

"You're on the board of directors. I need your vote. Marguerite Varick's agreed and so will everyone else."

"To what?"

"Oh, right. Marguerite's agreed to give up her position as director of the Delville Museum. I'm going to apply and I'm well qualified. All I need is your vote, Ralley."

"Go screw." She slammed the receiver down but in a second picked it up. She hadn't disconnected him. "My vote and Marguerite's are two out of nine. You'll never make it, Win."

"I will, Ralley."

"I see," she said after a moment's pause, "you're going to blackmail all nine directors of the Delville board."

"A barter, Ralley, that's all I ask."

"And might I remind you that barter requires an exchange of goods."

"Nah, in this case an exchange of promises. As long as I have your promise, you can trust me."

"I don't trust you. Believe me, if I ever see you in the flesh, I'll kill you."

"Hey listen—"

Ralley slammed the receiver down. The loft seemed to have got smaller; the air was heavy. She sat there surrounded by shadows. Until the world around her began to spin, she wasn't even aware of her holding her breath. She gulped in a lungful of air, drew herself to her feet, and went slowly to the liquor cabinet. She poured herself a Chivas. It flowed smoothly down and she let a sigh escape her parched lips. All Steyman Senior had to hear was that she had witnessed a killing in a drug bust and she'd be history. Ira's death was trouble enough.

Egon, the old bastard, had cajoled her life history out of her with a smile, when she was coming down from a failed affair and at her most vulnerable. He'd promised never to tell. Then why in the world had he told that little cretin about her? Perhaps he and Win were having a go at it, Egon regaling him with tidbits to keep him amused. She went to the window and opened it wide. A cool October breeze sifted through. The sky was an iridescent blue green that held the remnants of a spectacular sunset.

Leaning against the building opposite were some teenagers, smoking and bopping to the music that was going on in their heads. She gazed up over the roof of the building toward the river. She heard the burst of a foghorn.

The drink was beginning to work. Her body warmed, and the scaly feeling disappeared, although there was now a band of sweat on her upper lip. She was scared. If only she had kept a lower profile, gone with the right men, *grown up,* for God's sake.

She had always wanted to be elegant, cool, mysterious, wanted to wash the insanity of her mother from her flesh. She had looked for a place to hide the real Ralley and had come up with the staid, stable catalog of WASP virtues that Steyman's thought her. Yet she was still afraid of the real Rachel Sanders lurking beneath her skin, her mother's daughter. Maybe she was only killing time before she, too, would walk into the water like that strange woman who had borne her.

She realized she had probably been waiting twenty years for someone like Win Smith to surface, smiling Win Smith who so desperately wanted the directorship of the Delville Museum. Why hadn't he come out with it and asked Egon when they were fooling around in bed, discussing her?

No, all wrong, she decided. Rolling around in bed wasn't Egon's style. Win had something in hand. He'd turned Marguerite around and said he would turn the others. Ralley went back to the phone and dialed Marguerite's number. She got the machine, remembered Marguerite was leaving for the Continent, had probably already left.

He'd be on to Annalise next, or Jaybee or Kate, but about what? What in hell had Egon done? She dialed Annalise's number. The phone rang twice and was picked up by the butler who reported that Annalise wasn't home. Just then Zack's voice broke in on an extension.

"That you, Ralley?" He sounded cheerful enough. She took it as a good sign. She had known Zack for a long time, from before his well-publicized wedding to Annalise, at which she had been maid of honor. Ralley found him formidable although they'd never had a serious private conversation; they were at ease with each other, if only out of deference to Annalise. People called Zack Younger arrogant, self-centered and too wealthy for his own good; Annalise had always been guarded about her husband.

"I wanted to talk to Annalise," she told him, "but I gather she's not home."

"Talk to me instead."

"I wish I could, Zack." She tried to sound lighthearted, but her voice cracked unexpectedly. She reached for her glass, then saw that it was empty. What was happening nowadays when a slug of whiskey wore off in a matter of minutes?

"Ralley?" Zack sounded concerned.

"Just a minute." She put the receiver down and went over to her liquor cabinet and poured herself a drink, fully expecting Zack to have hung up when she returned.

He was still there. "What's wrong?" he asked when she came back on, his tone soft and sincere.

"I had a bad phone call. Nasty, that's all."

"Want to meet me for a drink and cry on my shoulder? Annalise won't be back until tomorrow."

"No, thanks, Zack, I'm not up to it."

"Give it a try. I'll come over, get you to change your mind. I won't take no for an answer."

"But—"

"See you in a half-hour."

He was there in less time than that, and she let him in silently.

"Are you all right?" he asked at once.

"Yes. I promise I won't break into little pieces." She was surprised to find him wearing a tuxedo; she realized he was probably just as puzzled to find her barefoot and in a robe.

"I'm sorry," she said, shrugging an apology. "The truth is I haven't been able to get my act together."

"I like your act just the way it is."

She nodded. "I'm afraid I caught you on your way somewhere."

"Saved me is more like it," he told her. "I was scheduled for dinner with two city officials. I think I even heard relief in their voices when I canceled."

"Relief? Somehow, Zack, I doubt that. You need their backing, I suppose."

"I guess that's as good a way as any to put it."

"Come on, I'll get you a drink." Ralley led him through the loft and over to the counter that divided the efficiency kitchen from the living room. "Where's Annalise?"

"Dallas."

"Neiman-Marcus, I remember now, she said something about a private showing of her cruise line. When did you say she'd be back?"

"Tomorrow."

"She's cutting it close, isn't she? Market week's just around the corner. Annalise is too much hands-on to let anything get away from her."

Zack laughed. "You know Annalise, she has this romantic vision of herself as one very sophisticated lady standing on an airfield somewhere waiting for a plane to take her to her next port of call. She likes teetering on the edge of her control."

He had a nice smile, Ralley thought, and now he was turning it on her. "I don't think you've ever been here before, have you, Zack? I've asked Annalise to bring you, but SoHo just isn't her scene."

"Next time ask me," he said sincerely, looking around. "Nice."

"A little short of artwork at the moment." Ralley found her cigarettes on the counter and lit one, taking the smoke deep into her lungs. She wondered what Annalise would think of his being there. Nothing, probably. They were sophisticated people and it couldn't be the first time in his marriage that Zack had been alone with a woman. As for Annalise, Ralley knew what she was like and suspected marriage couldn't have changed her completely. She and Annalise were close but oddly private about some parts of their lives.

As for Zack, even Ralley, from the beginning, had been impressed with her friend's prize. He was the quintessential catch, a self-made multimillionaire who was ready to back Annalise in her own business and to see her through it. "Can I get you a drink?" she asked.

"I was going to talk you into coming out with me, crying on my shoulder in public."

"I'm not sure what that would do for your image, Senator."

"Shove my image. Want to talk about it?"

"A drink first."

"Scotch on the rocks."

She busied herself with the drink, knowing his question needed answering and not certain she was up to it.

"We don't have to make small talk, Ralley," he said, taking the drink from her shaking hand. "Who called and what did he say?"

What did *he* say? Good Lord, was she that transparent? Or did Zack know something? She poured herself a strong drink and went over to the window and gazed out. He stood behind her. The teenagers were gone and night had fallen. Something was confusing her and in an effort not to face it, she turned and offered him a stiff smile. She couldn't tell him the truth about Win's call. "I know who the caller was, a scuzz bucket who seems to have kept up with my love life in boring detail. I'm afraid Steyman Senior wouldn't take kindly to his information."

"That what you wanted to talk to Annalise about?"

Win would be on to Annalise soon enough, and probably Zack as well. "I needed a shoulder to cry on," she said. "Annalise's padded one would have been just right." She felt the tears start and tried to move past him. She sensed his hesitation before he put his arms around her and gathered her close.

"Go ahead, cry," he said, stroking her hair.

"I hate my life. Nothing's ever gone right." Ralley heard the words and would have pulled them back if she could.

"Don't waste time wallowing in self-pity. It won't get you anywhere."

"What do you know about it?"

She heard him laugh softly. He smelled good, of something expensive and yet persuasively male. "You're rich, powerful," she murmured. "You have the whole world under control. Have you any idea what it's like to be helpless, to know you're completely alone?"

He stood holding her, rocking slightly, as though the motion would soothe her. "Being what you call rich and powerful doesn't leave me without feelings. And I don't want you ever to feel you're completely alone. I'll always be here for you, surely you know that."

"Yes, of course, the husband of my best friend."

"What about the call? Tell me more."

"I sowed a lot of wild oats once. This little turd knows it somehow. He has access to the secrets of my past, and now he's making demands. I can give in on one point, but blackmail's blackmail and I'm afraid he won't stop."

"If he calls again, let him know you have friends in high places who'll see him caught and prosecuted. Or worse," he added, smiling at her with great assurance as though the possibility were real, as if with a word he could have Win snuffed as easily as Ira had been in a restaurant in the garment district. "Is it money?"

"Barter. I do him a favor, he does me one." And if she didn't help Win, she could wind up in prison. She shivered at the thought, and Zack's grip on her tightened.

"Can you pay?"

"As a matter of fact, yes."

"Don't need my help there. Maybe you're taking this harder than you should, attaching too much importance to what he said." Zack's voice was low, a different voice from the public one, which resonated with confidence. "So he knows about some ill-chosen love affairs. It can't be the worst thing that's ever happened to you."

She shook her head. "He never mentioned the worst thing that ever happened to me." She took in a deep breath and then let it out in words she had never uttered aloud before. "I was raped when I was fifteen by one of my father's friends," she said at last. She saw his eyes shadow suddenly. "My father was in the army, stationed in Germany. His friend was a captain, and I suppose my father reasoned that no one would believe my word against that of a respected hero and army officer. Even, that is, if I'd worked up the courage to tell someone. My father's solution was to send me away. I don't know whom I hate more, the man who attacked me or my father."

A few moments went by in a claustrophobic silence. Ralley, in an instant of surprising clarity, understood that she had enlisted Zack as an ally because he now knew more about her than did Annalise. She had carved into her loneliness and fear and made a place for him.

"Thank you for telling me," he said. "It couldn't have been easy."

"It was a double betrayal. I've never come to grips with it."

"What happened to the man who raped you?"

"Are you a white knight coming to my rescue?"

"If I could kill him, I would."

"He's a four-star general and an adviser to the President."

Zack took in the information without comment. His grip on her hadn't lessened. She could feel his breath on her cheek.

"I've followed his career," Ralley said dully. "It's easy enough when you're signed, numbered, and dated by the army."

"Does he know you have?"

She shook her head no.

"And your father?"

Ralley recited the facts coldly. She might have been reading from a newspaper. "He died in a jeep accident in Germany years ago while I was in school in California. Full military funeral with honors. I always suspected he was involved with gun running, but if he left any exceptional amount of money his mistress was the beneficiary, I suppose. There *was* something for me to finish college, anyway. The army didn't let me down. I had no one," she added quietly.

He continued to study her for a long while. She remained still, not at all uncomfortable under his sober gaze. When he spoke, his tone was deliberate and strong. "Evidently under that cool, brilliant exterior you've been hiding a helluva lot, my girl."

"Hiding it, just about."

He crooked a finger under her chin. "You're much softer than you let on," he said. She knew then that he would kiss her and that she should move away. When he did kiss her, part of the rush through her was guilt over Annalise. She was taking one more step in the wrong direction, turning down another unknown road. Yet none of it felt strange, not his being there or his attention.

His kiss deepened and she let it happen without giving voice to questions that needed answering. All she felt was need of a greedy, ravenous kind and the desire to satisfy it. She clutched at him, feeling the floor slip out from under her. The liquor had gone to her head; the room spun around until he lifted her and with his mouth still on hers carried her to bed.

Their eyes held as he slowly opened her robe. With his head bent to her breast, he removed his jacket. Neither spoke as he stripped naked. She watched him hungrily, suspecting that it pleased him to be admired in such a way. And then he was on her again. His hands stroked her, not in the hard, careless way of some men who need satisfaction quickly, but in the heated manner of one intent on making love, on telling her something, on sharing.

It wasn't the rough scrappling she knew so well with Cliff or any of the others, the sweaty rumble fueled by mistrust and a courting of disaster. Her body was coming alive after a long hiatus in which she had managed to ignore all sensations.

She was surprised at the tentative way Zack touched her, as if he were discovering something new. His lovemaking was so liquid she had to arch her body to receive his long-drawn-out caresses. Her nerve endings tingled with desire.

"I forgot what it was like," he told her. "I didn't think I could do this anymore."

And then passion took control and his touch changed. Powerful hands held her enthralled, fingers probed, squeezed, enticed. His mouth slid down her body until he came to the soft curls between her legs. His tongue took over and he moved his body as if he sensed every thrill that shuddered through her. His tongue tapped at her clitoris and she felt the beginnings of a seawash of waves. His teeth caught and held on to the tiny button of flesh, nibbling and tasting as his fingers sought to fill her. Stirrings, seesawing between pain and an exquisite sensation that was brand new, had her gripping the sheet, crying out. She heard his own deep, pleased groan.

She twisted to receive him, opening herself to his thrusts, wrapping her legs around him and pulling him in deep. The room had become a small airless box, its walls pressing in, shutting the world away. He clutched at her, groping for her mouth, possessing her entirely. She gave herself for the first time totally and without doubt for a few precious, blind moments. Then it was over.

Zack left long after midnight. Ralley, roused from sleep by his kiss, had scarcely stirred. He had whispered that everything would be all right. She turned on her side and curled up, pushing her face deep into the pillow. She heard the door open and close, thought she should get up and lock it behind him. Instead she lay there knowing everything was far from all right. Somewhere along the line, as they lay in each other's arms, Annalise had slipped in between them. For the first time Ralley wondered seriously about Zack's relationship with Annalise, what it was really like. It couldn't have been stable if he had come running at her call, so easily slipping into bed with her. She wondered as she drifted away toward sleep if she was falling in love with Zack. It would be the forlorn, unsatisfied love that was barely acknowledged, that was clutched quietly to the heart to ease loneliness. Perhaps she had been in love with Zack for a long time and had kept it a secret from herself. Whatever was true, she was as guilty of betrayal as Cliff had been. She would sleep with the memory of Zack's body against hers, but in the morning, reality would face her square on.

CHAPTER 25

Zack was a man who thrived on no more than four hours sleep a night and when he returned to the apartment on Park Avenue at three in the morning he felt wide awake and vigorous. He did not at once head upstairs to his bedroom, but went to his study, surprised at a drift of light under the closed doors.

The doors were on sliding hinges, and Zack pulled them quickly apart. The room was a mellow one that never failed to please and soothe him, with navy matte walls, crowded bookcases behind an L-shaped desk, an Oriental rug on the dark-stained floor, and a seating arrangement near the fireplace. He was annoyed, however, to find his stepdaughter Elizabeth sitting cross-legged on the couch with two of her friends, the flickering light from the television screen holding them rapt.

His glance took them in, then swept across the room to the fax machine and his computer. He went over to his desk immediately. "Little late for you, isn't it?" he asked Elizabeth.

"We were going over the film once again." She held the automatic control in her hand and clicked the picture off.

"Why not use the screening room?"

She shrugged. Her companions were silent, two youngsters with unruly hair, wearing leather jackets. He noted they were drinking his brandy. "Mom called," she said absently. "I told her you were with Ralley."

He had been sifting through his fax messages, and was slow in registering what he'd just heard.

"I listened in on the extension," she said. Her tone was her usual truculent one, daring him to argue. Her gaze was steady although she seemed to have trouble hiding a small, triumphant smile that told him she had left out nothing of his conversation with Ralley.

When he returned to his messages, she explained, "I was waiting for a call."

He thought of what an unpleasant young woman she was, this little German baroness with her pretensions of a democratic caste. Underlying her contempt was a certain amount of anti-Semitism, learned very possibly at her parents' knees. It hadn't escaped Zack that anti-Jewish feeling was virulent in Argentina and that his wife, whether she admitted it or not, had certainly been indoctrinated. The time she had spent in France and Germany should have completed her education. Although no word had passed between them, Zack, who was sensitive to his Jewishness although he didn't practice his religion, often wondered just what her feeling was.

Odd that Ralley thought he could buy anything he wanted. Power and money couldn't purchase breathing space, as Elizabeth's presence certainly proved.

"This is Timmy Hendron, and Blake Connell," Elizabeth said. "My stepfather, Mr. Younger."

"How do you do," Zack said, smiling politely at them. "I like the work you're doing. Glad I could help."

The two youngsters scrambled to their feet while Elizabeth removed the film cassette from the VCR. "We have to spend so much time working up requests for grant money," she told him, "that we can't find the time for filming the project."

"You're running for senator, right?" one of the boys said, finally finding his voice.

"You're over eighteen, aren't you?" Zack asked and without waiting for an answer, went on, "Hope you're registered voters, both of you."

"Yes, sir."

Elizabeth sniffed audibly.

Zack switched on his computer, punched in a couple of codes, and sitting down, fixed his eyes on the screen. But his mind wasn't on numbers. It was back in Ralley's loft, focused on her long, slender torso.

"Mom said she'd be at La Guardia at twelve-fifteen tomorrow. She wants you to send the car."

"Thank you, Elizabeth. Is she all right? Did she sound tired?"

"She's never tired. Neither are you. Neither am I. It's kind of like a family sickness, except we're not a family." Elizabeth herded her friends from the room; as she pulled the doors closed, he caught her eye. He wondered if she knew what he had just come back from and thought perhaps what had happened between him and Ralley was stamped on his face. He got slowly to his feet and was on his way to his room when he stopped and slipped into Annalise's instead.

The familiar scent of potpourri filled the room. Zack went over to the full-length mirror that stood catercorner to the window and stared at himself, wondering what changes Elizabeth might have noted. His tuxedo showed no sign of having been carelessly tossed to the floor of Ralley's studio. His hair was untousled, his color unchanged.

He turned away and at her dressing table he picked up an informal photograph in an antique silver frame: Annalise and himself when they had first met, she in jodhpurs with her hair held back by a black band, he in tennis shorts. His arm was around her shoulders. He grinned for the camera; she gazed at him with a thoughtful smile. He put the photo back, behind a formal portrait of Elizabeth as a beautiful three-year-old child. Elizabeth was no mystery, although Annalise still was. He had bought the story of her lonely life as the only child of aging parents on a ranch in the Argentine pampas. He had even fallen in love with her mystery, her accent, her charm, the air of exotic origins that made New York seem like tepid bouillon. And over the years of their marriage, she had become more proficient in their lovemaking, more beautiful, and more remote. If he won his party's nomination in the spring for the Senate race, the opposition might seriously begin to wonder about Annalise, her two divorces and that distant country where she had neither kith nor kin. But then they might be equally curious about his dalliance with the beautiful vice president of Steyman's.

Annalise went straight from La Guardia to her office, where she showered and changed her clothes before taking phone calls and talking to her staff. It was after one-thirty when she sat down at her desk to dial Zack at his office. He wasn't there, his secretary informed her, and was expected back some time late in the afternoon. A check of her calendar revealed an appointment at four-thirty with a photographer from *Mirabella* in preparation for an article on fashion designers. Annalise wanted to give a hands-on feel to the shoot and had dressed in jeans and a white cotton shirt. She wore a bandeau to keep her hair out of her eyes. From every point of view except a close look into her wary eyes, she appeared youthful and full of attractive energy.

She found, checking her messages, that Ralley had been trying to reach her. She'd been feeling annoyed over the way Zack had rushed off to see Ralley; her daughter had been a little too dramatic about the phone call to which she'd apparently listened without the least guilt. If Ralley was in trouble, Annalise expected her husband to respond. Elizabeth's theatrics worried her, though. And she knew that Ralley, for all her toughness, was as vulnerable as a child, and men responded a little too easily. Zack was probably no exception, although she was fairly certain there had never been or could ever be anything between them.

"I heard you had a date with my husband," she said crisply to Ralley a few minutes later. Both she and Ralley had private lines and she wasn't afraid of speaking openly to her friend. "I hope he brought you a corsage."

"I called you, Annalise, but frankly I must have sounded as frantic as I felt. Zack rushed right over."

Annalise was suddenly on guard, although she couldn't have said exactly why, unless it was the note of apology in Ralley's voice. "Frantic?" she asked, her mind working on two levels, unable to blank out a picture of Ralley and Zack together. "What's wrong?"

"Nothing but a spot of blackmail."

"What are you talking about?" Annalise felt a slight headache coming on, as if events were crowding further in.

"Win Smith is trying to blackmail me and I'm afraid he'll be on to you next."

"Blackmail? Did you say blackmail?" Annalise felt long, cold fingers trace striations of fear down her spine. The word *puta*, never far from her consciousness, seemed to pound against her skull.

"Annalise, I've never known you to sound so dull-witted. He's crazy if he thinks he's going to get away with it, but he's trying."

"You're talking about Egon's little friend, the one running the gallery." She remembered his Buenos Aires patois that evening at Sotheby's.

"Would you believe the little twerp wants Marguerite's job; he wants to be the director of the Delville Museum." Ralley paused, then said, "I'm waiting for a nice loud *'What?'* "

"Good Lord, he sounds mad. What utter nonsense, director of the museum. And you say he's blackmailing you for your vote? Have you talked to Marguerite? What in hell can he blackmail you about? Certainly not Cliff." Annalise was aware of the sharpness in her voice, the way she spoke too quickly, how her Spanish accent was tripping her up.

"Marguerite's out of the country. He's discovered something about my past I'd as soon Steyman Senior didn't know. That simple enough? He claims Marguerite's already come around."

"Marguerite?"

"Annalise, don't keep asking questions. I called you last night because I wanted to find out if he'd already spoken to you."

"No." Again her response was a little too sharp.

"I don't know where he got his information."

"How does he think he's going to be named director of the museum?" Annalise asked. "He needs the votes of a majority of the board."

"From the sound of his voice, he doesn't think he'll have a problem. In other words, he's in possession of information about each and every one of us."

"You know that for a fact."

Ralley took a few seconds answering. "From his confidence in the matter, I'd say I know it for a fact."

Annalise had to think, organize what she might say if Win Smith took it into his head to call her. "I'll get back to you, Ralley," she began, then went on in a constrained way she couldn't conceal, "what did Zack suggest?"

"Your husband would like to take a contract out on Winthrop Smith. Trouble is I have no idea where he's living. But if I find out I won't need Zack to handle him, believe me. I called Reuben Newcombe first thing this morning to ask him about Smarts. I figured he'd know Win's whereabouts if anyone did. Reuben said Win just closed the door and disappeared. Left the estate with a lot of angry artists threatening lawsuits. I think Win's a cold, calculating little bastard, a genuine sociopath who may not get what he wants in the end but who's willing to take a lot of people with him when he goes. In a moment of candor he admitted to Cliff that his family told him to ship out or they'd have him hospitalized for good. Unfortunately he shipped out."

"All right, I more than get the drift. Let me get back to you," Annalise said, before hanging up. She checked quickly through her messages again and found nothing from Win Smith. She then told her secretary not to put through any calls from him.

At three o'clock Annalise was in her workroom with her premiere, Nance. Emphasis in the Milan collections had been on tailored jackets for spring, and word had it that Paris was combining similar soft-shouldered jackets with narrow skirts. With the New York collections less than a week away, Annalise had to make a decision about adding a couple of similar items to her line. She began to sketch a few possibilities, as Nance had agreed to make up two in shades of gray wool tweed ordered from an Italian mill but never used.

She checked her secretary a couple of times to make certain no calls had come in from Win Smith. None had. At four-thirty Nance, Annalise, and her fashion coordinator were in the workroom accessorizing the collection when her publicity assistant reached Annalise on the intercom. "The photographer's here from *Mirabella*. He wants to know if he can set up in your office."

"I thought they were doing a story on designers in their ateliers."

"He said he wants to shoot you at your desk looking over some fabric swatches."

"*Dios mio.* How do you say it? Mine not to question why."

"I'll send him back."

Annalise went quickly into her office, checked her makeup and hair, and was at her desk smiling when Win Smith walked in carrying expensive camera equipment.

Annalise twisted her fingers around a heavy silver-handled letter opener she had picked up just before Win Smith left her office. If he had remained in her presence one moment longer she would have plunged the knife into his chest. She let it fall with a clatter to the wooden surface of her desk and closed her eyes. Her heart resumed its normal beat although a dull throbbing in her head remained that no pain killer could relieve. After a moment she signaled her secretary on the intercom.

"Hold my calls until I tell you otherwise. All of them, please, including Mr. Younger's."

She got up from her desk and walked restlessly around the office. Egon had befriended her, introduced her to Zack, and lobbied for her when she had decided to establish her fashion house. He had been the most solicitous of friends, an old gossip whom she thought she could trust. And all the while he was collecting the bloodied moments of her life.

She dropped onto the taupe leather sofa and closed her eyes. Winthrop Smith had the means at his disposal to suck her dry as clearly as he did for Ralley and almost certainly for Marguerite. The blackmail he asked was simple enough to grant, but there was no reason to think he would stop there. Something would have to be done about him.

She had no idea where or when Egon had transmitted the information about her to Win Smith. She remembered the man's curiosity when they first met but never thought he'd follow up on it.

"The pampas? That's where you grew up?"

"You ask too many questions, Egon. I grew up far away from the big city on an *estancia* deep in the heart of the country."

"Ah, one of those glorious reconstructions of a Spanish hacienda in the middle of nowhere, surrounded by cattle. You see them in *House & Garden* and you *know* they cost ten million dollars."

"You'd be bored senseless, Egon. You don't even ride. Besides, I left when I was a teenager."

"Of course, I remember now," Egon said, reminding her of the story she had told him when they first met. "Wicked uncle takes over management of estate after parents die in tragic plane crash. Harried niece escapes, never to return."

"I believe the word was left for school, Egon. Don't exaggerate."

"Come with me to Buenos Aires, Annalise. We'll kick up some dust together."

She backed away in horror, saw the interested light in his eyes, the question form on his lips, then die away. He had gone to Buenos Aires well before she married Zack, had come back and greeted her without a word about his trip.

She remembered breathing a sigh of relief. Egon's interests, she had thought, were short-lived. She was engaged to Zack, Delville was launching a new fragrance, Kate came into his life. She thought Egon had forgotten all about her past and now she understood he had been a very busy man indeed in Buenos Aires.

Everything came back to her now in hot, putrid waves. She could no longer fight the hypnotic pull, the fragments of memory that shook her soul when she least expected them. Egon might have gleaned the facts of her past, but no one could ever grasp the essence.

The boots of the men she had serviced tramped through her dreams; even in her coolest, most collected moments, she could break out in a stinging sweat. She would never be free.

Señora Girard's Flora Vista was an old Italianate villa on Calle Alejandro near Alvear where the wives of the very men who came to visit spent their days shopping. Annalise learned many months later that she had been fortunate with Colonel Antonio Guzmán, although he ultimately gave her up to Señora Girard.

"Nina, Nina, *bella* Nina." She was beautiful. Men told her so as they touched her, probed her, reached in as if to grab her soul. Dark-haired, wild-eyed, she possessed a soft young body trained early to yield.

Annalise, then Nina, painted her young face each day with great care, losing her identity with each mark of the pencil, each trace of color. She would rouge her nipples. She would shape her pubic hair sometimes in a heart, sometimes in a diamond. She made her own clothes, each outfit more fantastical than the next. She made clothes for the others, too, and charged them, saving every penny.

She had been living at Flora Vista for a year when General Juan Molenos Garcia made his first visit to the house. Rumor was that his mistress had run away the previous week, some thought to Brazil. Others said she had learned too much about the general and that she would never be found.

When he chose Annalise, she shook with fear but learned quickly he was a man on the edge who required entertainment of the most unusual kind. He showed his appreciation by installing her in the apartment vacated by his previous mistress. "Your life will be better here," the general explained, his rough hand touching her cheek. "I am climbing up in the world, Nina."

She had hungrily taken in the lavish surroundings but recognized the ambitions of his previous mistress: she had wanted too much and had learned too much. Annalise resolved to learn nothing, to do only what was required of her, to hoard the money he gave her and to stay sane. She had learned the end could come when least expected.

They were in bed one Sunday night, the general on top of her, when the door crashed in and soldiers entered, firing guns. Garcia uttered a curse in her ear and slumped over her, blood gushing from his mouth, his heart, his buttocks. He breathed his last breath into her mouth. She held in her screams. They must think she was dead, too. The general's body was pulled away. She lay there covered with blood, her eyes open and staring as if in death.

"*Muerto.*" The face that gazed impassively down at her was that of Antonio Guzmán. He reached out after a moment's hesitation and in a quick gesture pulled the bloody quilt over her head.

"Finished here," he said to his men. "Let the police clean up the mess."

She waited until they were gone, then escaped with nothing more than the clothes on her back and the money she'd been hoarding, enough to buy her a passport in the name of Annalise Michelis and a one-way ticket to Paris.

CHAPTER 26

$\mathbf{H}$is name was Aaron Jaffee and he arrived at Kate Hayden two days after Ira's murder, a small, balding man with large, surprised gray eyes behind thick glasses. He spoke in a soft nasal voice, and had trouble pronouncing his *l*'s. Kate wasn't certain whether to be intimidated by or at ease with the conservator. She had expected a lion from the Justice Department and was awarded a lamb. That alone was worrisome.

Reuben Newcombe had advised Kate to act as though nothing was wrong, to volunteer little, and to ask no questions except the most necessary kind. Jaffee's manner wasn't confrontational, however, and Kate felt every muscle in her body relax.

She took him quickly through to the shipping room. The head of the department sat at his desk in front of the freight elevator; he was on the telephone when they arrived and took his time hanging up. His end of the conversation consisted of a series of noncommittal grunts. When he put the phone down he turned to Kate without a greeting. She disliked him and considered him rude, but Ira had trusted him, an idea she now found uncomfortable.

"Hal, this is Mr. Jaffee," she said. She realized she didn't even know his last name. "Mr. Jaffee's with the government and has come to oversee the operation for a while."

Hal got halfway out of his seat and nodded before sitting down.

"I'll be back to talk to you later," Jaffee said, "when I get settled."

"Right."

Kate was at the door to the packing room when she stopped and turned back to Hal. "Incidentally, who handles our local shipping?"

"NYC Trucking, like always."

"Is that the only company, besides United Parcel?"

"NYC handles all of our local trucking," he told her.

"Do we have a contract with them?"

"They've been handling our shipping from the beginning." It was no answer.

"If we have a contract, I want a copy of it. And I'd like bids from half a dozen trucking companies by the end of this week." She walked ahead of Jaffee into the packing department. "I never liked him," she said.

Jaffee laughed. "Feeling your oats?"

"Maybe. Maybe I've got nothing to lose."

"Gorgeously styled, but the heels are a little too high for my day look." Kate shook her head. "Uh-uh."

Elfie gave an impatient laugh. "She said to try them. I figured what the hell?"

Kate regarded the pale beige kid shoes with delicate spike heels, designed to be worn with very short skirts. Maud Frizon, with whom she worked closely, had delivered most of the order on target, including several pairs of intricately embroidered velvet slippers made to Kate's specifications.

"Nice, but not for me," Kate said. "If I wouldn't wear a heel that high during the day, neither would the Hayden ladies."

"Hayden ladies," Elfie repeated. "From your mouth to God's ear."

Fifty pairs of shoes were spread out on the showroom floor, and they went quickly over each with their color chart in hand. Classic evening pumps would double for several of her evening shapes. It took Kate and Elfie several hours to accessorize the collection, and then only because the original work had been done weeks before. After they had checked through the shoes and locked them in the storage room, they took on the gloves.

"I don't know," Kate said. "I'm thinking of cutting out gloves altogether. They show nicely, but nobody wears gloves in spring. It's an affectation."

"Let's put them on reserve," Elfie said.

"Scarves next," Kate said. She had ordered oversize paisley silk scarves from India in pale spring colors. They had arrived early but had been held up at Customs for a week. When the carton was opened, Kate discovered that half the order was missing but some beautiful silks were included in unusual shades of teal.

"Somebody else's order," Kate commented. "What the hell, let's use them where we can."

Next they chose soft, floppy straw hats to be worn with long black linen jackets over long black skirts of gazar.

Kate confined her jewelry to exaggerated hoop earrings in a narrow range of muted colors, and multistrand necklaces of tiny semiprecious stones. Kate wanted them for bias-cut, figure-flattering silk dresses that just grazed the knee.

"Wowee," Elfie remarked when Vivian came into the showroom modeling a dusty violet silk crepe dress, her necklace a twisted fall of citrine, amethyst, light jade, and coral beads.

"Try it with this," Kate said, producing a large square of paisley. "Draped *comme ça.*" With the necklace removed, the silk square completely changed the look of the short-sleeved collarless dress.

"Wrong stockings," Kate said, standing back.

"White, shimmery," Vivian said, walking to the full-length mirror near the window and appraising the dress in a completely dispassionate way.

"Check the stock," Kate said, joining her. "Try bare, also." The sling-back shoes had been dyed to match the dress. "We're showing the dress in how many colors?" She began to tick them off. Each color had been selected to match the semiprecious stones in the multistrand necklace. "Pale lemon, amethyst, light jade, coral."

"We're still awaiting delivery of the coral fabric," Elfie reminded her. The first sampling had arrived in an offshade with a little too much orange in it.

"Have you checked?"

"On the way, they said."

"And black."

"You never mentioned black, Kate."

"We need black."

"*Oy vey.* We don't have black silk crepe in stock."

"Smoky black. I seem to remember ordering a sample."

"Never showed. It's not on my list."

"We need smoky black, Elfie."

"I'll call them this minute." Elfie paused then asked suddenly, "Is it going to work out? I mean, with *him?*" She referred to Jaffee, the conservator, who had been wandering through the place all afternoon, asking questions in his pleasant manner, nodding regularly.

"It should." Kate had learned quickly enough that Jaffee was a careful man whose facade hid his opinions.

Elfie cast her a worried glance and left the showroom. Then Kate's secretary came to the door; she was already a wreck from a day on the telephone, fielding calls from the press about the show.

Now she looked terrified. "Mr. Jaffee asked if you wouldn't mind going back to see him," she said.

Kate, shoeless and in jeans and a white shirt, glanced at herself in the mirror. She had a smudge of dirt on her nose, and her hair appeared wind-blown. She rubbed the smudge away, slipped into her shoes, and drew her fingers through her hair. Mr. Jaffee wasn't a man to impress with cool, unruffled looks, she decided.

He was sitting at the desk with the accountant next to him. Piles of computer printouts took up most of the space on Ira's wide desk. She hesitated at the door, realizing that Ira's expensive scent still lingered in the air. Her eye was drawn to the sofa and then quickly back to Jaffee.

"Sit down," he said, motioning to a chair.

"Should I be worried?" she asked, exchanging a glance with the accountant who gave a slight shake of his head that she couldn't interpret.

"What do you know about the way the company is run?"

"I know it's a subsidiary of DAS and that we're expected to turn a profit." She paused. Her hands were shaking and she tried to hold them steady in her lap. "The arrangement with Mr. Gregory was that I would attend to the design side and he'd handle everything else. I did try to call Mr. Daguras in Zurich," she added, "but he's out of town, or incommunicado."

"I spoke with Mr. Daguras this afternoon," Jaffee said, watching her.

"He called?"

"I found him in Zurich. I suggested he fly over or send an accountant. He told me in so many words . . ." He paused and glanced at the accountant.

"To stuff it," the accountant said. "In much more polite terms—right, Aaron?"

"Daguras is cutting off your DAS credit line with your European fabric suppliers," Jaffee said.

Kate shot to her feet. "No, it's impossible."

"Wait," Jaffee said, motioning to her to sit down. "The Hong Kong factories will be at your disposal if you pay up front."

She sat down, feeling too weak to stand. "Can he do that?"

"He can do whatever he likes. It's his company. He feels you've been difficult to deal with—"

"What? I don't know what he's talking about."

"The designer market is a tough nut to crack. You've been adamant about not designing a bridge line or going private label. Those were his words, delivered in a charming Italian accent."

"I've been building my name first, Mr. Jaffee. That was my original arrangement. Everything will follow in good time."

"My guess is DAS is going to close the company down if your spring line fails. And you're going to have to familiarize yourself with company finances," he said. "I'm only here as a temporary stopgap. Eventually you're going to have to handle the business all by yourself."

"You mean if there *is* a business. How in hell am I going to get a line of credit with my European fabric suppliers?"

"Write paper as the result of next week's show—and plenty of it."

"And DAS will continue to let me use the Hong Kong factories."

"All you have to do is pay up front, Miss Hayden. If you're considering running this business by yourself, you won't be the first designer to think she can handle it all."

"Well, of course we'll hire a business manager." She realized almost at once the flightiness of her remark. "Ira ran everything," she said. "He was sales manager, business manager, promotion manager, everything rolled into one."

"A business manager costs money," Jaffee said without missing a beat.

"Perhaps Daguras—"

"Daguras is going to cut his losses, believe me."

She was silent for a long while. The accountant stirred in his chair. Jaffee tapped a pencil on Ira's desk.

"A quick look indicates approximately a million five in accounts receivable," he said at last. "Accounts payable a little under two million."

"The IRS already knows that," Kate said.

The accountant spoke up. "The company did a little more than ten million this year, Kate."

She let out a deep breath. "Including cash orders taken from South American stores for goods Hong Kong claims were delivered, and the stores say were never ordered."

"That accounted for maybe a million and a half. The money was sent to Hong Kong. The paperwork looks right," the accountant went on.

"But the goods were never delivered. Which is why you're here," she said to Jaffee.

He nodded, fingers at his lips.

"And we owe more at the moment than we're taking in," Kate added. "Because, I suppose, a lot more money has gone to Hong Kong than should have."

Jaffee said, "The point is your fall-winter collection did well. Sell-through was better than projected and spring should do even better, if you watch your price points," he went on. "You can't afford cash up front when you order fabric or trim. We're going to have to lay it on the line to department stores to pay their debts."

"I know," Kate said, "they're notoriously overdue."

"You can't go on financing their operations. One bad turn and you'll be way in over your head."

"What do you want me to do?"

"Learn to cost out each item. Eliminate your excesses, put a little less emphasis on silks and cashmeres. All you're doing is financing the greed of the Chinese."

"My ladies expect silk and cashmere."

He smiled and Kate was beginning to think his smile lethal. "A good designer should teach her ladies what to expect."

Kate felt her skin color.

"And plan on designing a second line someone else will produce. That's money in the bank. As for this operation, we can talk about approaching a factor if necessary."

She thought of Egon telling her to license her name for a perfume. And Ira with his bridge line. And now Jaffee. "I guess the time has come to bite the bullet."

He nodded, smiling in a kind way. "With three or four hours' sleep a night, you'll get along well."

The words "I have a son" were on the tip of her tongue, but she held back. The accountant was watching her with a dismayed, apologetic grin.

"Just tell me one thing," she said. "Am I in business?"

"Think of DAS as a partner who's strayed and is admiring the blonde up the road. Whether Kate Hayden survives or not is up to you," Jaffee said.

At six, after running home to see Matt through his dinner, Kate showered, changed, and hurried back to the office with a portable cassette player, a couple of tapes of thirties music, and the determination to string together enough tape for an hour-long show. The next day models were scheduled for fittings and discussions about makeup and hairstyles. Delville Perfumes was providing the makeup from its upcoming spring line. The company was also sending over one hundred fifty small gold shopping bags filled with samples of perfume and lipstick to be given away.

Five days were left to see every piece in the collection finished and matched with its correct accessories. Because Kate couldn't afford to hire free-lance help with the show, she planned to pull people out of the accounting office and workrooms; they seemed thrilled to have the extra work. For the showing she needed sixteen helpers in the dressing room, one for each model plus seamstresses for last-minute changes and emergencies.

"I'm heading home," her secretary said at eight, peering in the door. The staff, too, was working overtime. "Anything else I can do?"

Kate gave her an appreciative smile. "When we get through this I'm going to design a spring suit for you that will knock your socks off."

"Stockings, Kate, I only wear stockings."

"See you tomorrow."

Her secretary lingered at the door. "What are you planning on using for music?"

"I'm thinking Cole Porter."

"I get a kick out of you." She grinned and waved good-bye.

Jaffee was still in his office, as was the accountant. Kate put everything out of her mind, however, except the music. Fast and bouncy kept models moving. A heavy beat enhanced the air of excitement in the tonier hotel settings that the larger houses could afford. Kate, not having that luxury, didn't want the music to overwhelm her audience. She preferred mood and romance, although the models would be instructed to move quickly, almost in counterpoint to music evocative of a time when appearances were everything, when people pretended the world was a good place. She put the Cole Porter cassette on; the first number was "Don't Fence Me In."

She walked the length of the showroom to the music, picking up speed, jutting her hip forward, turning so that her skirt swirled. Back down the room and another swirl, then a quick, enticing walk with a certain sensuality.

She heard a rustle at the door and whipped around. Pete was standing there leaning against the sill, smiling, his head slightly tilted. She reached over and turned off the tape, feeling a little silly. "What are you doing here?"

"I like watching you work. Or is it walk?"

"I've got to put together an hour's worth of music for the showing. Not easy," she explained. "It might just take all night."

"Let me help. I'm an old hand at music."

Kate gazed at him skeptically and thought about how little they knew of each other. They were each holding back, afraid of the attraction they felt— for his reasons, for her reasons, or for his idea of what her reasons were, because Pete would certainly know, as everyone else did, that she'd been a fool in her love life.

"Trust me," he told her. He went over to the cassette player and switched on the tape. An obscure melody came on in the middle of a note.

"I'll—I'll make some fresh coffee," she stammered. "And send down for deli."

"I was about to invite you for dinner."

She shook her head. "Pete, I'm really on a tight schedule. I suppose Jaffee told you, it's sink-or-swim time. DAS has cut me loose. Meaning if I make a profit, Daguras will be there with his hand out. If I fail, he'll come and remove the light fixtures. I figure I'll always end up on my feet. If I don't have my own company, someone will hire me, but it's everybody else here. They can't be left swinging."

"I'll take pastrami on rye. If you set up a pot of coffee, I promise we'll get an hour's worth of music to your satisfaction."

She was about to turn away when she spontaneously reached out and grasped his hands. The time for distrust was past. "Thanks."

"You're welcome." They exchanged a smile that could have been construed as conspiratorial.

"The trouble is," he said suddenly, "I think I'm nuts about you."

"No, you're not."

A moment passed before he answered her. "That's your final assessment of my feelings."

"You're not supposed to have feelings. You're with the Justice Department, and Uncle Sam is trying to determine whether or not I'm involved in Ira's murder."

"You're not and I'm nuts about you."

"Dammit," she said, pulling her hands away. She trusted him but couldn't quite trust the future. She wanted to be happy, wanted to feel a surge of love race through her at his touch, but it was an added complication she couldn't handle. "Don't confuse me. Don't add to my troubles."

"Kate."

"What?" she asked on an expelled sigh. She ought to tell him to leave.

"Order the deli. We've got a lot of work ahead of us."

CHAPTER 27

From Egon's journal:

> *April 5, 1982. Reuben Newcombe decided to split from Pearce, Barr,*
> *Newcombe and Hanna over a point that has my vote. And he's taken*
> *with him a half-dozen bright young things. Insufficient advancement of*
> *women ticked him off; maybe his wife, France, prodded him, but I doubt*
> *it. He's fair, liberal, and brilliant and it's also possible his old law firm is*
> *growing too fat and self-gratifying. I told Reuben to take my account*
> *along with him. Trustworthy and faithful, I'd suspect there's nothing he*
> *wouldn't do to protect a client. Best of all, perhaps, is his demeanor—*
> *part hangdog, part neutral, part patsy. Worked like a charm when I took*
> *AMET Fragrances to court. We won the case in no time flat and put*
> *that perfume thief out of business. For ten minutes, was it? We'll get*
> *him again.*
>
> *Asked Reuben to set up a date about my will. An idea has been*
> *circling around in my mind.*

No, Win decided, Newcombe definitely wasn't a man to challenge. Annalise, Marguerite, and Ralley were already in the bag. Zack Younger, as well,
because he was married to Annalise. Kate Hayden was a problem. So far she
seemed too good to be believed, but then slogging his way through the
journals wasn't an easy task.

Kate Hayden was the problem. He remembered Cliff talking about her.
He had made it clear she wouldn't be of help in setting up Smarts. She was
just beginning a business of her own and didn't have a cent to her name.
Kate Hayden and Reuben Newcombe went to the bottom of the list. There
were others Win could approach.

"Jaybee, it's Win, Win Smith. I figured it's time we had that drink."

"That drink?"

"You know, when we met at Ralley's. Last thing I remember saying to you
was we ought to have a drink sometime."

"I don't recall. Listen, Win, I'm too busy by far right now. Market week's coming up. I don't have time to breathe. We'll have to make it some other time."

"A quick drink, that's all. While you're between appointments, say. I gave up the gallery business; I'm on to something a lot more stable."

"You gave up Smarts? You were so damn gung-ho the last time."

Jaybee sounded unexpectedly interested, then Win remembered she had told Cliff once that she had often thought about running an art gallery.

"Can't get artists," Win explained. "Plenty of people call themselves artists, but I'm not about to push the careers of a bunch of no-talents."

"Come on, the world's full of talent. You just have to look, Win. You're too lazy. You expect everything to come to you. What about Cliff Beal, anyway? I thought he was your hot talent."

"I didn't trust the materials he was using. Man, some of that stuff began to crack and it was only hours old."

"Listen, there's another call coming in." Her voice turned impatient. Win tried to remember whether she had something going with Cliff, but then of course she wouldn't. "We'll have to go into this some other time," she added.

"Wait, Jaybee, don't hang up. It won't take a minute, what I have to tell you."

"What?" The question was sharp, impatient, as though she considered him a turd.

"Quote," he said without trying to soften his words. Softening wasn't the way Jaybee operated. " 'A blackmailer, our little Jaybee. Not a term she uses, of course. *Barterer* is more like it. The mayor certainly agrees, having created a job for her that didn't exist—' "

Win stopped in midsentence when he heard the click of the receiver, then the dial tone. He smiled, patiently put another quarter in the slot, and dialed her again.

"Jaybee Olsen, please."

"She's not in her office."

"Sure she is. Just give her a message. Tell her I'll meet her at the Canal Bar in twenty minutes."

"To meet who?"

"Win."

"Win, right. I'll give her the message, but I won't promise anything."

"She'll be there."

Marguerite left her assistant, Jackie, in France to cover the spring openings and took the Concorde to New York with a promise to return in a day or two.

Even with the selling of *VFF* to Libby Publications, Marguerite felt compelled to exercise tight control over what went into her biweekly newspaper.

She'd miss a couple of the bigger houses—Chanel, Montana, and Scherrer —but had planned to emphasize younger talent in her overview. At any rate, the week in Milan had been torture: she had sat through an entire showing of Armani, whose talent for the unexpected and elegant she admired, and couldn't have said what appeared on the runway. At the end of the week, Marguerite knew she had to return to America.

She arrived in New York at ten in the morning, calling Kate the moment she stepped into her apartment.

"Marguerite, thank God you're back," Kate said, startling Marguerite and putting her on guard. "But you're back a little early." Then, without waiting for an explanation, Kate launched into a description of her own problems, which apparently didn't include a call from Win Smith.

"Stop by for a drink tonight," Marguerite told her when Kate paused for breath. "Six o'clock. We'll talk then."

"Perfect." With that one word Kate expressed relief, but after she'd hung up, Marguerite realized she had paid Kate's problems scant attention.

Marguerite hadn't mentioned that she intended to ask Annalise and the others to stop by at six as well. The meeting was to be a command performance. If they hadn't heard from Win Smith, they would soon enough.

"Egon kept a journal." The words were pronounced by Marguerite at precisely six-fifteen that evening. Her visitors were seated in her gold-toned living room, a cloistered, comfortable place with a fire crackling in the fireplace and subdued lighting from under pleated silk lampshades. "For years," Marguerite told them. "Leather-bound with ruled paper like a child's notebook. Took it everywhere with him."

A moment of silence ensued. Marguerite, who sat close to the fire on a straight-backed Queen Anne chair, at last broke the quiet. "I used to see him writing in it. 'My history of the world,' he'd tell me when I asked him what he was doing."

"Yes, of course. Win got his hands on Egon's little history." Annalise stood up and restlessly went over to the fireplace. She remained there with her back to the room, reaching her hands out and warming them. "One always confided in Egon. After all, wasn't he our father confessor? Didn't he help us over the rough spots in our lives? And we were only too eager to use him as a confidant when we trusted no one else."

" 'Tell me, darling, you look a trifle peaked,' " Ralley said, imitating Egon at his most solicitous. She held a cigarette in one hand and a martini glass in the other. "I remember Egon regarding me with those wide eyes of his absolutely moist with worry. A trifle peaked. Lovely bait, that 'Tell me everything, get it off your chest.' You wanted him to know *tutti*, the whole enchilada of how you ticked. Tell it to papa. Or maybe mama. Dammit."

"Great listener, though," Jaybee added. "Isn't that what we always said about him? The man really listens."

Kate wasn't quite certain why they were suddenly condemning Egon. "What's going on?" she asked impatiently. "I don't recall any journals."

Her four friends stared at her. "Obviously you never confided in him," Ralley said.

Kate reared up. "I didn't have to. My life all along has been a bloody open book that the whole world has read chapter by chapter: a husband, a child, a divorce, a famous boss who died of AIDS."

"Oh, damn," Ralley said, "I'm sorry, Kate. That was bitchy of me."

"Plus a mother whose divorces and remarriages regularly make the *National Enquirer*. And the final blow—a partner who died of bullet wounds before the whole world, but of course Egon wouldn't have known that," Kate went on. "Open the newspaper, turn on your television set, you'll see the rerun of Kate Hayden's life in full color. Today I had to put off David Orenstein who wants to do a story about me from the day I was conceived on. I told him to call Holly Good and interview her."

"The only thing you left out is a call from Win Smith," Marguerite said.

"Win Smith? Why would he call me?"

Annalise said, "Kate, he's blackmailing all of us. He's probably wondering just how he's going to handle you."

"Handle me! I don't even know him. I met him at your place, Ralley, had two words with him as I recall."

"They may have been two wrong words. He wants to become director of the Delville Museum," Ralley told her, "and he's using blackmail to get it."

Kate regarded her, nonplussed, then turned her gaze on each of them in turn. She was speechless, questions forming in her mind that she could never ask. "What about Reuben, Mortimer Quinlan, Locke Warren?" she managed at last. Kate hesitated, then added, "Zack?"

"He knows Zack won't be a problem because of me," Annalise said. "And I doubt Win will take on Reuben, who was stuck with the fallout from Smarts."

"The little turd thinks he's safe," Jaybee reminded Ralley. "He gave me a song and dance about the source of his information being in the hands of his lawyer, et cetera, et cetera."

"I suppose we ought to warn Locke and Mortimer," Ralley said.

Marguerite said, "I was thinking about that. Perhaps they've already heard from our little blackmailer."

"He has us by the *cojones*," Ralley said. "I suggest we find the little bastard and kill him. That's the best way to stop him. I'll take his throat. What about you, Jaybee?"

"His *cojones*, of course."

"It's no laughing matter. He could have us for the rest of our lives. Does anyone know where he lives?" Annalise came across the room, kicked off her shoes, sat down on the couch, and tucked her feet under her. She looked at each of them in turn. "We *do* have to stop him, you know."

"I've already talked to Reuben," Ralley went on. "Win just walked away from the gallery, leaving Reuben to sort everything out. No one knows where he's holing up. I've tried to find Cliff. I figured maybe he'd know. So far, no luck."

Jaybee gave a bitter laugh. "Win really sold me a bill of goods about why he gave up the gallery. I believed him."

"Call in the authorities," Kate said.

"Kate, this is blackmail," Ralley said tiredly. "We're not in a position to call the police."

Kate, however, was thinking of Pete. "Look, I have a friend—"

Jaybee cut in. "No police, no friends, not even enemies. What we've talked about doesn't leave this room."

A sudden quiet and a meeting of eyes followed, and Kate realized that whatever competition existed between them, whatever sharp words, or one person's success over another's, they were now bonded together irrevocably. They might have come from different directions and backgrounds, but the bitter experiences they had survived had come back to destroy them in the form of Win Smith. And if Marguerite was right, Egon Delville was still shaping their lives.

Egon had hated Ira and now Ira was dead. Perhaps that was why Kate had been spared a call from Win Smith. If Ira were alive, Kate reasoned, probably she would be a victim of blackmail, too. "If I do hear from Win—" she began and was interrupted by Marguerite.

"We want to find out where he lives," she said in a manner that indicated she had already given the possibility some thought. "Meet him somewhere. Agree to his terms. When he leaves, follow him."

"And then?"

"One or all of us will kidnap him and torture the journal out of him," Ralley said.

Kate laughed. "That's your solution? I'm beginning to think this whole thing is a joke."

"It's no joke," Marguerite said. "We agreed to his terms because we had no choice. The four of us acting in concert *will* have a choice. I propose that if we discover where Winthrop Smith is staying, we make it our business to learn whether he left the journal with someone, as he claims, or whether it's in his possession."

"It?" Annalise asked. "Surely he wrote more than one."

"Then we'll have to find them all," Marguerite said.

"I go this way," Kate said to Win Smith two days later when he'd surprised her with a phone call, and after they'd had lunch at a kosher delicatessen on Thirty-sixth Street off Broadway.

"I'm heading back downtown to the gallery."

"Well, good luck to your artist. I think he has talent."

"Thanks for the lead." He gave her a smile that Ralley warned her would be full of sincerity.

"Any time. As I explained, it's a tough town to make a go of it in. But it's for Egon's memory."

He waved good-bye and headed down Seventh Avenue. Kate began to tail him. She had trouble keeping him in view, although that worked to her advantage as well. The one o'clock lunchtime mob streamed out of office buildings, pouring into the streets like so much lava, only to end up at cross purposes with the clothes trolleys that were pushed relentlessly along the sidewalks.

Win didn't seem to be in a great hurry. He still carried the portfolio of fabric designs he was hawking for one of his artists, or that he claimed to be hawking.

When he reached the cross street, Win stepped out into traffic and tried to hail a cab going downtown. Kate watched him covertly through the passing traffic. After a few moments, he crossed the street and began to walk downtown. Kate, too, crossed the avenue and kept a discreet distance away. She was still puzzled by the conversation they'd had over lunch. He hadn't tried to blackmail her; he'd discussed Smarts as though it were still a viable business, and Win spent a lot of time reminiscing about Egon. Kate wasn't impressed. Egon had never mentioned him, and she had been warned by Ralley that he was a liar.

Win stopped at a light and Kate watched in amazement as he deposited the black portfolio, in which he carried the putative samples of fabric design, in a litter basket. A moment before she had been questioning why she was following him when her work called so desperately. Now she understood. She had all the confirmation she needed that Win Smith was on a fishing expedition of some kind but that he hadn't selected the bait quite yet. The traffic light turned green. Kate, waiting fifty feet back, almost missed seeing him hail a cab and step into it just before the light changed. The cab made it through and turned down Broadway. Kate ran out into the street, but Win's cab was long gone before one stopped to pick her up.

CHAPTER 28

$\mathbf{B}$roome Street," Win told the taxicab driver, giving him the address of the May Collins Gallery. He leaned back, gleefully watching the rapidly moving meter. Race on, Macduff, he said to himself, I can afford ye. He was on top of the world. He had a pocketful of cash, and prospects of a bright future. Kate Hayden, on the matter of Egon Delville, was as innocent as a newborn lamb.

The May Collins Gallery occupied the ground floor of a renovated cast-iron loft building. Peering in the window, Win saw that the gallery, but for the receptionist, was empty. The street was also deserted at that time of day. He didn't feel at all sorry for the gallery owner. May Collins did most of her business with museums, both domestic and international, as well as with serious collectors who were ushered in through side doors, unlike common folk. Standing there he experienced a moment of real anger over opportunities missed. If Egon had held on a couple of months more, Smarts would have hit the jackpot. Egon would have brought his rich friends around. It would have happened, it would have.

He opened the door to the gallery and felt a rush of nostalgia. The smell of varnish and paint was overwhelming. The walls were white, the floors smooth, pale, and shiny. The front of the gallery was hung with realistic drawings in silvertip—ocean waves, a detail of a tree trunk, closely observed flowers. At his approach the receptionist gave him a toothy smile. Win straightened his shoulders like a man about to make a major purchase.

"Yes, may I help you?"

"I'm looking for Cliff Beal," he said. "I've got those photos he wanted."

"Right." She gestured toward the rear of the gallery. "He was in there a while ago."

Win smiled his thanks. His shoes made a clicking noise on the highly polished floors as he headed back. He stopped at the open door to the workroom. Cliff was alone, standing at a table and gazing at a long, narrow canvas that lay facedown. Looking at him without Cliff's knowing it did something to Win. The craving escalated; he hadn't felt that way in a long time, but he had to be careful about his approach. With things going great, he might just get the artist back.

"Hey, Cliff, man, how you doing?" He came into the room and clapped Cliff's shoulder.

"Got my stuff?" Cliff didn't look up and with a quick movement brushed Win away.

"I have them, but you never showed up."

"You're so full of shit," Cliff said. He shook his head and with a quick, disgusted glance took Win in. "Jeez, you take the fuckin' cake. I know you closed the place up. I met Maxi Franilero, and he told me you screwed him out of his money."

"He's a liar. It just takes time. Too bad you left, Cliff, but listen, that's your business. Anyway, I got something really big coming down the pike."

"Fuck off." Cliff grabbed the picture and turned it right side up.

"Great stuff," Win said. He went around the table and pretended to be interested in the work encrusted with paint and found objects. "When's the show?"

"Next month."

"Well, May Collins is Connection City. You'll end up on museum walls. Maybe my museum walls."

"I don't know what the fuck you're talking about."

"They're turning Egon's town house into a museum and as the expert with the most knowledge about the place, yours truly has agreed to take the post of director."

Cliff turned and stared at him, his look of disbelief tempered with a certain interest as though with Win, anything was possible. "You've got a screw loose," he said at last. "Ralley said Egon was going to kick you the hell out of there and you know why."

"Egon died before he could kick a roach out of there. I'm going to be director of the museum, and I'm staying in the place for the duration."

"Sweet dreams."

"Come on, I'll take you there now. You can have the private guided tour, pick out the spot you want your painting hung."

Cliff suddenly looked interested. "Ralley always talked about that place. What the hell is it? A holy shrine?"

"Come on," Win said. "See for yourself."

Cliff grabbed Win by the collar. "If you're pulling my leg, I'm going to walk on your face."

"If I'm not telling you the truth, I'll lend you the spike boots."

When they entered the town house an hour later, Win turned off the burglar alarm with a flourish. He moved with a proprietary air, leading Cliff, who was clearly impressed, from room to room, explaining the salient points of the collection.

"Someone could steal this place blind," Cliff said when they reached Egon's room on the third floor, and regarded Win with something amounting to respect. "No one would ever know the difference."

"*I'd* know the difference," Win said importantly.

"This where you bed down?"

"No way, man. This was Egon's room. It's a fuckin' shrine, like you said. Come on, I'll show you where I bed down. It was good enough when Egon was alive," Win explained when they reached the fifth floor, "and it's good enough for me. I figure I'll turn the rest of the rooms up here into offices. Nothing like flopping out of bed and into work."

"I like it," Cliff said, striding into the room and throwing himself across the bed. "This place has definite possibilities."

"I thought you'd like it," Win said. He reached over and began to stroke Cliff's forehead. Then he climbed in beside him.

Cliff leaned back and put his hands behind his head. He lay there, staring up at the ceiling. "Well, listen, I mean May Collins figures my work is going to go through the roof."

"Great. Then we'll both make it."

"Yeah, right, well, I guess there's a time and place for everything."

Win knew what was expected of him. Carefully, with faintly trembling fingers, he unbuttoned Cliff's shirt and then ran his hand in a leisurely way across the artist's chest, through the crisp hair. Win was hot and ready, but he instinctively understood he'd have to control his desires for a while. With slow, deliberate movements he trailed his fingers down Cliff's thigh and across his crotch. Cliff was soft. To hide his disappointment, Win bent over his friend and bit his nipple. He felt the surprise rush through Cliff and was rewarded by the feel of an erection beginning under his ministering fingers.

"Hey, man, easy, easy," Cliff said.

"Sure, Cliff, whatever way you want it." Win figured he'd have to work for his reward, but a little work never hurt anybody.

An hour later, Win stirred, lifted himself on his elbow, and admired Cliff's sleeping profile. Things were definitely looking up. A few good moves and Cliff had responded by going down on Win and meaning it.

Feeling the brush of Win's breath on his face, Cliff opened his eyes, checked his watch, and leapt out of bed. "Shit, I'm due at the gallery. I've got an appointment with May." He groped for his pants.

"Wait just a minute," Win said, getting out of bed and grabbing a paisley robe. "I've got a little present for you. Back in a flash."

There was no reason for the crap Egon collected to molder away in some airless case to be gazed at by people who couldn't care less. He ran down to Egon's bedroom and opened a velvet-lined box on the dresser. Of the more than two dozen cuff links in the case, he selected a pair of heavy gold ones, lions' heads with ruby eyes. Egon's initials were engraved on the backs, but Cliff wouldn't even notice.

"Here," he said, coming into the bedroom where he found Cliff smoothing his hair with Win's brush.

Cliff took the present and assessed it carefully. "Just like that?" he asked. "Just like that."

"Son of a bitch," Cliff said. "Who the hell wears cuff links? But you wanna know something? You couldn't pry these out of me."

When Cliff was gone, Win felt unexpectedly flustered. Cliff hadn't said a word about where he was bedding down. Still, by the time Win was back in his room, the good mood had returned. His life was on a positive trail. He had to plan his moves, make no false starts, no mistakes. He yawned. Time to think about his future when he was wide awake. What he wanted now was a couple of hours of dreamless sleep. He dozed off and was awakened later by a sound, not quite identifiable. Street noise, perhaps. He lay in a pleasant daze, thinking of Cliff. There was another faint movement, more sensed than heard. In another moment he decided the noise had come from inside the house. The caretaker, probably. He quickly sat up but was frozen by the sound of a footstep outside his door.

He stared ahead as the door was pushed open; his unease deepened into fear. "Hey, listen," he said, making no attempt to hide his surprise. "We can talk."

CHAPTER 29

Pete walked through the station house, past the ringing telephones and loud talk, to the captain's office. He knocked twice and then stepped in. Mallory had the phone to his ear, a stogie between his lips, a couple of officers shuffling over some papers on a desk that was buried under a snowdrift of files, and a bootblack polishing his shoes. He gestured to Pete to come in.

Captain Mallory of the Nineteenth Precinct had no reason to believe the murders of Win Smith and Ira Gregory were related. Pete wouldn't have wondered about the connection, either, but for something Kate had said. When he picked her up on his way to work that morning, a habit he had every intention of preserving, she pointed to the Friday morning newspaper headline.

"Now, what do you suppose Win was doing at Egon's town house?"

She regarded Pete innocently enough but he detected a kind of elation behind her words. Her eyes held an unusual sparkle, one he thought of as triumph.

"Did you know him?" he asked.

"Not really. I talked to him once, maybe twice."

"Recently?" He glanced at the newspaper photograph, which revealed Win Smith as handsome but bland.

"He was at Ralley's party," Kate said, folding the newspaper and tucking it into her bag. "You were there."

Pete had never heard of Win Smith before that morning when he tuned into an all-news radio station.

"Nothing on Gregory," the captain said around the stogie. "Now there's been another fashion murder. At least," he added, "that's the way the media will view it. Ira Gregory, in the fashion business. The Delville town house, site of a fashion museum. What the hell's going on here?"

"Do you see a connection?"

The captain shook his head. "Win Smith shouldn't have been in that town house. He must have sneaked back in, because his clothes were there. They found him in his old bedroom, shot through the head, wearing a silk paisley robe the cleaning lady identified as belonging to Egon Delville. We'd guess Smith knew the intruder."

"Know much about the victim?" Pete asked.

"He ran a gallery called Smarts that was bankrolled first by Egon Delville, then by the Delville estate. He got deep into debt and walked away from the gallery owing money to at least one artist and to all his suppliers. He disappeared completely from the scene and fished up dead a couple of weeks later in the town house he should have had no access to."

Pete got to his feet as the telephone rang, fitting in a question. "Who found the body?"

The captain picked up the receiver, asked his caller to hold, and said, "There's a cleaning lady comes in to dust a couple of times a week, letting herself in through the service entrance."

"Did she know Win Smith?"

"Saw him coming and going when Delville was alive but didn't know him. No one was supposed to be in the house, incidentally. The caretaker has the basement apartment with a separate entrance. She's a college kid juggling her time and social life. The town house was at the bottom of her list of priorities, and incidentally, she hasn't been upstairs in two days. Or that's what she claims."

"Any idea how the killer got into the house?"

"The alarm was turned off. Smith died twenty-four hours before the cleaning lady found him. If the caretaker is telling the truth and had nothing to do with the murder, then the killer had plenty of time to act."

"Thanks, Captain." Pete went to the door and turned back to find Mallory watching him.

"One other question," Pete said.

Mallory frowned.

"The name of our cleaning lady."

"Check the detective on the job."

"No problem, Mrs. Kosrovski. I just want to ask you a few questions." Pete held his identification up to the peephole. He heard a series of locks unbolted one by one like the security system at Attica Prison.

"How do I know you're from the Justice Department?" The cleaning woman opened the door a fraction.

"Because I just showed you my identification card."

"Doesn't mean a damn." She unchained the door and stood there surveying him. She was a small pock-marked woman in her early fifties with hard eyes of a shiny green flecked with yellow. She clutched her flowered housedress close to her chest. Gazing past her into the kitchen, Pete saw a sullen-looking teenager sitting at a table eating a sandwich. The youngster got up and disappeared into another room. Pete figured he'd just caught the scent of the law.

"I'm not a cop, Mrs. Kosrovski. I'm an attorney with the Justice Department and you don't have to answer any of my questions, but I wish you would anyway." He was following tracks that had nothing to do with RICO and the garment district, only Kate.

"Come on in, then." Her voice held the resignation of someone who all her life had acquiesced to more important people's wishes. "I have some coffee on the boil if you want some."

"As a matter of fact, I would."

She bustled into the kitchen and with a swipe cleared the table of crumbs. "I don't mind talking about what I found, but it scared the hell out of me at the time. They were thinking of covering the furniture when Mr. Delville died," she went on, her tone taking on the self-importance of the eyewitness who will relive the experience at the slightest provocation. "You know, with sheets, but they decided to keep everything like a shrine, just the way it always was. Mr. Newcombe said Mr. Delville would turn over in his grave if he knew they were covering his furniture with sheets. So I vacuum, dust, do what has to be done, like I've always done."

"Which wasn't much, I imagine, until Mr. Smith moved in."

She cast a level gaze at him. "He didn't move in."

"The police say he was living there."

"He wasn't living there."

"You know that for a fact."

"He wasn't living there; I'd have known."

"Nonetheless, they found his clothes."

"In a closet, I never do closets."

"And he was wearing a bathrobe."

She blanched. "I know that better than you. And it was Mr. Delville's robe. Mrs. Varick gave it to him."

"Mrs. Varick?"

"Mr. Delville's friend. Sometimes I did for her when her maid was sick."

"Do you know if anything else was stolen?"

Her eyes glinted. "I noticed things were missing."

"And you told no one?"

"Sure, I told Mr. Newcombe when I first noticed. He said he'd send the insurance adjuster around."

"And did he?"

"How do I know?"

"And what precisely was missing?"

She shrugged. "Little things. I can't say exactly, some silver things, for instance. Mr. Delville, may he rest in peace, collected silver animals. Deer and rabbits and squirrels. And the books were gone. I noticed that right away, weeks ago. Mr. Newcombe said they were probably at the warehouse."

"What books, Mrs. Kosrovski?"

"Like notebooks. Leather-bound with gold dates on them. They were on the library shelf for years. He kept adding to them. I always figured he was writing in them."

"And you never looked them over, inside I mean. Just out of curiosity?"

She stared at him defiantly. "Once, just to satisfy myself. I wasn't a snoop. Once, a long time ago."

"And what did you read?"

She shrugged. "About fancy parties, things like that. He'd put in what people were wearing and stuff. His handwriting was tiny, hard to read."

He handed her his card. "If you can think of where they might be, call me at this number," he said.

"Mr. Newcombe would know."

CHAPTER 30

Captain Mallory called Pete at his office later that afternoon. "Tie-in time," he said in his gruff voice. "We found some notes the deceased left in his pants pocket. Thought you might like to know Win Smith had an appointment the day of his murder with Ira Gregory's partner, Kate Hayden."

Pete held the phone away from his ear for a moment. Damn, she had lied to him.

"There's a limit to coincidence," Mallory was saying.

"I suppose you pulled her in."

"It isn't against the law to have your name on a slip of paper, even if the owner of that note is dead. We have somebody at her office now taking a deposition."

After Pete hung up, he dialed Kate's number and was put through at once. "Are you alone?"

"Now, yes." She sounded tired, depressed.

"Why did you lie to me?"

"I didn't lie."

"Kate—"

"You don't know anything about anything. This—this doesn't even involve me. It involves . . . Dammit, just don't ask me, Pete."

"What time do you finish work?"

"We'll be going on all night, thanks to these bloody damn interruptions."

"I'll be at your office at ten."

"Pete, Win Smith wasn't a friend of mine; he wasn't even an enemy, I promise you."

"Ten o'clock." Then he added in a calmer voice, wanting to believe her, "Don't work too hard."

"Hard work is what's keeping me sane," she said, adding, "I'll see you at ten."

He put down the receiver and checked his watch. Nearly five. A backlog of work would keep him busy for the next five hours. Good, because he didn't want to think about Kate.

When he arrived at the showroom, he found half a dozen people still working, including Aaron Jaffee. The table was laden with partially eaten sandwiches, cans of soda with bent straws sticking out of them, copies of *W*, boxes of trim, and assorted materials he couldn't identify. The smell of deli pickles was mixed with that of stale coffee.

Kate sat on the floor at her model's feet, fixing the hem of a long sparkling gown. "She tripped," she explained to Pete, "and went right through it with her dagger heel."

"I'm sorry, I'm sorry, I'm sorry," Vivian said.

Kate, wearing black pants with a black blouse, got tiredly to her feet. A long white thread and some sequins clung to the pants.

"Oops," Elfie said, coming over to her. "You look as if you've been dipped in a vat of dust balls." She removed the thread and held it up in the air. "Reminds me of a cat I once owned."

Kate began brushing her pants. "It does belong to a cat you once owned. What am I talking about?"

Pete took Kate by the arm. "Come on, let's go. You need to get away from here for a while."

She made no effort to resist. "Okay, gang, let's call it a day. I think I'm bushed. Bright and early tomorrow morning."

"Bright and early?" Vivian said. "Tomorrow's Saturday. I'm never bright and early on Saturday."

"You'll make it," Kate said. She cast an exhausted smile at Pete. "Just let me throw some water on my face. Or somebody throw some water on my face, anybody."

Ten minutes later they left the building. Pete directed her to the pool car he had commandeered. "Let's go for a drive," he said.

"I'd just as soon go home and go to bed."

"I'll take you there the long way around. Don't fall asleep on me," he said when she slumped down and put her head against the back rest. "I want to talk to you."

"Why bother talking to me? You think I lied to you. You won't believe anything I say."

He headed toward the West Side Highway, figuring on taking the George Washington Bridge into New Jersey. A drive along the Palisades Parkway might be soothing and there was a lookout point that drew in fresh breezes from the river. "What did Win Smith see you about?"

"He was a jerk."

"That's your answer, he was a jerk."

"He tried to exploit my friendship with Egon. He thought I could help him with some fabric designs. I couldn't. That was all. I live on the East Side, remember?" She yawned.

"For somebody who should be worried, Kate, you're not."

"My life is going down the tubes. I'm too worried about the collection and my future to be worried about anything else."

"Odd Win Smith should call you the day he died."

"You'll have to ask him how that happened."

"That all you told the police?"

"There was nothing *to* tell. We had lunch, he showed me his portfolio—"

"You had lunch with someone you didn't know at the height of what you call the busiest week of the year."

"It was the easiest way to get rid of him," she said hotly.

"Remind me to sell you something. You sound like a soft touch."

"Dammit, he was a blackmailer, a *blackmailer*. You want me to tell that to the police?"

He drew the car screeching over to the curb and then slammed on the brake. It took him seconds to gain control of his feelings. He was afraid for her and for what he didn't know. "You were being blackmailed by Win Smith?"

"No, that's not what I said. I said he was a blackmailer and that's why I went out to lunch with him. But all he did was show me his portfolio. I made it clear I couldn't help him and passed along a couple of names, that's all. Oh, and he talked a lot about Egon. I let him, because . . . well, just because. After a while he seemed to run out of steam. He picked up the lunch tab, we parted, and that," she said, throwing Pete an odd, sidelong glance, "was that."

"Yet you call him a blackmailer."

"Right. He is. Was."

"What about the portfolio, anything strike you as funny about it?"

"Drawings that looked almost like wallpaper samples, but they were hidden behind acetate so I couldn't touch them. They were silk-screened, if you ask me. And I just remembered the most extraordinary thing," she added, furrowing her brow. "He threw the whole thing, portfolio and all, into a litter basket once he thought I was gone."

"A blackmailer throws his portfolio away and you watch him do it. You wouldn't happen to have been following him, would you?"

Kate turned from him with a truculent glance. "I told the police everything that was relevant to our meeting."

"Why didn't you come to me, not as someone from the Justice Department, but as a friend, Kate, a friend. You know I care what happens to you."

She was quiet for a moment, then said, "Let's go home."

The apartment was quiet when she invited him in. Although it was close to midnight, Pete half hoped to meet Matt again, as though the child could act as referee between him and Kate.

"My son's with his father for the weekend," she said.

Not his father's weekend with the boy, Pete remembered, hating himself for keeping track. He supposed it had something to do with Kate's busy schedule.

She led him into the kitchen and gestured to the table. "How about a drink? If you're hungry I can make some—"

"I'm not hungry. How about orange juice, a nice macho drink."

"Great. We're set up here for orange juice drinkers." She pulled a full bottle from the refrigerator and then with a conspiratorial smile took a cookie jar down and put it on the table.

"What makes you think Win was a blackmailer?"

"You wouldn't know if the police found some journals, would you? I mean with the body?"

He watched her evenly. What the hell, he was off duty, and he hadn't been going by the book since he'd first met her. "If they did, they haven't told me about them. Journals?"

"Egon kept journals. We think Win found them and used them to blackmail some people I know. We didn't know where he was staying, or even if they were actually in his possession. If the police have the books . . . Oh, hell," she said sitting down and leaning across the table toward him. "Pete, I wanted you to know the minute I learned about Win. I even suggested that I knew someone who might help them. They said no, they'd take care of it. Damn, I'm squealing on my own friends."

"Just tell me what happened, Kate, from the beginning."

She nodded. "Right. From the beginning. But off the record."

"He was killed around six o'clock that evening," Pete said when Kate finished telling her story. "Where were you?"

"That's in the deposition. Where I should have been. At home with Matt. I returned to my office at seven."

"Witnesses?"

"Not exactly. The gang got a couple of hours off around that time. Aaron Jaffee stuck me with a load of homework, and I was deep into that."

"I suppose you told your friends about losing Win in traffic. Anybody angry that you failed?"

She shook her head. "No, I don't think so. They said things like, 'Oh, too bad,' and 'We'll get the little bastard yet.' And there was speculation on how come I've led such an exemplary life that I can't be blackmailed." She got up and poured the coffee, which Pete finished in a gulp.

"Get some sleep," he told her. "I'll see you in the morning."

She accompanied him to the door and handed him his raincoat. "Do you believe me?"

He shrugged the raincoat on. "I want to."

"But you don't think I've led an exemplary life and therefore I'm suspect."

He lifted her chin and planted a kiss on her lips. "I don't dwell on the past, not even the recent past. Everything about you pleases me. Just don't lie to me."

"I haven't," she said simply. "I haven't, Pete."

CHAPTER 31

City streets were being wetted down by a light drizzle the next morning
when Pete headed for the Nineteenth Precinct, an old building of absolutely
no architectural refinement that nevertheless fit into the most elegant neighborhood in the city.

Inside, Pete confronted a lull that presaged the crush of the usual weekend
outrages. He found Captain Mallory talking to one of his lieutenants at the
outside desk.

"We got lucky on this one," Mallory said when he had Pete alone. "A call
came in from the May Collins Gallery in SoHo. The receptionist there recognized Win's picture, said he was there the day of the murder looking for one
of their artists, Cliff Beal."

"Cliff Beal, son of a bitch," Pete exclaimed. The artist who was sharing
Ralley's loft.

"You know him."

"I knew he was hanging out in a loft belonging to Ralley Littlehurst."

Mallory looked surprised. "And Littlehurst was present at Raven's when
Ira Gregory was murdered. The long arm of coincidence meets the long arm
of the law, except that Cliff Beal has been staying at a sublet belonging to an
art historian, a man. Smith showed up at the May Collins Gallery asking for
Beal. They left together a little while later. Beal admitted readily that he
knew the victim, that he spent the afternoon with him, and said he left him
well and alive. He claimed Smith was director of the Delville Museum and
that he was living in the town house legitimately. But Beal was running
scared. He voluntarily showed us a pair of gold cuff links with the initials
E. D. on them, said Win had given them to him. Cartier identified them as
having been made specifically for Delville."

"Where's Beal now?"

"We didn't book him. He was with the owner of the gallery at the time of
Smith's death. But we have someone else. When Beal got back to the Collins
gallery, he met another artist, Maxi Franilero, and a pal of his, a character
called Doherty, Chuck Doherty. Beal told them about Win's setup. Franilero
had been one of Smith's artists, and Smith apparently owed him money.

Hearing that he'd fallen into a pot of gold, the two took off to see him, no doubt with the idea of taking the debt out in merchandise. Come on," Mallory said, leading the way to an interrogation room. "You can hear the rest of the story from the perpetrator himself."

"Franilero?"

"Franilero's dead. His sidekick, Doherty."

Pete let out a low whistle.

Chuck Doherty was sitting where Kate had sat earlier that week. He was a big man who must have weighed in at two hundred fifty pounds. He wore a leather jacket with a slash down the back. His pale blond hair was cut short on the sides. The two detectives who had questioned Kate were now questioning him. Doherty didn't look up when Mallory and Pete stepped into the room. Big as he was, he was clearly scared and sweating. He clenched his huge hands together on the tabletop.

The interrogating detective looked up at the captain, then at Pete before turning back to Doherty. His tone was that of a sympathetic friend who had to get at the truth in order to set Doherty free. "Franilero was about half your size, but he was a mean bugger, that what you mean?"

"Look, he came at me with a knife. We were having an argument, he came at me. I thought it was a friendly discussion, maybe a little heated, but so what, wouldn't be the first time. He took it serious."

"He came at you with a knife."

"Yeah."

"Then what?"

"I pulled the gun in self-defense."

"You were scared of a guy half your size."

"I said it was self-defense."

"Was he your lover?"

Doherty's head snapped up. "Go fuck."

"You were friends."

"It was a business arrangement, goddammit. I'm big and I can fight. Plenty of buggers get their brains beat out because they're gay. I hire out as a bodyguard when one of them thinks he's got trouble."

"That was your relationship with Maxi."

"Yeah."

"As a matter of fact, you did your pal a favor by beating up Win Smith a couple of weeks ago, right?"

"He owed Maxi money. He was a little creep, living high on the hog on money that belonged to Maxi."

"So why'd you kill Smith?"

"I didn't kill him."

His interrogator turned to the captain for a second, then back to Doherty. "Okay, let's forget Smith for the time being. What happened between you and Maxi Franilero?"

"We were arguing over money."

"You were arguing over killing Win Smith and about robbing the town house."

"I said I didn't kill that little creep."

"But you killed Maxi Franilero."

At that point the second detective jumped in. "Hey, Doherty, you've got a record as long as your arm. You're wanted in Ohio on a murder-robbery charge. The police in San Francisco have a warrant out on you. Murder of a loan shark who was preying on the gay community. You've been one busy boy, a private vigilante army of one."

Doherty took his jacket off. Semicircles of sweat dampened his armpits. He stretched his legs, then tucked them under his chair.

"You'll need an alibi for the time of Smith's death."

"I was with Maxi."

"Gee, too bad he isn't around as a witness."

"He came at me."

"And Smith? He came at you, too?"

"He was dead when we got there. . . . I mean we were never there. . . . Oh, shit."

"We found your fingerprints all over the house."

"I didn't kill him."

The detective got up, turned his chair around, and then straddled it. "This is how it happened," he said to Doherty. "You and Maxi went to the town house to settle the debt with Win Smith. You got into a fight with him and shot him dead. Then maybe you and Franilero got into an argument over the spoils of the town house . . . how to fence the stuff . . . how to divide it up. That's what happened, Doherty. Don't waste our time trying to deny it."

"Okay, okay, *okay,* so we were there, what the hell, the son of a bitch owed Maxi money. The door was open and we went in and looked for him and found him in bed in a pool of blood."

"So you left without calling the police."

"What'd you expect me to do with my record?"

"What about Maxi?"

"We figured we maybe got lucky," Doherty said. "If we could get our hands on a truck, we could back it up and clean the place out before anybody found the body."

"But you and Maxi had a lovers' quarrel," the other detective put in.

Once again Doherty wiped his fingers across his mouth. "We got into a stupid fuckin' argument over how to fence the stuff."

"And you killed Maxi like you killed Win Smith."

"I said I didn't kill that creep."

"Okay," Mickey said. "Let's start all over again."

CHAPTER 32

G o!"

Elfie's kid brother, who was in his senior year at the Juilliard School of Music gave Kate an impish, important little grin. He sat at the controls of the tape recorder that had been hooked up to loudspeakers in the showroom. The music began softly at first, Cole Porter's "Night and Day."

Kate caught Elfie in the act of crossing herself. She bit her lip, reflecting that she had no such crutch, only nerves, fear, and insubstantial ambition. All of which added up to a swarm of killer bees in her stomach and a splitting headache. Fine substitutes, though, for a genuine anxiety attack that could render her helpless.

Her promotion assistant peered through the curtain that separated the activity in the rear from the crowded noisy showroom. "Should we start the video camera now?" she asked Kate, "or wait until the show begins?"

"It might be nice to show we had an audience."

"Elle's here, Grace Mirabella's here in the flesh, also somebody new from the *New York Times.* Ruth Finley of the *Fashion Calendar;* but she's keen, she tries to cover every show. Let's see, *Harper's* and somebody's third assistant from *Vogue."*

"Women's Wear Daily?"

"Also someone new. But since the important thing is coverage in *Women's Wear,* we've seated her down front, and I'm thinking of kissing every one of her fingers if that'll help."

"News services? Television?"

"I'll get back to you, Kate. Caught Saks, Bonwit's, the fashion director of Associated Merchandising."

"Bloomingdale's?"

"Not Kal Ruttenstein, but the fourth-floor buyer and a couple of assistants."

"Bergdorf?"

"I'll get back to you, Kate. Incidentally, we've got a whole bunch of the Ladies who Lunch, thanks to Marguerite."

"Name one."

"Nan Kempner."

Kate grinned. "Hey!"

"Bianca Jagger. Isabelle Leeds."

"Hey!" But no Egon. Kate experienced a momentary disappointment, as though the possibility might remotely exist. Still, with all those honchos out there, it was make-or-break time.

The music was turned up a decible. The noise in the showroom subsided to a scraping of chairs and the sound of applause led, no doubt, by Ralley, followed by Marguerite and Jaybee.

"Let's go, let's go," Kate said, herding her first three models up the wooden steps of the small runway that led through a beige curtain into the showroom. Her fear subsided; all that was left was fierce concentration. One by one, moving quickly, the models stepped up to the runway, then proceeded forward, hipbones first, heads haughty on long necks, placing one foot in front of the other in a sensual but refined manner.

Kate ran quickly into the dressing room, where clothing was systematically taken from hangers, and matched to boxes of shoes, hats, jewelry, and gloves. Talk was subdued but hurried, through an air of suppressed hysteria. There were breathless questions about the sudden disappearance of a pair of shoes here or a bangle there. Time moved too quickly; models dashed out and back in what seemed like seconds.

Four models in narrow-legged jumpsuits were headed for the runway when Kate discovered a scarf that needed re-tying.

"Hold on," she said, quickly handling the mistake.

"You're the only one can do that, Kate," the model remarked. "You should issue a book of instructions."

"Good idea. Off you go, now."

Another, stripped of her pants suit, stood helplessly in her bra and white pantyhose.

"Everything goes," her dresser said, "but the bra and your underpants, my dear."

"Right, now I remember." The model pulled off the pantyhose and threw them in a ball to the floor. "Excuse my dust." Her dresser, sheet of instructions between her teeth, handed her a pair of black stockings.

"Don't run, please don't run," the model intoned as she drew the pair on.

"At fifteen dollars a pair, they don't run."

"Next." Kate checked her clipboard as though she hadn't memorized the show, its lineup, and every accessory.

She heard a round of applause and guessed it was for a lightweight silk crepe dress called Daydreams, with delicate tucking at the bodice, in an avocado so pale it bordered on cream.

The model wearing Daydreams came back grinning. "Did you hear the applause? I almost fell into the first row but managed to turn it into a pirouette."

"Thanks," Kate said dryly. "I thought the applause was for the dress."

"It was. Sigourney Weaver is sitting in the front row. Why didn't you tell me?" She was stripped of her dress and, while she was talking, had slipped into a dazzling light wool day suit in paisley jersey. She changed her shoes, clipped on some earrings. Someone thrust a pair of gloves into her hands.

"Don't put them on," Kate said. "Just carry them."

"Get a move on," Elfie said, standing at the door and motioning to the next row of models.

Kate could hear the volume turned up on "Just One of Those Things." Loud, she thought. Perhaps too loud, perhaps her audience wouldn't be able to concentrate.

"It's okay," Elfie said, as if reading her mind. "Gives everybody a little *Lebensraum*. My brother's a pretty smart cookie."

There was applause, not led by Ralley this time, Kate saw, peering past the curtain. The next model strutted out wearing a taupe washed-silk jacket over a short chemise in a matching fabric. Kate let the curtain drop and walked back to the dressing room thinking of Ira and how he had, for good or ill, set her on this road. A wash of emotion roiled through her when she realized she hadn't been allowing herself to dwell on him.

For a moment she was almost unmindful of the frenetic activity in the dressing room, where the racks of discarded garments were filling up.

"Break a leg, kid." She looked up sharply. She had suddenly felt Egon at her shoulder. Her support system, for what it was worth, had been Egon and Ira. They were gone and she was alone. Well, it was all hers now, design, sales, success or failure.

A model brushed past her heading for the runway. Another returned. They threw quips at each other which Kate didn't quite catch. She went back to the curtain once more and looked through to the audience. They were attentive, rapt, some even hungrily watching each turn of the model. Her heart filled with the most unexpected happiness. Next year, she promised herself, she'd use the Pierre or the Puck Building, where she'd have a longer runway and a lot more room for the overflow crowd. And more clothes. She felt the high that came from the creative act fulfilled. Kate had no idea what the outcome of the collection might be, but for now her audience seemed won.

The dinner dresses were shown in quick succession until the small runway was crowded with half a dozen models wearing dresses with uneven handkerchief hems and soft draping at the shoulders. The colors were muted, the fabric, silk mousseline, crepe de chine and chiffon. The skirts had a swing that flattered a woman's walk and made her legs the focus of attention. Waists were shown off, arms bared, necklines filled with a king's ransom of tiny beads giving emphasis to the color of skin, of hair, of makeup.

When at last the long evening dresses were assembled backstage, the models were columns of black silk with tiny diamonds at their ears. As soon as the black gowns filled the runway, Kate's final gown made its entrance—a remembered and well-loved color combination from her childhood, based on a dress her mother had worn: another silk column, but in fiery red flowers on white, the distribution of colors equal. The columns of black parted. The model took the course of the runway slowly, head high. The line across the neck was straight but when she turned, she revealed a bare back dipped to the waist, with a diamond clip emphasizing the point.

The music stopped. Kate, just behind the curtain, heard an outburst of applause. Someone shouted her name. It was all over and Kate, who had decided against the traditional ending of a bridal gown, wasn't sure if she felt elated or sad. Soon there'd be a scrape of chairs as her audience prepared to dash to the next showing on their lists.

The curtain parted and her model in red and white came toward her smiling. "C'mon, Kate, they want to see you."

She waited a second, then bounced up on the runway in jeans, discovering as she came through the curtain that her audience was genuinely applauding the collection. She shivered with happiness, and stumbled on her first step, which elicited a relieved laugh from the audience as her models led her down the runway and back. Out of the corner of her eye, she was astonished to see Pete standing with Aaron Jaffee at the back of the room. He grinned and flashed her a V for victory sign.

When the curtain closed behind her and Elfie and her assistants had finished their shouting and hugging, Kate came to her senses. "What we want to know now is will they write paper?"

Amid the euphoria and confusion of the crowd that soon materialized around her, she felt a hand on her shoulder.

"Egon would be proud of his little girl," Marguerite said in French while planting a kiss on each cheek.

"Nice, all of a piece, very original," someone else said, pumping her hand. Marguerite faded away before Kate had a chance to talk to her.

"Love the fabrics. I'll give you a call, Kate. I've got just so many price points, however. May be spread a little thin but I'm anxious to talk to you. Ta-ta."

"We'll work it out," Kate managed, recognizing the buyer from Marshall Field.

"No problems?" The owner of an elegant boutique in Palm Springs gave her a curious smile, one that asked for intimate details of Ira's death and the way the company would survive.

"No problems of delivery," Kate said cheerfully. "DAS is behind me every step of the way."

"I'll give you a call, make an appointment as soon as possible."

Kate was distracted from wondering about the meaning of the double-edged smile offered her by a tall, thin man who said, "I don't know if you remember me; I'm David Orenstein."

Someone jostled her from the rear and she turned to find herself pumping the hand of one of Marguerite's society ladies, who talked hurriedly about a projected charity fashion show at the Metropolitan Museum of Art.

David Orenstein was still with her, however. "I'm on that story about mob infiltration of the garment industry," he told her. "I was interested in catching your collection."

"I don't think this is the time for an interview, Mr. Orenstein." Kate could scarcely make sense of his words. In spite of the crush she thought she had never felt more alone and without direction. She looked past the crowd and saw Pete standing with Aaron Jaffee. He caught her eye and she relaxed a little.

"Right," Orenstein was saying. "I mean, this is your crowning moment. I'll get back to you. The only thing I'm curious about now is how you're going to handle DAS putting your company up for sale. I understand they own world rights to your name."

"Aaron, how did this happen?"

Kate, standing over his desk in Ira's office, pounded her hand on the wooden surface. "And why in hell didn't you tell me? I had to hear it from a reporter when probably the whole world knows." She collapsed into a chair. "How can DAS sell the company? I thought you were keeping their assets intact."

"We are. Outside of that, DAS can do what it wants, as long as taxes are duly paid and they aren't breaking any United States laws. They obviously want to sell the company while the name Kate Hayden is a viable one."

"But my name, they're going to sell *my name.*"

He reached across the desk as though to pat her hand. "Take it easy, Kate. Offers don't come that easy when the designer herself isn't available. Your name, I'm sorry to say," he added with an apologetic air, "isn't exactly a household word on the Asian steppes. Let's see how much paper you write as a result of the collection."

"And then?"

"First things first, Kate. You sold your name, not your soul. The buyer wasn't the devil, just a mob figure. He'll be open for negotiation." After a moment, during which time Aaron smiled benevolently at her, he said, "Mollified?"

She shook her head. "I've been so incredibly stupid."

"Ambitious, that's all."

She got to her feet feeling exhausted and depressed. "Well, I guess the next week should tell. What if DAS sells?"

He waved her away. "We'll put out a contract on Daguras."

Click.

The picture came on the small video screen to Latin music with a particularly Brazilian tempo. Annalise had decided at the last minute to switch from Vivaldi to bossa nova to underscore the collection. The beat worked although she had worried about her choice all through the showing.

Four models stepped quickly onto the runway at the Plaza Hotel, wearing black Puritan-collared dresses of identical prints, thin black stripes on champagne linen, the same black stripes against emerald, white against black, and black against pale brick; the sleeves were full and gathered at the shoulder, with black cuffs. They wore huge black straw hats and shaded stockings with black pumps, four schoolgirls moving sexily to the Latin beat, hips forward, arms swinging.

Alone in her Greenwich country house, for the servants had gone to their quarters over the garage shortly after her arrival, Annalise watched the tape analytically. But something was pulling at her, interrupting her concentration, and it had nothing to do with the collection. She dragged in a long breath and forced herself to go on studying the tape.

The wools were cashmere or alpaca; the silks five and six ply; embroidery was done in India; buttonholes handmade. Jackets were weighted with chains at the inside hem to keep them hanging right. Pants, lined with silk, were pleated and curved to flatter any figure.

For late day and formal wear, the collection contained sequined jackets topping short skirts that were slit high and buttoned at the hip, black "smoking" jackets with short slit skirts that paid homage to Yves Saint Laurent. There were great evening capes in satin with monks' hoods over long silk chiffon gowns gathered below bodice knots.

Unlike Kate, who elected not to end her show with the traditional bridal gown, Annalise produced a demure wedding dress of white chiffon studded with white, pale turquoise and pink beads, intertwined with silver embroidery.

The music stopped abruptly. Annalise switched the VCR off. The clothes were absolutely correct for her ladies, though she could all but hear Marguerite banging away at her typewriter: "Annalise is playing it safe, happy with the status quo, but then isn't that what her ladies want?"

She checked her watch. It was nearly nine o'clock. She had come up to the estate for the weekend and was expecting Zack to join her. He was running late but hadn't called. She went over to the French doors that led to the terrace and stepped out into a cool fall night. She was glad to be alone, to wander through the house and collect herself before her husband's arrival.

She gazed around as if for the first and last time. Lanterns cast a blue haze over the pool, shadows seeming to float and sink into its smooth surface. Cabanas on the far side stood against the trees like sentinels guarding a palace. The night was crystal clear; Annalise breathed in the scented fall air as if it might be the last breath she'd take in this kind of life. It seemed to her that no amount of money or success could cut through the shadowy demons that taunted her.

Suddenly she felt chilled and with a last glance around, returned to the library. She closed and locked the doors, unable to shake the feeling that time was running out. She'd wait for Zack upstairs.

Annalise sat in the dark in Zack's room, listening for the sounds that would tell her he was home. She always knew when he had been with another woman, and she always kept her distance. The parameters of their marriage called for no other response. Zack, of course, never mentioned where he'd been or with whom, but she knew the signs: the sated glow and the scent of strange soap after a shower.

She also knew what had changed this time. The woman was Ralley. Any other wife might have considered it a double betrayal: friend and husband, husband and best friend. The whole situation was a cliché. But Annalise understood that Ralley wasn't propelled by greed or avarice or a desire to climb socially. Zack had answered a telephone call for help, responding as Annalise expected her husband to; there was no conspiracy between them and no desire to hurt her.

She envied Ralley her quick animal instincts, her ability to grab what was near in an effort to satisfy her hunger. Annalise never blindly surrendered to passion, to the most feared emotion of all. She always damned the consequences when she needed the quick fix of pulverizing sex. She shivered thinking of Zack, of what he might have felt when he made love to Ralley.

Annalise marveled that she could live with Zack, touch his flesh, breathe his breath and know nothing of the man, nothing of what he thought or felt. Annalise's bones had been held together by fraud, deceit, and denial. She could feel them cracking in an effort to loosen. Her life was in danger of coming apart. She had known all along that it would happen.

There was a slight rustle at the doorway; Annalise whipped around, startled, pulling her silk dressing gown closer. Zack stood in the doorway for an instant, as if he smelled her presence in the darkened room. He loosened his tie and came striding in. He reached for the bedside lamp and saw her as soon as its amber glow lit the room.

"Why are you sitting in the dark?"

"Do you want a divorce?" She asked the question so softly she could hear his sudden intake of breath.

"Why ask that now?" He did not even bother to inquire how she knew. He shrugged his jacket off and tossed it on a chair, then stripped off his tie and undid his collar. "You never demanded absolute fidelity. Do you think this is different from the others?"

She stirred, realizing he wasn't going to insult her by denying his affair with Ralley; they were way past that. "The others were anonymous," she said, "bodies that had no names. Ralley Littlehurst belongs to me, to my past, to the moments of my life."

"It happened, Anna. It's nothing."

"I don't believe you."

"I can't help that."

"I won't have it." The determination in her voice surprised her and with it came an astonishing fact she hadn't faced before. Fear had always made her deny her feelings for him. Now, when she might lose him, Annalise wanted her husband's love. She wanted to hear him say he loved her and had always loved her. Instead, she was forced to watch helplessly as he began to laugh.

"You won't have it? Tell me what you won't have." His eyes had turned to hard, brittle slits edged in ice.

"Why Ralley? Of all the women you could have."

"Because she needed me. *Me*, and it had nothing to do with money or power. I'm talking about need as an emotion, something you've been a stranger to, Annalise."

"Don't be ridiculous," she said, but the words came out faint and half-hearted.

"Our marriage is a charade, a play staged for business reasons, for the columnists, for dinner party gossip. At this point I could use a little honest compassion."

"I asked you a simple question. Do you want a divorce?"

He was a long time answering. "You know I can't afford a scandal now."

She moved restlessly out of her chair. "And that's your answer. Damn, we've always been too civilized to argue about how our lives are arranged. How have we managed so long?"

"Easily enough if all we have to do is cross and crisscross each other's paths, smiling when we meet and waving as we move out of sight. We've always skirted the hard edges. We never needed each other for emotional support."

"What's Ralley giving you that I can't?"

"Are you confusing what you and I do with making love?"

Annalise steadied the trembling in her arms by hugging herself.

"You initiated the fun and games, Annalise. First you held me off. I was intrigued. Women have always been an easy conquest for me. It was as if you were circling me, sending out whispers of exotic doings, of a strange journey only you and I would share. You breathed something enticing, some wildness, your accent, your look, your damn mystery. And you were beautiful, so beautiful, the way you walked, held your head. Your hair, pale, shimmering—the way you hid behind it, hide behind it still, using it as a shield, not letting anyone near. I took it all in. I was hungry for you; I wanted you, convinced myself I needed you the way a man needs a great work of art, and if I had to pay, so be it. And to keep you, I let you deal."

He waited a moment, assessing her, shaking his head slightly. Annalise thought she had never seen him more vulnerable. She longed to reach for him, but instead kept her distance, hugging her arms.

"You needed power," he told her, "to rule, to fit our sex into your idea of what I needed, and God help me, I was ripe for seduction. I wanted the pain because it excised all kinds of guilt and put sex on a new plane. And, dammit, because it seemed the only way to reach you."

She was frozen by his words and only half heard the rest.

"You married me because I was the means to conquer a world you thought important. I married you because you were a unique prize in a world where I already owned everything." He stood apart, studying her as if seeing her in a new way. "You're still so beautiful. A cold marble statue of a woman who can feel nothing, not even jealousy. I think I would have appreciated a gun in my face more than a question about whether or not I want a divorce. Tell me, my wife, have you ever felt anything—pain, humiliation, defeat? Love?"

"Love? Are you asking me about love?" She began to laugh at his last words, the hysteria rising, tears forming at the back of her eyes. When the howling began in her ears, she was totally out of control. She saw him start for her, anger etched across his face, his mouth curled, a cruel, dark enemy. He grabbed her. She heard his voice from far away.

"Annie, dammit, get hold of yourself."

Get hold of yourself. The idea struck her as funny and the laughter rising from her throat was high-pitched and hysterical.

The slap across her face stung and yet was oddly painless. "I said calm *down.*" He was shaking her as she managed to pull in a choking sob.

"Damn you. It's still you." His lips came down on hers in a hard, punishing kiss. He ripped her robe away and shoved her down on the bed, then tore his clothes off and flung them aside. With a deep groan he was on her, pulling at her breast with his teeth. Annalise felt the slow start of wings in her stomach, the beginnings of a sensation she had dreamed of but never experienced, not in all those years of being in men's arms.

Zack lifted his head, locking his eyes with hers in a silent struggle neither expected to win. Annalise wanted to say something, to reveal the deepest part of her feelings, but she couldn't find the words, and the moment passed. Zack took her mouth as he parted her legs and plunged into her, thrusting with a power she hadn't known before with him. She felt him pulsing inside her, and a thrill like a distant wave rolled closer. At that moment she knew she had won something precious, something she had no right to.

He stopped moving suddenly and gazed down at her. "Say it."

She clasped her hands behind his neck, feeling unexpectedly shy. She held herself still, the moment of perfect completion balancing upon her words. "I want you, Zack," she said after a moment's hesitation. "I always have."

He shook his head. "Say it."

She pulled him close and pressed her lips against his. "I love you, as I've never loved anyone else."

It happened then, a rockslide of emotions. He let her know him slowly. He was deep within her; she could feel the pressure against her womb and when he came, it was with a pouring out of her name. This time her tears were for him.

Afterward he didn't speak. He lay back and gazed at the ceiling. Annalise barely breathed, the bitter irony consuming her. She had spoken the fateful words, I love you, and yet the means for destroying him were still there. The journals had disappeared and her life was no different from before. She turned and moved into his arms. She should tell him everything, have done with it.

"*Te amo,*" he said unexpectedly.

"Oh, my darling," she said and put her lips against his. She had no choice but to find her way alone out of the shadows.

"I won't see Ralley anymore," he offered quietly when she was just dropping off to sleep, "or anyone."

CHAPTER 33

Ralley knew the moment she opened the door to Zack that it was all over. His eyes briefly met hers, then slid away. Ralley had known many endings and couldn't remember one that hadn't left her blindfolded and walking the plank.

She held the door wide nevertheless and offered a broad smile of welcome. If she'd had any class at all, she would have dressed for the part, perhaps in something by Kate Hayden, one of those black, drapey Giselle things, a double strand of pearls at her throat, and her hair piled high on her head. Mustn't forget the bright red lipstick and silver cigarette holder, she thought. Only it wasn't funny; Annalise was the other woman.

Zack came in carrying a dozen long-stemmed white roses, which he thrust at her. She buried her face in the petals and thought inconsequentially that the more splendid the flower, the less fragrant it was. Well, she'd let him say his piece and wish him farewell. She would ask no questions, strike no attitude. What the hell had she expected, anyway? Moonlight along with the roses? She put the flowers on the table without bothering to arrange them in a vase. She'd dump them in the garbage along with her emotions as soon as he was gone.

"Listen, Ralley," he began.

"Does Annalise know?" She gave him a throwaway smile.

"Yes."

"Careless of you."

"Not careless at all, except with the telephone hookup at home. My step-daughter listened in when you called and promptly told her mother."

"That kid always liked to get her kicks in." Ralley lit a cigarette and took in a deep drag. "And Annalise doesn't need details to figure out the results of your coming here. I suppose she's in a fury about me."

"No, she doesn't blame you at all. She realizes it was something that happened, that it didn't mean anything."

His words hurt and she looked away before bringing her eyes back to his. "She wouldn't want to share you, would she?" Ralley gave a husky laugh. "You know, Tuesdays and Thursdays and the occasional weekend?"

"Ralley, don't." He reached for her, but she moved away.

"Listen, Zack, don't get sappy on me. We're all sophisticated; we're talking sophistication of the highest order. We can still meet at parties. Hell, we don't have a choice; we're going to meet at parties. We'll blow kisses in the air, chat away like old friends. We *are* old friends. Annalise and I are decidedly old friends. Hell, she called me this week and said *nada.* Now that's *savoir faire.*" She stubbed her cigarette out and reached for another.

Zack took the cigarette away and pulled her close. "Listen, Ralley, you weren't just a quick screw. For some reason I can't explain, what we had changed things for me with my wife."

My wife. Annalise, my wife. "Oh, sure," she said, twisting out of his arms. "That's what I'm well known for. I mean, you can read it in the gossip columns every day. 'Fuck Ralley and see the light.' "

"Why do you do this?" he asked.

"Get out of here, Zack. Just let me sulk by myself. In a few days' time, we'll both forget what happened. Oh, excuse me, you've forgotten already. Me, I was more afraid of Annalise's wrath than anything. You know what they say about Latin tempers." She took him by the hand and led him to the door. "Remember nice things about me. I like to think of myself as lingering in men's minds."

Zack seemed about to say something, then kissed her swiftly and left. Ignoring the elevator, he took the stairs. Ralley waited at the door until she could no longer hear the sound of his footsteps.

She went back into her apartment. He was a self-serving son of a bitch just like the rest of them. Money gave him power but no class. She didn't envy Annalise one bit.

The whiskey bottle was half full, or was it half empty? She decided upon half empty and poured a drink, wondering if the liquor store was still open. She hated racing down late at night as if she were a lush dying for a drink.

She raised her glass. "To you, sweetheart," she said, staring at herself in the mirror above the bar. "And to every mistake you ever made in your life that taught you absolutely nothing."

She wondered whether her falling for Zack was the result of being tired, sated, bored, or confused. And while Win was out of the picture, Egon's journals were still missing, meaning someone else could have them, could read them, and could start the blackmailing all over again.

Ralley thought about taking a leave of absence from Steyman's, spending the winter in the Caribbean or the south of France. Right, that's what she'd do, get out of it for a while. She had tried to steal Annalise's husband as she once stole Thierry Saul, not out of malice but because the opportunity presented itself. The guilt was part of the fun. Well, she was glad about Annalise having the spring cover of Steyman's catalog. It didn't make up for anything but auld lang syne; still, it was better than nothing.

The glass of liquor she held on to as though it afforded emotional support suddenly seemed to take on additional weight. It was half empty, decidedly not half full. She stopped short of refilling the glass. What was needed, besides the truth, was a month's visit to some mountain hideaway where they dried lushes out and made them new.

Egon's journal:

Christmas Eve, 1979: Marguerite apparently decided she'd fudged her history long enough, at least with me. I know I have an inherited tendency to dig. All those years down on a hard-scrabble farm, no doubt.

The truth, she told me this evening over espresso and chocolate truffles in front of her fireplace (roaring fire, of course, one of those movie fires that never seem to go out but burn with a steady fury through a half-hour of dialogue). The truth, because she must have caught the cut-the-crap-Maggie look in my eye. I always bought the business of the aristocratic childhood (although the Auvergne was a little too romantic). After all, Maggie has the formidable French nose for it—long enough to look down it at lesser beings and short enough to turn up in disdain.

And so, nibbling des truffes I heard it all, le petit château fifty miles south of Paris, the father who collaborated with the Nazis and lost his head over it through the offices of the partisans and all the rest.

Pierre Varick was a distinguished and prosperous French Moroccan who had come to Paris carrying a shady past having to do with the Germans that Marguerite did not dare question. But when his past was about to catch up to him, which would also have revealed her father's collaboration during the war, Maggie did what the partisans in Morocco should have done. She dispatched the man she loved d'après guerre, so to speak, with a bullet to the brain. Apparently self-preservation beat more strongly in her breast than love. During the war, she'd have been a heroine. After the war, shooting M. Varick was a crime. But a crime not even Maigret could have solved, she confided. No one suspected his wife, Marguerite, who was in Portugal at the time on a fashion shoot (if you'll pardon the expression). No one checked airline schedules between Lisbon and Paris during the relevant hours.

"Why are you telling me this now?" I asked. "You're not in any trouble, are you?"

"No," she said. She reached over and patted my hand. "You are my best friend."

Am I? I think not. You reach the pinnacle, carrying a collection of neuroses no one can share or understand. She told me because she wanted to confess and was certain the secret was safe with me.

"Pete?"

Pete, picking up his own calls because his secretary was out to lunch, recognized Jaybee's deep, melodious voice. "Hey, how ya doin', Jaybee?"

"Thought I could treat you to a chopped chicken liver sandwich today. You game?"

The invitation surprised him, but he liked Jaybee in spite of her best efforts to let him know he didn't figure in her life. "How about coming over my way? I'll order in."

"Sure, great. Grilled cheese on rye and coffee for me, with a couple of pickles thrown in. Say about forty minutes?"

"I'm in the Federal Office Building, three blocks south of your office."

"I know where. See you." She clicked off.

Pete suspected that Jaybee had access to information about the way the murder case was going. She probably knew about Doherty but maybe, like Pete, didn't quite have the faith the police did that Chuck Doherty killed both Maxi Franilero and Win Smith. No, you don't confess to killing your lover while denying a second murder. You start crying for your lawyer.

Jaybee's sexual preference wasn't a blackmailable offense. Whatever she had done, Win had scared her into compliance, or maybe even into killing him.

Jaybee came briskly into his office just after the delivery of the lunch order. He remarked once again how beautiful she was: tough-jawed, dimpled, with light blue eyes, a stunning figure, and shapely legs. A smile that some might call mysterious came a little too easily to her.

"I've been meaning to call you," he said, gesturing to a chair.

"Oh?"

"Not to pick your brain." He cleared a spot on his desk and laid out her sandwich and a paper plate of pickles.

"I was wondering what other damage you were going to do to Seventh Avenue before your boys packed their bags and went back to Washington."

"We've got an investigation in progress, Jaybee. Gregory's death ought to serve as a warning to others to stop doing business with the mob. But it won't."

"What happened to Ira Gregory was a result of your taking him in on flimsy RICO evidence, I'll just bet. You have a conservator at Hayden now, haven't you?"

Pete nodded. "Kate would've told you. She send you here?"

"She told me she talked to you . . . about everything."

"Ah." Now they were getting down to business. Kate had called her friends and told them Pete knew about the journals.

"We don't know if Doherty took any evidence with him," Jaybee said, "or whether the police found the *evidence* or whether Doherty wasn't the killer and the evidence is in someone else's hand."

"And you've been sent as a committee of one to find out what I know or what I can find out for you."

She nodded.

"Have you got an alibi?"

"For the time when he was murdered?" Jaybee thought for a moment. "Yes, but . . ."

"There's someone else involved."

"Yes."

"Let's go on to Annalise Michelis," Pete said. "Does she have an alibi?"

"Yes."

"But there's someone else involved."

"She, like Kate, was in the midst of getting her fashion show under way."

"And so she has an alibi."

"Half a dozen people were with her at the time," Jaybee said.

"Marguerite?"

"Has a newspaper to get out, tight deadlines, scores of people around."

"At all times?"

"No doubt," Jaybee said, not trying to hide the sarcasm in her voice. She had apparently come completely armed.

"Ralley Littlehurst?"

"Alibi." After a beat or two she added, "Someone else's husband."

"And even though you're in the mayor's office, you believe I have better access to information."

She blanched. "I can't afford to seem the least bit interested. Look," she said after a moment, "I haven't lived a blameless life, all right? Am I sorry I did things the way I did? Sure. Am I convinced you can get where you're going by talent and virtue? You can, but there are faster ways, all of which is beside the point. The little worm deserved to die and I'm for subscribing to a monument built in honor of his murderer, how's that?"

Pete reached into his pocket and withdrew a quarter. "From everything I've heard about Win Smith, I'll be happy to make a donation. But better than that," he said, flipping the coin and catching it on the back of his hand, "I'll see what I can find out about the journals, if they're being held for evidence, for instance."

Jaybee carefully wrapped the uneaten sandwich in her napkin and shoved it with her coffee cup across his desk. "Thanks for lunch, Pete. And for whatever you can do." She swiftly made her way to the door. "Let's make it a real lunch next time, treat's on me." She was halfway through the door, her hand still on the knob, when Pete reached her.

"Jaybee," he said, "tell me."

She hesitated but came back into the room.

"Off the record," he said softly.

She gazed at him with faint distaste and shook her head. She hates men, he thought, but he still persisted. "What did you do that's so bad, that you live in daily terror of being found out?"

As if coming to her senses, she directed a smile at him, her eyes dancing with merriment. "I'd better trust you. You might find the journal and learn everything anyway." She gave a dry laugh and stated flatly, "I blackmailed my way into this job. The mayor lives in dread fear of me. I understood Win's ambition, you see." She was defying him to call her a liar.

"What do you know about the mayor that isn't already known?"

"The mayor is a past master at covering his tracks. You don't think I could uncover them, do you?"

"I hate to think you're in trouble, Jaybee."

"Thanks for being concerned," she said. "You're an attractive man and I think a good man." This time when she opened the door, he let her go.

As soon as Jaybee left, Pete dialed Kate's office. When she came on line, he said in his best Oliver Hardy voice, "It's a fine mess you got me into."

"You saw Jaybee."

"What the hell possessed you to have a conference with your blackmail buddies involving me?"

"Because we can't go on not knowing about the fate of the journals."

"The journals. You're putting a lot of faith in a supposition."

"Marguerite swears that's where Win got his information."

"I'd like to talk to Marguerite."

"I'm having dinner with her this evening. Come along."

"Can't." He had an appointment with the comptroller of a fashion house far larger than Kate Hayden; the man had a grievance against his bosses. The grievance might be backbiting, or it might be a real payoff about mob control on Seventh Avenue. It was a date Pete couldn't miss.

"Bring your date," Kate was saying.

He laughed. "Tell Marguerite I'm going to drop in on her at work any day now."

CHAPTER 34

The cab whizzed up Eighth Avenue to Columbus Circle before Kate even noticed she was being taken home the long way around.

"Driver, I said Sixty-fourth Street and Madison Avenue. Why are we on the West Side?"

The cabbie looked at her in his rearview mirror. In an accent she could barely understand, he said, "Raydy, I ask you. I say Sixy-forse Stree, Wes Sye, you say yes."

"That's not what I said. All right, let's repair the damage. Go along Central Park West and then east through the park. It's six of one and half a dozen of another anyway. And don't be so unpleasant," she added in her best urban guerrilla voice.

"You say Wes Sye," he murmured under his breath.

After a couple of blocks more, Kate leaned forward. "Driver, stop here."

He pulled up, clicking the meter off. "Wha now?"

"I'm getting out." She handed him the exact change, deciding not to tip him, then added as if an explanation for her behavior were necessary at eleven o'clock at night, "I'm going to walk a bit."

He turned and after glancing at the tipless fare, laughed. "Craycee."

Craycee, maybe, but she needed some quiet time to order her priorities. Market week was over; the collection, according to *Women's Wear Daily* and *VFF*, was a success. Words like *ideas, talent, trendy, classic, drama, innovative* had become part of her vocabulary. But then, so had a brief article on page two of *WWD*, about DAS putting Kate Hayden on the market.

She walked one block west. Other people went to museums; Kate relaxed by checking out store windows and the fashion parade. On a friendly autumn night, with Lincoln Center nearby, the cafés and restaurants along Columbus Avenue were crowded and busy. The women were attractive. They wore expensive designer fashions by Donna Karan, Louis dell' Olio, Ralph Lauren. No Kate Hayden, she thought with a bitter smile. One needed backing, public relations, promotion, *time*, and Ira had afforded her none. He wasn't finished with her yet. Even with the interment of his ashes Kate suspected that she'd feel his touch on her career.

At Seventy-third Street, she started east, expecting to pick up a cab that would take her through the park to Madison Avenue. But halfway down the block, Kate knew precisely where she was and what it had taken her to get there.

She found the brownstone easily, having memorized Pete's address from the note he had scrawled on his business card. Maybe he was asleep, maybe he was working, maybe he had a woman in bed. She climbed slowly up the stone steps and checked the directory for his name. He was on the top floor. She pushed the bell, but there was no answer. If she had any brains she'd take it as an omen and get the hell out of there. Then the door opened and a young man came out followed by two laughing women who hardly noticed her. She slipped into the hallway before the door slammed shut.

Her steps were silent as she made her way up, trying not to think of what she was doing. She had never been forward or aggressive with men; she didn't have the confidence. Ira had made all the moves, as had Tim, and she had fallen willingly into their arms.

Kate found Pete's apartment and knocked softly, but with no response. She decided to wait a few minutes and sat down on the stairway leading to the roof. She leaned her head against the wall, closed her eyes, and drifted into sleep.

A noise startled her. Kate was awake at once but didn't move. Pete was there juggling a package and trying to maneuver his key into the lock. Her moment of truth. "Need any help?" she asked.

He turned abruptly. When he saw her, his surprise worked into a broad grin. "Who says prayers aren't answered?"

She came over to him and took the key. "Incidentally, it's an easy building to break into." She unlocked the door and pushed it open. "After you."

He waved her in. "After you."

"I guess you don't mind surprises."

"Not when they're packaged the way you are. You're in luck," he said, putting the bag of groceries down. "I gathered all my dirty shirts and socks and took them to the laundry this morning." He went quickly over to the coffee table, which was covered with books and newspapers, and made a feint at gathering them into a pile.

"Pete." Kate stood at the door in her coat. "Don't bother."

He regarded her from across the room. "No, of course not. What is it?" His question was gently asked. "Slumming? In trouble? Have questions that need answering?"

"None of the above."

They remained standing apart, not speaking. Then Kate said with a barely perceptible shrug, "I need a friend." In spite of the fact that she was wearing her coat, she shivered.

"Kate," he began, but stopped, went over to her, and helped her out of her coat.

"I should've gone home," she said. "Instead I grabbed a cab and—"

"Came here?"

"No, not quite. I had a dummy for a driver. Yes, yes, perhaps it was all planned, going home the long way around. Without consciously—" She began to wander about the room, a big floor-through with beamed ceilings and walls with wainscoting typical of old brownstones. The view outside tall windows was of the side street with similar buildings on both sides.

The long, narrow room had a fireplace, and was furnished with an attractive mix of antiques, plush chairs, and Danish modern. "I walked along Columbus Avenue," she told him, "saw all the pretty people in restaurants, nobody alone, and incidentally nobody in a Kate Hayden. Pretty nifty apartment you have here."

"I inherited it from a friend in the State Department. He was given an assignment in Paris just as I was posted to New York."

She continued to wander around, putting her hand on chair backs, touching lampshades. "I've spent the last couple of years in a strange kind of time warp—" she said. "Twenty-seven hour days, living nothing but the business. The business, the business, the business. I think I missed something like all of my twenties. I never sat in a restaurant on Columbus Avenue smiling at eleven o'clock at night after seeing the ballet with my boyfriend." She was talking just to keep space between them.

"Sounds like the story of my life," he told her. "I've spent entirely too much time hiding behind long days and short nights."

She went over to a bookshelf and found it full of law books. "You just moved in encumbered only by law books."

"Those are my friend's, too. Mine are in my apartment in Washington."

"Which somebody else is babysitting." She watched him narrowly, expecting him to mention his wife.

"Which somebody else is babysitting. I may sell out lock, stock, and barrel if I decided to stay in these parts. I haven't wanted to own much since my divorce. Somehow possessions seem to slow you down."

"You're talking to the ace who's spent her adult life talking women into adding just one more possession to their wardrobes."

"And you're having second thoughts about it."

She went over to the sofa and sat down. "I'm at a crossroads. Did you find out about the journals?"

"That what you came to see me about, the journals?"

"No. I'm not in them. At least not that way. I think." She sank deeper into the sofa. "DAS has put my name up for grabs. What in hell am I going to do about it?"

"Change your name."

"Thanks. Any suggestions?"

"Kate Frank. Has a good honest tone to it."

"Don't kid around." She closed her eyes for a moment, aware of his waiting and watching. She was comfortable there in the apartment he didn't own, among effects that weren't his. "No children," she said at last. "I mean, when you and your wife split there weren't any children involved."

"Just our egos."

"Are you an only child? I never did ask."

"You've never asked anything. I consider this a sign of progress. I have an older sister. She's a lawyer, too, in Washington. Married a lawyer and has two boys. Anything else you'd like to know?"

Scads of things, but she was tired, exhausted in fact. She felt herself dozing comfortably off. "Mmmm."

"Kate."

She came awake suddenly.

He was bent over her, holding her coat in his hand. "I called a cab. Time for you to make tracks." He reached out, pulled her to her feet, and for a long moment gazed at her without saying anything. "I don't think I can be a friend," he told her at last.

"Because of DAS and Ira?"

He brushed his lips against hers. "Them, too." He released her and went to the window. "There's your cab."

CHAPTER 35

C hiChi called from Greece at four o'clock Saturday morning, her usual time for reaching Kate, along with the usual laughing excuse that she was never able to figure the time zone correctly.

Kate, as usual, took several moments to calm down. She always assumed the worst when the phone rang at four o'clock in the morning.

"Well, I just read about Ira," ChiChi said, as though the event had occurred that day. "My heart's still pounding. He was murdered, *murdered*. Like John Kennedy with his head in Jackie's lap. And it happened *gangland* style in a *restaurant*. You were there. Good God, you could've been murdered, too. Why didn't you call me? Why must I find these things out on my own?"

"The restaurant phones were all busy," Kate said.

"And you were covered with blood, I suppose. Very nice. You can give your outfit to Egon's museum for display. Hayden Original Splattered with Blood. I suppose you made the headlines from one end of the country to the other. Very nice way to make your label known. And why *didn't* you call me? I'd have come running if you'd had the decency to call me."

"Mom, take it easy, please. Everything's all right."

"But he was a *mobster*. Couldn't you *tell*? Just one look at him!"

"Mom—"

"Good Lord, you'll never have a day of rest in your life. Are you in any danger? What's happening to the company?"

"The company—"

"What in hell's going on? I mean, all this death and transfiguration in your backyard. Kate, I'm beginning to think you're a menace. If I were a man I'd give you a pretty wide berth. First Egon, now Ira. Apparently no man is safe around you. What are you going to do? Don't tell me his wife has decided to take over. She's some piece of goods from what I hear."

"Mom, will you slow down? It's four o'clock in the morning. You're talking about something that happened more than a month ago; no, his wife hasn't taken over, I haven't seen or heard from her—"

"And you're left without a soul to advise you. I have a good mind to come back this instant. I suppose Tim has been making the usual noises about his son. Ira getting it in a mob killing should have your ex walking out of family court with Matt for good. How's my darling Matt?"

"Safe and sound. I'm hanging up now."

"If you'd played your cards right with Egon. He wanted to help you. He adored you from the start. He even thought you had talent. You wouldn't be in this pickle. Exactly what kind of pickle are you in?"

"It's too complicated to go into now, but there's nothing to worry about," Kate said. "How are you feeling?"

"How am I supposed to feel, knowing a gangster died in my daughter's arms?"

"Mom, I love you. Everything's all right. Call me again when you've calmed down." Kate replaced the receiver with a careful little bang, resisting the urge to rip the cord from the wall.

There was no getting to sleep after that. She pulled herself up in bed, hands behind her head. The call from ChiChi was no worse than expected, and it came later rather than sooner, when events were far enough in the past to keep her detached. She had no doubt her mother would come racing back, beautiful, silly, and meddlesome. But the onset of cold weather, Thanksgiving, and Christmas would distract her and after a while, snuggling in her sable coat, ChiChi would make her way down to Palm Beach or one of the islands and Kate would take her first breath of relief.

She had no idea what Pete would make of her mother, or what her mother would make of Pete. ChiChi had disliked Tim from the start, as she had every other man Kate brought around whose prospects for material success seemed poor. Pete was a working stiff on a salary; ChiChi would be impressed neither with his job nor with his law degree.

ChiChi, a piranha when it came to men, decided her daughter was a menace because both Ira and Egon had died. What would she have made of Win, who died the same day he had lunch with Kate?

The only important question was what Win had discovered in Egon's journals about Kate that did not qualify her for blackmail.

Did Win feel his charm would win her over? Why hadn't he brought up the subject of the museum? It was all too puzzling. She slid back down under the covers, resisting the temptation to call Pete at four in the morning to discuss it all.

"Where's Matt?" Pete stood at the door to his apartment as Kate came upstairs later that afternoon. "Why'd I think you were bringing him?"

"I would've, except he's having a busy, very social weekend, a party and then his first sleep-over. Which is why I could come here in the first place."

She stopped on the landing and took in a deep breath. "I'm beginning to think I'm a bit out of shape."

"Really?" Pete grinned at her. "You'd have to prove it to me."

She walked past him into the apartment, pulling off her raincoat and dropping it on a chair. There was a fire in the fireplace, a smell of wood smoke and freshly brewed coffee in the air.

"Nice. This is what you dream about when you dream about New York."

"How's the weather out there?"

"New York chilly." She went over to the fireplace and warmed her hands.

Pete came up behind her and rested his chin on the top of her head. "What did you want to talk to me about?"

She turned to face him. She could have invited him to her apartment. Jeannette had the day off, her son was gone, she could have lit a fire in her living room, brewed coffee, set a cozy scene; but her mother's call still rankled. The memory of Ira was never stronger. She had felt stifled, anxious to be away. Pete was watching her, worried. He tipped her chin with his finger. "What is it?"

Kate shrugged. No use bringing up ChiChi.

"Hold everything," Pete said, heading for his kitchen and returning moments later with coffee and cannoli. He set the tray down, poured coffee, and joined her on the sofa.

"Win not blackmailing me," Kate said, "is a little like Sherlock Holmes and the dog that didn't bark in the night. Why didn't Win try to blackmail me? I mean, you do believe I'm telling the truth about the conversation I had with him the day he died?"

"Kate, I believe everything about you."

"And that I didn't kill him?"

He bent toward her and placed his lips on hers in a long kiss. Kate returned the kiss, drawing her arms around his neck. It would be so easy, she reflected, to let the kiss deepen, to forget everything but the two of them.

Yet when he released her all she said was "How can you be so sure I didn't kill Win?"

"The police have his killer in custody, remember? Anyway, I love you. I don't have to be sure of anything."

"Pete, be serious." The time wasn't right for professions of love, although Kate understood that being loved by Pete Frank might be the one constant, besides her son, in a life that could, if she wasn't careful, parallel her mother's in craziness. "I didn't come here to talk about love," she said quietly.

"It's all I think about."

"Look, there's something concerning Egon," she began hurriedly, trying to deflect him. "Dammit, the man won't stay buried. He—he bought my apartment for me. Did you know that?"

Pete pressed his lips together, then seemed about to say something but held back.

"I was in a bind," Kate said, feeling the need to explain away the loan and how grateful to Egon she'd been. "I couldn't raise the money for the mortgage and maintenance, and Egon said he was giving me the money and there'd be no further discussion about it. That's when I was going into business. With Ira," she added as if the notion were new to her. "Egon was pissed about my decision. He hated Ira. But still, he insisted I buy the apartment, insisted he was lending me the money interest-free, to be paid back at some unspecified date."

Pete leaned back against the sofa, uttering a curse under his breath. "I'll be damned. He hated your going into business with Ira Gregory, but tied you to a mortgage."

"Well, I always figured he was jealous, but after a while he sort of pretended Ira didn't exist."

"Since the parties of the first and second part are both dead," Pete said, interrupting her, "I'm going to tell you something I learned a couple of days ago. Your friend Egon was the one who contacted the IRS about Kate Hayden suggesting the company was a money-laundering operation."

"What?" Kate jumped angrily to her feet. "He *what?* He did that to Ira? Without even realizing the repercussions? And how the hell did he know?" She sat down abruptly. "He'd know. Egon would make it his business to know. Oh, I could kill him, kill him, the selfish, self-centered . . . Oh, damn, he's dead and he's manipulating us even now with that journal of his."

"Sit down, Kate. He rid your company of a tumor—"

"And nearly put me out of business."

"I, personally, will be eternally grateful to the man."

"Egon would've hated you, too, just because you came knocking at my door."

"Was he in love with you?" Pete asked.

"Maybe. I shamelessly accepted his loan without even a note, promising blithely to pay him back, knowing I had all the time in the world and then some."

"There was nothing between you."

"Physical?" Her face expressed pure surprise. Egon might have been in love with her but it had nothing to do with sex. "Good heavens, no, he hated to be touched, although he certainly adored my son and wasn't above heaving him around and playing with him like a good grandpa."

Pete picked up on the word. "Grandpa? Is that what your son called him?"

"No." She laughed a little self-consciously. "Matt called him Uncle Eggie, although the nickname ordinarily drove Egon into a frenzy. He put a lot of store in sophistication and dignity."

"And left a tremendous legacy for a blackmailer," Pete remarked.

"Where do you think the journals are, Pete?"

He shrugged. "If Win had them, and if he was killed by Doherty—who wouldn't have known they were valuable—then I'd say they're somewhere in the town house."

"And if Win was killed because he was a blackmailer?"

"Then his killer has them."

"Let's go to the town house and ferret around," Kate said. "I can ask Reuben Newcombe for the key, although I doubt he'll be in his office on Saturday," she added. "I'll have to call him at home. He lives close to the town house; one couldn't be Egon's lawyer and do otherwise."

Kate went for her coat and Pete caught up with her at the door.

"Kate, wait a minute." His expression was serious, and for a moment she thought he might refuse to go. She was searching for a way to handle him when he put his arms around her. "And if Win found an entry indicating that Egon meant you to be his heir?"

She stared at him, confused. "What in hell do you mean by that?"

"If you were," he persisted.

"He left his estate to the museum."

"Or . . ." He stopped.

"Or what?"

"Suppose you were somehow related to him. You could sue the estate and come away with it."

"What are you talking about?" she asked, turning from him and reaching for the door.

"Kate, forget the journals."

She spun around. He made no sense at all. "You're crazy, I am *not* related to Egon, and there was never anything between us, period." More quietly she added, "I'm not after his money."

"Neither am I."

She gazed at him, perplexed. "What the devil does that mean?"

"I love you. I want to marry you. The broker the better."

Relief flooded over her. "Oh, Pete." She threw her arms around him and kissed him. "How dear you are and good, and why you love me I'll never understand, when I'm one step south of being as off-the-wall as my mother. I love you, but I don't trust what I feel. Just let me make myself whole again, complete, a *mensch* and then, and then—"

"Let's find Reuben," he said, taking her arm and drawing her gently through the door, "and that key to your history."

CHAPTER 36

E gon's journal:

October 31, 1987. This evening, Halloween, Kate insisted I accompany her and Matt down to the Village to view the Halloween parade. She claimed we were making the trip for Matt's sake, but I knew Kate was seeking ideas, eager to see what people were wearing, wanting confirmation that she's working in the right direction. She's full of plans for her enterprise. I began the litany all over again, knowing in advance what her reaction would be. "I'll back you."

"I need my independence."

I took Matt's hand in mine, then raised him to my shoulders. For the first time in my life I felt the purest, most selfless, and incandescent love for another human being. Matt was thrilled with the parade. He has his father's stolid appearance but Kate's good humor. As for ChiChi, it would seem she's been left out of his gene pool entirely. Except, of course, for the fact that she was extraordinarily dazzling as a youngster; perhaps more so now. When I first saw her thirty years ago—even I, no slouch when it came to judging pulchritude, it was my business, after all —gazed upon her with awe.

I haven't for years thought of those early days when ChiChi came to New York to model and into my life. Now with Matt's laughter still in my ears, it's all come back. She was tall, slender, swan-necked, wide-eyed, and just off the farm. Her hair—shiny, blond, silken and worn down to her waist—was all wrong, of course. Underneath the hayseed was the most sensual, sophisticated look I'd ever seen.

Ambition was also written all over her face. In no time at all ChiChi learned to walk, smile, and pose. We made a great team, ChiChi and I. I used her as Kate now uses Vivian, as the living, breathing inspiration for my hats.

Thirty years ago I wasn't half bad looking myself. My stomach was flat, my derriere where it was supposed to be, and I had a certain flair. I was stone, however, when it came to women, even ChiChi, who thought

*when I began developing Delville Perfumes that she might have some-
thing going with me.*

*I worked alone, I lived alone, I slept alone. Truth be told, I couldn't
bear to be touched. And I've never speculated on the psychological reasons for my behavior. I leave that to anyone courageous enough to inquire.*

*Most models require rest and are careful about what they eat. Not
ChiChi. She went where she wished, ate what pleased her, never seemed
tired, never gained weight. She was certain she'd never have to pay the
piper. She was friendly with everyone, she was invited everywhere. Occasionally she'd drag me along, as Kate did this evening, and most times I
refused to go.*

*"You're a party pooper," she'd say, pouting. "You've got to change
your ways. I'm personally going to see to it."*

*One night early in the winter, when I felt a cold coming on and was in
no mood for company, she showed up unannounced, as usual, and ready
for fun, as usual. She swept into my studio wearing a mink over an
evening dress. The crowd that followed her in echoed her laughter.*

*"Come on, Egon, you old sourpuss, we're here to cheer you up." She
invited her friends, an attractive bunch of models, artists, photographers,
and the like, to make themselves at home.*

*But being at home in my studio wasn't enough. After a while ChiChi
Who Must Be Obeyed ordered everyone, including me, up and out. We
rolled into the Copacabana at about midnight, a large, noisy crowd, all
hugs and kisses. Liquor flowed and the music played on. Around one we
left and sloshed out to the Stork Club. Walter Winchell was sitting at
his usual table, and his narrow, cranky face lit up when he spotted
ChiChi. She went over and sat on his lap for a while. I remember
thinking she could have a good time in a shoe box.*

*My cold worsened and at last I made my excuses and headed for my
studio. I wasn't fated to be alone, however. ChiChi and her gang tagged
noisily along. I had a splitting headache by that time and stupidly kept
on drinking to make it go away. Things got a bit foggy and I sulked off to
bed. I had just closed my eyes when ChiChi leaned over me.*

*"Come on, Eggie, wake up and join the fun." Her speech was slurred.
She pulled at my jacket and I yanked it from her.*

"Beat it, ChiChi, I've got a headache."

*"A headache." She laughed hilariously. "Hey, everybody, Eggie has a
headache. Not tonight, dear, I've got a headache." That tickled the
collective funnybone. The room was too warm, and everyone crowded*

around me, pretending to be worried about the state of my health. Some-
one handed me a drink: "Solves the headache problems."

My head began to swim; I suffered a feeling of dislocation. I lay back
down again. People pushed closer, there was a rustle of clothes being
removed, of whiskey breath even I couldn't ignore, of huddling together.
For an instant I was transported back to my childhood, to the comfort
and softness of the quiet, closed-in space I shared the last time I touched
someone.

I awakened the next morning with a head the size of a watermelon,
the kind that wins prizes at the county fair. ChiChi was still there,
asleep on the couch. Two of her pals were sprawled on the floor. I got
up, made some coffee. When we all regained consciousness, everyone
was silent about the previous evening. I put it out of my mind entirely; it
was back to business as usual.

Two months went by before I saw ChiChi again. She showed up one
night subdued and a bit depressed. I went on working at my desk. She
sat silently on the other side, chewing on a fingernail and when the
silence began to turn leaden, she blurted it out: "I'm pregnant, Eggie,
and it's you."

"What's me?"

"You're the father, idiot."

I stared at her. For a few moments the words made no sense. "You
don't know what you're talking about."

"I don't?" Her mouth curled in a smile. "That night we all had a
blast and ended up back at your place? Good God, I ought to take your
remark as the final insult."

"I'm the father of your child?" I let the anger seethe quietly. Delville
perfume was moving briskly throughout the country. One didn't need a
hundred million dollars in those days to launch a fragrance. I figured she
was looking for a marriage license and a comfortable place to roost.

"It's you, Eggie. I haven't been with anyone else since I broke up with
Jackson Reed. I don't blame you for pretending not to remember. It was
stupid. We were all drunk, and I thought it would be cute; you're such a
fuckin' old stiff."

"Sorry, ChiChi, don't think you're going to pawn off some passing
fancy's kid on me. Get an abortion."

"An abortion?" She shook her head. "Uh-uh, no way. I'm going to
have a little girl, a little girl like a doll, a perfectly gorgeous little girl
who takes after her mommy."

"The father must be some handsome sucker, then."

She got up and for a moment bent across the desk and gazed at me.

"You aren't bad looking, Eggie, just a fuckin' old stiff." She turned and went out and I didn't hear from her again. *Several months later I read in Walter Winchell that ChiChi had married some Wall Street tycoon and was living in Connecticut. Then I read that she had a baby girl named Kate. Not Katherine, just Kate. The same Kate who believes her father moved to France and died there. Kate, with my eyes, mother to my grandson. Kate, born only a few months after the beginning of ChiChi's life with the tycoon. I knew the moment I laid eyes on her that she was my daughter.*

And so there it was, the truth about Kate Hayden in Egon's own handwriting, which Kate must never see.

The room was dark except for a spectral light cast by the kerosene lamp. Shadows danced among the books and fancy clutter of Egon's library. The room, shuttered against the gray November day outside, seemed airless in an alien and uncertain world.

Marguerite found a paper clip and slipped it over the edge of the page. She sank back into the worn leather chair and stroked the smooth surface of Egon's journal. She and Egon had both loved Kate, but now she wondered whether she could afford to be sentimental. Clearly Egon had wanted the museum brought to fruition, else why not leave his fortune to his daughter?

"You grand old fool," she whispered as the phantoms glided and sputtered around her, "and so you admit to fathering Kate Hayden. If you only knew the trouble you've caused us all with your foolish equivocation. A museum I am to direct. A daughter you refuse to acknowledge publicly." If Kate ever learned the truth, she'd have every right to sue the estate.

No, Egon wanted the museum, and he wanted his old friend as director. He loved Kate and her son, but knew that history would remember the man because of his unselfish gift to society. Besides, he expected Kate to succeed in her own right. She would not need his money, and had refused his help all along, except in the matter of her mortgage.

Nevertheless, Marguerite wanted to be angry at Egon, to rail and scream, but an ennui, primeval and sucking at her bones, prevented her from moving. Yet she knew she must hurry; she was running out of time. Reuben Newcombe had decided to board up the town house until the museum was a fait accompli. The premises would be secured the next day.

Using the duplicate set of keys she'd had made, Marguerite calmly let herself in through the basement entrance, as she had once before, on the day she followed Win in a taxicab long after he had eluded Kate.

Now, after having discovered, in a fever of activity, the cache of leather-bound journals, she sat in Egon's chair, in his library, the room he used so cunningly all those years to collect the memories and lives of his friends.

"It's really all your fault, Egon." She spoke the words aloud as though they could conjure up the man himself. "What right did you have to burrow your way into our secrets?"

She shifted in her chair, stirring the pile of journals at her feet. She had been there alone for hours, sitting in the half-light, reading Egon's small, spidery words, learning the secrets that had cost Win Smith his life.

That stupid boy, lying on the bed in the paisley robe she had given Egon for Christmas, with Egon's silk scarf wrapped around his neck. Perhaps it was the sight of the robe that infuriated her most. He had caught the black look on her face at once, perhaps even before he spied the gun.

He shot to his feet. Marguerite had tightened her finger, certain that one jar, one wrong word would cause the gun to go off.

"Hey," Win had said, holding his hands up and smiling at her, "we can talk."

"You're wearing Egon's robe," she said. "And his scarf. How dare you?"

"This?" He grimaced as though he had been the charitable beneficiary of the man's bad taste, "he gave this to me." Win put his hands down and made a pretense of tightening the belt, which only succeeded in further infuriating Marguerite.

"I've come for the journals, Mr. Smith."

"Journals?" He creased his brow. "I'm not sure I know what you're talking about."

"Of course you do. The journals, please."

He gazed shrewdly at her for a moment, then seemed to make up his mind about her and about the gun leveled at him.

"You made pretty interesting reading, Mrs. Varick. I mean, you can say anything you want about Egon, but he had a real gift for writing. Those young studs, those friends of yours, I mean, the way Egon wrote about them, if I didn't know him better, I'd figure he was salivating as he wrote."

"I'm not interested in what you have to say, Mr. Smith. I intend to leave with the journals, the sooner the better."

He clearly caught the determination in her eyes. "Yeah, well, maybe you're right," he said, adding as if it were an afterthought, "You're a very interesting lady, but you did kill your husband. I know when to back away."

She flinched, saw the look of surprise Win gave her and said, gesturing with the gun, "Where are the journals?"

"In the attic storeroom. Hidden."

"Get them."

"Sure, because, I mean, there are two ways to skin a cat. If we could work as a team, say." He moved past her quickly, almost as though he had forgotten the gun, but when Marguerite turned to follow him, he whipped around and lunged for it.

She heard the sound of gunfire. She hadn't intended to kill him. Fool. She only wanted the journals; he had no right to them. His blood sprayed everywhere, his eyes wide with disbelief. Even as he fell, he tried a smile. "Fucked up, didn't I?"

Marguerite had left hurriedly with neither time nor energy to look for the books. They were hidden in the storeroom and would have to remain there.

By planning to seal the town house however, Reuben had forced her hand. And now in the flickering darkness she could almost feel Egon's presence.

As if she were shooing him away, Marguerite struck her hand out, hitting the kerosene lamp, sending it rolling along the rug and spilling its contents. In a flash the rug caught fire, casting sparks into the air.

Marguerite stood her ground uncertainly, then without quite knowing what she was doing, she grabbed the journal and clutched it, mesmerized by the way the fire moved, quickly, like a shopper at a closing-out sale. An old paisley wrap on the window seat shot a flame to the curtains above.

The sight galvanized Marguerite. "Oh, my God, Egon," she called, rushing around, grabbing precious objects, then dropping them as though they were already in flames, "it will all be lost, all lost, your precious museum."

The ceiling alarm went off, a high-pitched scream that seemed to mock her. The alarm was connected to the nearest firehouse, and as the flames raced along the bookshelves toward the library door, Marguerite realized she was wasting precious minutes.

She had to get away before anyone found her there. Still clutching the journal, she ran to the door. Flames shot out after her, spreading to the stairway and blocking her passage down. Feeling as if her heart would give way, she raced up the stairs, remembering that the top-floor windows were unshuttered.

The door to Win's room was ajar. Marguerite stepped in and closed the door behind her. She thought of the blood and gore so recently there and was surprised to find the bed freshly made. Smoke seeped into the room as she scurried, scarcely breathing, to the window. She dropped the journal and pushed the curtains aside. The window was sealed shut. Her chest seemed to cave in as she struggled for a breath of air. She grabbed a lamp, and using strength she no longer thought she possessed, heaved it at the window. The glass smashed just as Marguerite felt a wrenching pain in her chest. She slid to the floor, spying the journal just before she closed her eyes. She reached for it, wrapping her fingers around the soft leather binding. A most unusual calm invaded her body.

Marguerite opened the door upon a long, winding tunnel bathed in bright light. A sunset glow, she thought. Someone was beckoning to her. She reached a hand out, still clutching the journal. "Egon?"

"Do you have the hat, Marguerite? It was always my favorite."

"Are you relatives of Mrs. Varick?" The young resident who met Pete and Kate in the hospital corridor fixed them with an interested eye.

"I'm a close friend," Kate said. "She has no family here. I'd appreciate knowing her condition."

Pete considered hauling out some identification to cut through the formalities but the doctor seemed to take Kate's word for it. "All right. We have her in intensive care and her condition is critical but stable. Apparently the effort to escape the fire put a strain on her heart."

"Is she badly burned?" Kate asked.

The doctor shook his head. "No, not at all. She's one lucky lady. It's her heart we're monitoring closely. Do you know the name of her doctor?"

"As a matter of fact I do." Kate gave him the name of a prominent East Side doctor, one she used herself.

"Do you know anything of her medical history?"

Kate shook her head. "She never complained about her heart, if that's what you mean. Can I see her now?"

"Sorry," he said. "Hospital policy. I'm afraid we can only let in close relatives."

"She has no close relatives," Kate reiterated, biting down on her words.

Pete put a restraining hand on Kate's arm, to let her know not to pursue the subject.

"Well, I'll get back to you," the doctor said with a sympathetic smile, moving off in the direction of the nurses' station.

"We're going to find Intensive Care and barge in," Kate said to Pete.

"I'll handle it," Pete told her. "You stay put."

Kate regarded him uneasily, as if she sensed the doctor and Pete were in collusion, that Marguerite's condition was far worse than reported. "Oh, I get it," she said at last. "You're going to pull rank. Okay, okay, I've got to call the others, get them down here. Then I'm going in to see her."

"Fair enough," Pete said.

They had come upon the town house in time to see the entire edifice go up in flames. By then the paramedic unit had already taken Marguerite to Lenox Hill Hospital.

Kate hurried along the hospital corridor in search of a telephone. Pete waited a moment, then headed for a door marked Intensive Care, reaching it just as a stocky nurse came out. "Who's Agar or Egar?" she asked, as though he were standing there just to answer her question.

"Who?" Pete straightened. "Possibly Egon?"

"She keeps asking for him. She's very agitated. Are you a member of her family?"

"Her son." He went past her into the intensive care unit, a long narrow room with a dozen occupied beds. He found Marguerite at the far end. She was hooked up to a heart monitor, an oxygen tube, and an I.V. Her mouth was moving, although no sound issued forth. Her bright red-orange hair lay limp and damp against the pillow. Her eyes were sunken and her skin had a bluish cast. He remembered the elegant and self-possessed woman at Egon's funeral and saw little resemblance. He bent close and whispered her name. "Marguerite."

After a moment, she opened her eyes and stared at him.

"I'm Kate's friend, Pete Frank. You're going to be all right," he told her.

She muttered something Pete didn't understand, then he realized she was speaking French. He reached out and touched her hand.

"Egon, I didn't mean to," she said suddenly in English, in a tiny voice that was scratched out of her throat. Her eyes rolled back in her head and for an instant Pete thought he had lost her. "The fire. Everything gone," she said. "Your lovely museum, gone. And the journals, your journals, those abysmal things, gone too."

So the journals had disappeared into smoke, destroying whatever there was in Kate's past that might have come between them. Pete stayed very still, knowing any movement could disturb Marguerite, break her chain of thought.

"Egon, he was wearing the paisley robe I gave you for Christmas. A nasty little blackmailer and he was in your robe. I was furious. My finger tightened on the trigger." She lapsed into silence, her eyes still on Pete. "How did you know I was here, eh? Clever of you to find me, Egon. Are you looking for the journal? I saved one, you know, about Kate. All the rest are gone."

A transparent veil seemed to drift across her eyes. She loosed a sigh. "I saved the journal for her, for Kate, so she'd know. But later, not now . . . You wanted me to be director of the museum. That comes first, doesn't it? Kate can wait. She has her whole life."

Pete leaned forward and in the silence that followed, asked the one question he had already answered. He asked not as an attorney with the Justice Department but as a suitor to Kate Hayden. "Marguerite, you killed Win Smith, didn't you?"

"Who?"

"Sir, if you'll excuse us."

Pete turned. The resident had come in with the nurse. "I'm afraid you'll have to leave," he said to Pete.

Pete reached out and touched Marguerite's hand once again. "I'll be outside," he said. She didn't move. He was at the door when the nurse came up behind him.

"Mr. Varick, if you wouldn't mind?" She walked out with him and took him over to the nurses' station. "Your mother was clutching a notebook when the firemen rescued her. They had trouble prying it out of her hands. We really don't want to be responsible." She went behind the desk and took a leather-bound notebook out of a drawer. She handed it to Pete. "I'll tell her you have it, in case she asks."

"Yes," he said, "do that. Thank you."

She hurried off while Pete flipped nervously through the pages until he reached one marked with a paper clip.

"Pete?"

He looked up. Kate was headed toward him. He slapped the journal shut. It was a little bulky but with the soft leather binding it rolled easily into a cylinder, which he slipped into his jacket pocket.

"I'm glad you're with me," Kate said, leaning against him. "I don't think I could face all this without you."

"I wouldn't want you to." There was time enough to discover what secrets the journal held. Sometime in the future, when all was settled between them, he'd present Egon's legacy to her and they'd go over the contents together for better or worse. He wrapped his arms around her and pulled her close.